Maitland '95

Roy Peplow

To Jo,
A small token,
thankyou for helping
my family,

Roy Peplow

To all those who embark on the adventure ahead, I thank you.

To all those who wish to rekindle that spark of childhood and the unknown. This is a love letter to the 1990s and to all those who made mine one to remember, I thank you.

To my beautiful partner and her constant, unfaltering support through all my endeavours in life. I thank you.

To my family, growing up was about the bonds and memories we shared. Creating loving moments and teaching life affirming lessons. I thank you.

And finally. To my own little brother. Without you, this book would not exist. For there would be no memories and fond times to look back upon, there would be no adventures into unknown worlds. To the adventures we had and to our own children's now, I hope the lessons and loyalties in this book guide you all!

Thankyou

Roy Peplow

<u>Chapter 1</u>

Lightning Cracked overhead, illuminating the midnight sky, as the rain pattered heavily against the dark canopy of the dense forest below. The trees waved their long, leafy branches back and forth as the steady wind howled through their cold, wet limbs, making them dance in the crisp night air.

The Forest was a wall of darkness that was lit, only by the sudden outbursts of the flashes above, as it clapped its monstrous bolts and reflected through the heavy rainfall. Thousands of tiny lights momentarily coming to life then disappearing forever. The rainfall had turned the once solid forest floor into a slippery, mud surface, unwelcoming and ever changing as the falling water carved its paths.

Through the desolate and deafening wall of precipitation, that beat down on the earth like skeletal fingers on a drum, there came a cry.

"This way."

A voice called out in the dark as beams of light shone through the underbrush of the woods, darting in all directions. The torchlight slowed it's swinging as two men came to a sudden halt by a nearby tree.

The first of the men to approach the scene was Sheriff Dale Johnson. A balding, round faced man in his fifties, with a thick moustache that was slowly greying. An attribute, Sheriff Johnson held his days on the force as a city cop, to blame.

In his adventures, in his younger years, he had witnessed many atrocities as a detective and faced more adversity than he would have liked and more than he would ever care to tell another soul about. So, the sheriff would have everyone believe that it was through these exploits that the hair he had left on his head was greying and not the inevitable result of a full life falling into its autumn coat.

He had replaced his fast-paced city job, and the harsh criminal underworld that resided there, with the more tranquil and serene setting of Maitland, New Hampshire.

The change came with all the benefits a small-town sheriff could require, a fresh box of Dunkin' Donuts on his desk daily, a hot pot of Jerry Murphy's homemade coffee to start the day and the one thing more precious to Johnson than the surplus amount of fishing spots. The chance to know the people of the town. Maybe some not as well as he would have wished but he knew them. He was a people person, with a kind smile and a good heart. There wasn't the politics and faceless evil that was found in the larger cities. Maitland was his town and he was proud to know the people he helped protect.

Sadly though, on this cold, dreary night in early November, 1990, he found he was battling with himself to believe he could successfully look after his own.

The onset of middle age spread from a veritable diet of baked goods and cosy living, mixed with the gradual disappearance of youth, had led the sheriff to become out of shape. As the rain beat down on the rim of his hat, he placed his hand on the trunk of a nearby tree and crouched, resting his free hand on his leg to catch his breath. His face red with exhaustion, he looked through the forest, his vision obscured by the unforgiving, cold rain.

"Chief, you okay?" One of the deputies yelled out above the thunder and wind from behind.

"Yeah I'm fine," He waved him off. "Just catching my breath is all."

"Chief, we've been out here for hours. Don't you think we should have found something by now?"

The sheriff looked up under the rim of his soaked hat at the younger deputy.

"These woods go on for miles, besides in this weather it would be easy to miss something. This area is where they spotted the light, if there's anything out here it shouldn't be far."

The deputy leant in close to the sheriff and whispered in his ear. He didn't want to admit his doubts out loud.

"Chief, erm... all due respect, running around out here in the middle of the night, what are we even looking for?"

"Honestly Danny? I don't know, I just don't know. All I *do* know is that when that poor family lost their babies, we received a call at the station about the same time to say someone had spotted strange lights in the woods."

Johnson paused. he ran his hand over his moustache as a look of sadness crept over him.

"It was Halloween night. I just thought it was kids, you know how it gets. Busiest night of the year for punks wasting our time. Spooks and U.F.O. stories. But tonight, I see those same damn lights out here, not a click from where they reported it just a week before. Now we haven't had so much as a trace in the past week since it happened and I'm damned if I'm gonna give up on the only lead and more importantly, the only hope these folks have."

The deputy remained silent in thought. This was Maitland, nothing like this happened. Yeah sure they had small burglaries here and there and the odd vandalism, usually from some of the older kids with nothing better to do. But this was a good town and a missing persons case was rare. He also knew that no one lived in these woods so the sighting of light from within, again, made him curious.

Still, the deputy thought this a goose chase, in these conditions they could barely see a thing.

With that, a fork of electric white shot through the sky. It lit up the forest floor in front, the light bouncing off an object up ahead. The sheriff stood to attention forgetting his breathlessness and the pain in his knees, as if newly envigored by the sight of the strange object.

"Danny over there! I think it's them!"

The officers ran over to the spot where the object lay, they glided to a halt on the loose, wet earth. Sheriff Johnson dropped to his knees without care of the mud beneath him. Lightning cracked above as he rolled the object over with care and a pale white face looked up at him from the cold, dark ground.

"My God... We found her."

He paused momentarily, looking the fragile shape over. Despite the fortunate finding the sheriff couldn't help feel subdued in his triumph as he saw the terrible condition the poor young girl was in. She was soaking wet with a small scratch above her right eye. Probably from one of the branches thought the sheriff. The mud from the forest floor had turned her once yellow, night dress brown.

"What's wrong with her chief"

"Shh Danny, hang on a minute." He turned back to the young girl, wary not to move her in case she was injured.

"Are you okay darlin'?"

The frailty in the sheriff's voice was noted by the officer. He too couldn't help but feel a little on edge. The girl was alive but as the pale moon shone on her face through the gaps in the trees canopy, the men could see she looked frozen in fear but her gaze wasn't on them. She must have been about six years old Johnson thought, seven, tops. She was shivering all over. Her lips were blue and her face drained of all colour from the elements.

"Are you okay?" he said again, louder and slower in the event she was most likely in shock and serious threat of being ill. Still she said nothing, no noise at all but it was her eyes that haunted the sheriff. She just stared at him in silence

"What happened to you sweetheart?" he muttered aloud. He paused, looking at the frightened figure, considering his options.

"C'mon Danny, we gotta get her out of here and into the warm. We'll take her to the Hospital, it ain't far!"

As he picked her up, Danny looked at him and asked.

"What about the other one?"

Johnson half ignored his question and lifted the girl up and started back on the trail to their vehicle.

"Danny, I'm gonna need you to drive while I look after this one okay?! I'll Get Skeeter to come down, carry on searching the area with the dog, I'll come back myself, soon as she's safe inside... I promise"

Sherriff Johnson laid the girl gently in the rear of the 1987 Ford Explorer and climbed into the rear passenger seat to sit with her. He reached into the back and grabbed a couple of blankets and wrapped her tightly to help stop the wet and cold setting in.

"Step on it, Danny. We don't know how long she's been out there."

"You got it boss." Danny sped away from the forest and towards Maitland General Hospital.

Johnson grabbed his walkie and radioed the other officers.

"Skeet... Skeet come in. We got the youngest! Repeat we found the little one. Roughly a half mile south west from you guys when we found her. Bring the canine unit, we're heading to General. Keep me updated over..."

"*Copy chief will do... and chief... over.*"

"Yeah... over."

"*...Good work... over!*"

"Night's not over yet Skeet. I'll be back to help find the other one... but thanks. Over and out."

He focused his attention back on the girl and wondered how long she had been laying there, alone.

"Hey sweetheart. Are you in any pain?"

She stared blankly.

"Can you feel your fingers? Toes?"

There was no reply, she just stared up at the roof of the vehicle without blinking. The sheriff leaned in. He could check her over better now they were out of the rain. Her eyes, her head, there were no marks other than that of the scratch above her eye and dehydration and exhaustion. He sat back up and pondered to himself. He had never seen anything like it. He leant forward and tapped Danny on the shoulder.

"You ever see-"

All of a sudden Johnson felt the girl lunge and grab him a sudden shriek interrupted his words and filled the car, she was hysterical, he spun round and set her back in the chair.

"Keep your eyes on the damn road will ya!" He shouted at Danny as he swerved left and right in the commotion.

She calmed and turned to Sheriff Johnson with a tear welling in her eyes. She took his hand and said with a soft, calm voice almost as if pleading...

"It should have been me!"

The car sped into the horizon. The dim lights flickered out of sight as the rain beat down on the woods below.

Chapter 2

Five years later

Swish, swish, thwack!

The long, New England grass crashed and parted and the peaceful undergrowth came alive with a stir under heavy, rapid footsteps. The slender limbs of the shape pressed on at great pace through the forest. Along the winding paths that connected the primeval looking swamp to the peaceful port town of Maitland.

The autumnal sun glistened on the rusted leaves in the canopies of the sea of trees as it stretched its half-light across the landscape with the shades of colour that could only be witnessed at this time of year.

The late October twilight was a thing of beauty and every year the town of Maitland was plunged into a picture postcard full of orange and purple hues that were both awe inspiring and mystical. Maitland was neither a big, nor small town. It had most facilities and pros that you'd expect to find in such a typical North American town but it kept it's "small town" charm and was filled with independent stores and a sense of community.

Along Mainstreet you had your typical stores with their green, outstretched awnings over the sidewalk. The Maitland Bank and Post Office sat alongside each other opposite the western face of the bandstand pagoda, which resided in the centre of the town on the big, green lawn with its park benches and year-round bunting that was changed to reflect the seasonal events of the year. Red, white and blue on the fourth of July. Red and green at Christmas and now orange, black and purple for Halloween.

Maitland was a small port town and so, shellfish was a big staple and this could be sampled at a few little eateries around the harbour. The town had a single screen cinema "The Waterside Picture House" and a small but popular arcade both just south of Main Square.

But this isn't a story about picture postcards or things of beauty. Today the woods that surrounded the lake were home to an evil that was in pursuit of its next victims.

The sounds of heavy breathing could be heard above everything else through the undergrowth. Growing increasingly rapid with each heavy footstep. The chase continued through the forest along the winding dirt paths, the shapes ducking and diving through the ferns and shrubs. The pace picked up as the pack of wild beasts grew closer to their victims, the prey in turn willing each other on to escape as the pursuit shifted direction towards the peaceful town.

As nature and manmade structures entwined, the edge of the dark forest abruptly ended as it met the asphalt of the outer suburbs like an invisible line drawn in the ground where the two worlds couldn't cross. There was a burst of noise and leaves and the skidding of four feet as the prey emerged onto the pavement and stopped. The voracious predators could be heard, not too far behind. As the creature spun its head left and right, its eyes grew large with fear and it's breathing, heavy with fatigue and panic. Then it opened its mouth and cried.

"Quick, that way!"

It was two boys, brothers. Marshall and Randy Sanderson. Marshall was the oldest at 14 and Randy was 8 and not far behind them was an evil that Marshall feared more than anything. Tenth grade bullies.

The previous day

The autumn leaves flickered their rust and golden shades over the red bricks of Maitland Junior High in the early afternoon.

It was 30th October, 1995 and the bell had rung to sound the start of last period for the students. Soon they would all be free to put the finishing touches on their plans before they embarked on their Halloween adventures on the following evening.

Like every kid across the country, the students of Maitland High had spent the last few weeks mapping out the best trick or treating routes and finding the materials for their costumes. Each trying to outdo the other. Everyone knew the good spots and the houses that gave the best hauls, but each troop had their own route that they thought was best for scoring the most candy, in the least time.

Sally Waters knew that Dante Boulevard was rich in chocolate bars but she preferred lollipops so she always started at Mayfield Street. Eddy Dean and Jerry Thompson knew that Freling Drive was best for quantity but it was also the *safest* neighbourhood to go to and so you had to fight with all the kindergarteners and their parents to get to each door, so valuable time was wasted.

Then there were the costumes. Masks obscured visibility and could land you in an unwanted bush or treading on the neighbours' cat but Donny Chesler who was six years old, preferred masks any day to face paint because his Mother always made him wash his face spotless before he was allowed a single piece of candy and all he wanted was to come home and savour his horde.

So, Halloween night was different for everybody but to all it was the culmination of weeks of planning and strategy and something all the kids at Maitland Junior High were currently counting down the minutes to.

Maitland Junior High was like most small-town schools. It had the *finest* lunch in the canteen. Some kids had stopped asking for the food by its name and rather by its colour, as the lunch ladies served their gruel, like witches from a pot.

It was also the home of the Maitland Mud Crabs and their mascot Murray the Mud Crab. Whose likeness was plastered all over the school walls. They weren't the best team in their league but they had spirit and their coach had unfaltering hope that each year might be the year to put Maitland on the map for its sporting accomplishments.

It had all the other typical social cliques you might find at any school across the country. You had your jocks and cheerleaders. The preppy kids who had more money than everyone but whose parents still didn't have enough to get out of the Maitland area.

There were the grunge kids who kept to themselves behind the bike sheds listening in a close circle around their boomboxes to cassette tapes of Nirvana and Pearl Jam, nodding their heads in unison to the beat of the drums.

There were those who were dubbed geeks or the *academically strong* as they called themselves, who spent their time talking about the previous night's X-Files episode and whether or not the conspiracies were true. They followed that by a round of homework, both theirs and that of the other, more intimidating, students.

You had the notorious Butcher Boys, who were led by Josh Butcheson who himself coasted on the exploits of his older, meaner brother Mike Butcheson. Mike had been expelled from school at an early age and now worked at his dad's garage on Maple.

Lastly there were the social chameleons that never quite fit to any group. Like Marshall Sanderson. Marshall was a typical teenager, of average height, with dark brown hair that parted in the centre. He wasn't much into sports but he was athletic looking. His mom said with the amount he could put away on a family movie night he should be three times bigger than he was and like most kids his age, he loved video games and T.V. but he wasn't one for staying in, cooped up indoors. He was always out with friends on their bikes or exploring the lakes and woods of Maitland. He had lived in town all his life.

He had an after school and Saturday job sweeping the floor for the elderly owner of the local hardware store and also did general odd jobs that the owner, Mr. Abernathy, was now unable to do due to his age. He spent most of the rest of his time either out on his bike with his best friend Joe or with his younger brother Randy.

He was close with his brother but he could feel, as he grew older, that the bond was being tested, which made him sad. Randy was six years younger and Marshall had grown out of playing with action figures and make believe. He had recently found his attentions wandering to other areas.

For example, the bleached blonde, popular girl that was currently walking his way as he retrieved his things from his locker. In Marshall's mind time slowed and her hair flowed in the wind as she brushed it away in slow motion. He could almost hear Boyz II Men playing in the air as she flicked her locks.

Vinessa Marsden, everything about her was perfect. Marshall had had a crush on Vinessa for as long as he could remember. She was tall and skinny with golden hair that cascaded over her shoulders.

Marshall thought her eyes were the brightest blue, as if Angels had painted them themselves. All the boys at school would try to impress her and all the girls wanted to be her... even those who hated her.

In all that time though, he had probably only said three words to her in total.

She was chatting to her group of friends about that week's "Loser list" and who had frustrated her enough to be on it. The people with less money, the less attractive people in her mind and anyone that wasn't wearing the latest fashion. As you can imagine it was rather a long list and she and her gang took great pleasure in running down each individual at length as they walked along the hall.

Unfortunately for her though, she hadn't spotted the doomed eighth grader crouched on the floor, tying his laces. She stumbled as she walked into his crouched form. Managing to stay on her feet, her books, along with the eighth grader spilled into the hallway and she let out a yelp.

"Like, watch where you're going." Scowled one of Vinessa's followers at the eighth grader.

"What a dweeb!" Said another.

"I... I'm sorry." Said the kid in fear and he ran off.

"You will be!" Said the first girl with a frown and then they giggled in unison at each other like a cackling coven.

Marshall, watching the events unfold, seized his chance and ran over to help pick Vinessa's books up.

"H... here you go." He said, behind a goofy smile and a fumbling of his words. He brushed the curtained hair out of his eyes as he stood back up with a handful of study books.

"Uh... Thanks," she replied, rolling her eyes with a sarcastic glance to her friends who laughed as if on cue. She turned back to him. "Mitchell, right?"

"Uh yeah." He said awkwardly. His stomach was a flutter and his hands were getting sweaty with nerves. She had just spoken directly to him. He wasn't about to ruin it by correcting her on his name. It was close enough he decided.

"Well... thanks." She said patronisingly, ushering him to leave them. Her friends laughed. There was an awkward silence between them both. She glanced back at her friends then turned back to him.

"Anyways..." She hinted.

"Oh right, yeah, sorry." He realised he had overstayed his presence.

The girls turned to leave and they muttered under their breath about the awkwardness. But as they left, he noticed something glistening on the floor to his right, by the lockers. He bent down and picked it up It was an old, small earing.

"Hey wait!" He called out.

"God, like what now?!" murmured one of the other girls.

"I think you dropped this?!" He held out his hand and showed the sparkling object in his palm.

"My earring!" Vinessa exclaimed with a genuine display of panic as she felt the empty hole in her lobe.

Her expression changed from the bravado act that she gave her friends to a softer, "human" side.

"Thankyou." She said softly in shock as she took the jewellery. "That was my Gramma's."

"I'm sure she's as beautiful as *it* is!" Marshall replied humbly with a smile, just happy that he could redeem the awkwardness of the previous conversation.

"She was..." Vinessa paused and gave a sad smile at Marshall. She quickly brushed the display of raw emotion away and resorted back to the bubbly, in control façade everyone was used to. "My Hero" she said and gave him a peck on the cheek.

She turned and ran back to the group of girls waiting for her, who instantly continued their inane conversation about something trivial and inaudible and as they walked up the hallway, Vinessa turned and shot Marshall another smile.

Marshall filled with joy. For that brief moment Marshall's world stopped around him and it was just them. In his mind it was just like in the old movies. He wanted to call out some charming and witty parting words that would sweep her off her feet as she left. Like mentioning he thought her voice was like a dawn chorus's song or her hair was like strands of gold, brightening the day wherever she went... but instead his nerves got the better of him, as ever, and what came out was a splutter of words and noises that resembled those that could only be heard in a barnyard. She turned to look at him curiously and giggled, he felt his face grow red with embarrassment. Her friends laughed mockingly before they rounded the corner and headed to class.

"Stupid, stupid, stupid!" He scolded himself as he pretended to bang his head against the nearby wall of the hallway. He felt a slap on his left shoulder from behind.

"Smooth moves Casanova." It was Joe Miller, Marshall's best friend. Joe was lean and gangly, with short, black frizzy hair. He wore a pair of black framed glasses that rested on the nose of a spotted face. Joe was an only child and extremely clever but it meant he got bored quick and so he had an accidental tendency to come off as irritating. But he and Marshall became best friends some years before when Joe moved to Maitland with his mom.

"You know you HAVE to show me how you do it one day! That whole *'pleugh'* move... genius!" He said, mimicking the sound that had emerged from Marshall like an involuntary cough.

Marshall playfully punched Joe's shoulder as they headed to class.

"You're such a jerk, you know that?" He laughed.
"Besides this year is gonna be different!"

"Oh yeah, how so?"

"Well, you know... I'm gonna..." he stopped himself
while he tried to think of an achievable goal but his head
overruled his Heart. "I don't know yet, but I'm telling you,
this is my year!"

Joe laughed, "Yeah pal, you're dreaming, it doesn't
matter what you say, girls like that are never gonna go for
guys like us!"

Marshall looked at Joe and laughed.

"Who said anything about you!"

Joe clutched at his chest.

"You're breaking my heart Marsh'."

They laughed and Marshall pushed him away.

"I dunno, maybe you're right Joe..."

He was staring at the direction Vinessa exited. "What
would she see in a loser like me?"

Joe went quiet and took Marshall reassuringly by the
shoulders. He looked him square in the eyes, as if
searching for something.

"Wow man." said Joe. He looked surprised.

"What is it?" Asked Marshall curiously checking his
face with his hands.

Joe raised an eyebrow inquisitively. "You know what
Marshall?"

"W... What?" He replied.

Joe paused. "I never knew you were that smart!" He
burst out laughing.

"Nice!" Said Marshall rolling his eyes. "C'mon we're
gonna be late for class."

The last period seemed to drag for an age but finally the bell sounded and the class dispersed.

Marshall and Joe made their way through the hallway to the front of the school, through the crowd of kids, towards the busses.

"You're not gonna believe my costume this year!" said Joe clapping his hands with glee. "Okay so... I was gonna go with Red Power Ranger until my uncle caught me trying to spray his motorcycle helmet red so, instead, I thought go big!" He broadened his shoulders and cleared his throat. "Hasta La Vista... Baby!"

"Let me guess, a European nerd?" Marshall said, laughing at the impression.

Deflated, Joe hung his head. "No, well I mean I'll have the jacket and everything too, so picture that, and I'm gonna glue some foil to my face to complete the look!"

"'Cos that sounds safe!" Laughed Marshall

"Wow, you're going as The Terminator!" said an excitable voice from behind.

It was Eddie Dean. Eddie was pudgy and a little clumsy but he meant well. He was also one of the boy's closest friends. Eddie had close knit, blonde, curly hair and a collection of freckles on his rosy cheeks. He was wearing his favourite T-shirt, the one with a skateboarding Bart Simpson and a speech bubble that read 'Don't have a cow, man'.

"Wow that's awesome! My mom won't let me watch that film, she says I'm too young but the poster at the video store looks awesome!"

With Eddie's new interest in Joe's costume, he began to indulge the attention.

"Yeah, I even have one of the real guns from the movie! They were gonna lend me the bike but I said it was too much."

"No way that's true" exclaimed Marshall.

"Yeah huh!"

"Prove it then!"

"Well it's expensive and I have to give it back so I can't really risk breaking it."

"You are so full of it Joe." Said Marshall with a smile, waving him away.

"How about you Eddie?" Joe asked, trying to change the subject quickly. "What you going as?"

"Ah, I'm not."

"What do you mean?" asked Marshall. "You not coming to the diner tomorrow? It's the Horrorthon!"

"Nah. My mom's all panicked that it's not safe again."

"Ah, not this again!" Joe exclaimed raising his hands and arms in the air in protest.

"What have I missed?" asked Marshall

"You know, the *Dennison girl*." said Joe.

"Oh, that... that was years ago. And in a completely different town." Said Marshall.

"Precisely!" Said Eddie.

"No, see that's the thing," Joe said, resting his arms on the other boys' shoulders as they walked slowly to the bus. "She was *from* Dennison but she went missing right here in Maitland, out in the swamps."

Naturally, news as big as this in a small town travelled fast and it wasn't long before the facts, and many other accounts that were less than reputable, had skipped to Maitland and kids being kids, they all had their own version of the account.

"She was my Cousin. I'll tell you the whole story as it happened." One boy would say.

"I saw her ghost in the woods!" Another fabricated.

"I heard she was abducted by space frogs and that's not really her that came back!" Was one of the more *exotic* stories that circled the playground at recess.

But nonetheless the sad truth was a family was broken that day in 1990 and a poor little girl's life was transformed forever. They never found her sister and they never found the person or people responsible for her disappearance. There wasn't a parent in three counties after that, that was going to risk their son or daughter being next and Sheriff Johnson called a town wide curfew for a good six months after the event. Marshall remembered that summer spent indoors with his brother, missing out on all that fresh air and Sun. His mom had said that if it could happen to a nice family in Dennison then it could happen again at home and she didn't want them going out again, even after the curfew ended. She eventually loosened her reigns and when school resumed again that fall, she allowed him to go to Joe's house but only if his mom called to let them know he had arrived. He missed out on Halloween that year too on the anniversary of the disappearance, as did most kids his age. So, he knew how Eddie was feeling but that was old news, Eddie's Mom was overreacting he thought.

"I heard the Police had said that she had gone missing for a *whole* week before they found her in the woods north of town. Between here and Dennison. And when they did, she wouldn't say a thing." Said Eddie.

"I heard that she kept shouting crazy talk and they put her in the nut house." Said Joe, less subtly. "And no one's seen or heard of her since."

"They say that's why Sheriff Johnson retired." Added Eddie.

"How so?" asked Marshall.

Eddie went to reply but Joe stepped in, eager to add to the story. He lifted his arms off of the boys' shoulders and stepped between them to face them as he recanted his tale.

"It was Johnson who found her, apparently there was someone else out there but he never found them or the person who took them. He went crazy trying to find them. Spending days and nights in the woods looking for clues, but he never found them. Apparently, he wouldn't stop, he was on a one-track path straight to Coocoo-Ville and eventually he just broke!" As he said the words, he snapped his fingers to accentuate the point. "They say he's a mad man roaming the swamps, living off the land. Driven crazy by the *one that got away*. Some nights you can hear him howling at the Moon."

Eddie went quiet with fear.

"*Hooooowllllllll!*"

Joe let out a loud howl making Eddie jump.

"Not funny you guys!" Eddie batted Joe away in fright and frustration.

Joe laughed and Marshall shot him a glare to show he didn't approve but he did think it a little funny as a small smile crept across his face.

"I... I didn't know that though." Replied Eddie after he caught his breath.

"That's 'cos it's not true Eddie" replied Marshall sharply.

"It is so" shot back Joe.

Marshall rolled his Eyes. "How do you know all of that then?"

"I heard my uncle talking to a guy ages ago in the diner, and that's why Sheriff Danny is in charge now."

"Please." Scoffed Marshall.

"Fine don't believe me, but now as soon as anything slightly wrong happens this town goes crazy and panics. Point in case Eddie's Mom, no offense Eddie but... well it sucks." Joe patted him on the shoulder reassuringly as if to comfort the loss of his Halloween plans.

"Ah jeez, thanks guys but I'm not too bothered. I'm allowed to stay up later and play Nintendo so not a total loss. Anyways... I best get my bus!"

Eddie waved goodbye enthusiastically and ran for the bus.

"Hey wait, what happened?" Marshall shouted to Eddie as he ran off.

"What do you mean?"

"You said something happened? To make your mom worry. What was it?"

"I didn't ask!" He shouted back. "When my mom has a head on, it's best just to go along with it. But she did mention about some creepy guy? Bumped into him at the supermarket said he'd just bought a new store over on Kingston... must've looked creepy enough to make her worry though! Well, see ya guys tomorrow." He ran for the bus and hiked up his jeans clumsily.

Joe laughed "He's such a clutz."

Marshall couldn't help but be intrigued. *A new store on Kingston*, he thought. Why was that any reason to stop Halloween?

26

He felt a sharp pain in his shoulder. It was Joe's bony fist as he gave him a jab.

"Earth to Marshall! Hey man wanna go out on bikes?"

"Er... sure." Said Marshall snapping back to reality. "Oh wait. I gotta take Dash out first. It's my turn."

Dash was the family dog, a 7-year-old Golden Labrador.

"Wanna come?"

"Sure, as long as I'm not on poop duty!" Joe Laughed holding his nose.

Marshall laughed and the boys headed to The Sanderson home.

Chapter 3

Joe only lived a block away from Marshall and they made the trip home together every day. They had walked the route so many times together over the years that they would often reach their destination without realising it as they chatted about their plans for their evening, which was usually consisted of playing outdoors, video games and exploring. The School wasn't that far and often they would ride their bikes but on days like this when the sun was out and the air was filled with that crisp autumnal feel you get around Halloween in the fall, they preferred the walk.

They crossed the road just down from the school entrance and made a turn down one of the smaller streets. On foot they knew it was a shortcut. Marshall could hear Joe talking about a new game he had on his Mega Drive and how he could beat him under the table at it but he wasn't really listening. His mind had wandered onto Vinessa and how he was going to try and rectify his goofy attempt at a conversation with her. Marshall didn't live too far from the lake and Joe just a little closer to town by a block or two.

As they reached Marshall's house, they could hear Dash barking from inside. They walked up the short wooden steps and opened the front door into the house. Before he could even get the door fully opened, Marshall was pounced on by 70lbs of fur and drool.

"Dash! Ah get down, down boy. Ew!!" he wiped his face and regained his balance. He gave the lovable dog a petting.

"Hello!" Marshall called out as he threw his backpack onto the staircase opposite.

"Hmm, nobody home, must still be at work or something."

"C'mon boy let's go." He grabbed the lead hanging on the nearby coat rack and turned to Joe and ushered him back out of the house.

They passed through a few of the surrounding neighbourhoods as they grew closer to the edge of the woods that surrounded the west and north west of the town. Joe was mumbling about aliens and high scores and Marshall had his head in the clouds when they both stopped in unison as they heard Dash begin to bark. Suddenly, he pulled himself free of Marshall's grip as he gave chase to something he had spotted in the shadows.

"Dash! Dash, you stupid dog, get back here!"

The boys charged after the Labrador, following it around a few corners until they reached the entrance to the woods. They darted in and stopped suddenly as they saw the dog sat at the base of a tree near the entrance to the forest. Marshall ran over to him and grabbed his lead.

"Hey boy, what was all that about?!"

The boys looked up at the tree where the dog stopped. "Must've been a cat." Laughed Joe. "Man, I need a break!" He said panting as he sat down on the leafy floor.

They both looked around but there was nothing. Marshall ruffled Dash's fur, sat down next to Joe and patted the ground to invite Dash next to them. He was about to ask him what they should do for the evening when all of a sudden Dash started barking again, his tail waving like mad. They heard a thud in the leaves behind the tree and a rustle. Then, without warning, the chase erupted again and they found themselves leaping from their spots in pursuit of Dash once again.

The dog zigged and zagged through the bushes. They chased it for a couple of minutes until it reached a path in the woods that ended at a small wooden building. The boys followed the path and nearly caught up with him but they skidded to a halt and watched, it had something small and black in its mouth as it played with it at the base of the steps.

Before they could get to it and prize it out Dash let out a high-pitched yelp and they watched as the animal scurried through a hole in the doorframe and into the hut. Dash swiftly followed and bounded through the wooden door nearly knocking it from its hinges.

"Woah." They both exclaimed looking at the building. It was an old hunting cabin, by the looks of it. Marshall thought. The hut was made of wooden logs on the outside and old tiles on the roof, the porch was full of leaves and the windows looked dusted up. The windows were cracked and cobwebs covered the entire outside of it. It hadn't looked used in decades.

"Well, that's that then." Joe laughed as he stopped to take a breath. "Gonna have to get a new dog?"

"Give me a break." Marshall replied laughing. "What was that thing though? It certainly wasn't a cat... or a squirrel... I've never seen anything like it... kind of like a scaly rat?!

"Are you gonna go in there?" Joe asked as if the matter was already closed.

"Where's your sense of adventure huh? Asked Marshall. "C'mon, let's take a look."

"Are you kidding? What if somebody lives there?" Joe exclaimed as he grabbed Marshall's arm to stop him.

"What? Don't tell me you think that someone *actually* lives in there do you? Besides I'm more worried what that thing will do to my dog. Anyway, it looks cool, don't you wanna see inside!"

"I don't know, but we can't just go in can we. What would we say if we got caught?"

"Erm... how about we say we lost our dog?" Marshall replied laughing, slightly sarcastically.

"Okay to be fair that would work." Said Joe feeling a little foolish. "Okay, but two minutes then we're gone okay?"

"Alright." Agreed Marshall.

They walked up the steps and pulled open the screen door that had bounced back shut. It gave a loud creak as it moved on its hinges. Marshall took the lead and knocked on the wooden doorframe. He looked at Joe who had a look of questioning on his face. A fully-grown dog had just barged through unannounced and here they were, knocking first.

"What?!" Asked Marshall. "It's still polite."

There was no response.

"See!" He smiled. "Nobody home!"

They stepped inside. There was a pair of old boots by the doorway and a few jackets hung up. They all looked old and faded and the boots had seen better days too. As they closed the door, Marshall called out.

"Hello?"

Nothing. They walked into the main room of the hut and they couldn't help but be instantly drawn to the back wall. They walked over to take a better look.

"Whoa, someone's been busy!" Said Joe almost in a whisper to himself. "What is all this?".

On the wall, were hundreds of newspaper clippings and a large map with drawing pins, marking points of interest, each linked with a piece of string. Dotted all around were notes and scribbles, sketches of strange objects with dates written next to them. One note in particular that Marshall noticed was repeated all over the wall was *The Lights.*

Pinned around the map were photos of missing people, lost dogs, even an entire gap where a house used to be.

"Who do you reckon all these people are?" whispered Marshall, staring up close at the faces.

A large, round man with glasses, an elderly couple, a young, pretty woman. The wall was covered in people of all ages and types.

"That map is of Maitland." Marshall pointed. "Look, that's the main square and there, that's the port. The School is around here somewhere. So, we must be-"

"Trespassing!" A large booming voice came from behind them, they froze, their hands in the air.

"What are ya doing here?!" Asked the voice.

"We... er..." Joe Froze and looked sideways at Marshall with a grimace. "...lost our dog?"

"Pfft... a likely story... more likely come to tease an old man you mean! When are you kids gonna learn to leave me alone?!"

The boys looked at each other confused. Marshall slowly lowered his hands.

"I'm sorry Sir. We meant no harm. Truthfully..." He looked at Joe for reassurance. "Truthfully, we were chasing my dog it came through here, we saw some weird rat creature run under the hole in the front door there. That was all, promise. We thought this place was abandoned."

The air was silent and the boys wondered what the stranger was doing, they daren't turn around to face him.

"Weird creature you say?" The stranger asked, softer in his approach and inquisitive.

"Y... Yes Sir." Marshall stuttered.

"I don't suppose it had black fur did it?" The stranger asked.

Marshall was a little shocked at the question but answered. "I'm not sure, it was only quick, it attacked my dog when he caught it but it looked more like scales than fur, but it looked more like a rat."

"Ha, I knew it!!" Cried the stranger with Joy, making the boys jump. "How big was it? big as a dog?"

"No actually it was like a squirrel, smaller than a racoon." Marshall replied.

"They're breeding, I knew it." He clapped his hands and the boys heard him rummaging through some papers nearby. He stopped and looked at the boys, still stood there with their backs turned to him. "I... I'm sorry to startle you boys, just I get a lot of hooligans coming through here playing mischief and such. Sorry, you can turn 'round it's quite safe."

The boys slowly turned around, still unsure whether to trust the stranger's voice or not but as they faced him fully Marshall recognised the old stranger behind his greyed beard.

"Sheriff Johnson!?" Marshall muttered with his mouth wide open.

He was wearing an old coat like the ones hanging up, just as scruffy and his beard had grown and aged with him.

The Man looked a little embarrassed. "Well, Just Dale Johnson now, my friends call me Dale... at least they used to before..." he waved his arms at the room of notes and diagrams. "...well, all this."

"What happened to you?" Asked Joe.

Marshall Interrupted. "I think what we mean is how come you're living out here all alone?"

Johnson stopped rummaging through the mess of papers on his desk. "That my eagled eyed nature lovers, is a very good question! One that requires a lot longer answer than we have time for. Ah yes here we are." He said as he found the sheet of paper he was looking for.

He walked over to the boys and showed them a rough pencil sketch on the white paper. "Was this what you saw?"

They looked at it and nodded their heads. "We couldn't see the head but yeah that's it alright."

"Man, it's even uglier from the front." said Joe looking at the sketch. The creature Dale Johnson had drawn had a flat face, with large green eyes and small pointed teeth. "What is it?" Asked Marshall.

"Darned if I know boys," Replied Johnson. "but up until now I thought I was the only one who had seen one. Everyone on the force thought I was crazy but I knew there was something going on here."

With that Dash came walking into the room from the back of the hut. He had given up on his chase and returned to the boys. Great guard dog he would make! Thought Marshall.

"Well what do you know, there was a dog!" chuckled Johnson, looking surprised.

"How do you mean?" Asked Marshall stroking Dash and telling him to go lay down. "...Something going on?"

Johnson patted the seat of his armchair and sunk into it as the dust settled around him. "It started a few years back. I took a case up North-"

"The Dennison Girl!" Joe interrupted.

"I see your familiar with my handywork." He said with a raised eyebrow and inquisitive tone over his aging moustache.

Joe, realising he had overstepped apologised for interrupting. "It's just that I had heard-"

"I know the stories you probably heard alright." He said staring at him. "The one where I saw aliens? Or how about the one where I created a huge conspiracy and was secretly kidnapping people so I could make the police look the hero when they found them?"

Joe opened his mouth to speak but the sheriff continued.

"No? How about the one where I turned absolutely crazy?" He paused and softened his tone, realising he was getting agitated. He took a deep breath, calmed himself and stared out the window in front.

"How about the one where I did everything I could to look for a missing little girl and return her to her family? Including carrying on way after my team did, after her parents did. Just so I could be called obsessive, deranged, mad. I bet you never heard that one huh!?"

Joe hung his head and answered awkwardly, slightly ashamed. "No Sir."

"No... I didn't think so. Trouble is the night that little girl and her sister went missing there had been reports of weird lights, not in the sky like the UFO stories but here, in the woods. The night I found that youngest one I saw those exact same lights, in the woods, in the same damn area.

"Now apart from me these past years, there's been no one living out here, nor are there any camping spots and with the weather we had that night I can guarantee you there were no fisherman and the like out here that night. So, I started looking a bit deeper at the records on our database and in the public library and it turns out that our little town has had its history of missing items, from way back when, and people's pets turning up half eaten. Now we don't get any coyotes and I can't see a raccoon eating a sheepdog so I went on the inter web thing-"

"The internet?!" Joe interrupted again, this time trying to help.

"That's the ticket, damn thing took nearly a half hour to click in. Making its whurry noises, I thought it was gonna take off. Any who, I came across some articles about hikers spotting things in the woods to the north and a few other similar stories."

"Why didn't your officers believe you?" Asked Marshall.

"That's the thing, I had to dig hard just to find that and it was on a page called *The Weird Wide Web*. Not exactly the most reputable source. But the peculiar thing is all the reports and stories stop after that night. I knew it had to be connected somehow. The guys down at the office nearly laughed me right out there and then. All except one of my deputies, Danny."

"You mean Sheriff Danny Pullman?" Asked Joe

"Yeah, one and the same, he was always a good kid but he saw that girl that night and he knew something was wrong. See when we found her, she wouldn't say a thing but eventually, when we got her back with her parents, she started talking about monsters and being trapped in a dark room. Supposedly these *monsters* had tried to kidnap her and her Sister.

"I figured, same as her folks that she was manifesting the people that took her into monsters. Poor girl must have had a fright, who knows what happened. After a while her folks had her see a shrink up in Dennison. I went up to visit her a couple o' times but all she would repeat to anyone is that 'It should have been her' and something about a locket.

"We looked for the locket too, even just to make her smile again or make her remember something who knows, but we never found it or her sister. Problem was the rain came down so hard that night we found her that any trace of either was long washed away or buried under the mud. Must have meant a lot to her though as that's all she would talk about. Any who, I couldn't just stop looking for the sister and after finding these strange articles I decided to stay out here longer."

He forced himself up, out of the chair with a groan and flicked the coffee pot on and it started making its bubbling sound as it brewed. He stared out of the window in silence as if reliving that night all over again in his head.

The boys looked around at the room, it was clear that Johnson hadn't stopped caring about the town even to his own risk. The sink was full of dirty cups and dust. Too busy to look after himself. They looked at each other and without a need for words they decided to stay and sat down on the nearby sofa. Joe coughed as the dust plumed up from the cushion.

Johnson, brought back to the room from his thoughts by the bubbling of hot coffee, turned to the kids.

"You boys thirsty?" He offered.

The boys politely declined after seeing the dirty sink. He ran his fingers round the rim of the nearest cup.

"I suppose I have let this place go a little." He said in a quiet murmur to himself, embarrassed.

He rinsed his cup under the tap and filled it with the hot coffee and took his seat again to continue his story.

"I had this old cabin from when you used to be able to hunt around here but I used to use it when I took a weekend to get away fishing. I was out here so much and driving home late it made sense to work from here. I could get back out, and on the trail, nice and early. But the longer time passed, the more the force was leaning on me to stop and get back to the other, day to day issues, the town was going through. But I couldn't see how a ruined flower bed or small bit of graffiti measured up to a missing person let alone a child. So, I up and quit. All my time solving crime in the big city and it was a little town like this that broke me. Thing is, I know I was right. I figured the day we stop caring about people is the day things ain't right and after I tracked down a few of these leads from the..." He looked at Joe who smiled.

"Internet."

"Right!" He put his thumb up. "Once I started following those leads, I started coming across some weird items of my own but I noticed that all the stories stopped the night that girl showed up. Then one day down by the river I spotted one of those beasts. I've seen it twice but until you showed up and broke into my home, I thought I was the only one." He smiled.

"Uh technically we didn't break in." Replied Joe. "The door was already open when we knocked."

"Was it really?" Johnson looked up from his chair at the hook on the wall behind him with a set of keys hanging on it. "Well now, would you look at that. Well I guess I'm not crazy but I am going mad." He laughed.

"You're not crazy!" Marshall laughed nervously.

"Well that makes three of us!" Johnson said, he looked at Joe to check it was actually three. Joe Nodded reassuringly.

"I first saw it about two weeks back, down by the water's edge but if you kids saw a little one in town it means whatever they are, they're getting braver... or desperate. Either way can't imagine it bodes well for us folk."

He stood up from his armchair and ran his hand through his beard as he stared at the map and the various articles dotted around.

"It's like I have all the pieces but I'm looking at the wrong jigsaw box. Something made these incidents stop five years ago and something has happened now to start it all up again. I can feel it."

He lost himself staring into the map. Then he remembered his company.

"Anyways... you best be getting on! People will start poking fun at you if they see you hanging around the town kook. Besides it'll be getting dark soon. You'll never spot that critter out here now! Leave it to me."

The boys nodded and after another quick glance at the wall of strange, they headed out the front door. Though secretly they both wanted to stay and see what else Johnson had discovered since moving out to the swamps. Whatever it was had to be more exciting than the school assignments they had waiting for them at home.

"You be careful now you hear!" Johnson shouted as he watched them leave the swampy area.

They both couldn't stop thinking about Johnson's collection of weird articles and the creature. Joe came up with a few ideas to try and trap the creature, which made Marshall laugh as all he could picture was Joe sat there like the coyote waiting for the road runner, suffering fail after fail.

They decided they'd had enough excitement for one night and enough of the weird even with Halloween so close. Joe even said he might have a night off the video games. They parted as they got to Joe's house and decided it best to keep their discovery to themselves for now, judging on how the town reacted to Johnson and the Dennison girl's stories.

"Hey do you think we get to name it, the creature I mean." Said Joe. "You know, if it's a new species."
Marshall laughed. "Hey, we have to see it again first and prove it before we start thinking about naming it. I'm not sure I even want to see it again though, that drawing was too gross."
The boys laughed and ran back home. Marshall didn't sleep much that night. He dreamt of giant, black squirrel creatures chasing him through the streets and just as they opened their mouths to chomp down on him, he turned to see they all had Johnson's face, opened wide and laughing. He woke in a cold sweat in his bed. He rolled over and tried to put the thought out of his mind.

Chapter 4

The next morning was like any other. Almost as if the previous evening had all been a dream itself. Despite it being Halloween, the day passed by, largely uneventful. Josh and his gang had managed to slip some fake plastic creepy crawlies into the vat of yellow pudding in the cafeteria, causing a few entertaining outbursts. But other than that, it was a typical school day.

Marshal walked into his last class of the day, 9th grade English. He passed the teacher, Mr. Neidernaim and took his seat with a smile. English was his favourite subject. Not particularly for his love of the English language or even what they studied in the lesson. But because last period English meant he was sat two seats behind Vinessa and for one solid period he could bask in her radiance.

"Alright class, settle down." Cried the teacher over the buzz of chatter in the room as the kids found their seats. "I said settle down! Now, as some of you may have noticed, today is Halloween!"

"Mwahaha!"

A few seats back from Marshall, sat Josh Butcheson, who had grabbed the girl in front of him with a devilish laugh and made her jump. The class erupted into laughter, save the poor spooked girl. As Marshall turned back to face the teacher, he spotted Vinessa laughing at the outburst and as she turned back to the front of the class, she caught Marshall looking her way and gave him a smile.

"Thankyou Mr. Butcheson. We can discuss your idea of a trick in detention, which I can assure will be no treat for me either"

Josh Groaned.

"Very well, now who can tell me -"

As Mr. Neidernaim continued to ask the class the origins of Halloween, Marshall felt himself falling in a daze. Thinking about the smile Vinessa had given him.

"...Sanderson! Well?!"

Marshall jumped and came to. He looked up from his desk to see Mr. Neidernaim standing directly in front of his desk, staring at him. The other kids in the class around him giggled.

"Huh?"

"I was asking if anyone knew why we give candy to trick or treaters on Halloween and by the vacant expression on your face, I assumed you knew and had time to drift into dreamland." He mimicked a waving motion with his hand as he said it.

The class giggled again.

"Um..." Marshall hadn't realised he had drifted so heavily into a daydream. "Well... I guess -"

"Guesses! Guesses won't do Mr. Sanderson. Maybe next time spend more time using these," He pointed to his own ears. "and less time with this in the clouds." he said as he tapped his head.

"Y... Yes Sir."

"Right class for your *seasonal* assignment I want an essay on my desk on the origins of Halloween and why we still celebrate it. And try not to fill it with guesses."

The class let out a groan.

The bell rang and the class started packing their things into their bags and leaving.

"And remember, by the end of the week people!" Mr. Neidernaim managed to yell out as the sea of faces left his class.

As Marshall began to leave the room, he noticed Vinessa get up from her seat and head to the front of the class. She was speaking to the Teacher about something. This was it he thought, this was his moment, the class was nearly empty, there was no one to look a fool in front of. He cleared his throat and headed towards the door.

She had appeared to finish her conversation with Mr. Neidernaim. As he got nearer, he could see she looked upset after her conversation with the teacher.

"Are you okay?" He asked.

"Oh, Mitchell, right?"

"Marshall actually, but it doesn't matter."

"No, I'm not alright, stupid Neider- *Lame*." She said sarcastically. "I was supposed to be going to the big party at Jason Ricci's tonight you know."

"Oh yeah the big party," He said realising he had been missed off the invite list again. "Yeah I was thinking about that but I'm not sure, I'm so busy." He said, trying to act casually.

44

"Anyway, now we have this stupid assignment and I can't go. I explained it to that fossil but he hates me or something because he said something about the world not revolving around me and everybody else... something blah, I don't know, I stopped listening. Anyway, I have cheerleader practice tonight and then I'm super busy in the week, so now I have to go straight home after School and do this stupid assignment. It's not fair." She pouted.

"I er... I could write yours if you like?" He said eagerly. He quickly tried to sound less desperate. "If you wanted that is... I mean I totally get it if you don't need my help... Why would you need *my* help?"

"Oh Mitchell!" She said, forgetting his name again. "That would be amazing, thank you! You would do that?" She asked.

"Yeah sure I'd do anything for you!" He said goofily in a daze. "I mean for your school work." He quickly retracted, realising what he had said.

She smiled, she had him wrapped around her finger. "My Hero" she said, reeling him in.

Filled with a new sense of confidence he suggested giving him her number so he could call when it was ready, in case she wanted to check through it before handing it in at school. She didn't fall for it but was amused by his boldness and teased him.

"No, it's okay, you can print it for me." She grinned.

"We don't own a printer" He replied quickly trying to push for her number.

"Then how are you doing yours?" She countered, again giving him a smile, enjoying the game.

"I uh..." Darn, he thought she was good at this. "Floppy disc... Yeah I was going to bring it on a floppy disc."

"Great." She exclaimed then you can do the same with mine.

"I... uh" he was losing the game. "I only have one." He had dozens at home he used to save work and computer games on but she didn't know that.

"Hmm." She pondered and smiled "Okay Mitchell, you win"

"So, you'll give me your number." he asked confidently.

"I tell you what, I have to drop my sister at that silly Halloween thing at the diner later on so how about I meet you there tonight and I can give you a floppy disc to save it onto when you're finished?"

"Uh, Yeah. That sounds awesome." he said with slight disappointment.

"Okay, it's a date." she smiled, getting her own way. She cocked her head to the side and waved a little goodbye then skipped down the hallway.

"It's a date..." He repeated in a whisper as he watched her disappear down the hallway to meet up with her friends. He grinned from ear to ear.

"Yes!" He exclaimed throwing a fist in the air in excitement.

"Hey watch it!"

"Oh my God, I'm so sorry!" he apologised, as he nearly hit a younger kid in the face with his celebrations. He quickly withdrew his hand in embarrassment. "Sorry!" He yelled as the kid walked off in a huff.

"What's got you all worked up?" Asked a voice from behind. It was Joe.

"I have a date with a Miss Vinessa Marsden tonight!" He said beaming with pride.

Joe scoffed and dismissed him.

"Yeah right and I'm Michael Jordan." Joe replied throwing an invisible three pointer and mimicking the crowd's cheer with cupped hands to his mouth.

"No, I'm serious," Said Marshall, waving Joe's hands away from his mouth. "she just left. She's meeting me at the diner tonight."

Joe reached over and spread Marshall's eyelids wide open, checking his eyes then mouth "Hm ze patient seems okay, say ah! You don't *look* sick but zees delirious dreams you are having just have me vorried." He mimicked like a mad scientist. He laughed. "Have you been eating the Halloween candy too early?"

Marshall pushed him away with a grin. "Get off, I'm serious! You'll have to wait and see tonight!"

"Speaking of tonight what time are you coming over?" Asked Joe.

"Well I have to take my brother trick or treating first but then I'll be over."

"Okay, my uncle's asked if I can help out this year, wanna come early and give me a hand? you can bring Randy too if you like?!"

"Sure," replied Marshall, "why not!"

"Are you sure?" asked Joe, "You don't wanna get too dusty for your big date." He laughed and pretended to kiss, with his arms wrapped around himself.

"You'll see," Said Marshall. "So, meet you at the diner yeah?"

Joe turned to him with two thumbs up and a grin.

"Sweet, yeah see you then!"

Joe only lived a block away from Marshall but the diner was the other side of town so he rode his bike and Marshall walked the other direction back home.

Marshall made his way down the leaf strewn pathway right of the school gates. He followed the path that ran parallel with the main road alongside the metal school chain fencing. There was the unmistakable smell of damp autumn leaves in the air as he heard them crunch under his step. He watched as some of the school buses passed him taking the next left to the east side of town. Marshall lived on the west side of town past the old church, towards the woods and lake that surrounded the far edge of town.

As Marshall arrived home, he made his way up the white, wooden steps to the porch. He could hear Dash barking in the backyard. He opened the front door and as he did, the feint aroma of cinnamon and apple greeted him. yes, he thought, his mom must be baking for the trick or treaters.

"Hey." he hollered as he took his bag off and dumped it on the stairs by the entrance.

He could hear the television set from the front room. His dad must be home already he thought.

"Hey hunnie, I'm in the kitchen. How was school?" His mom called out through the hallway.

He walked through, into the kitchen. His mom was taking a fresh batch of cookies out of the oven and by the conveyor belt of trays and baking ingredients all over the work surfaces he could see they wouldn't be the last.

"Oh, you know." He said. "The usual." trying to keep calm about his encounter with Vinessa. He was close to his parents but there were just some things you didn't talk to your parents about he had decided. They would be all embarrassing about it and make a fuss. Besides, his parents were old, they probably couldn't even remember dating and if they did, he didn't want to know their advice.

"Smells great Mom." He complimented while eyeing up any strays that he considered easy picking, like a lion hunting a sick zebra.

"Thank you, Sweetheart. Shall we make sure that they all reach the kids who knock on the door tonight?" She questioned with a smile, eyeing him as he picked out his prey.

"I was just checking they were all the same, you'd hate to make the kids jealous if one was smaller Mom."

"Well thankyou Marshall. You know what, that's awfully sweet of you but..."

"Let me guess, Dad's already *checked* this batch"

"Uh Huh" She grinned

"And they were delicious!" Exclaimed his father as he came in from the living room, swiping another as he walked past.

Marshall noticed he had not long got home himself. He recognised the half-loosened tie around his neck as a show of defiance that the moment he left the office he wouldn't be governed by its rules.

"Dennis N. Sanderson, you drop that now if you know what's good for you!" She slapped the back of his dad's hand playfully and gave a less playful scowl his way as she took the cookie from him. "You'll just have to wait." She laughed and shooed them both from the counter, like a mother hen with her eggs.

"So, I haven't had a chance to cook anything yet, so how does pizza sound tonight? What d'ya say?"

"Uh, I say... great!" Marshall laughed.

The Sandersons didn't order out much. Mrs. Sanderson liked to make a homecooked meal each night. So, the promise of pizza came as a very welcomed treat.

The phone rang and Mrs. Sanderson set her things on the counter and wiped her flour covered hands on a nearby cloth. She took the phone off the wall and stretched the cord as she quickly spoke to Marshall.

"Great, I'll let you order Hunnie okay. Just check with Randy what toppings he wants first. He's up in his room." She took her hand away from the receiver and carried on her conversation with the person at the other end of the line.

Marshall walked to the entrance of the kitchen and leaning against the frame, he yelled.

"RAND!!"

His dad jumped at the outburst and gave him his newspaper, which he had rolled up into a cone.

"Here you go Champ. I don't think they heard you on the Moon" he said sarcastically with a smile and walked back into the living room to watch T.V.

"I meant go *up* there." his mom scolded in a harsher tone. She had gotten off the phone. A quick call to say her guests would be a little late. "Sorry," She said, realising she had snapped. "He's not talking to me. I've grounded him tonight and he isn't happy."

"Grounded? Tonight? You do know what tonight is right mom?" Asked Marshall. "What did he do?" He knew how much his brother loved Halloween, he must have done something *real* bad to risk missing out, he thought.

"He can tell you himself when you go get him for dinner. I've tried and I've tried but he keeps testing me! I mean I'm meant to be the cool mom, right? you know, grow up get married have kids so I can pretend to be 25 again, I'm "da bomb"" she said using her fingers to make air quotes. "Did I say that right? ...Da bomb?" She turned to Dennis for reassurance of her knowledge of the secret language of teenagers.

"Word!!" He replied from his spot without looking up from the T.V. The back of his head visible above the top of the sofa, he raised a thumbs up.

"He needs to know he was wrong and I still have at least two batches of these to do before I get ready for the neighbour's coming over. Are you and Joe Trick or treating this year?"

"No, I think we're a little too old now but we're still going to the diner for the Horrorthon. If that's okay? In fact, Joe's asked me to help him decorate so I was going to go after I took Randy trick or treating but... I guess that's not happening now is it?" He gave his mom a disappointed glance under his brow whilst he fiddled with the cookie cutters. He knew his brother could be irritating but even with the age gap they were thick as thieves and he wanted to help him out.

"Come on Marshall, don't you give me that look. I feel terrible already that I've had to ground him, let alone have him miss out on the fun tonight but he needs to learn."

Marshall faked a pout with his lips then burst into a grin as he saw his mother smile.

"Okay, okay, God you win, okay, but I'll compromise. I stand by my decision no trick or treating *but* he can come with you to the diner. He needs to learn some responsibility and I don't have the time to argue with you boys tonight before getting ready for the neighbours so maybe Joe's uncle can give him some jobs at the diner to help you boys out. But no candy and just to the diner okay?"

"Okay Mom, you're the best" Marshall leaned over the counter and gave her a peck on the cheek as he rushed to tell his little brother the news.

"Why do I feel like I just rolled right over on that one?" she called as he ran upstairs.

Whipush... Marshall's dad could be seen imitating the noise and motion of the cracking of a whip from the sofa in the front room.

"You're the devil Dear, you know how to punish them."

She smiled and came in the front room, white flour covering her hands from the baking, she placed her hands on his cheeks from behind and laughed. "You're a regular stickler for punishment too Mister. I wonder where they get it from?"

White hand prints covered his face. He laughed and chased her back into the kitchen, relenting as she cried in laughter for him to stop but not before swiping a couple more cookies for his return to the living room.

Marshall blocked the sounds of his parents acting like a couple of lovebirds and called out again to his brother.

"Rand!... Rand, come on it's time for dinner buddy!"

There was no answer so Marshall made his way to Randy's bedroom. He could get to the diner a little earlier now he didn't have to take his little brother trick or treating but he was also a little sad at that thought. Marshall was five years older and was often asked to change his plans to help his mom with Randy. Like with school work or looking after him while she did the groceries but for their differences, he and his brother were very close and they did everything together. He knew though that the days of trick or treating, bike rides and exploring wouldn't last forever. They were both growing up and this might have been one of the last years they got to do this together. One last adventure.

He walked along the light blue painted hallway, passed the bathroom, to Randy's room. He knocked high near the top once, then lower down, around the middle twice then the top again once more. They had a secret knock they made up when they were younger and they used it for everything.

"Hey Rand..." Silence... "Rand?" Marshall asked a little softer. It was usual for his brother to ignore his mom's calls but unusual for him not to reply to Marshall. He pressed his head against the door.

"Look, Mom told me about getting grounded, you okay?" There was nothing, not a sound. Marshall tried the handle and opened the door. "I got some good-" The room was empty... "news."

He scanned the room. It was pretty tidy apart from some sheets of paper on the floor and some crayons, he smiled as he spotted some familiar tatty posters of his on the walls that he thrown out a while ago. Randy must have taken them out of the waste paper bin and put them up. Marshall had gotten hold of the two posters from the video store when their displays changed. The Land Before Time had been his favourite movie when he was younger. He was always trying to copy Marshall or be like him.

"Hiding from me now huh? You know I'm not the enemy right?"

He walked over to the large white wooden louvred doors of the walk in Closet and opened the doors with a rush but there was nothing. He turned and crouched on his knees and lifted the duvet of the single bed up a bit and looked underneath but again there was nothing, except some action figures and some board games that Randy had thrown under hastily in a previous attempt to clean his room. Marshall didn't have time for games, he needed to get ready and head to the diner to help Joe and more importantly be ready for when Vinessa arrived.

"Hey Rand, c'mon. I spoke to Mom and she's cool but maybe you could tell her you're sorry okay?! You know one of these days you're-"

He stopped himself short when he cast his eyes upon the open window. He ran over and looked out but there was nothing, no sign of Randy but a chair was propped against the bedroom wall underneath the window with an old shoe box next to it.

The lid was ajar, so Marshall lifted it off and looked in. Marshall didn't need the label, that was written in marker pen on the side, to know that this box held Randy's "treasures" as he called them, which he had collected on his travels while playing on his own or exploring with Marshall. Amongst other things, there was some fishing line wrapped up, some old marbles, the leg of a He-Man figure, a small bird's nest made of twigs and moss. Half a pair of reading glasses that had broken on the bridge, various trading cards and Pogs and some black tape that come from a cassette tape. Who knew his designs and plans for these "treasures" but to Randy they were special and valuable and Marshall could see that the box was missing a few items. He breathed a sigh of relief, quickly followed by a shake of his head in frustration. He knew exactly where his little brother was.

Marshall needed to leave the house but he couldn't risk his parents knowing his brother had snuck out. If they did that would be the end of it and Marshall would be made to watch over him while they entertained the neighbours instead of meeting Vinessa and Joe at the diner. He crept out the window the same way his younger brother had. He was going to be in so much trouble.

Chapter 5

There in the clearing by the edge of the water was a strange, small creature. Bright white, crouched down facing the water. It was hunting, watching the water for every little ripple as it scooped and collected its prize.

"Ya know, it would be easier with a net!"

As the voice spoke out, the creature slowly raised its body from the ground, still facing the water. Dark brown tufts of curly hair poked out the top of the white robe.

Marshall gave a little smile. As frustrated as he was that he had to make his way out here, he was relieved that his brother was okay and where he knew he would be.

"Hey!" He called out, warmly.

Randy spun round, he had been focused on catching frogs so much so that he hadn't heard his older brother approaching or anything else for that matter.

Randy was more of a free spirit than Marshall, something Marshall knew all too well, as he was often bailing him out of situations and smooth talking his parents to go easy on him. He could keep himself occupied for hours but he loved nothing more than hanging out with his older brother. He loved how they did everything together, fishing, action figures, bike rides, fancy dress for Halloween. You name it, they were inseparable.

He stood around four feet tall and had short, wild, curly Brown hair and today he was dressed all in white in some sort of sheet that Marshall didn't recognise.

Marshall could see by the red of his eyes that he had been crying not so long ago. All his frustration left him and he walked over and gave his little brother a big hug.

"I like your costume..." He smiled. "Marshmallow?" he laughed

Randy wiped his nose on his sleeve and raised his arms outstretched in front of him.

"I'm a Ghost."

"What you doing out here on your own!"

"It wasn't my fault!" Said Randy instantly on the defence hanging his head down, staring at the floor.

"What wasn't?"

"The old china lady, it wasn't my fault."

"The old china lady? You mean Mom's porcelain statue?"

Randy nodded his head "I can't say Porlecain"

He looked upset with himself that he was unable to pronounce it correctly.

That explained it, Marshall thought. His mom had a small porcelain statue of a woman that she kept on a dresser on the landing of the house. It was very old, no wonder she was so angry. He hadn't noticed it missing when he came up the stairs but it had been there so long it had blended in to the décor.

Randy sniffled. "I get bored... and I get.... Breaky." He said, slowly looking up at Marshall. "I was waiting for you to come home from school so we could go trick or treating. I got bored, so I made some paper airplanes. The first ones didn't fly but then one went amazing, you would have loved it! It went out the room *whoosh.*" He mimicked its path with his hand. "Then it crash-landed... and so did the old china lady. I didn't mean to. Mom heard the noise and caught me. She told me I couldn't come trick or treating with you and that I was grounded. I would have saved my allowance for a new one but she wouldn't listen."

He turned to face the water. Marshall knew he was trying to hide the tears that were coming back.

"She never listens to me." He paused. "So, I came to catch frogs, it makes me happy." He said with a smile and a new vigour in him. "And look!" He exclaimed with a huge smile as he turned back to Marshall with a complete change in mood, wiping his eyes, almost forgetting his upset.

He grabbed the metal pail he had brought with him and showed Marshall with pride, as if it were a trophy. Marshall peered into the metal bucket and could see the large bullfrog submerged in a pool of pond water. It was huge.

"Wow cried Marshall that's the biggest I've ever seen!"

"I know right, he was just sitting here, so I crept over and bam trapped him in the bucket. I call him *Jeremiah Bullfrog.* I just need to catch his wife *Betty Croaker.* There must be some good ones over the next bank too, I can hear people over there."

"And what about the bedsheet?" Marshall interrupted, finally realising what Randy's costume was made from. He could see better now he was up close that it was a white duvet, tied at the waist with a toy lasso.

"Mom took my cowboy costume away when she grounded me so I made a new one, she forgot the lasso." He smiled, sneakily. "I used a marker for the eyes. What do you think?" He said with excitement as he flipped the hood over his head, making the ghost complete, raising his arms in front moaning like a ghost.

Marshall could see by the ragged hole his head had been through that Randy had used scissors to cut the bedsheet to make a hood he could remove. He knew their Mom was going to be even angrier but right now he knew Randy hadn't thought of that and he didn't want to upset him all over again and make him worry. He would try and lose it somewhere when they got back. Plus, he was actually impressed with his little brothers' ingenuity in such a short time.

Marshall knew his brother had a terrible habit of doing the wrong thing with the right intentions but he was really a sweet kid with a Heart of Gold. He Loved his brother but he was so random, he wondered if that's where his parents got his name from, and it was partly why he shortened it to Rand. Because if random wasn't his first name it was surely his middle name.

"Look, it's getting dark and we need to head back okay, how about we come back out here tomorrow and try this together?"

Randy scratched his chin and pondered his choices.

"How about two more spots quickly, then we come back tomorrow if we don't find anything?" He negotiated, testing his big brother.

"How about one more spot now and I don't tell Mom about the bedsheet you cut up?" He said with a smile.

Realising all of a sudden, the trouble he might be in. He stuck his hand out in front of him.

"You sir, have a deal."

The brothers shook hands and sealed the agreement.

"Eurgh!!" Cried Marshall as he wiped the frog slime on Randy's shoulder. Randy giggled.

"Get off, that tickles." He laughed.

"It's grim. Wash your hands in the water." Marshall smiled.

"Ah, it's okay besides, it's good luck." Said Randy.

"Good luck?! Who told you that?"

"I did!" Randy laughed again.

"Let's go. Oh, also I convinced Mom to let you come with me to the diner tonight to help put the decorations up."

Randy stopped in his tracks with a huge smile and wide eyes.

"So, I can still have Halloween?" he asked with joy.

"Sort of, no trick or treating. But you can come to the start of the Horrorthon!"

Randy wrapped his arms around his big brother and squeezed tightly.

"Just until the kids show ends okay!"

"Okay, thankyou Marshall!"

The two boys started walking to the next spot, a little south westerly from where they were. As they got closer, they could hear the voices of other kids just as Randy had said.

"Hey, you're right, sounds like it's a good spot. I hope they left some for us!" said Marshall teasing Randy.

Randy looked up at Marshall with a serious face and then the thought of all the good frogs being taken already crossed him and he started running, pail in hand. Jeremiah Bullfrog sloshing in the bottom as he ran.

"Hey I was... kidding." cried Marshall after him. But it was too late Randy had shot off like a rocket across the grass and through the bushes. Marshall carried on walking but as he got closer, he could make out one of the voices and terror filled him in a flash.

"Wait!" He shouted in panic. Marshall broke into a run and caught up to his brother at the bushes and grabbed Randy's shoulder firmly.

"Ow!" cried Randy "That hurts."

"Shh!" said Marshall pressing his finger to his lips. They peered through the bushes and saw the group of kids.

It was Josh Butcheson and The Butcher Boys.

"We need to go now!" Whispered Marshall.

"Why?"

"This one looks crowded that's all." He didn't want to scare his little brother. He also knew how much he looked up to him and he didn't want to show just how scared he was, out here without teachers or friends to stop the boys. He grabbed Randy's wrist and was about to turn to walk back the way they came when he heard the familiar wheezy voice of Terry Deagle.

"Leaving so soon?"

Marshall was well liked at his school but for some reason Josh Butcheson and the rest of the Butcher Boys, as everyone at Maitland High called them. Seemed to take great delight in making the time to torment him daily or at least as often as they could in between their rounds at the school.

They found any excuse to cause mischief and mayhem. Just last week they decided setting firecrackers off in the girls bathroom was the most productive way to spend their day avoiding classes and despite everyone knowing it was them, they simply replied with shrugged shoulders and a *helpful* suggestion that it was in fact the new kid as they had seen him not five minutes before the end of recess in that direction.

But for all the pleasure they got and attention they directed at the unfortunate architecture of the high school and its inhabitants, Marshall always seemed to garner the award for "best target" and today was no exception.

"H... Hey guys we were just passing through."

"Oh really?!" replied Josh.

"Hey, they did catch a big one!" Shouted Randy, not realising the situation they were in. "See Marsh I told you this was a good spot."

Josh looked angrily behind him at the buckets of frogs and snarled. They had seen their haul and he knew they would tell the principal what they were up to and the last thing they needed was more detention time.

"Trouble is, you know our little secret now pipsqueak. So, when Principal Wade asks who had the genius idea of putting frogs in the teachers' lounge then I'm thinking we have some problems."

"Um, they never knew we were putting them in the lounge Josh."

"Shut up Terry, how many other kids you think are out here collecting frogs?"

"I am!"

Marshall groaned as his brother joined in.

"I won't say a word Josh, I promise" Marshall said. "I just came to get my brother."

Josh smiled and looked at Randy.

"Now, I believe you Marshall... I really do. But my boys here, they aren't so sure. Me and you have history but they need some reassurances and you know this is our lake, so there's a fee for trespassing! I'll tell you what you pay our little toll and *maybe* we let you pass and we ALL forget what we saw here. So how about it, kid. What you got?" He asked Randy as he noticed him fumbling under his costume.

"Nothing!" Replied randy, panicked. He was suddenly worried he would be forced to part with his treasures he had in his pocket."

"Don't be shy kid." Called Terry.

"Hey, Leave him alone." Marshall shouted.

"Stay out of this Marsh," Josh looked up and stared at him. "I'm talking to Casper here. So how about it, what you got under there?"

Randy looked over his shoulder at Marshall and saw how worried his big brother was. He smiled a fiendish smile and Marshall groaned, he knew what was coming next and got ready to run!

"Show him Randy!" Marshall shouted.

Randy grinned and turned to face Josh and the other boys and in one swift move he lifted his costume and threw the metal bucket and its foul-smelling contents at the boys. Pond weed, stale water and Jeremiah covered Josh's face and the brothers turned and ran as fast as they could towards town.

They made their way through the trees and bushes and didn't look back once. As Marshall Approached the spot the boys had left their bikes, he shouted for Randy to carry on. He thought, with a sense of self satisfaction, about letting their tires down but he could hear the boys not far behind and the thought was swiftly dashed from his mind as he continued running along the path with the main road in sight. They could hear they were now on their bikes and they knew they would catch up at any minute.

"Quick, That way!" Cried Marshall.

They took a left onto Fisher street where they could hopefully navigate the small alleyways of the suburbs that surrounded the outside of the town and hopefully shake them from their tail.

Once firmly in the neighbourhood they ducked behind a big industrial waste bin behind one of the first stores that led to the centre of town. Ms. Thackery's Flower Emporium, an artisanal looking shop, duck egg blue on the outside with a more worn out yellow on the inside.

The exterior had just been painted that spring in an attempt to bring in more custom but the inside hadn't changed since the day her father opened the store some 70 years previous. Some folks thought the yellow décor suited the feel of the pretty, yet dated flower shop. Others thought that because there was so much clutter and the store was in constant, direct sunlight, the once fuchsia paint had now yellowed with age and lack of cleaning due to Ms. Thackery's own aging. But there were those who knew that when Mr. Thackery suddenly left town years ago, she didn't want to change a thing, like an everlasting memory and nostalgia piece to times with her father.

He heard The Butcher Boys shoot past the front of the store, past the hardware store next door and carry on to town.

"They can't have gone far." Cried Josh, he pointed to a slight and gangly looking boy to his right, Billy Mcfadden. Billy's face was covered in freckles and he had jet black hair that poked out around his Red Sox baseball cap. Billy was Josh's right hand man, more out of fear than loyalty. Despite his wickedness Josh wasn't the strongest or the smartest, but Josh's older brother, Mike Butcheson, was and everyone in Maitland knew better than to mess with Josh or they would have Mike Butcheson to contend with. Even some of the grownup members of the Maitland community could be seen to skip across the other side of the street or avert their glance if they were in Mike's path. They themselves bullied in their day by Mike Sr. And so the trend carried on through history by generations of Butchesons that never left town and never amounted to anything other than the future inheritor of the Butcheson family garage, and with each hands that the family business was passed, the anger and bitterness grew with the knowledge that they would be the next town failure. The future Maitland High dropout, and so instead of breaking the trend and standing up to the current "Mr. Butcheson" they would take it out on everything and anything smaller and weaker than them.

Billy took one of the other boys with him and the two groups split up in search. Josh headed north, towards the town hall and Billy circled back towards the woods and the pond.

Just as Marshall thought they were in the clear, *thump...* he felt a heavy hand on his shoulder from behind.

"Marshall! What're you up to out here?" a hoarse but welcoming voice cried. It was "Old Man" Abernathy.

Mr. Abernathy owned the hardware store in town that served as Marshall's part time workplace. He was a kind old man in his 70's. Slight of shape and could always be seen proudly sporting his short sleeved, "Abernathy's" monogrammed, white, cotton shirts. His wife had made a whole bunch of them when he purchased the store in the fifties and though the wording had been re stitched on some a few times and the odd tear had been sewn back together, he still wore them today. Though a little more threadbare after his wife had passed.

He had tufts of white hair combed neatly back from under his blue baseball cap, which again, was stitched with the company's logo. He would always wear a pair of grey work pants to complete the professional look with the only exception being his tattered grey sneakers. He said *if a man was to be working on his feet all day then he should be doing so in comfort.*

He kept a clean-shaven face and a year-long farmer's tan on his frail, sun dried arms. He was a man set firm in his beliefs and morals and went out of his way to help others. He had lost his wife some years before and the store had become his life. In recent years, with bigger D.I.Y. depots opening up in Dennison nearby, he hadn't been as busy as he used to and in is elderly years, he found it increasingly harder to clean and run the store alone, even with the loss of trade. And so, he hired Marshall after putting a "help wanted" sign in the window. He could afford to pay Marshall what equated a decent wage to a teenager but also have the odd jobs and heavier lifting jobs attended to that he found harder to do now.

He could see, all too well from the expressions on their faces and the redness in their cheeks, that they had been running away from something... or someone.

"Those Butcheson Boys at it again?" He asked, shooting a disapproving glance out into the ether as if searching out for the thugs himself.

"Ah it's okay, nothing I can't handle." Marshall said, trying to don a sense of bravado, a little embarrassed he had been caught hiding.

"Oh, I wasn't doubting for a second Son." Replied Abernathy, noticing the boys abashed expression and trying to reassure him of his bravery. "But no shame in taking the high road."

He leant his old leathered arm outstretched onto the lid of the waste bin and pointed at Marshall. "You could give that Josh Butcheson a lick three ways to Sunday, your smart too." He said wagging his finger to emphasise the point. "But that older brother of his..." He sighed. "I'd hate to think what he'd do, the little punk."

"I threw a bucket!!" Confessed Randy with pride from the shadows. Peering his head from his hiding spot near the bin.

"Hehehe, well I can see you're just as brave as your brother. I can imagine he rightly deserved it too! Did you get 'em?"

"Yeah, got him good" he smiled a cheeky grin.

"Atta boy" Mr. Abernathy jostled Randy's curly hair. He reminded him of himself in his youth.

"But I lost my Frog... and my bucket!" Randy suddenly realised.

"Well that won't do." Exclaimed the Old man. He had heard the clicking of bike gears shifting in the distance and could tell the gang were still in the area. He turned back to the boys. "I tell you what, why don't you come inside the store. I reckon I have a spare bucket around here somewhere that you can borrow until you get yours back." He opened the back door of the store and ushered the kids in to safety, peering around as he closed the door behind him to make sure they hadn't been seen.

The back room of the store was a familiar sight to Marshall. He would unload any deliveries for the Old man here and he would eat his packed lunch on a Saturday in the back room. Although, he would always prop the back door open. The smell of white spirit and old wood could get potent in the summer heat and was enough to put him off his lunch. Today though that familiar smell of spilled varnish and old tools felt safe and comforting.

"Here, take a seat Scamp" The old man, patted an old stool for Randy to sit on. Randy laughed to himself at being called a scamp.

"Marshall, grab that box up there will ya, I think we got some metal buckets here somewhere."

Marshall reached up and grabbed the box the old man had pointed out. He reached in and took out a shiny new bucket.

"There we go!" Smiled Abernathy.

Marshall turned around to show Randy but he wasn't in his seat. He was over by a workbench just off to the side but when he saw it, he had a big smile on his face.

"It's perfect. Thankyou."

"You're quite welcome." Abernathy smiled.

They walked through to the front of the store. The shelves were stacked high behind the counter on the right, all along the back wall, with boxes of different size screws and fixings. To the left were a mixture of tools that had been on display for years and the odd promotional stand selling newer products in a bid to stay current.

"So, why are you out catching frogs anyway, it's Halloween! Shouldn't you be out with your friends?"

JOE! Marshall suddenly thought. The old man was right! In the unfolding of the events at the lake he had completely forgotten about Joe and about his date with Vinessa.

"We need to go! Thanks Mr. Abernathy." Marshall opened the door at the front of the store and waved his brother through.

"No trouble at all, just remember, there's no harm in hiding but a bully will always be a bully if you let them!"

Mr. Abernathy stood in the doorway and waved them off, grabbing a broom near the entrance to sweep down the path outside the store.

The kids waved back and ran without pause all the way to Futterman's, the best diner in town.

Chapter 6

Marshall loved coming to Futterman's. He loved looking at all the paraphernalia on the walls from different movies. It was also like a second home ever since Marshall met Joe all those years ago.

Futterman's was the place that everybody in town would go. Whether it was just to meet up, celebrate birthdays, have their first date and even break up. Anything that happened in Maitland probably happened at Futterman's.

Sure, there were other restaurants in town like the Italian bistro and pizzeria. There was the Asian kitchen and the burgers at the local bar and some people liked Mrs. Harvey's Coffee shop on main street. But that seldom did more than a piece of fruit pie with your hot beverage and that was only around the time of Apricot Fest or when Mrs. Harvey harvested the pitiful looking apple tree growing in her yard. But none of them came with the atmosphere that could be found at Futterman's.

Complete with full kitchen, a modest bar, outside area for the summer nights and a host of entertainment nights. There were three things that drew the people in.

Firstly, was the menu, which had a range of dishes all playfully named with a play on words after the owners' favourite cult movies.

The "Mogwai Burger" had a decent helping of green food dye added to the burger bun and came with its own warning "*not to be eaten after midnight.*" You could get a side of "Marty McFries" with any meal and wash it all down with a cold refreshing glass of his homebrewed "B-Eerie, Indiana." Maybe a healthier option was your thing? The "Edward Caesar-Hands" salad was a popular choice and the new dish "The Prawnshank Redemption" the surf and turf meal based on the years Blockbuster hit "The Shawshank Redemption", was proving a firm favourite amongst the diners.

The children had their own menu entitled "Honey, I Shrunk the Kids-Meal" and on "Steak and Cinema" night you could enjoy a movie on the drop-down projector screen with a prime cut of beef all for $6.95 with unlimited salad and potatoes. You could even watch "The Breakfast Club" at the breakfast club!

Secondly, was the owner. One Robert Lawrence Futterman, or "Big Bob" as the town called him. Some say due to the size of his heart and the sheer amount of joy he gave to everyone in town, some say due to his waist band that matched and some say due to the roaring belly laugh he would emit at any opportunity. But regardless the reason, everybody in Maitland loved Big Bob.

He was a lovable, giant of a man that brought a presence to the room, he was funny and witty and liked to make people laugh. He had a pair of chubby cheeks that lifted almost past his Eyes when he smiled. He wore a pair of glasses for reading that tucked into the remainder of his tight knit hair that encircled his bolding head. His facial hair was trimmed into a small goatee that rested on his double chin. Which looked too delicate for him to have shaved himself given the size of his oversized, sausage-like fingers. He could fill a room with joy and with his booming voice that still retained his southern *N'Orleans* drawl, despite living the last three decades on the East Coast.

Lastly, everyone in town knew to meet there for a night out, like an unwritten rule. So, it was always a hive of activity. From families enjoying a meal out, teens meeting for a shake and some "Marty Mcfries", to the blue-collar workers of the town that would meet for a beer after work. Everyone would flock to Futterman's, especially tonight!

This was because every Halloween, "Big Bob" Futterman would spend the week decorating the diner. Transforming it into a one stop extravaganza, full of handmade decorations. Props from horror movies which Bob was certain were genuine like his "original" book of the dead and various other trinkets and artefacts that were so real looking, some people questioned where Bob would get such items. Some of the older kids in town would try to outdo each other and tell the younger one's stories of how Bob got them, each story more gruesome and unbelievable than the rest. Every year there would be at least one outbreak of tears or screams before the night's events.

This included Big Bob's Nephew, Joe. Marshall always enjoyed coming to Futterman's. Joe and Marshall had met when Joe moved to town after his dad passed away.

He was only young but when they arrived in Maitland, Big Bob took him under his wing, or more appropriate to his size, his "Paw". When Joe started school that fall, Marshall was the one who stepped in and prevented Josh Butcheson from making an easy target of the new kid. Joe was an only child and as such tried that bit extra to fit in and be liked. Marshall knew that his stories about his uncle's knick-knacks were more out of boredom than actually trying to scare the younger kids, truth be told most were nothing but old newspaper, PVA glue and a creative eye. But some, even Joe couldn't be sure of. Like the supposed monkey paw, frozen in a partially clenched fist waiting to grant wishes. So, life like. So, disgusting. *Too* disgusting to be real and on display in the diner thought Marshall.

Aside from the visual wonderland that the venue transformed into every year, was the main event "Horrorthon". Every year people would gather from all over town and come join in the Movie marathon that Bob provided. Set amidst the trinkets and Halloween decorations to give that extra authentic feel. Each Year Bob would visit the local video store and see what new horror VHS tapes were out. He would pick the most freakishly fun new movies and then invite the town to spend Halloween evening at the diner. There, he would screen various classics and new Halloween themed movies. Starting always with a special showing of "It's the Great Pumpkin, Charlie Brown" for the younger ones and their parents after Trick or Treating. Then proceeding to raise the scare factor incrementally as the night continued.

He always served a host of Halloween themed food too. From his "Severed Finger" hot dogs, to his famous "Spine

Chilling Chilli" which he prided himself on keeping his secret recipe. This would go on into the night until the last people left.

This year he was showing a screening of the creature feature "Critters" and the new horror release, "A New Nightmare", which he was very excited to unleash on the townspeople of Maitland.

Out of breath and a little red in the cheeks, Marshall arrived at the diner to find Joe tapping his wristwatch mockingly.

"Hey Colonel Sanders, what time d'ya call this?"

"You want help or not?" replied Marshall with a scowl. The two burst out laughing and brought it in with a pat on the back.

"And I told you I hate that name ...Smeller" Jeered Marshall.

"It's Miller, not Smeller... Chicken Boy." Replied Joe.

He paused and grinned a side glance to Marshall as they were walking to the entrance of the diner.

"But as you wish... Colonel." he raised his right hand in salute with a wide grin on his face.

When the two were young they had a run in with Josh Butcheson on one of his daily attempts to ruin Marshall's schooldays. He thought it would be funny to steal Marshall's Walkman and he proceeded to throw it back and forth with Billy Mcfadden. Marshall stood up to Josh and the kids gasped.

"This was it." Thought Joe. "That bully is finally going to get what he deserves."

He braced himself and tried to stand tall in defiance of the bully's threats. But the crowd's cheers soon turned to whispers as Marshall could hear the loud, heavy footsteps of Mike Butcheson coming up the hall. The crowd parted and Mike towered over Marshall. Before Marshall could even say a word, he received a quick sucker punch for his efforts and the crowd erupted into a single "Oooohh". They felt every bit of pain as Marshall took the blow and fell to the ground.

He tried standing upright but he was winded too bad and whilst every fibre of his being wanted to stand up to the Butcheson brothers and tell them exactly what he thought of them. That they were nothing but losers and dumb losers at that, with nothing to do but pick on people smaller because they were cowards themselves. All he could muster was a dry sounding "quark" that resembled a chicken clucking and his eyes filled with tears that he would refuse to release.

Josh looked at him and mimicked the sound in jest. "Quark" he flapped his arms then pointed at Marshall. "Look at the big chicken! Not so tough now huh Sanderson!!"

Marshall ran, with Joe swiftly and loyally chasing him through the corridor and out of sight. All the while they could hear the Butcheson brothers shouting "Chicken, Sanderson's a Chicken". The other kids joined in cruelly.

Once around the corner, Joe proceeded to tell Marshall how he would have taken the two on and he was in fact just about to make his move but he thought he should stay with his friend in case he was hurt.

Marshall smiled from under his tears. There were days he just wanted to escape the bullying, why was it always him, why did they have to hurt other kids at all? He wondered.

From then on, he was labelled as Chicken Sanderson but Joe tried to change that for the best to "Colonel Sanders" because, he reasoned, it was a fact that everybody loved the colonel and his famous fried chicken. To Joe's upset it didn't make it any better at school but Marshall appreciated it and always remembered his friend for trying that day.

In truth, Joe knew Marshall was tougher than he gave himself credit for. If only he had the confidence in himself. He looked up to him like the brother he never had. If only he was given a chance to prove himself.

"So, where have you been?" asked Joe.

Marshall and Randy explained the chaos that had ensued from leaving school to them meeting Joe. Randy didn't hold back on the frog details.

"So, what's the damage, how much still needs doing before your uncle opens?"

Joe went to answer but the booming voice of "Big Bob" beat him to it. Albeit muffled by a stack of boxes he was carrying in both arms, that towered past his enormous shoulders. He dumped the boxes on the hood of his Pontiac with force.

"We got two boxes of Pumpkin lights need untangling and stringing up around the screen. We got a few dozen hot dog rolls still need slicing for my "Zombie's Finger Rolls" and the pet cemetery display on the grass over there is missing a few cats, they're in one of these boxes somewhere, and maybe add a few more werewolf footprints, ya know, for extra effect." he said with a devilish smile and fiendish laugh.

"Joe, you know where the keys are right?"

"Uh yeah" said Joe a little surprised "But you're telling us this all because? Asked Joe "Aren't we doing this with you?"

"Yeah, well you will be but your mom just called and her car done broke down on the way home from work, I keep telling her to get an American engine but... anyway, so now I gotta go pick her up and wait for the mechanic to arrive with a pickup. So, with a very heavy heart I'm relying on you guys to make this thing happen until I'm back. You think you can handle it?" He pointed at the trio with a stare like an owl.

"Uh yeah."

"That's the spirit... get it spirit." He guffawed.

The boys looked at each other and rolled their eyes.

"Oh, and if I'm not back before the young'uns arrive, you know what to do!" he said, handing a VHS cassette to Joe.

"I know, I know, put the Great Pumpkin on, you think one year we could maybe change it?... everybody in town has watched that movie as a kid."

"Exactly" cried Bob with joy. "*EVERYBODY* has grown up with it, it's a yearly tradition at Futterman's, it's a classic, and it's my legacy to the town. No, my boy, you don't change what ain't broke."

"How about we slightly... *adjust* tradition?" asked Joe, groaning at the thought of having to sit through another half hour of Snoopy and the gang waiting for an oversized fruit to appear.

"Or slightly wobble tradition... I'm willing to give room here on the level of wobbling we do as far as tradition." He tried negotiating.

Big Bob looked him sternly beneath his furrowed brow, without movement, not even a blink.

"Slightly?" Joe winced, breaking the silence, motioning a pincer movement with his thumb and index finger to illustrate just how small a change he was willing to go.

Big Bob's stern expression suddenly melted into a huge smile.

"I'll tell you what, if you can get *all* this done before I'm back, you get to pick the Kid's movie next year!"

Joe's face lit up "Really?!"

"Hell No!" Bob shot back quickly and laughed his booming laugh, pleased with himself and tussled Joe's hair.

Joe slumped his shoulders and pulled a face.

"Hilarious." He said sarcastically.

Marshall had seen them do this dance a thousand times before and he could never quite tell if Joe always fell for it or secretly, he enjoyed the bond they shared and indulged the little game.

Big Bob had, after all, taken over the Father role in Joe's life after his dad had died. Joe was only young when it happened, he wouldn't talk about it but Marshall knew it must have been bad. A year later Joe and his Mom moved up to Maitland and Big Bob stepped in and filled the gap, and then some. Having never married and with no kids of his own, Bob was saddened at the news of his brother in law but filled with love and a sense of responsibility to his sister and her only son.

He treated his nephew like his own, with all the joking and mocking only an uncle could get away with. Marshall wondered why Bob hadn't settled down, he would make a great dad, he thought.

"Ah dang it, one last thing." Bob said as he turned to the boys before getting into his car.

"I almost forgot. There's a new store opened up. Real cool looking, got tons of neat stuff. I stopped by a couple days ago, spotted the owner outside, unpacking. I'm gonna go take a decent look around soon but he was going to put a few bits aside that I spotted. I was supposed to pick them up for tonight but I straight up forgot. Here's Sixty bucks he never said how much they were but take it in case and if it's any more tell him I'll swing by tomorrow with the rest. Could you guys run over and grab them for me? He'll probably be closed before I'm back."

"What, more horror crap!" exclaimed Joe.

"Joseph Miller! You watch your cussing!! And besides..." Bob said with bruised pride "It's not *crap* it's..." he thought a second.

"Collectable… Replicas... And... Props!"

Bob exclaimed with a beaming grin.

"Exactly!" Joe sighed. "C.R.A.P."

Bob smiled. "Yes, it is!" He said proudly. "It's over on Kingston, can't miss it!"

The Boys stopped laughing and looked at each other, both taking a huge gulp.

"Wait, a new store on Kingston?" Marshall asked.

"Yes Sir'ee. "Worlds Apart" or something. You good?"

"Uh yeah, we're good." Joe let out a small smile.

"Thanks kiddo."

He pulled Joe in for a hug and tussled his hair again. He got in his car and started up the road. The brake lights glowed red as he slowed down and leaned out of the rolled down window and shouted "And I'll be counting my change mister!"

"Go already!" Joe shouted back with a smile.

The car pulled away and drifted out of sight.

Marshall spun round to Joe.

"Joe, we are most certainly not good! That's the store, the store Eddie's Mom must have been talking about, creepy guy, selling creepy stuff. No way we can go there!"

"What store? I wanna go!" Asked Randy, but the older kids ignored him.

"Relax Marsh, I got it covered." Said Joe acting cool and calm. "He said if we get all these things done! Sooo... we just need to find a reason not to have gotten over there in time!"

"That's actually a good idea!" Marshall said, surprised. "So, where do we start first?"

The three boys smiled and looked at each other and with mirrored expressions shouted "Ice Cream!!"

After a few generous scoops of the diner's stock and enough time wasted, they set to work with the lights and the other decorations they had been tasked with.

They set up the diner the way it had been laid out every year. They knew where each skeleton limb should hand, where every cobweb should be placed from spending way too many Halloweens there. With the exception of a few items Randy was left in charge of. They went up to the attic space of the diner to get the last of the boxes, the attic was filled with junk and cobwebs.

"I think he stores them over here." Said Joe.

Marshall saw a large cardboard box similar to those downstairs but with no markings, it wasn't sealed.

"Hey I think this might be one!" He opened it and on the top was an old yellowed photo in a frame. In the photo was a man and a woman. Underneath the photo was a Mauve suit, covered in dust and cobwebs.

"Hey, I think this is this your uncle?" Marshall handed Joe the old photo. "I didn't think your he was ever married."

"He's not." said Joe. He walked over to Marshall.

"That's strange." Joe frowned. "I've never seen this woman before."

"It's strange." Replied Marshall. "I feel like I have but I can't think why?"

"Oooh Marshall has a guurlfriend." Randy taunted.

Marshall ignored Randy's taunts as he stared at the woman in the photo. He shrugged and carefully laid the photo back down on the top of the box and they took the remaining boxes of decorations and clambered over the debris in the attic to the loft hatch.

It was getting dark as the boys were putting the finishing touches to the Diner. Bob's car pulled up and Joe's Mom got out.

"Wow this looks great guys, you did a great job. Bob told me you were holding down the fort." She looked up at Randy, who was sat on the counter "And how about you Randy? Are ya having fun?"

"Am I" He Exclaimed loudly as he spun around to face her. "I ate four Ice creams" he said with his spoon held high and his hand rubbing his stomach.

She laughed as she wiped the remnants of chocolate ice cream from around Randy's mouth.

"My brother won't have any left for *paying* customers if you keep at it. I tell you what, how about we get you cleared up and you can give me a hand in the kitchen getting things ready while the boys and Bob finish up the decorations okay? Maybe we can find you a special snack for the movie?"

"Ooh yeah." Randy shouted as he jumped off the counter with excitement at the thought of some candy or other goodies.

Bob locked the car and stopped a while outside to admire the boys work.

"Mighty fine if I do say so myself guys."

The Diner had been transformed, there were fake spider webs hanging from the top of the windows. Pumpkins illuminated the path up to the entrance. Fake gravestones and body parts littered the grass outside and the inside, full of its props and movie treasures was lit with purples and greens with orange crepe paper tied over the chairs set around for the movie.

"Thanks Uncle Bob. We did everything on the list we just didn't have time to get to that store, we're real sorry but it looks cool we think without the extra bits!" Joe commented, hoping he would be satisfied.

"Wow that's great guys, really appreciated. I knew I could trust you Joseph!" He was still looking at the display smiling while he tussled his nephew's hair.

The boys sighed a relief, it looked like they wouldn't have to venture to the store after all.

"Hey, Uncle Bob... were you ever married?" Joe asked partially out of curiosity and also to make sure the conversation moved on quickly.

The happy go lucky demeanour, permanently plastered on Big Bobs face changed for the first time Joe could remember and he knew he had asked something he shouldn't.

"Why would you ask that?"

He sounded as shocked to be asked as Joe was to see his reaction to being asked.

"You know I've been out here on my own until you and your ma showed up to give me a thorn in ma side."

"I know... it's just we were looking at some of the boxes for decorations and we found a photo... A photo that looked like you and a woman but you were really young in it... it was on an old suit and so I thought-"

"Dammit Joseph no, I ain't never been married okay. Now drop it" Bob snapped and rubbed his large paws over his mouth and head.

"I'm sorry... I didn't mean ta yell... I... I mean... well it's just been a really long time is all. Look sit here a sec."

Marshall began to leave to give them space.

"Nah, you can stay too Marshall."

The two boys still in shock from seeing Big Bob so upset and feeling guilty for touching on a nerve took a seat on the bench outside the diner and listened to Bob's story.

Bob took a seat on one of the benches outside and breathed a deep sigh. Then, as he stared into the abyss, he smiled a little from the corners of his mouth.

"Her name was April and she was just as pretty as the month and then some!" He said as he stared into the crisp, October sky.

"This was a long time ago and I mean looong. I'd only been in town a few months before I met her, she was the one who convinced me to get the Diner. She told me *dreams weren't for fools, they were for fools with the courage to dream*. I knew the moment I met her I wanted to spend the rest of my life with her. We'd go on picnics... we'd go for walks that lasted all day and we wouldn't see another soul until we got back home. Just us. We'd talk about all the places we were gonna travel, she used to tell me we'd have fifteen kids, can you believe that fifteen! I'd laugh. She said then one day, when we got old and the babies had gone their own way, we'd sell the diner and build a place in the woods on one of those walks that took all day, and not come back."

Joe had never seen this side of his uncle. He always showed compassion for others and took great joy in the fun and work at the diner. But what he was seeing was something new. Why had he never spoken of this April before.

"So... what happened." Joe asked softly.

"Well, we had been together a couple years, and I'd finally saved enough to buy the diner and some spare to get a ring..."

He paused. His face grew solemn, he knew how hard the next few sentences were going to be. He composed himself and continued.

"Like I say, this was way back when and you gotta remember I was just a slither of a thing back then. I was rather handsome too like Shaft without the moustache" He said with a faint smile, trying to lighten the mood.

He sighed and bit his lip.

"It was Halloween and I was going to open the Diner that night! I figured everybody would be wanting to go out and so it would make a great opening night. I also decided I was gonna make an honest woman out of her and what better way to celebrate than having all our friends around us... if she'd have me that is. And so, I asked her to meet me that evening around sunset at the lake where we spent our first date. I got myself a suit jacket and some decent pants and done the best I could with this."

He pointed to his face and forced a little smile for the boys.

"Anywho..." A tear welled in his eye.

"I got held up and I was running late by about a quarter hour. I got to our spot... an' she weren't there. I figured maybe she was running a little late herself, so I waited... and I waited..." He trailed off in thought and looked at the ground.

"She didn't come?" asked Joe with mouth a gasp.

Bob sighed a heavy sigh.

"I thought maybe she had guessed ma plan and she had seen sense and left or somethin'... y'know, didn't wanna settle down yet and that's when I noticed this."

Bob reached for a threadbare wallet in his pocket and pulled out a faded white ribbon. He held it up for the boys to see.

"She was wearing this in her hair the morning I left her to work on the Diner. It was on the ground between my feet where I stood." He said, still looking at the floor as if staring back at that spot.

"I searched the area 'case she had taken a walk elsewhere but I couldn't see her. Well I got worried and when I realised I couldn't find her, I drove back to town. She wasn't at home and no one had seen her so I went and spoke to the sheriff told him she was missing. They searched the whole area. Hours turned to days. Days turned into weeks, weeks to months. The Police never found her. No one ever saw her again. The Police thought maybe she'd run away but I done told 'em, she was happy she had no reason to. I was the only family she had." He paused in thought.

"No, the truth was she had come, she had been there, waiting for me... and I was late. Whatever befell her it was 'cos of me... I failed her."

A single tear strolled down his large, solemn cheek.

He looked up and at the diner with all its Halloween decorations.

"Those fifteen minutes have haunted me more than any of these decorations will haunt a man."

He looked over at the two boys, who wanted to be supportive but they just didn't have the words.

"Ah jeez, what am I saying." He snapped back into the jolly Bob the town new and wiped the tear away from his face. He put the mask back on and played the character he was expected to be, just slightly ashamed.

"You kids have heard enough of an old fool's sorry ass story!"

Marshall didn't know what to say. Joe had questions firing through his mind but he knew now wasn't the time. Instead he stood up and without a word just gave his uncle a hug as far around his big stomach as his arms would let him.

"How about you get those last few items and I'll have a special new *spoooky* shake ready for you both when you're back? That store will be closing before you even get there at this rate."

"Say what?" Asked Joe Mortified both from the story and Big Bob's last comment.

"The store, it's still open boy, so you best be gettin', don't think I forgot."

The Boys felt sick all of a sudden. "Are you sure? I mean it's getting late and it's Halloween too."

Bob gave the boys the look and they knew they would have to go.

"Mr. Futterman. Is it okay to leave my brother with you guys?" Marshall asked. He really didn't want to go but he felt better if he knew his brother was safe.

"Course it is, Marshall. Now go safe and come right back, it's gonna be a full moon out and you don't wanna be late! *Oooooooh!*"

He raised his hands up like a ghost and chuckled to himself before silently walking back to the store trying to shake himself back into the party mood.

Chapter 7

As the streetlamps flickered on for their evening service, the two boys headed out to the new store on Kingston Street, towards the outskirts of town. The sky glowing red and purple behind them with the last of the setting sun's light. Kingston Street was on the old side of town which was run down and although safe, it could be creepy at night.

"So, what do you think is *in* this store?" Asked Marshall. "I didn't even know it had opened!"

"Is that any surprise?" Said Joe. "This side of town is a bit of a dump."

The trouble was that the stretch of road was so far away from the rest of town that nobody really went there, which meant it was cheap to hold a store here but the standard of places that went in there were more *unsavoury,* or just not needed. A second Barbershop had lasted a week, then there was a Chinese massage parlour run by a man who looked like he'd never heard of Asia let alone could run a functioning centre that practiced the arts of the orient. But it came complete with tropical fish and one of those *lucky* golden cats with the paw that moves up and down and so he had to be the real deal... right?

The whole precinct was planned to be bulldozed and a strip mall built in its place. Complete with new stores, a cinema and artisanal coffee shops to rival Dennison or at least stop people leaving town to shop there so much. But a small group of protestors claimed it was part of Maitland history, being the original main street in the town's inception and all the local business owners seconded the motion. More for fear the new allure of modern shops would run them out of business and so the plans were abandoned and Kingston Street was left as it was. A lonely reminder of yesteryear, fallen into disrepair and right in the middle was the store that Big Bob had mentioned and somewhere inside was the mysterious owner.

"The shops are always changing here." Said Joe. "Did you know there was even a mob hideout, until the cops came and shut it down?!"

"No way!" Scoffed Marshall.

"Yeah I saw it with my own eyes and everything."

"You're full of it, you know that, right?"

"Well either way, I don't like this side of town and now we have to go see this creep. So, can we just get in and go as quick as possible?"

"You're not scared, are you?" asked Marshall smiling.

"No!" protested Joe. "I just don't want to miss out on the Horrorthon that's all."

"I thought you'd be glad to miss that cartoon you said you loved so much." Marshall Laughed.

"I... I am. But... look that must be the place."

The boys came to a stop in front of an old store. The wooden black frames around the large windows made the store feel cold and sinister. There were red curtains hung in the window tied with a yellow sash at each side. There were no signs on the window or above the door but from the strange objects in the display window, they knew this must be the store Big Bob was talking about.

Tentatively, Marshall turned the door knob and opened the door inwards. The smell of dust and incense hit them almost instantly in a battle to overpower each other. The little bell above the door rung above his head.

Ding a ding ding

Almost like an alarm to warn the store owner something from the modern world had arrived. The boys entered and Joe shut the door behind him carefully. Everything in the shop seemed delicate and fragile. As they looked around at the strange objects for sale, they saw a variety of items. Ancient looking, full of mystery and long forgotten memories as the incense subsided and the dust prevailed, Marshall thought it like the smell you get at a library. That of old leather books and times long gone, with everything waiting for its story to be told.

They walked along the bare wooden floor slowly in awe and caution as they took in the sights around. There were artefacts and trinkets of every description covering the dark stained mahogany shelves that ran along the dark green and beige papered walls. There were display benches with pedestals and stands that held strange masks and books open. Tall black armoires, positioned on the left side of the store, stood under the high shelves. They were decorated with strange golden symbols and filled with various items and candles.

There were metal pendants and small ornate boxes with gems on, which Joe thought must be fake. There were glass jars with what appeared to be creatures, or at least pieces of creatures, in but Marshall couldn't make out the resemblance to any animal he'd ever seen before. Some items were labelled with a description, most were not. Leaving its purpose to the imagination and its origin known only to the most serious of collectors.

There were pieces of parchment on one wooden rack of shelving, some rolled into a scroll and some flat out on display but all of which were in a language the boys couldn't read and some they weren't even sure were written using letters at all. Marshall noticed that nothing had a price either. No sticker even. There were old bird cages hanging from the ceiling in one of the corners and at the back of the store, in the centre, like a royal throne amongst the dark walls and macabre trinkets, stood an old copper cashier's desk. Detailed like neither had ever seen before. Everything about this store was awe inspiring and terrifying all at once.

As they walked slowly towards the desk, Marshall ran his hand along a long blade on a rack of what looked like ancient samurai swords.

"Ouch..."

The blade was paper thin and sliced the tip of his finger with no effort. He put his finger to his mouth and could taste blood instantly but it was only a small scratch.

"Hey I thought this store was new?" said Marshall. "It's covered in cobwebs and dust."

"Relax." said Joe. "Most of this is probably old movie stuff that's why my uncle must have loved it so much it's probably stolen or fake that's why there's no labels."

"But why would anyone bring Hollywood props to Maitland... Nothing interesting happens here."

"I don't know, makes sense, if you'd stolen a load of movie props you wouldn't stick around the big city where everyone would know. You'd play it cool in small towns, less conspicuous. You see it on the TV all the time."

Joe went on to talk about a case he'd seen on "Cops" on the TV once but Marshall had stopped listening, instead he was trying to work out where that noise was coming from. It was soft, and calling to him from the right-hand side of the shop somewhere at the back.

He followed the noise. It was like music. Was there someone else in the store, the owner maybe? It sounded soft and high pitched like the music of a jewellery box but sad. Where was it coming from? Thought Marshall. The shelving racks obscured his view to the origin of the noise. So, he made his way around the corner and towards the back corner of the store. As he got closer the music grew louder. Marshall was hypnotised, the song was like a lullaby calling to him. He was fixated on the mysterious sound.

La la DA dah
La la DA dah

The room disappeared in his mind and all he could hear was the mysterious music, he must be close.

La la DA dah
La la DA dah

"*Heeeelpp...*" A voice echoed in the back of his mind like a whisper.

"Huh?" thought Marshall

"Heeeeeelpp..."

Something was talking to him over the mysterious sound.

"Caaan Iiii Heeeelppp..." this time it sounded behind him and increasingly clearer to hear. He spun round and snapped out of his daze.

"Can I help!" Came a sharp voice.

"Marshall you okay?" Shouted Joe.

Marshall shook his head and came to. Joe was stood behind him and next to Joe was the shopkeeper. An older man, in Brown corduroy trousers and wearing a dark Green sleeveless V-neck, sweater over a white cotton shirt. He was gangly with a wry smile and a slight comb-over of the last hair he had left. He had a hooked, beak like nose that jutted out almost as far as his thin, pointed chin.

This was the guy? Marshall thought. This was the evil, maniacal man who had spooked Eddie's Mom.? Sure, he was creepy looking but nothing serious. Once again, the townsfolk of Maitland had overreacted and a poor kid was losing out on Halloween, Marshall thought.

He calmed at once after seeing the man and began to take in more of the store now he felt at ease. As spooky as its contents were.

"Can I help!" The Shopkeeper repeated, impatiently this time and perfectly clear. The music had gone.

"Uh yeah..." said Joe glancing to his side, eyes fixed on Marshal still checking he was okay. "We uh... We came to pick up some things for my uncle. Bob Futterman. He said you had them put aside."

"Ah..." said the shopkeeper also glancing at Marshall but with more of a questioning tone. "Yes, *Big Bob*" He pronounced with exaggerated B's almost in detest.

Marshall didn't know what Bob had asked for but Bob's taste in the strange looked oddly mainstream compared to the rarities found here and Marshall could almost sense the disdain the shopkeeper had had for his mediocrity.

"I know exactly the items you mean. Let me retrieve Mr. Futterman's items from out back. I won't be a moment, please have a look around if you wish, but don't touch anything!" He said angrily. Joe shook his head vigorously in silence and looked for reassurance from Marshall.

Realising his effect on the kids, the shopkeeper smiled a crooked smile.

"There are a lot of dangerous items and we wouldn't want anything to happen to them... or you, would we?"

Despite his smile Marshall couldn't work out if he meant it or not. The boys looked at each other and decided to stay at the counter.

"We're okay thanks, we'll just wait here. We have to get back anyways... to the diner..." Joe called out.

"Ah yes, the *Horrorthon*." Said the shopkeeper, spinning back round on his heel with an heir of disgust. "Mr. Futterman mentioned his... *show*."

"Are you coming?" Asked Joe. "Everyone in town will be there."

"Unfortunately, not." replied the shopkeeper sarcastically. "I'm afraid in my line of work you become rather desensitized to the paranormal and the things that go *bump in the night*. Pumpkins, costumes and hot dogs do not exactly strike fear into the soul I'm afraid."

"And what exactly is that?" asked Marshall

"I beg your pardon" replied the shopkeeper.

"Your line of work" asked Marshall... I mean do you collect these? Make these?... these things... are they... are they..."

"Real?" Asked the shopkeeper, stroking the side of a stuffed animal.

He leant in close to Marshall with a grin and whispered.

"What do you think?" There was a pause, Marshall was trying to work him out.

"I'll be right back!" He said softly with a devilish smile and he turned slowly and went into the back of the store, through a dark curtain behind the counter.

Joe continued to talk to the man, even after he disappeared out of sight.

"Your loss Mister, everyone's going to be there. So, what made you move to Maitland in the first place anyway?" He raised his voice a little. "I mean, no offence some of this stuff is cool but the people here in town aren't... and again, no offence... *voodoo freaks.*"

The Shopkeeper returned from behind the dark curtain with a box. He was wearing that little smile of his again.

"You see, I travel from... no offense. Little town, to little town, with this... s*tuff.*" He said in a tone mimicking Joe's. "You see my collection is... rather special shall we say, one of a kind."

"But why do you have to move a lot, is it because no one wants it?" Asked Joe.

"Cut it out." Said Marshall, tapping Joe's side. "He didn't mean that sir."

"Of course he did. But that's quite alright! The reason I have to move so much is because the items I bring are shall we say... rare... desired by certain people and the attention that brings isn't always desirable. So, I keep on the road stopping just long enough in each place to make a living without drawing too much attention to myself or the store." The shopkeeper turned to grab some paper to wrap the items.

Joe whispered to Marshall. "See, I told you, stolen!!"

"I don't think that's what he means?" Marshall whispered back with a thoughtful look.

The Shopkeeper had wrapped the items in some old paper with some twine to secure.

"What, no bow" Joe asked with a sarcastic grin.

The shopkeeper grimaced. "I like to be old fashioned."

He Continued his story. "No, I travelled through here some years ago on my way to acquiring some new items. Stayed the night in a wretched motel on the outer edges. It looked the perfect town but I never made it back until now."

Joe started asking the Shopkeeper more questions but Marshall tuned out again and instead he noticed the music a second time but this time a glistening blueish light caught the corner of his eye to the right.

La la DA dah

La la DA dah

Again, he found himself drawn to the music and the glowing light. The melodic call got louder as he made his way back to the corner of the store and the light, which was more of a haze, grew more focused as he got closer.

He slowly stepped around the end of one of the racks and there... In the corner was a large wooden dresser with a small wooden stand upon it and on the stand was a turquoise amulet. It was glowing! He turned to Joe and the Shopkeeper but they were deep in conversation.

From his position he could see the edges were silver in colour, with strange symbols carved into the metal and set in the middle was a deep blue/ green stone. As he got closer to the object, the music slowed and the light grew dim but now the centre of the stone started to swirl. He looked in disbelief. He reached his hand out and the swirl grew faster with every cautious step he took. He took another step closer and the light grew again this time from the centre of the swirl and the smoke that was trapped inside increased its pace.

"What was it?" Thought Marshall. "How was it moving like that? It couldn't be clockwork it was too... liquid" he thought. "But it couldn't be moving on its own!" He stepped closer again, closer...closer... he could feel heat coming from the curious object. It grew warmer.

He could barely breath as he reached out to take it with his hand. With one final and cautious reach, he picked up the Amulet.

It hummed in his palm like an insect buzzing... It seemed alive although solid metal. The smoke swirled mesmerisingly... It was slower and the music had stopped. It was almost as if the Amulet had *wanted* Marshall to pick it up and now, he had, it had calmed.

"But that was impossible!" Marshall thought. For all the noise and mysterious happenings before, the amulet seemed rather ordinary. He began to turn it over and he realised there was a hidden compartment on the back, like a pocket watch. He opened the clasp and a folded piece of old, yellowed paper fell out onto the dresser sideboard below. Written inside the folded paper, there were words scrawled in dark red. He read them in his head.

Mortal worlds and souls combine.
Speak the words and leave behind.
Journeys from the light begin.
Tread forth unto the depths within.

"Speak the words?" Marshall muttered to himself.

"Hey Colonel!!" Shouted Joe. "You ready?"

Marshall jumped with a fright. "Y... yeah." When he looked back down at the amulet it was dark and cold... he looked around him and everything was normal, no light, no music. Was he imagining it? He set the amulet back on its stand and walked back over to the counter, keeping his gaze on the amulet.

"You okay?" asked Joe noticing his pale expression.

"Yeah, no... yeah. Didn't you just see that?" replied Marshall.

"You have a keen eye boy." Said the shopkeeper.

"I was just looking." Replied Marshall sheepishly. "Besides it must be expensive, like everything here, there's no price on anything."

"Everything here has a price lad. It just depends what you're willing to pay!"

"That's another way of saying you can't afford it Marsh. C'mon let's go." Said Joe.

Joe grabbed the box of items from the counter and the boys left the store. The Shopkeeper watched with a smile as they left. Then, he retreated to the back room, to attend to business.

On the walk back from the store to the diner, Joe was talking about how excited he was to try out his costume but all Marshall could think about was the amulet.

"That stone, how did it move like that?" He thought. "Why didn't anyone else notice it?"

As they made their way back through the streets, they passed groups of trick or treaters, mainly younger kids who had gone out early with their parents before their bedtime.

One family had a duckling and a mini Frankenstein in their group. Another group of slightly older children wore a mix of creepy classics like Dracula and The Mummy but some had gone for alternative costumes. Most noticeably, the leader of the herd who was wearing a loud, Hawaiin shirt and a pair of sunglasses. He had his hair slicked back into a huge quiff and thought it funny to greet everyone who opened the door with an over confident-

"Ace Ventura, Candy Detective... Aaaallrighty then."

Marshall laughed but imagined it would have gotten old by the end of the night. His poor friends, he thought.

They made their way back to Futterman's and it had started to get busy. People were turning up in elaborate costumes. The younger kids who had finished trick or treating, were already there with their parents, grabbing a seat for the show. Music was playing in the background, people were laughing and the chilli was smelling delicious as it wafted through the building, right up to the boys' noses.

"Mmm hmm." The boys both liked the smell of Bob's secret chilli and raced each other to the door. As they reached the door Joe jokingly pushed Marshall to beat him to the finish line.

"Loser" he cried with his finger and his thumb in the shape of an "L" on his fore-head.

As they stepped inside, Randy came running up to them with a pen and pad in his hand.

"You've been gone aaaages."

"Sorry buddy." Said Marshall. "You been okay?"

"Yeah, Mrs. Miller had me take people's food orders while you were gone."

"Orders?" Cried Joe. "Isn't Bob doing counter servic-"

"My little helper has been busy!" said Mrs. Miller interrupting and giving her son a wink. "He's managed to help and stay out of trouble." She said with a grin. She leant in and whispered to Joe. "Thanks to all that Ice cream you fed him he hasn't stopped chattin', I couldn't get a thing done."

Marshall laughed. "Okay, let's have a look at those orders."

Randy handed the older boys the notepad. It was sticky and it only had a few scribbles and a picture of a stick man with a burger.

"I wasn't listening and I didn't know how to spell chilli so I just gave everyone in here burgers, also you might be running low on ketchup."

"I think we're safe, my uncle has hundreds of those little packets." Said Joe, laughing as he handed back the notepad. "Besides who has ketchup with chilli?"

"Oh, no one." Said Randy "Just lettin' you know you're out." He said, wiping his mouth on his sleeve. As he walked back over to the chilli stand, they saw the mound of opened ketchup packets on the counter and realised why the notepad was so sticky… the older boys looked at each other.

"My uncle's gonna freak." Joe said shaking his head and laughing in shock. "Where does he put it all?"

"I don't know man, that kid just doesn't stop eating."

"Oh, and Marshall there's someone asking for you!" shouted Randy over his shoulder, taking another family's fake order as they sat and watched the kids cartoon on the screen.

"For me?" Asked Marshall confused.

"Yeah, it's a gurrrl." Randy turned around and held his hand over his mouth and laughed in embarrassment.

Marshall looked at Joe, who had a shocked smile on his face and pointed over to one of the booths at the back. Vinessa was sat alone.

"Okay Romeo, you weren't lying. I'll sort this stuff with my uncle and get into my costume and you go do your thing so she can let you down quickly and we can get the night started."

How could he have forgotten! The thoughts and questions he had about the amulet suddenly left his head and his hands started getting sweaty. She was here, here to see him and he wanted to make a good impression. He walked over to her booth. *You can do this Marshall. You can do this!*

He stood by her booth and coughed. She hadn't heard him over the kid's movie in the background and people talking. He decided to just sit down opposite her in the booth.

"Hi, Hey, I... I... I uh-" he knocked over the salt as he climbed into the booth.

"Hey watch it nerd!" Vinessa shouted as she jumped up, off the seat to avoid the spilled salt. She was wearing a sky-blue princess dress cut short at the skirt.

"Oh man, I'm so sorry!" He apologised. "I like your costume." He added, trying to save the encounter.

"Oh Mitchell... it's you, thanks. That's okay at least it wasn't my drink." She slurped her straw. "Speaking of which..." She motioned with her eyes towards the empty glass.

"Oh right, of course!" He turned behind him, raised his hand and shouted "Can we get another..." he turned back to Vinessa. "What was it?"

"Oh my God... cherry cola!"

"Regular or diet co-" He cut his question short, realising he didn't want to anger the girl of his dreams any more than he already had and ruining this encounter any more than he had. He spun back to shout out the order but was interrupted.

"And what can I get for the lovely couple tonight?"

"Oh my God Randy, where's the real waitress? Go away, please!" Marshall wondered if his night could get any worse. Randy ignored the protests of his brother and assumed his role.

"Can I recommend the burger, and can I not recommend the ice cream. I'm not done with it yet and I'd rather not share."

"Please go away!" Marshall begged through closed fingertips. "We don't want any food. I just need a new cherry cola. Besides, there aren't any burgers and you don't even work here."

"Bob's helping Joe with the movie and Mrs. Miller's serving the chilli. I'm not allowed to touch it 'cos it's hot. But I can take your order... or draw the pretty lady a picture if you want?"

Vinessa lost her temper and stood up and pointed at Randy. "Listen dweeb, get lost okay. Like, I don't want a stupid picture, I don't want a stupid burger, I just want you to take this stupid glass and fill it with cherry cola. Got it?!" She sat back down and adjusted her hair with a sigh.

Randy's eyes started to well up and his bottom lip began to quiver. He spun round and ran out into the back room, abandoning his notepad on the table. Marshall saw his crude sketch strewn on the metal surface. His brother had drawn him as a caped superhero holding hands with a princess. His stomach felt ill with guilt at how much his younger brother looked up to him and how he had been a jerk to him.

"Don't you think that was a bit harsh? He's just a kid!"

"Mitchell are you gonna help me or not I'm already in danger of being nearly late for this party and I'm worried any longer and my costume is gonna smell of this dump."

Marshall hung his head. She realised she was losing him.

"Besides, if my hero helps me out, I can repay him with a princess's kiss." She smiled at him and lured him in with her eyes.

Conflicted, Marshall pushed his brothers upset aside and fell for her spell.

"Thank you *sooo* much." She said as she handed him a floppy disc. "You are a lifesaver and a sweetie." She leaned over and gave him a peck on his cheek which turned red and he couldn't hide the smile on his face.

"So, uh you wanna grab a seat for the show?" He asked.

"Haha, yeah sure! Oh, wait you're serious, oh *noo*. I couldn't think of anything worse. I mean how tacky are these decorations and the films are always lame. I mean it's full of kids and old people. All my friends are at the party and besides my boyfriend will be waiting for me!"

"B... Boyfriend?!" Marshall's Heart sunk to his feet and the room span. "Oh yeah I... I mean, I knew that for sure. And *pfft* yeah totally agree, this place is lame. I'm just here to..." He looked around for an excuse, rather than tell her how much he actually enjoyed the annual Horrorthon. "...to look after my little brother before I come to the party, I don't like getting to those things too early."

"Hmmm." She smiled, she liked this casual side of him and measured him up with her eyes and gave a smile. "Well maybe *boyfriend* is too strong a word." She smiled flirtingly.

"Hey Marsh, saved you a seat." Joe interrupted. "Hey Vinessa." He said with a smile and nod of the head. "How's it going?" He smiled at her.

"Eww, no!" She replied. "You're as lame as these decorations."

"Ah this place is way cool. It'll grow on you." He pretended to be grabbed by the nearby skeleton hand dangling down. "See." He laughed.

"Whatever. I'm gonna head to a *real* party!" She turned away from Joe. "I tell you what Mitchell. If you can find something that's *really* eerie and cool why don't you bring it to the party? Maybe I'll save you a dance?!" She gave a smile, turned and left the diner, pushing the door open onto a family entering with two small children.

"Rude!" She yelled at the woman. "Walk much?" She sighed and left the diner in a huff. The Woman and her husband consoled the two small children.

Marshall stared as she left, with a goofy grin all over his face.

"Oh boy what a-" Joe cut himself short and realised Marshall was still stood there mesmerised.

"Hey, Earth to Marshall." He waved his hand in front of Marshall's face. Marshall grabbed his hand and turned to him eyes wide with excitement.

"What's the coolest thing your uncle has here?"

"Are you kidding? He would freak if you took any of his things besides you *do* realise, she's using you, right?!"

"No way, you're just jealous."

"I'm really not." Joe protested.

"C'mon it will be just for the night, something small, besides with all this stuff do you really think he will miss it?"

Joe sighed a heavy sigh "Okay, okay but just for a night and you don't let it leave your sight, right?!"

The Boys looked across the walls and in the displays. There was a hockey mask. Too cliché. There was a jar labelled "Ectoplasm", too gross. Besides it looked like it was already leaking.

"It's no use." said Marshall, deflated. "Who am I kidding?" He slumped against the diner counter and sunk to the floor. Then as he looked up out the window with despair at the glowing moon in the night sky it hit him. He jumped to his feet.

"Hey, I just realised I left my... Walkman at the store."

"Your Walkman? I didn't see you with it!" Said Joe.

"Yeah it was under my shirt. It must have fallen out."

"Okay, well let's go grab it."

"No, it's okay, I'll go alone. Your mom needs the help anyway, I'll be right back." He headed towards the door.

"Okay, but be careful." Called Joe.

"Relax." Said Marshall. "It's just a store."

"Yeah but it's the creepy things with eyes and pointy bits inside the store that freak me out!"

"Hey, where you going?" Shouted Randy who had spotted his brother leaving.

"Back to the store quick."

"Can I come this time?" Asked Randy.

"Not this time bud, Joe needs you to look after him okay?" He smiled at Joe. "I'll be five minutes! There and back."

It was dark by the time Marshall reached the store. He turned onto the dimly lit Kingston Street. The lamp light at the entrance to the road flickered and the only lights left on were those of the store and the phone box on the corner at the opposite end of the road. There was a small light that Illuminated the crude sign above the store but despite the small glow coming from inside, the Store looked shut.

Great. Thought Marshall, as he got closer. He peered through the window, the Store looked eerier in the evening, if that was possible. He couldn't see the shopkeeper but there was a small light on in the back. He tried the door and to his surprise the handle turned cleanly in his hand and the door opened.

Ding a ding ding.

He Jumped, as the bell above the door rang out and cut through the eerie silence as he stepped across the threshold into the dimly lit store.

"Hello." He called out. Nothing. "Are you still open?" Silence... The Shopkeeper must be in the back, he thought. He walked towards the rear of the Store. As he did, he passed the artefacts, which in the low light looked more ominous. "

"Hello." He called out again. "I came in earlier with my friend, small annoying guy with a lot of questions... Remember us?"

He picked up a few jars and trinkets inquisitively as he made his way to the counter.

"Hello!" Marshall called... nothing.

He walked towards the back of the store and peered through curtain in the alcove that led to the ominous back of the store. It seemed to drift off into the distance in the dark without end. He wasn't sure whether to cross the barrier and head to the back of the store or call out again. But then he noticed the light again from the corner of his eye. He turned and there it was, the amulet! Glowing its mysterious blue/ green, almost calling to him. He took a few tentative steps towards it. *Vinessa would Love it!* He picked it up as it did its magnificent song and dance. He stared at the swirling smoke in the centre. It was freaky and cool and he was sure it would win her over. He turned it over to look at the piece of paper inside again.

"Speak the words?" As he held the amulet and paper in his hands, he heard a noise and snapped the clasp shut. There it was again. Like a knocking. Maybe it was just the wind. Maybe there was a window open, he thought.

Ding a ding ding.

It was the bell at the front of the store.

"Wow this place is *cooool!*" Said Randy with a sense of wonder as he entered.

"Randy, what are you doing here? I thought I told you to stay at the diner!"

"And we thought you came to find your Walkman?!" Said Joe who came in behind him, he shot him a raised eyebrow and shut the door behind him.

Randy began wandering around the store looking at the items. Joe turned back to Marshall.

"He said you're Walkman's been broken for ages!?"

"No, it hasn't" replied Marshall quickly in defence.

"It has too... I broke it!" laughed Randy from behind one of the aisles.

Marshall frowned at him.

"So, why are you really here? Or can we go already? 'Cos, I want to get back and get into my costume, it's gonna blow your mind."

All of a sudden, a loud, eerie howl from outside cut through the air.

"What was that?" Asked Joe.

"It sounded like an animal..." Replied Randy hiding behind the large black armoire, peeking his head out to spy a look.

"No... I know that sound." Marshall trembled. "Quick hide, its Josh Butcheson!!"

They ducked down behind the shelving racks, out of view from the window.

"Did they see you come here Joe?" Asked Marshall.

"No way, I would have seen them, or smelt them at least." He Jested holding his nose.

They both turned to look behind Randy who in turn looked behind himself as if there were another person in the room.

"What're you looking at me for?"

"It's okay." Marshall whispered. They must have been still looking for the brothers from earlier he thought, what was it that made them hate him so much!

The familiar whirring sound of the Butcher Boys bikes came closer and closer until they heard the tires skid to a halt outside the store.

"Hey, here's the place! Ohhh Marshall. Come out, come out!" They heard Billy taunt.

"Yeah, we know you're in there! We saw Frogboy and the nerd come in here. Make it easy on yourself and come out and we may take it easy on you..."

"That was Terry Deagle." Whispered Joe.

Terry winked to the other boys, who knew he had no intention of taking it easy.

"What do we do Marshall?" Asked Randy, scared.

"We can't get out the front door without them seeing us and they might come in here any second now." Replied Marshall.

"D'you think we can reach the bolt on the door?" Asked Joe.

"Not without them seein' us through the glass. Quick, there may be a back way we can sneak out!"

The trio made their way to the back room of the store behind the counter and down the long tunnel hallway.

"If the owner is still here, he can scare them away, that guy gives me the creeps easy enough." Said Joe.

"Over there, the exit, I see it!" Shouted Marshall.

They ran over to the door but stopped abruptly and their hearts sank. It was padlocked with a chain... from the inside! Why would they need to lock it from the inside? Thought Marshall.

Ding a ding ding

It was the front door!! The bullies were inside the building. They were trapped with no way of escape. Joe gulped. Randy grabbed Marshall's hand. They heard the boys enter the store and Marshall instantly started to think how he could lead them all to safety. He looked around the back room. There was a workbench and an old leather armchair with a small TV facing it. Some news clippings hung on the wall but it was too dark to read. The room was pretty empty but in the back corner to the left, there were a stack of old boxes. They must have been left from the move, he thought and he wondered if they might have anything left inside, they could use to prize the door open. But they didn't have time, they could hear the bullies inside and it wouldn't be long before they checked the back room. With that he heard an almighty crash. He turned to see Joe on the floor with a goofy grin of apology.

"Shhh." Marshall rolled his eyes.

"Sorrrrry" Whispered Joe. As he dusted his trousers off from the fall. He looked to see what he had tripped on.

"Hey, look!" Joe pointed to the curled corner of a large, old looking rug on the floor.

"Look, it looks like something's underneath."

Marshall and Joe rolled the carpet back. It was a hatch.

"It might lead us out somewhere Marsh?"

"Where?" Cried Randy in fear.

"Who knows, but it's gotta be safer than here at the moment." Marshall reasoned. "We can hide at least."

Marshall got a hold of the hatch door but it was solid and heavy.

"Here!" Said Joe as he grabbed the other side. "If we're going down, we're going down together." He smiled at Marshall.

"Randy, can you grab the end?" Marshall said. "If we do this together, it might budge!"

The boys grabbed a side each and carefully lifted the heavy hatch together. They saw a set of wooden steps leading down into the pitch-black emptiness below. They looked at each other for reassurance but they were all as nervous as the other to go down there first. Eventually Marshall took the lead, then when he knew it was safe, Randy followed then Marshall came back to help Joe pull the hatch shut. They were careful to drag the carpet with it as best they could to hide the entrance.

Once down there, with the door shut, their eyes adjusted to the shafts of light that pierced the darkness from the gaps in the beams of the wooden flooring above. The floor was bare soil and to their utter disappointment, there were no windows or doors to escape. They would have to lie low and wait it out and hope not to be discovered, at least until the owner returned or the bullies gave up their hunt.

Marshall placed a finger over his lips and pointed upwards. They could hear footsteps above, followed by the shadows of the tenth graders as they entered the room.

"Hey... Chicken! We know you're in here." Josh called out.

"Yeah Chicken, come out now and we won't hurt your friends." Teased Billy Mcfadden.

They made their way through the store, towards the back.

"They're gonna find us!" Joe whispered.

"Shh!" Randy hushed.

"Hey what's that?" Said Joe, pointing at Marshall's right jacket pocket.

Something was glowing a bluey colour through the fabric. Marshall reached into his pocket and slowly pulled out the glowing amulet from his pocket.

"Are you serious? You stole that from the shop? Well I suppose they can't arrest you if you're already dead." Joe said angrily.

"Shh..." Whispered Randy again.

"What is it anyway? A mood necklace?" Joe asked, trying to stay calm.

"I don't know." Replied Marshall

"So why take it?"

"I uh..." Marshall's cheeks turned a little red with embarrassment.

"I don't believe you!" Said Joe, a little louder. "We're sat here waiting for our demise, for... for a girl!!"

"Shh." Repeated Randy.

Joe lowered his voice "*That's* why you came back?! To steal something to impress a girl, who's clearly using you?"

"Hey." Marshall pushed Joe. "She's not using me. We have a date, which I should be on right now! Instead I'm hiding out in a dusty old basement. Besides I wasn't going to steal it, I was going to pay but the store guy wasn't there and then you spooked me. Then when we had to run, I don't know I just panicked and kept hold of it!"

"SHHHHHH!!!" Randy broke the argument and pointed sternly up top. He whispered lowly "They're right above us."

They looked up and their breathing slowed in anticipation... They were safe still. They hadn't been heard.

"Why's it glowing though?"

"I don't know... it... does that, plus it sings."

"What?" asked Joe surprised.

"Well not actual singing but it... makes a tune somehow. look I don't know how or why it does those things, but it does. Does anything in this shop look normal to you?"

"Well whatever the reason, hide it! If those creeps see that light we're doomed!"

Marshall placed the Amulet back in his pocket and tried to cover the glow with his hands. The boys waited.

"He ain't here Josh! None of them are... lets go check the diner." Said Terry.

"Nah, let's go steal some trick or treats, or smash some Jack-O-Lanterns." Josh laughed. "We'll get them later."

The boys heard the gang walk back towards the entrance and they all relaxed and breathed a sigh of relief. Joe looked at Marshall with a smile.

"That was close."

La la DA dah

La la DA dah

They all froze at the sound and Marshall knew it was the Amulet. He scrambled to get it out of his pocket to try and stop it. But it was too late.

"They're downstairs!" Yelled Josh.

The pounding of heavy footsteps echoed in the basement and the boys started to panic.

"They're coming." Whispered Randy, his eyes filled with fear.

"Oh, we're coming for you now dweebs!" Cried Billy.

There was nowhere to hide and only one way in or out and at any minute the Butcheson boys would discover the hatch and they'd be for it.

"What are we going to do?" Asked Randy.

"Well, nice knowing you all." Said Joe jokingly "Hey Marsh thanks for getting us, you know... killed."

But Marshall was deep in thought. He opened his eyes and pointed over to the far corner of the basement.

"Get over there, under that sheet." He pointed to an old dust sheet. On the stack of boxes. "They don't know we're all still here. I'll face them, it's my fault we're here in the first place."

Joe was speechless which was a rare thing for him.

"No Marsh, you can't face them alone, they'll pulverise you!"

"Better just me than all of us." Said Marshall.

113

"Marshall, you're my big brother, I won't let you do this alone."

"That's sweet Randy." Marshall smiled at his brother.

Randy looked at the floor and shook his head and sighed.

"I have way too many chores already and I hate chores and there is no way I'm doing yours, as well as mine, while you're in the hospital. If you're getting out of it by being murderlated by big kids then so am I!" He folded his arms and adopted a serious look on his face as if settling the matter there and then.

Marshall tried not to smile when he knew how much danger they were in. He felt a bit more relieved with his brother and best friend by his side but he knew they were no match for the full gang.

Suddenly, the hatch flew open and Josh poked his head in.

"Gotcha!"

He grinned his evil grin and the gang descended the stairs, into the dusty basement. First Josh, then Billy. Before Billy could finish, Terry Deagle jumped down the side of the steps, too impatient to wait for the others to climb down. Marshall could see the blue denim of Josh's jacket still soaked from the pond water.

The Amulet's song grew louder and the light shone brighter in Marshall's hand.

"Boy oh boy, what do we have here?! Three little pigs in the dirt! Well now the big bad wolf is here!" Josh smiled as he closed in on the trio. "And he has some friends!" He laughed as the three bullies closed in.

"This is gonna be fun!" Sneered Billy.

"We just want Frogboy." Smiled Josh, manacingly.

"Not happening!" Marshall shot back. "You can't have him!"

"Oh, we aint askin'." Replied Josh.

The Amulet felt warm in Marshall's hand, he looked down at it and it looked brighter than ever, down there in the dark basement. An idea struck him. He turned to Joe and Randy and stuck out his hand and whispered.

"Quick get ready to run."

"Where?" Asked Joe.

"Up the stairs!" Marshall smiled.

Joe looked puzzled, how were they to get past the Butcheson Boys?

"I'm gonna use this to distract them! Close your eyes and take my hand. I'll shine it in their faces and then we'll make a run for it."

"Are you sure?"

"I'm sure Joe."

"Okay, lead the way Colonel!"

Marshall flashed him a smile. He just had to convince himself now that the crazy plan would actually work. The amulet was glowing a brilliant light blue now, this was the time.

Josh stepped forward and the others started to chuckle in a sinister frenzy, like a pack of hyenas closing in on the kill.

Almost, thought Marshal, just a little closer. He would only have one chance. Too close and they could still grab them. Too far and the light wouldn't blind them or they wouldn't be clear of the ladder. He squeezed his left hand around Randy's and Randy grabbed Joe's. The amulets soft song grew louder as Josh stepped another space forward. This was it he thought!

Marshall raised his hand outstretched in front of him and uncovered the amulet fully. A dazzling beam of light shone from the centre and filled the room in front with a bright blue. Josh and the rest of the Butcheson Boys raised their arms to shield their eyes.

He was just about to lead the charge forward but he spotted Terry at the back stumble back in a daze and crash against the ladder. Their route was blocked! What were they to do?

He knew he had to think fast. But that's when he noticed the back of the amulet. Amidst the forward-facing glow he could see the back of the amulet and on it were four words, etched into the metal.

Ramus
Venke
Hudo
Danray

"The words!" He thought to himself. "That was what the rhyme meant. But what do they mean?" They didn't make sense to him at all but as his fingers ran over the etched words, he realised they were soon to be out of time to try anything else. He read the first one aloud.

"Ramus!" No change.

He read the second. "Venke!"

The amulet got warmer. He could feel it humming in his hand.

"Hudo!" Something was happening. As Marshall prepared to utter the last of the words a brilliant light shone from the centre again but this time towards him and it filled the room.

He had to look away to shield his eyes it was so bright. He shouted the last of the words.

"Danray!"

The light from the amulet filled the room and then disappeared completely, as if someone had flicked a switch.

The Butcheson Boys lowered their arms as the room became dark again. Their Eyes adjusted and they looked about the basement for Marshall.

"Where are they Josh?" Asked Terry.

Josh turned to his gang and with a bewildered look, replied.

"They're gone!"

Chapter 8

Marshall coughed, as his lungs filled with air again after the heavy thud winded him. He spat out a mouthful of leaves. He was lying face flat on the ground. He groaned as he struggled to stand up. As he stretched his legs, he brushed himself off and looked about, he was outside.

As he took in his surroundings and cleared his head, he remembered Josh. He quickly surveyed the area but the boys were gone. Instead he was surrounded by trees and bushes... and water. He was at the lake, but how was that possible? He thought.

There was something else too, something was off. Everything looked a lot eerier somehow, not just in the evening light. The lake and its surroundings we more like a swamp than the parts of the lake he was used to playing in. The sky in the west was still bathed in a low purple glow from the small amount of light he could make out through the trees. All around were the chirps of crickets and other noises he wasn't so familiar with, like the shrieks of larger bird life.

He panicked, disorientated and realising he was on his own. Where was his brother?

"Randy!... Hey Rand!" He cupped his hands to his mouth in an attempt to project his voice further. His voice echoed as the shrieks from above called out invisibly in the air above him.

"Rand!" He called out once more.

"Ughh... Over here!" His bother called out as he crawled out of a tall patch of nearby weeds and bushes.

His white Ghost costume covered in dirt stains and bits of plant, hooked on by the barbed thorns.

"How did we get outside?" He asked his older brother in a daze.

"I don't know. But somehow, we're at the lake. That's miles from the store."

"Are you sure it's the lake?" asked Randy rubbing his eyes clear and looking at the horizon.

"Course I am, there's a great big lake in front of us, what would you call it?"

"I don't know, nothing looks the same. The trees are weird."

Marshall laughed. "It's probably 'cos you've never been here in the dark."

"Oh yeah... maybe." Randy replied with a frown as he took in the sights around him. "Still, I say we've not been to this part before."

"Well it's a big lake maybe-" Marshall stopped and looked at his brother. "Hey, wait. Where's Joe?"

"Joe!" Randy called.

"Let's check out over here." Marshall said as he pointed to a clearing in the trees.

"Joe! Jooooe." The brothers called in unison.

"Hey Joe." Randy shouted again.

Then a voice in the wind whispered.

"*Joooooooe*"

"*Jooooooooooe*"

The brothers looked at each other puzzled.

"Must be an echo." Marshall said, but he couldn't even convince himself that that was what it was. It sounded like a whisper, scratching through the wind, soft but gravelly.

They called out again.

The wind rustled through the trees and they heard the voice again.

"*Heeeeerreee*"

"*Thiiiissss Waaayyyy...*"

The brothers made their way through the undergrowth. All around were strange noises. They belonged to various creatures in the night. Some were far away and low pitched and some were shrieks high above their heads from things flying in the dark night sky but they didn't recognise any of them.

Marshall took the lead as the path grew narrower. They followed the voice through the bushes along a dirt track. Thorns and leaves jutted out making the trail harder to follow but the voice was getting louder, the further down the path they walked. Marshall was trying to stay calm, how had Joe wound up so far from them. How had *they* even got outside in the first place. Vinessa would be waiting. Marshall and Randy's parents were going to pitch a fit if they knew they were out this late in the dark. All these thoughts were running through his mind as he walked the narrow path to Joe but behind came a small crashing sound that kept interrupting his concentration every few seconds.

Bam... bam... bam...

Marshall lost his train of thought again and spun round.
"Rand, what're you doing? Quit it."

"I'm testing stuff!" He replied proudly, armed with a
beaten stick held high in the air like a cavalry soldier
charging into battle with his sword. He carried on hitting
various objects as they walked along. A log here, a strange
Mushroom there, as he hit each one, various insects and
creepy crawlies scurried from their dark hiding places and
Randy smiled with joy.

"Why have you got that?" Asked Marshall in
frustration.

"I found it. you can't go through the woods without a
stick. That's a rule right there!"

"Well cut it out, it's annoying."

Randy stopped and looked at Marshall then he drooped
his head, with his stick held down by his side.

"I was just..."

He sighed a sad and heavy sigh.

Marshall stopped walking. He forgot sometimes how
much younger Randy was, he was a little scared himself
with their current situation and he realised Randy must be
even more so.

"I'm sorry man. Look, it's just we don't know what's
going on or even exactly where we are. We just need to be
careful that's all I don't recognise this part of the woods or
anything about where we are. We just need to focus okay."

"Okay." Replied Randy realising he needed to stop
testing the forest's durability and help his big brother. He
wiped his nose on his sleeve and gave one last big
almighty whack on a nearby log and left the stick on the
ground. The boys picked up their pace and carried on their
way but as they left and carried on along the narrow

winding path, a low growl came from the foliage and a large, scaly, clawed foot stretched out from the bushes and with one swift thud it crushed Randy's stick, dragging the remains, slowly into the bushes.

The brothers came off of the narrow path and into a clearing along the water's edge. The ground was flat and the grass low. There was a network of roots and trees in front of them but it didn't look too thick. They should be able to get through, thought Marshall. He gave another yell into the night sky for his best friend.

"Jooooooooooe!... Where you at man?"

"Jooooooe... heeeeerre. Oooovveerr... heeeeerrrre"

Theis time the voice was close.

"He must be the other side of those bushes Randy, quick let's go? We're coming dude!"

The boys rushed towards the wall but Randy stopped in his tracks with his head in the air.

"Do you Smell that?" Said Randy sniffing the air around him.

"Yeah... I do." replied Marshall who had stopped to see what had caught his brother's attention. The feint aroma hung in the air. Randy's stomach grumbled.

"I think my tummy likes it?!" He giggled.

"It does smell good." Said Marshall. "It's coming from behind the bushes.

"Maybe Joe found the way out, maybe they were at the edge of town?" Marshall thought.

"Heerrre... ooovvveer heeerre... Joooooe"

The boys followed the call and the smell through the bushes. They parted the vines and tried to dodge the thick thorns until eventually they collapsed the other side. To their disappointment, the forest running along the water's edge was even denser the other side. But to their surprise, perched on the lake's edge, glowing softly in the cool dark evening was a large wooden shack.

"Funny, I've never seen this before." said Marshall cautiously.

"I've never been in this deep before!" added Randy "I think I may have found my new favourite frog hunting spot!"

The shack was lit with the orange glow of candlelight and the old stone chimney at the back was smoking nicely. Despite the rickety appearance it looked very warm and welcoming.

They picked themselves up from the spot that they had spilled out from and slowly walked towards the wooden building. The voices had stopped but the strong aroma of cooking was billowing from the chimney. They reached the bottom of the wooden steps that led to the porch.

"Joe must be inside, probably stuffing his face with whatever smells so good. Should we knock?" Asked Marshall, looking at his brother for support.

Before they had a chance to decide, a dry squeaky voice from within called out.

"C'mon in children, don't be shy." The voice sang out from inside.

"Okay." Randy smiled and marched in without hesitation.

"No, wait." cried Marshall but it was too late.

They entered but they couldn't see anyone. He ran to Randy, who was stood in the centre of the small front room. The walls were made of wood with various animal hides nailed to them. There was an old stone fire place roaring and crackling to the left of the entrance with a circle of chairs around an old wooden table just in front of it. A set of stairs trailed along the right-hand wall going away from the entrance and at the back to the right was a light flickering from what Marshall imagined to be the kitchen.

"H... Hello?" called Marshall. The fire was roaring and a large, black pot was hung over it. The contents were bubbling away, it smelt delicious Marshall thought.

There was a large wooden table set for a meal. Everything was rustic, it all looked homemade. The table looked like one solid slab of naturally formed wood."

H... Hello." He called out again.

They heard a rattling coming through the doorway. Randy took a step back towards Marshall. A large shadow loomed on the wall as the figure entered through the doorway. It was an old lady.

She stood, hunched over as she walked. She had striking, white hair that was tied up at the back in a bun, with small beady eyes and a kind expression on her aged, thin skin. She wore a long dress covered on top with a dark cardigan but what Marshall found strange was she wore no shoes. Instead she crept along the hard, wooden floor on her bare feet. He could make out her yellowed, cracked toenails.

She was precariously carrying a wooden tray with a cup of what Marshall thought could be tea and an empty bowl. She was shaking as she walked, unsteady on her legs from the ravages of time.

"Well lookun at you, such han'some strong boys."

Randy stood tall and proud and smiled as if exaggerating the compliment.

"We don't get new folk through here much. It's been such a long time." She placed the tray on the large wooden table, it sounded light as she placed it down but she made it look three times heavier.

"C'mon in young'uns, sit a spell." She patted a seat near a large armchair, made from the hide of something large and leathery, Randy went to sit down. Marshall placed his hand on his shoulder to stop him going any further into the stranger's home.

"Uh thanks but we're actually lost. And-"

"Oh, it breaks a poor woman's heart to hear of such nice children lost out here. Come, have some stew." She interrupted.

"Uh, no thanks. We actually were just looking for our friend Joe, we heard him shouting from this way and wondered if he was here and if you could direct us towards town?"

"Yeah or maybe give us a ride there?" Randy added. Marshall hit Randy's arm. She clearly struggled to walk, let alone be able to drive anywhere.

"Oh, nonsense you must be starving, town can wait. Walking around here, lost and alone out there in the woods! It's not safe! Come... sit.... eat." She insisted. "A nice warm bowl of stew will sort you right out. There's plenty to go around. Besides, I'll be making more."

She didn't wait around for an answer, instead she grabbed the empty bowl and started scooping the chunky brown substance into the dish from the boiling hot pot. Randy's eyes widened as she passed him the bowl. Marshall's stomach grumbled as he thought back to the cookies in his kitchen and the pot of chilli waiting back at the diner.

She turned around and put the bowl on the table and waved Randy to the seat ushering him to stay.

"Besides your little friend is safe."

"He is? Where is he? Marshall asked relieved looking around for him.

"Oh, he was in such a way when we found him. All covered in mud and such. I sent him out the back to get washed up for some food. Come... sit... eat."

"We?" he asked.

"Pardon?" answered the old lady.

"You said, *we* don't get new folk through here much. And just now again, you mentioned, when *we* found him. It looked like you were alone out here."

"Yes." She smiled and pointed at the seat at the table.

Marshall hesitated. The lady was strange but he figured if she was kind enough to help Joe, they might as well have something whilst waiting for him to finish cleaning up at least, just a small bite.

"Well if you're sure we're not imposing? He asked hesitantly, his hunger getting the better of him. He smiled and took a seat. "So, what way is town from here?" He asked as he pulled his seat closer to the table.

"Yes, Come sit." She said, ignoring Marshall's question on the town and focussing on setting another space at the table. "Plenty, yes plenty." She laughed amusedly to herself. "I'll go get you a bowl" She said as she went back out the doorway, humming a tune to herself as she did.

Marshall waited until they were out of earshot from the old woman. He could hear her humming to herself as she fussed about the kitchen, she sounded far enough away. He leant in across the table and motioned with a wave of his hand for Randy to come in closer.

"Doesn't this all seem a little strange?"

"She seems nice enough to me." Said Randy as he tried to scoop up as much of the remaining stew as possible, never one to let anything go to waste.

"I know... A little too nice don't you think?"

"What do you mean?" asked Randy.

"Well firstly, she's a complete stranger, living in the middle of the woods. Sheriff Johnson said no one else lived out here besides him now. And why won't she say anything about which way town is? It's like she's avoiding it completely."

"Maybe she's just lonely?" Randy replied. "Hey wait, who's sheriff Johnson?"

"Never mind, but that's another thing. She completely ignored me when I asked her about why she kept saying *we*. We've seen no one else here and why did she only have the *one* bowl ready for serving? Something just doesn't feel right to me."

"Shh. She's coming back." whispered Randy as he put another spoonful in.

"Mutter, mutter, mutter!" The Old Lady said as she focused on the floor for guidance, walking back in with the bowl. "Good children shouldn't whisper..." She looked up at the kids with a stern stare and placed the bowl on the table with force. "It's *very* rude!"

How did she hear that? Marshall thought. Randy stopped eating and glanced sideways to his brother for what to do or say next.

"You... uh... have a lovely home." Marshall said trying to change the subject.

She smiled again. "Well thank you, I try to keep it clear and clutter free." She said as she brushed a cobweb off a frame hanging on the wall that Marshall could tell wasn't fresh. "But it's so hard these days, what with my eyesight and not having as many visitors anymore."

She sat in her chair and rocked on it, but Marshall noticed it was not a rocking chair just an ordinary chair. Weird, He thought.

"What's with all the candles. Don't you have electricity?" Randy asked.

"I like the dark more." She said. "Electricity is so bright. candles are softer on my old eyes."

An uneasy feeling came over Marshall.

"So, I was thinking maybe I'd check on Joe... He's been a while."

The Creaking of the Chair came to a sudden silence. "I told you he's fine! He just needed to grab some sleep is all!" The old woman replied sharply.

Marshall's Heart started to beat faster.

"I thought you said he needed to clean himself up?" He tried to sound calm as he questioned the lady's response.

At that moment, Randy scraped his spoon on the bottom of the dish as he scooped the last morsels up and a high-pitched screech filled the room.

The Old lady held her ears and turned to the young child and screamed at him in a low growl.

How did that come from the old woman? Though Marshall.

The boys both jumped out of their seats and took a step back.

"We're taking our friend now and we're going, okay!" Marshall said trying not to let his voice tremble.

"You couldn't just sit and eat could you." The Old Woman said calmly with an angry smile. "No, the others, they sat and they ate but you had to keep on."

Her voice slowly getting deeper and angrier as she lifted herself up, off the chair and stood tall.

"We don't get visitors much now these days." Her voice now a gurgling deep growl, chuckling evilly.

"No energy left to hunt... no energy left-" she bent over and scrunched her form in tight to her body as if her stomach were in pain. "-TO FEED."

As she yelled out, she burst upright and the little old lady with beady eyes that had entered, with that kind expression on her face, ripped into shreds. Pieces of clothing and old lady were thrown everywhere as a large, brown furred beast exploded from the centre. It rose six feet tall as it extended from the spot where the lady had sat.

Two muscly arms, both with a set of razor-sharp claws attached, raised up towards the sky. It arched its head back as a pair of large, pointed ears unfolded and the shafts of moonlight shone through the thin membrane, down onto the creature's mangled face and its scrunched, pig like nose that was sniffing around, tasting the air. When it had locked onto the children's scent, the beast screamed into the night and two tattered wings shot out as it leapt forward to pounce on the brothers.

Randy screamed as the creature leapt up onto the dinner table and took a swipe at him narrowly missing his face.

"What the *fudge* is that" cried Randy.

Marshall watched in disbelief as the form had taken shape in front of them. He had watched it shed its "Old

Lady" skin and was reborn as this monster. He watched as its long spindly arms clambered for the table and gripped it with its claws. Then as the beast made a line for his brother, he grabbed the table and tipped it, flipping its end into the fireplace and making the beast just miss Randy.

"Quick over here." He shouted to Randy.

Randy ran to his brother and crouched behind him. The beast picked itself up and shook its long snout. It panted and sniffed the air. It caught the boy's scent and lunged forward. Marshall saw the broken leg of the table in the embers of the fireplace and grabbing it at the bottom, he brandished the flaming weapon and waved it in front of the charging beast. It skidded to a halt and snapped its vicious jaws at the flames as they flickered.

"It's bright." Shouted Randy, remembering the Old Lady's comments about the candles and electricity.

"Exactly." Said Marshall. "Its eyesight is sensitive. It's going by scent. No wonder it preferred the dark. Here, just stay behind me and we'll be okay."

The brothers backed towards the front door. The beast snarling and snapping its jaws trying to get to them.

"Nearly there!" Marshall cried.

But at that moment the beast leapt into the air and flapped it's ripped and battered wings until it reached the ceiling and then beat its wings at the kids and the sudden gust extinguished the flame on the end of the table leg.

They looked at each other for ideas as the creature thudded back to the ground with a low chuckle. It crouched onto all fours and stalked its way to them. They weren't close enough to the door to run for it, the creature was too fast, but it would be upon them in no time.

Randy suddenly had an idea and he leapt to the side to grab a bowl that had fallen on the floor from the overturned table and held it up high. He reached into his pocket under his costume and pulled out a small screwdriver.

"Hey, you old bat!" He yelled, trying to grab its attention. Then he struck the bowl with the tip of the screwdriver and began to scratch the surface back and forth, emitting an unpleasant, grinding, high-pitched squeak.

The beast screamed in pain and held its claws over its Ears.

"It's working." Shouted Randy with a smile.

The Creature cowered and backed up to the table. It tried to escape and opened its wings, fanning the flames of the table, half submerged in the fireplace. The flames took light and roared up the leathery old armchairs, across the wooden beam walls. The building glowed with orange as the flames crept higher. The beast startled and unable to escape the flames or the sound of Randy's screwdriver. It flung itself across the room in a frenzy.

"Quick!" Yelled Marshall as the heat of the flames grew more intense and the house started filling with smoke. "Let's get out of here."

Randy dropped the bowl and they ran for the front door. They ran down the wooden porch step and onto the grass.

The Beast still trapped inside dropped to the floor. Wheezing from the smoke. And trapped by the flames that had now engulfed it.

It started charging at the walls with what little strength it had, trying to break free. But as the creature darted back and forth and the flames weakened the wooden building, the structure started groaning.

Outside, on the grass. The Boys looked on as the wooden building slowly listed to the left and toppled in flames, into the murky waters of the swamp.

Heeerree... Ooooovvvvvverrrrrr Heeeerrre...

The whispers faded as the structure sunk and bubbles rose, as the pockets of the house filled with water. Within seconds the welcoming wooden shack with the little, old lady was gone forever.

The Boys stood up.

"Do you think it's dead? Asked Randy, looking up at his brother.

"Let's not wait to find out! We need to get away from here." But as Marshall went to leave the horrible spot he stopped and felt ill to his core. He turned and walked to the water's edge and looked down passed his own reflection to the murky depths below. He could see his own horrified look on his face. "Joe!?"

In their haste, they hadn't managed to free Joe, wherever he was. He sunk onto the grass and looked up at the star filled sky as he laid down. How could he have let his best friend die. He heard Randy shuffle in his costume as he stood by his side.

"Maybe he wasn't in there? You heard the whispers just then! That creature tricked us there to eat us. Maybe Joe was never there all along?" He reached out his hand and helped his brother up. "C'mon, let's go find him." He Smiled.

Marshall smiled back at his brother. "How do you always stay so positive?"

"I don't know what positive means." He said and shrugged his shoulders. "I take it back though. This is a terrible frog hunting spot!"

Marshall laughed and pulled him in by his shoulders as they walked back on the route they started.

"And another thing." Marshall asked. "Where did you get that screwdriver from?"

Randy looked up and smiled a playful grin as he placed it back into his pocket underneath his costume, hoping not to be in trouble.

"I found it... at the hardware store. When you were looking for buckets."

"You stole it?"

"I like my treasures."

"Well I guess we lucked out this time... you're so strange, you know that, right?"

"Thankyou." Randy smiled, pleased with the compliment he thought he had received and content with the title.

"You know you're using your allowance to pay Mr. Abernathy back, right!?"

The brothers walked on, tired, frightened and bruised, until they got to a clearing and stopped beneath a large tree and looked up. Marshall stood with a smile and a tear and Randy covered his mouth, trying not to laugh so hard.

Chapter 9

Joe was hanging by his jeans from one of the thick branches, dangling in the wind.

"About time." Joe shouted, twisting back and forth. "What took you guys?"

"I found a stick. We burnt down a house and I had some stew... oh, and a crazy old lady turned into a bat monster and tried to eat us. Oh man, I wish I had Dad's camera." Said Randy.

"I think I've been upside down too long. I don't think I can hear properly. Marsh, what did he say?"

"Erm... yeah, I'll fill you in in a minute, let's get you down first. We got a lot to talk about. Speaking of which what're you doing up there?"

"Oh, you know, hanging around!" Joe screamed impatiently.

Randy erupted into laughter. He raised his hands in the air and turned around.

"I'm done!" He walked away to try and catch his breath from laughing so hard.

"Yeah, it's a riot. Now, can you get me down?"

"Ha-ha okay." Said Marshall trying to keep the peace. "Hang on a minute."

Joe Looked at him. "Not going anywhere!"

Marshall heard Randy erupt again in the background. At least he was laughing again, he thought.

Marshall looked around the clearing for anything that might help unhook Joe. Randy tried climbing the tree but couldn't get a grip. Marshall looked for something that could be used as a lasso to pulled him down. Some rope or vine maybe, but they were surrounded by shrubs and trees full of thorns, there was nothing. Then Marshall spotted it, a large branch had fallen and was laying on the ground. It would need both of the brothers to lift and manoeuvre it but Marshall was positive it would work.

"Okay Joe." Marshall called up. "We couldn't find a way up but we did find a way down." He paused.

"But..." asked Joe, worried.

"But, you might wanna brace yourself." Marshall replied, with a grimace.

"Huh?" asked Joe puzzled. Then he realised the plan. "No, wait!" Joe pleaded with the brothers when he saw the branch.

"It's okay, we're just gonna use the branch to… *gently* knock you off!" Marshall replied.

"What, no!" Joe Begged.

The brothers counted to three.

"One..."

"Two..."

"...Hey wait guys." Joe protested as he noticed something from his elevated position. Something that was glowing in the distance.

"No use begging Joe, it's like pulling off a band aid, one quick strike and we'll be done." Shouted Randy reciting words he had heard his mom repeat so many times before.

"No Marshall it's-" Joe tried to explain.

"Ready?" Marshall interrupted turning to Randy.

"Ready!" Randy said eagerly, with a wicked smile and his tongue out in concentration. He was going to enjoy this. He made a thumbs up gesture, wiping his nose in the sleeve of his costume.

"...THREE!"

Bam!

Crash!

Thud!

"See... gently." Marshall whimpered as he realised just how hard Joe had tumbled down.

"You could have killed me!" Shouted Joe hysterically. "That was crazy... that was reckless!"

"That was *awesome!*" shouted Randy. "Can I go next?!"

"What no, no one's going next." replied Marshall, helping Joe to his feet. Randy sulked and kicked a pebble into some nearby bushes. "It's not fair."

The kids started walking towards a clearing and the bush that the stone landed in began to rustle.

"I'm sorry Joe." said Marshall. "I just didn't know how else to get you down and I didn't want to hang around out here. It's not safe!"

"You're telling me, we've got Josh and his jerks after us and somehow we've ended up here, wherever here is? I've never seen these parts of the woods before"

"We've got bigger things to worry about!"

Marshall began to tell Josh about the old lady and the shack, with some exaggerated sound effects from Randy.

136

"...And then that's when we found you and realised you weren't in there at all. Now we just have to find out which way town is."

Joe was in shock. His blood had had a chance to return to his feet again, now he was up the right way but he still didn't believe what he was hearing.

"First of all, you guys are crazy if you think I'm gonna believe that. But more importantly. The way back... that's what I was trying to say before you turned me into a human pinata. I saw the town. Well at least I think it's the town. I couldn't see any buildings but there was a large clearing and there must have been houses or shops or something because I could see lights. The strangest thing though was that the lights were almost blue like that amulet."

"The amulet!" Marshall suddenly panicked, feeling his pockets. "Where did it go? I had it in the basement and then... I don't know when I saw it last." He suddenly felt a knot of despair in his stomach.

"Maybe it's in the basement still or maybe it went down with the house?" Randy cut in, while Marshall was retracing his steps.

"Speaking of the basement... how did we get from inside that creepy store to here?" Asked Joe.

"Maybe we slept walked." Said randy trying to help.

"All of us?" Said Joe. "And at the same time?"

"I don't know." Said Randy "Stranger things have happened!" he proceeded to try on various large leaves he had picked from the surrounding bushes like a mask, poking holes for eyes and pushing his tongue through the mouth hole.

Marshall shook his head, there's something wrong with that boy, he thought.

"I don't know how we got here but all I know is Josh and those jerks aren't here and that's a win!" Said Joe.

"Where do you think they could be?" asked Randy, his mouth sticking through a ripped hole in the leaf.

"I don't know." Randy said. "Last thing I remember was waiting to be creamed by those guys and then a huge light and then *'bam'* I'm a human dreamcatcher. I think we must have got beaten so hard we blacked out, then they dragged us out here and left us to find a way home. Do I have a black eye?"

"I don't know." Marshall said. "I think it has something to do with the amulet, and if you say that place was glowing too maybe we should go check it out?"

"The amulet?" Asked Joe. "What do you mean the amulet?"

"Well said Marshall, this is gonna sound strange... "

Marshall told them how the Amulet played its song in the store and about the light, then again in the basement, the words and how, when he spoke them, the room glowed and they wound up outside.

"So, let me get this straight... and I think I'm being pretty calm right now Marsh. But you're saying instead of waiting for someone to come along and help, we should march straight toward the strange glowing town, that matches the strange glowing necklace, that *magically* transported us into the middle of the woods? Am I getting it right? 'Cos, I mean that sounds a great idea Marsh!"

Randy tugged Marshall's jacket and whispered.

"I don't think it sounds a very good idea at all, I think he's crazy." He grimaced as he made a whirling gesture with his finger by his head to indicate Joe had lost it. Marshall smiled, one day he'd have to teach his brother about sarcasm.

"I don't know where we are but I think somehow the amulet saved us. I mean, we're not dead and we're not Josh's punching bag. It was you that mentioned the town Joe."

"Yeah before I know about cursed jewellery and strange lights beaming us to strange places. I just wanna get back to the diner... oh man, Bob's gonna kill me!"

"Maybe the glowing saved us and if you say that town had the same strange light then maybe we should follow it, it might be a way home like a beacon or something in the store? Besides, has anyone else seen anything that even remotely looks like a path back to town?"

The boys looked around and all they could see were trees, bushes and darkness.

"I guess you're right... but for the record, I say this is a bad idea." Joe sighed.

"Okay, it's settled then." Said Marshall. "We'll head towards the lights Joe saw and see if we can find where we are or someone that can help us get back to the diner."

The trio set off, now that they had regrouped and headed towards the direction Joe had seen the glowing lights. Joe led the way as best he could with Marshall at his side and Randy, fresh stick in hand, brought up the rear. As they came out of the woods, they emerged on a hilltop which overlooked the vista. To the groups surprise there was a clearing down below with what looked like a cluster of large rocks in the distance in the dark, but after that, there was nothing but clear black skies and a canvas of treetops as far as the eye could see. Marshall wondered if

Joe had led them the wrong way? Marshall's Heart sank and for the first time since arriving he truly felt he didn't know where they were. And more importantly, he realised he didn't know how they would get home!

Chapter 10

Standing on the edge of the rounded hill, looking far below to the base of the opening, Marshall tried to hide his concern from Randy. He needed them to keep strong and not panic. He turned to Joe, who shot him a side glance with the same expression of fear on his face that he was trying to hide. He looked down briefly at Randy, who was stood between them, with eyes glistening in wonder at the amazing view before them. He had a smile on his face as if he had been told he could have all the free ice cream he could imagine. Joe looked back up and nodded silently at Marshall as if understanding the necessity not to concern Randy about the severity of their situation. But then something caught Marshall's Eye. A small blue spark in the distance, like blinking fireflies in the night sky but now increasing in size and brightness, dotted all throughout the rocks.

Hold up, they aren't rocks Marshall thought. He looked closer from his vantage point where he could see the lights slowly illuminating the area around them as their glow bounced off the shapes. *They were Houses! And... The glowing dots... They were people! It was a town.*

He turned to Joe with a grin. It wasn't Maitland but it was the first sign of being close since they arrived. Maybe someone down there could help them. There were houses of different shapes and sizes nestled together from what he could now make out with the glowing specks of light. And as the flashes of lights moved, he could see it wasn't just a "clump of rocks" but a larger group that filled the basin of the clearing.

The whole clearing and town were bordered by a dense and impenetrable looking jungle which towered over the landscape some 200ft above the peaceful looking town for the entire horizon. Like a naturally formed wall. Save for what looked like a small, dark archway that was revealing itself in the light of the moon at the back, northern most side of the town, that cut into the wall of trees and undergrowth.

"Hey Look. People!" Said Joe. "Finally, civilization! We can get home!" He said with a sigh of relief. "Hey!"

Marshall grabbed him and pulled him down behind a large rock nearby before he could call out again.

"Are you crazy?! You didn't see that thing back there, but we did! they might not be friendly either."

Randy gulped and gave a pause.

"They might not even be people!" His eyes grew wide as he said the words out loud and the sudden realisation came upon him. Then he smiled and looked up at Marshall. "We should *definitely* go!" He smiled, fumbling his pocket for his screwdriver.

"Let's not get too carried away." Said Marshall trying to quell the instant jump to aliens and the unexplained that

Randy's imagination always went to. "But we don't know where we are and things definitely aren't normal around here! I still don't know what that was back there, I barely believe it myself. But there could be more. Besides does anyone else think it's weird to be walking around with Blue torches in the dark?"

"Maybe their power went out?" Asked Joe

"'Cos of the aliens!" Said Randy with a smile, pushing the notion once more.

Marshall rolled his eyes, he looked at Joe. "Look *maybe* their power did go out?" He quickly turned to randy with his index finger stretched out, pointed at him. Randy closed his mouth silently and kept his ideas in. "But the fact is that's even more reason it could be dangerous. Maybe those things attacked the village and we're safer up here."

"If they attacked, then people might be hurt." Joe countered "We can't just not look. It could be our only way to get home, maybe someone there can give us a ride back to Maitland?"

"Look, I'm not saying we don't look, I'm just saying I think we need to be sensible about it. It could be dangerous. Let's at least try and get a closer look without being spotted before we jump in without a plan. Okay?"

The other boys agreed and they picked out a decent looking hiding spot from their vantage point. It wasn't too far from the village and they could get a better look without being spotted.

"Okay" said Marshall. "We have to be careful when we go down there. The moon is bright and there's no cover between here and there, so they'll see us if we're not careful. We need to time it right. Randy, Joe, when I say,

143

we make a break for it to the houses at the back over there. I can't see any lights over there so I think we should be safe."

"Okay Marsh, we're right behind you!" replied Randy.

"Okay... three... twwooo..." He paused, checking one more time that the coast was clear. "One, c'mon!"

They made a dash from their spot at the edge of the woods, on the hilltop and ran down the bank of the hill, towards the village. Although there were no streetlights, the piercing white of the moon bathed the exposed hillside in light and Marshall knew they had to crouch and run as fast as they could to the stony outcrop just south of the village. As they sped down the hillside, their hearts beating fast with adrenalin, they kept constant watch on the nearing town.

It was hard to make out any real distinguishable features in the dark, other than the edges of roofs in the moonlight.

As they reached the foot of the hill Joe stumbled and rolled to a stop at the bottom. He wasn't hurt but he was worried it might have caused unwanted attention. Marshall, who had reached the base of the hill already, shook his head and checked he was okay. They looked up but there was no movement. They hadn't been spotted.

They resumed their descent until they made it to the rocky hiding place. Although they were a lot closer, they were now level with the small village and the houses which were now visible fully, blocked their view. They needed to get to a better viewpoint.

"Over there!" Marshall said pointing to one of the houses on the edge of the village. "It looks empty. It's pitch-black and I don't see anyone around. They must have moved over to the other side of the town!"

The trio snuck along the side of a few of the old buildings that dotted the outskirts of the small town. Gingerly making their way from house to house trying to get closer. The buildings on the outskirts were old, almost crumbling. They were mostly wooden with the odd one having a grey stone foundation made of various sized, circular rocks. They reminded Marshall of those he'd seen in the Pioneer Village in Salem. He had visited the historic site with Randy when he was younger whilst staying with his grandparents in Boston. But these were all in a terrible state of disrepair. The outsides were covered in dark green moss and lichen and the wood looked half rotten on some of the beams.

There were no paths, just wild grass growing in-between the dotted houses. The air was damp and cool and Marshall felt a chill come over him. The houses all looked empty and unused for years and it was eerily silent.

"Where is everyone?" Joe Whispered.

"I... I don't know it's like they've vanished. The town doesn't look lived in for years, like a lot of years... the houses look ancient." Marshall replied.

"That can't be, we saw them literally minutes ago!" Joe puzzled.

As they walked past the empty houses, they became bolder and withdrew from hiding in the shadows. As they left the outskirts and entered the heart of the town, they noticed the buildings looked newer, still old, but more like that of the artisanal stores found in some cities nowadays.

Wooden boards hung from carved brackets that would once have displayed the goods which could have been purchased from there. When that may have been, Marshall could not tell but he assumed anything left in the stores was like the buildings themselves, well and truly rotting and of no use to anyone.

Randy took a step and heard a little knocking. He looked down and it was a pebble, he had kicked it by accident in the grass and it had bounced its way along until, they saw in front, the grass stopped and was replaced by a pathway of moonlit cobbled stones. It was a street. The join between the old wooden houses and grass and the newer houses and stone streets was almost clinical as if cut with a large knife precisely.

As they passed the buildings, out of sight, small spider like creatures darted for the rafters along elaborately constructed purple webs that hung in the porches as their peace was disrupted by the presence of life.

"What is this place Marsh?" Asked Joe.

"It was a town I guess, once."

"Was?" Asked Joe. "I mean what happened to those people we saw with the torches? They can't be living here but they couldn't have just vanished."

"Like I said... I don't know what's going on or where we are but we need to be careful, something isn't right." Marshall spoke softly whilst taking in his surroundings.

"Maybe we should try a house or shop see if they have a phone or radio that we can call someone on?" Said Randy.

"The Power's out Doofus, how can we use the phone?" Replied Joe sarcastically.

"Actually, he has a point." Interrupted Marshall, defending his brother's idea. "The phone lines are separate. We can use them if we find one. Maybe in one of the newer looking buildings they'll have one?"

Randy blew a raspberry at Joe and laughed.

"Okay, well the phones I've used all needed power, so I'm just saying." Replied Joe sulking, not wanting to admit he was wrong.

Marshall laughed. He was used to Joe always having an answer, even if it wasn't right.

"Okay well let's start looking."

They made their way up the creaking porch steps of a nearby house that looked like it was at home in the 20th century once. As Joe and Randy reached the top of the steps, they turned to see Marshall waiting at the bottom staring up at the house.

"What's a matter Colonel, you're aren't scared, are you?" Joe laughed.

"No." Marshall said with a distant look on his face. "I recognise this house, but not this block."

Joe hopped back down the stairs and paused as he took a look at the front of the house.

"I don't know what to say man, it looks like any other house in our neighbourhood!"

They shrugged their shoulders and met Randy back at the top.

Randy reached out and tried the handle. With a click of the latch the door swung open and moaned on its hinges. The interior was dark at first, it was impossible to see where to go but as the moonlight shone through small holes in the wooden shell of the house, their eyes adjusted.

They made their way through the doorway and into the hallway.

"Hello?" Marshall called out, still trying to be quiet.

"Honey, we're home." Cried Joe, not as quiet.

"Quit it." Marshall shot back.

"You quit it, it's not like there's anyone around this dump to answer back."

A loud knocking made them jump. Joe retreated back to the porch, suddenly spooked and afraid he could be wrong.

"It's just the wind." Marshall said reassuringly, after jumping himself. "Let's split up then, if you're so sure no one's around."

"Well maybe its best we stay together. Ya know, just in case we find anything?" Joe replied sheepishly, the strange noises of the old house evoking a sense of fear.

Marshall laughed. "Whatever. C'mon let's *all* try over here."

They searched the entire downstairs of the house but there was nothing except a few items of furniture, they entered the kitchen and they tried the cupboards and refrigerator but they were all cleaned out. Despite Randy's disappointment, Marshall thought that possibly a good thing, given the age of decay of the house. Any food left there without power would be less than desirable to the nose or taste buds.

Joe ran to the sink.

"I'm so thirsty!" He stuck his head under the Fawcett and turned the handle but nothing happened. Then an almighty groan came from the pipes below, followed by a rattling sound coming from under the sink. Then *spludge*, a huge black blob of ooze spat out of the tap and covered

Joe's face. Randy fell on the floor, unable to stand, with laughter.

"Ah man!" He wiped his face with his sleeve. "Eeeew, gross." He cried. He spat out the rest of the muddy substance. "Taps are dry... pretty much."

Randy was still laughing, Marshall whispered to them both. "Shh, keep it down. Let's try upstairs. Maybe they have a phone or something up there."

Slowly, they made their way up the wooden stairs. The floorboards underneath creaked under their cautious footsteps. As they scaled the old staircase, past the torn, patterned wallpaper, they could see the soft light of the moon floating in through the large window on the landing of the first floor.

At the top of the stairs there were three rooms, the doors to which were all shut.

"Okay, room each?" Marshall asked as he looked at his cohorts.

"Sure Marsh." Joe agreed. "But maybe we should have some sort of codeword or signal in case we find anything or get into trouble?!"

"Yeah that's sounds smart... hmm, let me see. How about *help*?" Marshall laughed as he held his hands up in a sarcastic suggestion.

"Oh yeah... that'll work." Joe said smiling, realising how foolish he sounded.

Joe wandered over to the furthest door. He tentatively grabbed the round, copper handle. He shut his eyes and let out a deep breath and prepared to open it. He heard a giggle next to him, he peered to his right slightly and saw Randy looking at him with a smile. He sighed.

The cold metal made him shiver as he twisted the smooth round handle until he heard the click of the mechanism opening up. He pushed the door open in a single, gentle glide.

It was dark inside, save from the moonlight coming through from outside. It was a small bedroom, with a single bed against the far-right wall. Maybe a child's? He thought. The cool light of the moon, shone through the rectangular window to the left of the bed's headboard.

There was no phone here but he decided to check if there was anything left that could be used. He walked across the wooden floorboards and approached a wooden dresser. There were some small wooden carvings laid on top. Roughly cut with a penknife by the looks of it he thought and smoothed afterwards into the shape of different animals. He picked up the nearest one, they were toys! He was right, this must have been a child's room.

"Way to go Joe." He thought to himself for guessing correctly. But then a sudden chilling thought came over him at the thought that he was right. What had happened to this family? What had happened to the child who owned these toys who couldn't have been much younger than him?

He thought he heard a strange sound like the sound of running water but it soon vanished and the house was in silence again.

He turned around and looked about the room but there were no hints, no signs of anything wrong, other than the mould and cracks in the walls that served as an indicator to the length of time it had been left empty. As he turned, the moon kissed the edges of the carving he held in his hands and he realised that this was no animal he had seen before. The hairs on the back of his neck prickled and he decided he had been here long enough.

He placed the carving back on the dresser with reverence and care out of respect for the previous owner and he stepped back into the hallway. Casually pulling the door shut as he left.

Slowly, as the door closed, the wall that lay behind it was revealed. Upon it there was a scrap of fresh paper stuck to the wall about half way up. It had a crayon drawing of a family and the house that the three boys were in, in the background. They were all there. There was the father figure holding hands with the mother and next to them the small child. All of them dressed in their best clothes, all of them happy... all of them glowing blue... all of them grinning... through the crudely drawn, pointed teeth... dripping red! The clouds rolled over the night sky and the child's picture was plunged into darkness once more.

Joe stood in the hallway, waiting for the others, thinking about the missing family. He looked at his watch it must be getting late. But It had stopped, oddly, about the time they got to the antique store.

"Wooow!"

He looked up, it was Randy, standing in the doorway next to him, smiling and staring at something outside the window at the top of the stairs. Then he heard it... outside in the streets, a little further off. The deep bloodcurdling screech.

****

Randy opened the middle door at the top of the stairs to the Right of Joe's. He watched as Joe fumbled with the handle and giggled. He was such a scaredy-cat thought Randy.

He reached out and in one swift movement he opened the door and stepped in. It was the bathroom. He reached up and tried the switch for the lights but they wouldn't work. He left the door open for some light and walked in.

There was a silver coloured tub, at the back of the room. Facing out, through a large circular wooden framed window. The walls had no paint or paper left on any of them and a long, broken mirror, above the sink, was set amongst cracked, discoloured, pink tiles.

Underneath was a mint green sink and a set of wooden drawers. He wandered over to the sink unit and opened the drawers that ran down the left side of the cabinet. The first contained the standard bathroom objects, nail clippers, cotton swabs, spare toothbrush, hair clips... He took the clippers and nail trimmer, which easily fit into his pocket under his costume. He opened the second, deeper drawer. There was a wash cloth and a small hand mirror. He picked it up and tried to look at his reflection in the mirror but when he tilted it into the little light there was coming into the room, he could see it was cracked badly and any reflection was distorted.

"Ah jeez." He said in disappointment but he noticed the small, blue gem that adorned the top of the mirror's frame,

"Alrigghht Treasure!" He said with a smile. "Very profitable!"

He used the end of the trimmers to pick the gemstone out and put them both in his pocket.

He considered if it were rude to use the facilities in a stranger's house without their permission. But he reasoned with himself that it was barely a house anymore and there were, in fact, no strangers present to protest. And so, with his bladder calling the shots he made use of the old toilet.

He whistled as he filled the bowl, glancing around the rest of the room for anything of interest. He tried the taps in the sink after to give his hands a wash but just like the kitchen, there was nothing. He made his way over to the old tub in search of running water and as he got closer a stench hit him. He wrinkled his nose and flipped his hood over to cover his mouth. It was like the pond water at his frog spot at home, he thought but worse and it grew stronger the closer he got to the tub.

He peered over the edge of the metal basin and stopped himself from vomiting, the liquid was green with mould and whatever else had fallen in by the looks of it. But it was certainly no longer used for sanitary purposes. As he stared at it in disgust, a bubble surfaced and made a large *plop* sound.

He heard one of the boys come out of their room and onto the upstairs hallway. *They must be done.* He thought to himself. Deciding he had also searched all he could and content with his haul, he turned to leave the room. As he reached the doorway and onto the landing, he noticed through the window at the top of the stairs, a blue spark in the air, through the trees outside.

"Wooow!"

He smiled in surprise, then he froze in terror as all of a sudden, a piercing cry filled the air outside.
****

Marshall watched his brother and friend enter their rooms and after knowing they were safe, he tried the door at the beginning of the hallway. It was stiff but with a bit of a nudge with his shoulder, he worked it loose.

Dust plumed into the air as the breeze disturbed its rest. It was the master bedroom. He saw a large armoire and dresser table, complete with vanity mirror and on the other side, was a large bed.

He reached for the switch but again to no effect, that's when it hit him. *Power.* He had seen no power cables, no phone lines. Back home you couldn't go a block without a dozen telegraph poles or power cables running above the street. But in all the time they had spent skulking in the shadows to get here, he hadn't seen a single one. Maybe this town had no power, because there was no power in the first place? But then why the light switch and the light fixtures, the refrigerator in the kitchen. It made no sense! It was almost as though the houses had been plucked from their spot and placed on the grass as was. He puzzled it over in his mind as he walked over to the old wooden armoire.

It was still solid despite its aging. Marshall opened the door. He spluttered as more dust filled the air and he fanned it away. He flipped through some dress shirts and suit jackets all lined with dust and full of moth holes. There was an old, black pair of shoes in the bottom but nothing of importance.

He sat on the bed and looked around the room. He couldn't work out what had happened to the town, to its residents Why was there no power lines but items that needed power? Where had the people with the blue torches gone and who were they?

So many questions ran through his head then he turned to the dresser table to his right and he began to tremble, eyes wide at what he saw there.

The dresser itself wasn't particularly uncommon. But the frames, which laid upon it, were. Marshall picked up the larger of the frames and gasped.

"We need to leave!"

As he looked at the photo in horror, he heard muttering in the hallway then he heard a scream outside in the streets. At least, the first one sounded like a scream but the second and third sounded more like a call, like the bark of a fox or the screech of an owl in the haunting, night sky. He ran to the hallway.

"Marshall, look." said Randy pointing out the window.

"No time, guys we need to leave!"

"But look, the light!" Randy insisted.

"Right now! We're in real danger if we stay here!" Cried Marshall.

They ran downstairs to the front door and checked to make sure the streets were clear.

"Which way?" Cried Joe. "Should we carry on or go back the way we came?"

"We can't stay in this town." Said Marshall.

"Why not?"

"The houses, they don't belong to people, not anymore!"

"What?" shrieked Joe in disbelief. "Are you kidding me? More of these monsters in old lady skins?"

"Aliens..." Randy calmly said to himself. "...I knew it."

"No, worse Joe. But good point we can't go back to the woods... There, the big arch in the trees! We go through there, away from the town, away from the swamp. It must lead away somewhere."

"We don't know where that noise was coming from, it could be *in there*." said Joe.

155

"Look, the lights!" shouted Randy pointing at the large arch in the trees in the distance. The soft pale blue light was flickering through the gaps in the wall of trees.

"See there are still people here, maybe they're hunting whatever you saw Marshall. And if they're hunting, they might have guns and if they have guns then that's the safest place to be. And if they aren't hunters then at least we won't be alone anymore out here and we can finally get home."

Randy and Joe made a mad dash without hesitation towards the arch and the blue lights.

"No wait!" Called Marshall. But it was too late they were too far ahead of him. He had no choice but to follow after them and hope that Joe was right. And that maybe this nightmare was over.

They darted through the streets and old houses in the shadows in a line towards the wall of trees. As they got closer to the hole, they could see it was actually a lot bigger than it appeared from afar. It was larger than the house they had fled and deeper. It reminded Marshall of the old, stone viaducts he had seen under train bridges. But the thick walls of the tunnel like passage were made of very large, hard thorns and vines. He could barely wrap both hands around the larger thorns. The borders of the forest were Impenetrable.

As they stepped into the entrance of the passage, they glimpsed the passing blue light. Illuminating the sides of the curved arch ceiling as it slunk across the top and sides, around the corner and then shimmered out the other side, filling the passage with darkness once more. They crept left, around the slight bend in the tunnel, towards the exit to see a flat expanse with more ram shackled wooden houses. This time though there were only a couple either side of a cobbled path that stretched up towards a large stately looking Manor. But along the borders of this path were people, the people with the lights!

From behind, in the shadows of the tunnel, they could make out the shapes of men, women, children. All dressed in suits and old, Victorian style clothing. They heard the laughter of play from up ahead. They were all following an invisible line marching towards a large, eerie looking manor house. As the moon's light shone down onto the towering building the kids could see it was all black and dark green stone, with cast iron adorning the edges of the roof. It continued onto the sloped Window frames that stuck out.

The building was an irregular shape. As it grew from the ground towards the night sky it reached up and out into circular turrets at each corner and judging by the amount of circular and odd shaped windows, there must have been hundreds of rooms inside.

The old-fashioned clad figures walked towards the strange looking mansion, dozens of them. It looked like they were off to a party.

Maybe a Halloween party or something similar Marshall had thought, as laughter and chatter filled the air. They must have been holding the lanterns in front because every so often the flicker of pale blue light shone momentarily into view. As they watched, Marshall felt the odd patter of a few drops from above. The clouds had slowly rolled over covering the moonlight and It looked like there might be some rain soon.

As the procession made their way up the street, Randy spotted a tall thin figure dressed in a faded suit, boots and a top hat at the back. He had a young child walking next to him. He noticed the young child drop something as they walked. Randy bolted out of the tunnel after the young boy and ran to pick up his toy to return it.

As he left the confines of the cave like shelter of the trees, the clouds above grew thick and grey and cast a dark shadow over the land below. The rain started to drop a little as Randy grabbed the small wooden toy and called to the pair in front to return it and ask for help. As he called out, he heard his brother scream from behind.

"RANDY, NO!!"

As the light diminished and the clouds began to pour their drops down heavily, Marshall and Joe had watched in horror as all the figures began to glow bright blue. Like dozens of neon torches up ahead. *They* were the lights that the kids had seen dancing in the distance!

It was too late. Randy had tugged at the bottom of the jacket tails of the tall figure with the child.

As the figure turned around to face the boy, the first bolt of lightning cracked overhead. Illuminating the pair and as the heavy rain thudded against the figures black top hat, the lightning shone its light over the white grotesque animal-like skull that sat underneath. Its long, jagged tooth jaw opened wide. Showing its two, sharp, powerful incisors at the front as it stretched its mouth wide. The lightning crackled wildly overhead again as the creature bellowed an almighty roar at the startled boy.

Randy saw its horns like a ram, curled at the side of his head around its baboon like skull. Its dark empty sockets glaring at Randy. Thick, blue ooze dripped down its mighty fangs as the figure bent down and continued its loud howl towards him. Randy tripped backwards onto the ground in shock. He could see bugs crawling through the few tufts of long black hair it had coming from under the hat.

He scurried along the floor, back to the other boys on his palms, not taking his eyes of the creature in the long black jacket and boots.

The child like figure turned and gave a similar, yet higher pitched, screech from his smaller, hornless skull face as if backing up his Father's annoyance. It turned and grinned its skeletal grin at his father as if for approval. Then they both turned back around and followed the crowd to the mansion without any further interruption.

The other boys ran over to help Randy to his feet.

"What... Was... That!" Shrieked Joe.

Safely behind the cover of the archway the boys looked on through the pouring rain as the group marched slowly towards the large manor.

"I believe you. I believe you. I wanna go home, I believe you." Joe burst out, unable to control his fear.

Marshall picked his brother up and checked him all over.

"Are you okay, did he get you?" He panicked.

"No..." Randy said calmly, in shock. "They didn't touch me."

"We need to run!" Whispered Joe. "We need to leave!" He turned to go back down the arch hallway of thorns.

Randy was unusually quiet and followed Joe.

Marshall, almost mesmerised, stayed and watched, as the creatures marched, almost to a silent rhythm up into the manor. Their bodies, glowing radiant blue now that the light from the moon had diminished.

He turned to speak but noticed the other two had made their way back to the arch opening at the other end.

He ran through the short tunnel to the two boys.

"They aren't bothered about us. Isn't that weird?!"

"Did you not just see that thing?!" Shrieked Joe. "How is it even possible? Let alone whether we bothered it or not."

Randy remained quiet. Marshall noticed and asked again if he were alright. Randy nodded and Marshall told him it was okay to be scared.

Randy sighed. "I'm fine, they didn't scare me... It's just... They're just like Mom."

"Huh?" Marshall answered, bewildered.

"They're just like Mom. I tried to help that little boy and I get shouted at, I was just trying to do the right thing, there's no need to yell, and another thing-"

"Wait." Interrupted Joe. "That's all you got from what just happened, that they're rude?! Is anyone else not seeing what I just saw back there."

With that a large growl filled the night air and the boys turned to their left as they looked out from the archway, back across the old town they had originally come from and above the canopy line of the wall of trees that curved round to the right from their spot.

The thorny walls of the archway seem to come to life as creepy crawlies of all shapes and colours came scuttling out of the thick, entwined mesh of weeds. In the thick, dense forest behind, the tree tops started waving, something big was nearby.

As the thick branches rustled, a flock of strange flying animals erupted into the sky, their large, long bodies visible even from where the boys stood and as soon as they erupted from their perches in the trees, they were lost against the black night and the whole jungle came to life with a symphony of howls, shrieks, hisses, and growls, far into the distance.

Marshall's stomach felt sick at the final realisation.

"Guys... I don't think we're anywhere near home. In fact... I don't think we're in our world at all!"

Chapter 11

The Clouds rolled in and the thunder let out its cry. But elsewhere, far to the west, the air was still and the jungle was alive with the sound of the shrieks and calls of a plethora of different creatures.

The jungle itself teaming with life and the high shrill call of winged creatures circling amongst the black and purple sky above.

Deep In the thick of the undergrowth lay a fallen tree. Its trunk hollowed by insects, weather and time. As the moon shone it's dappled white light through the vines and tree tops above, it glistened against the soft light green moss that covered the top ridge of the tree.

Four little feet came scurrying over the top of the fallen tree into the spotlight. Each with a small claw at the end of each toe and skin just as green as the moss itself. It was a scutterstrike. A scaly creature, no bigger than the palm of your hand. It had a crest atop its head that rattled like a snake as if alerting its presence. It cocked its strange head, listening to the various noises in the background. It lifted its chin and with a ruffle it shook a flap of purple skin under its chin that called out, as it expanded, with a low whooping sound.

"*Whoophoop, whoophoop.*"

Unanswered, it scurried from its mossy perch and darted along the jungle floor looking for its next perch. It's feet barely touching the dark, leaf strewn ground as it sped through the jungle. It came to a brief halt at the bottom of a large smooth tree. It's trunk as wide as a car with roots that fanned out like sails as it met the ground. It latched on to the side of the tree and climbed up to the top branches with ease.

It reached a thick branch that led to a gap in the canopy but its path was blocked by a sleeping creature that much resembled a bear but smaller. With large ears and sharp pointed teeth that stuck out from its jaws like knives. Its paws dangled over the branch and hung mid-air as it slept. Its jet-black fur was lined at the bottom with a mauve stripe. The scutterstrike scurried up and over the soft, black fur, undeterred in its course but as it hopped off the creatures back it felt a squeeze around its body. The creature had awoken with the ruffling of its fur and had curled its whip like tail around the creature. The sleeping animal rose and gave a growl. It brought its tail close to his face to see what had disturbed his slumber but as quick as it was to anger, it licked the small animal, nuzzled it with its nose and returned it safely on the branch with its tail. The bear like creature then slumped back to its spot and quickly resumed its heavy snoring. Safely, the scutterstrike crept along the remainder of the branch and up to one of the top branches, with precision, that overhung the forest floor below.

As it pattered its tiny feet across the bark, it suddenly froze and lowered its body, tight against the branch making itself blend in with the gnarled wood of the tree.

Silently, a large, dark blue, three toed foot dangled down slowly from the branches above, followed by a second. Then three more pairs of three toed feet dropped down onto the branch next to it, making no noise at all as the rough undersoles of the feet gripped the branch tightly.

Although the night was dark, the glowing white eyes reflecting in the moon were unmistakable. They belonged to a pack of shrewd and cunning creatures that stalked the night canopy, picking off smaller creatures as they slept. Walking upright on two legs they stood about five feet tall but crouched on all fours they could slink between the branches with ease, unseen. Whilst their hands and arms were used for gripping and climbing trees, each of their three toes were topped with sharp claws like the talons of an eagle, made specifically for one thing.

They had spotted the sleeping beast that had released the lizard creature and although it was bigger than them, it was no match for a small pack of the deadly hunters. Especially when they had the upper hand.

They made gestures to one another as they grinned an evil grin, teeth gleaming in the moonlight. The first one crawled head first down the trunk to where the beast lay. The rest of the group followed like a trained unit. They hopped down silently to its resting spot and like assassins in the shadows they circled around the unsuspecting beast as it lay asleep.

They closed in around it quietly and before the sleeping beast could open its eyes, the pack of dark blue monsters slowly opened their jaws wide, brandishing a set of razor-sharp teeth and the short cry of the sleeping beast was soon lost into the night forever.

The scutterstrike swiftly left it's hiding place amongst the branches and away from the pack of monsters before it was spotted. It scurried to the end of the branch and leapt across a gap in the thick trees that was far too big to cross. At the peak of its leap it flapped open a set of hidden wings on its back and flew over the streams of the jungle floor below.

It left the perils of the jungle for the predators of the night sky, as various bats and other winged creatures of the night tried to catch it with their claws and jaws mid-flight. Some swooped from perches hidden in the shadows like the slender legged scrob-grobble who waited in the darkness for unsuspecting animals to wander by, then it would strike out with its outstretched claws, cradling its victims. Or the small frog like creature that waited patiently, who's mouth resembled that of a hole in a tree or log and when unwitting smaller prey would stumble upon it as an ideal resting spot or place to make a nest, it would shut its mouth quickly, leaving the inhabitant to befall a terrible fate inside.

Some creatures flew high in the night sky, circling and hovering for hours waiting for something to pass through then it would dive through the trees like a speeding train in the hopes of taking the critters by surprise.

But the plucky little scutterstrike swooped this way and that, dodging the various predators of the evening. It flew through the exotic jungle and landed on a small rock, near the edge of a river that cut through the tropical flora.

It rested for a second as the cool water splashed against the edge of the rocks as it ran its course downstream. Before it could settle, the little scutterstrike hopped off its rock just in time as a giant amphibious monster came crashing out of the river and onto the rocky banks, nearly crushing the critter with its enormous, soft belly as it ran on all fours snarling into the night.

The scutterstrike continued its journey through the wild jungle. It hopped from rock to rock, up and over crooked trees that were covered in dangling moss then shone in the night's light. Past a symphony of insects and creepy crawlies all singing in the night.

It clambered over the furry back of a colossal blue bocine, a large beast with long, light blue shaggy hair that peacefully grazed along the forest floor. Undeterred by its hitchhiker the bocine travelled through the dark, mysterious jungle with its purple mists and creatures that hid in the dark. As it reached an opening in the jungle, a small winged insect landed in front of the bocine. It was glowing green and it lit the stony pile of rocks it had chosen to land upon.

The little scutterstrike spotted the insect and hopped from its spot on the back of the bocine and crawled up the side of the rocky outcrop.

It looked at the small, glowing insect with curiosity. It twitched its head side to side, making out the strange bug, deciding if it was a meal or not. As it deliberated, a spot of water hit the stone and the insect took flight. It had started to rain and the scutterstrike gave chase. Even with its spindly legs it struggled to keep up with the flying insect. It flapped it's wings here and there to give it height as it jumped and climbed over rocks and bumps in the grassy ground. The pair danced, left and right as they came to a patch of vines that covered a set of wide, stony steps.

The scutterstrike continued to chase its prey up the vine covered steps and into a tiny hole in the side of the giant stone wall of the building they led to. As it emerged the other side it scuttled its little legs down a bleak, circular stone staircase and into the darkness.

Water dripped and echoed in the distance and the wind howled through the abandoned dungeon as the storm grew close outside, filling the air with an eerie presence.

Various small creatures of different shapes and sizes hid in the shadows. Eyes glowed red and yellow from the various dark holes in the walls. Some spooked by the chase and others watched on eagerly in the hopes of a free meal.

The insect flew into the dark abyss of the dungeon passage way and stopped beating its wings as it landed on a small round stone in the middle of the room. The scutterstrike topped just in front of the rock. It held its position steadily, like a spear fisherman waiting in the stream. It had it in its sights. It edged ever so slightly forward, towards the bug, so that it was within striking distance.

Just as the creature was about to pounce, a low rumble filled the air and the insect flew away.

The round stone where the insect had perched had cracked and a bright light emitted from inside. The glowing green light beamed from the cracks forming in the stone. The cracks jaggedly ran from the stone and up the wall connected to it. The light grew stronger and as the dungeon became brighter the scutterstrike could see that the stone wasn't a stone at all but rather a toe, connected to the wall, which was now visibly not a wall. It was surrounded by three more similar shapes, all of which started to crack and emit the strange glowing light too.

The scutterstrike sensed the danger and scurried off as a low, sinister laughing could be heard from inside the glowing cracks of the boulders connected to the stone.

Outside, clouds drew in overhead and swirled as the calm night sky turned purple and green in a vortex. Lightning flickered outside and inside a mist circled from the ground around the boulders and the glowing lights and as it spun it peeled the cracked rocks off of the shapes. The stones were hatching.

The sounds of night creatures outside stopped almost instantly as if foreshadowing the next moments. With a final shrug the large rocky structure came tumbling down and the fog and cloud swirled and settled.

A large, dark purple, muscly arm reached up towards the sky and came crashing down upon the ground lifting a heaving body up, silhouetted in the low light.

Then another, slightly smaller but heftier deep, dark green figure rose. It was followed by a tall, spindly, shadowy blue shape that rose slowly above the ground cackling devilishly as it sprung to life, four arms raised it from the ground.

Then finally, with a wild gnashing of teeth and claws, a small dark Red shape darted out of the smoke and climbed up onto the last piece of nearby rock from where they had emerged, bringing it level with the first ominous silhouette, eyes glowing.

Between the grunts and growls came a sinister deep laughter followed by a chorus of cackles and wheezing shrieks. As the air cleared and the swirling of the clouds subsided, four grotesque figures stood in the remaining light.

"Heh heh heh..." A low, eerie voice chuckled. "Boys!... We're back!"

Chapter 12

"Nope, nope and nooope!" cried Joe. "Are you kidding? You want us to go in there?"

"I don't *want* to go in there," Replied Marshall. "but I think we should." He replied, wiping his brow as the rain poured down making his hair droop over his eyes.

"We don't know where we are at all or even how we got here for sure. We're lost, cold, a creature tried to eat me and Randy... I don't know what's in that building but as crazy as it may seem, all I *do* know is that apart from looking freaky and having a bad temper, that thing didn't try to eat us and right now that's a win. Maybe it was protecting its kid. Maybe, to it, *we're* the creepy ones. who knows? But I'm tired of walking and those old houses we saw won't keep out the rain, you saw the holes in the roofs and walls."

Joe sighed. "You're right... you're always right. But I'm telling you, one sign of a human cookbook or teenager sized oven tray and I'm outta there, okay!"

Marshall smiled. "Okay." He looked at Randy. "You good with this bud?"

Randy flipped the hood over on his ghost costume like a knight donning his helmet.

"I was born ready." He said with attitude, as he proceeded to walk off at a slight right.

Marshall grabbed him by the shoulder to stop him going any further in the wrong direction and pulled the hood back down.

"Here." He said as he grabbed a nearby thorn from the giant wall. He cut two eye holes where Randy had drawn them in marker pen. "Any better?" He chuckled.

Randy flipped the hood back up and put his thumb up again.

"Perfect!"

"Right then, that's that, let's go." Said Marshall taking the lead.

They ran up the wide concrete steps that led to the entrance of the mansion and out of the rain. The concrete figures that adorned the ends of the rails either side of the steps had fallen into disrepair and vines could be seen coming up, through the steps and curling through the railings.

They pushed the large wooden doors that opened into the dark abyss inside. Candlelight lit the large entrance Hallway but it was empty, not a shred of blue light to be soon anywhere.

Where were they? Thought Marshall.

They stepped into the large room and the large doors creaked slowly. They looked around at the dimly lit room and its dark mahogany coloured walls.

The decorative ceiling loomed high above them, full of ornate carvings and gold leaf work. Despite its decadence, the old hallway seemed faded and forgotten.

The patterned walls were ripped and covered in cobwebs and all the framed portraits that dotted across the walls had their faces scratched away.

Small, cockroach like bugs darted through the cracks and broken walls.

In the centre of the large hallway was an enormous set of ornate stairs that led up and to the left as it met the adjoining landing area. The ends of the bannisters had creepy faces carved into them. As he scanned the upstairs area behind the railing, Marshall could make out several doors and hallways leading off of the upstairs balcony area that looked down upon the huge front door. Back on the ground, a dark and dreary looking alcove tunnelled under the stairs.

"Which way?" Asked Randy.

"Up or Down?" Asked Joe. Gulping as he looked down the dark hallway on the ground floor.

"I don't see any of those lights." Said Marshall, trying to work out where such a crowd could have disappeared too.

The air was silent, save for the rain and thunder outside. They couldn't have just vanished Marshall thought. But at the same time the mansion looked so big it could have easily swallowed them up between all the winding passages and doorways.

A flash of lightening cracked through the sky, making the boys jump and it made the decision for them, as instinct kicked in and they ran swiftly up the staircase in fear. They clambered over each other as they ascended the steps.

They came to a halt at the top. There, they caught their breath and surveyed their new hiding spot. They were a little embarrassed by just how scared they were all feeling.

"So, upstairs it is then." Laughed Marshall nervously.

"Yeah, but where to now?" Replied Joe as he pointed in front.

Now they were level with the first floor they could see that the purple and black striped wallpaper corridors stretched on and on in front of them with doors filling the left and right and the path winding round to the right at the end.

"Maybe we split up and start checking?" Said Randy, ready to go.

"No way, look what happened the last time." argued Joe.

"Yeah in all honesty, now we know what's *living*... and I use the term lightly, in here. I don't think splitting up's a good idea anymore." Said Marshall.

"We need to find a way home but I'm pretty sure even if we found a phone now, we won't get an operator that's human. So, we need to find someone to help us."

"Yeah, and preferably someone with meat that covers their bones!" Joe replied shakily.

They tried the first few doors of the corridor but they were all locked. The last one had a gaping hole in the door and from the view outside in the corridor, they could see it was abandoned and of no use. They decided to take one of the lit candelabras and follow the winding passages to see where it may lead.

The halls were like a maze, they all looked the same. The only difference were the portraits that hung on the red patterned wallpaper. Some had been scratched away like in the foyer of the mansion but others had regal looking paintings in them. Randy felt as though they were being watched by the eerie carvings and spooky décor that filled the halls.

The older boys walked on, talking about anything to keep their mind off of their current situation. They jiggled the handles to some of the doors along the hallway, submitting to the fact that most of this house had been locked down.

Randy slowed his pace as he stopped to look harder at some of the portraits on the wall. These ones hadn't been scratched out.

The first was of a large, round looking fellow. With a long, pointed noise and a white masquerade wig. He was sat in front of a large bookcase with a roaring fireplace beside his chair.

His eyes seemed to follow Randy whichever way he moved his head and he was creeped out by the yellow, crooked smile that he wore.

The plaque at the bottom of the painting was engraved:
Lord Montague Hayne, 1528.

The one next to it on the right was of a similar sized man with a wry smile. He had deep sunken eyes, with large black bags underneath. He had a wicked expression on his face and again it had a small plaque underneath the painting which read:
Lord Montague Hayne, the 2nd, 1568.

The next along was the same, a portly chap this time with a Moustache, an equally horrid visage and a plaque. This one read:

Lord Montague Hayne, the 3rd, 1608.

Randy was noticing a pattern as he made his way along the wall but there was something oddly different about the next painting.

It was of a tall, broad shouldered man with a chiselled chin and dark bushy eyebrows. It read:

Lord Samuel Hayne, 1648.

Which in its self wasn't too strange other than the subject being significantly thinner than his relatives and bore a kinder smile, with a more original name. It was when Randy looked beyond this member of the family that he noticed something strange. The next painting was a duplicate right down to the bushy eyebrows but it was engraved:

Lord Samuel Hayne, 1748.

The only change was that the smile was slightly sadder.

The next was the same but entitled:

Lord Samuel Hayne, 1848.

But this couldn't be, the paintings were two hundred years apart but the man in them all looked in his forties.

Randy moved to the next one and covered his mouth in shock.

It was entitled:

Lord Samuel Hayne, 1908.

The picture was completely torn out as though it had been scratched away by knives.

The last painting on the wall made Randy shout for his brother to come look.

The boys came over and after being shown the pattern, they all looked in confusion at the last one. Sat in the seat was a hideous dark purple creature. It was large, muscular with glistening yellow eyes that made his maniacal grin worse. He was sat with three others surrounding him. The first was the taller of the four, pulling at a book from the bookcase. Another, dark green, picking his nose and the last, the smallest, was about to touch one of the flickering flames with his clawed finger outstretched.

The Plaque at the bottom was engraved but not like the others. It looked like it had been carved by claws. Scratched into the plaque was the word

"KASSIR - 1908"

"Woah!" Cried Joe. "That's one messed up family tree!"

"But what happened to the 4th dude? And who are they?" Asked Marshall.

Randy leant in closer to get a better glance at the monsters, when-

Sploosh

A screaming face came leaping out of the middle of the painting and covered them in blue ooze as the apparition passed right through them and knocked them to the ground.

"Ah, man. That's nasty." shouted Joe as he spat some of the goo out and cleared his eyes.

"Sorry, I'm sorry... I'm in so much trouble. Sorry again." The babbling figure said, as it helped joe up from the ground.

Joe having fully cleared his eyes, saw the bony glowing hand that had helped him up, it was connected to a bony arm, which joined to a bony body and atop it sat a smiling skull. Joe shrieked a high-pitched scream. The Creature shrieked back. Joe scuttled backwards against the wall as far as he could.

"Woah, woah, woah! Hold on fella it's okay, it's okay." The glowing Skeleton tried calming him down.

"Breathe, just breathe." He said in a calm voice then he held his mouth open and paused still.

Joe and Marshall looked at him in fear but also confusion.

"What are you doing?"

The Skeleton noticed their confusion "You can't tell? I'm trying to blow, the curse of having no lips, no skin at all to be honest!" He shrugged his bony shoulders and turned back to Joe.

"Just breathe meat bag, you can do it!"

"Who, what... Who are you?" Marshall finally asked.

The skeleton stretched out and hovered over to them.

"Pleased to meet ya!" He held an outstretched, skeletal hand.

Randy smiled, and shook it hard. The Skeleton's jaw rattled, which made Randy laugh but his smiled was replaced with a look of surprise when the arm came off in his hand.

"Uh sorry." Randy said with a grimace, handing him back the arm.

"Ah don't worry my friend, it's always doing that, ever since the accident."

"The accident?" Marshall asked. "I'm sorry, is that how you died?"

"Died? No, I got hit by a passing car, a crazy boglet hit me at ninety and broke my arm years ago."

"Oh..." said Marshall still confused at the whole line of events.

"No truth is, I've always been a skeleton, same as my Pappy, and my Grand' Pappy before him. Long line of no-bodies... get it!" He burst into a laughter.

Randy couldn't help letting out a little laugh.

"Name's Jimmy. The T is silent!" The skeleton said.

Joe was confused. "There's no T in Jimmy!"

"That's why it's silent, jeez keep up kid!" Jimmy leaned in to Randy and whispered. "Not too smart is he!"

"Well I'm Marshall, this is my little brother Randy and you already bumped into my friend, Joe."

"How do you talk if you have no tongue?" Randy asked.

Marshall nudged him. "I'm sorry, he likes to ask questions... even when he should mind his own business!" He said to Jimmy as he scowled at Randy.

"No harm there fella, best way to be! A youngster can't understand the world without making a few mistakes and asking plenty of questions!"

Jimmy crouched and leant on his knees with his elbows so he was eye height with Randy. "Honestly, I don't know kid. I just open up and it comes out, some say too much!"

"I get that!" Randy said, empathising with him. "I'm always being told I talk too much too."

"Honesty and curiosity my boy! I like it!" Reminds me of a younger me... you know, except with the hair... eyes... Skin... peas in a pod you an' me!" He smiled and stretched back up and looked back at Joe who had been quiet this whole time, still in shock and covered in drying, blue ooze.

"I really am sorry my friend, I took a wrong turn in this place looking for the kitchen and was in such a rush... I still am to be fair."

"Wait, kitchen? You're a skeleton... can you even eat food?" Joe asked.

"Not if I wanna keep this figure!" He burst out laughing again.

"But seriously, no I can't, but it's not for me. Surely you all know that though. That's why you're here right?! The party..."

"The party?" Marshall asked.

"Yeah, It's Crossover..." Jimmy made a frown as best he could with his skull and the blue ooze that covered him like a see-through skin as he hovered.

"You mean Halloween?" Asked Marshall, curiously.

"Hallow- What? No, you know... Crossover. The one night of the year we can visit the other worlds. Well used to anyway. But the big boss is still hosting the party and I'm kinda stuck on waiting duties-" He looked at the three boys faces.

"Why does it look like I'm talking to you in tongues?"

"You don't have a tongue." Randy added quickly, laughing.

"Ha!" Jimmy gave a laugh and high fived him.

"But seriously... where are you guys from?" He sounded concerned!

Marshall stepped forward. He looked either side of him at his brother and friend who both nodded.

"We're from Maitland..." He winced, hoping it would sound familiar.

"Is that up near Shockton? Or Terrortown?" Jimmy asked, curiously.

Marshall sighed. It was as he suspected. He felt a little silly saying the words.

"We're from Earth!"

Jimmy's eye sockets grew wide and he fainted with a heavy thud.

"Are you okay?" Asked randy, slapping Jimmy's face, trying to bring him round.

Jimmy sprung back up.

"Yeah I'm good. I can't actually faint, I have no blood. I thought it helped to add dramatic affect though! But thanks kid. I don't even think I can fall... I kinda just float. But that's irrelevant!" He said, snapping back into focus.

"You guys are... humans?"

"Last time we checked, yeah. Why?" Replied Joe.

"You need to get out of here now!"

"What do you think we're trying to do? We're trying to get home." Said Marshall.

"No, I mean, you need to get out of *here*, this building, now! It's not safe. Not after the last one! If the boss knew there were humans here-" He stopped his sentence short for fear of scaring his new friends.

"How do we escape? Like, to our home?" Asked Marshall.

"That, I don't know." Replied Jimmy. "But I can get you out of here. Besides if I was caught with you then it would be unthinkable."

"You mentioned you got hit by a car?" Asked Marshall. "So, you have cars? So, maybe you have a way of getting us back to Maitland, our Home town?"

"You're not getting it my friend. That's not how it works. Okay, so as I said we're celebrating 'Crossover' tonight." He said, making bony air quotation marks. "Right, so for as long as anyone can remember this one night a year we're allowed to travel. Like, long distance, you get me? To anywhere we wanted in your world from this very spot.

Some would use it to gather various items for potions and the like, some would use it to do some exotic shopping for things that just can't be found here. A buddy of mine, goes by the name Glopthark, used to visit a pen pal in some far-off place called New Jersey but he stopped going because he said it was too scary. Every so often, a traveller would bring something back. A little trinket or token 'Earth souvenir'."

"You mean like a snow globe?" Asked Joe.

"Yeah, sure, something like that or sometimes like those houses you see down there in the village."

"An entire house?" Randy said, with wide eyes.

"I knew I recognised that house!" Shouted Marshall. "It was on Sheriff Johnson's wall! You guys took all those missing things?"

"Hey, you guys have your own crime too! It wasn't all this place but you telling me you've never taken a rock from a holiday spot or shell from the beach? Anyway, as I was saying, this was all because of a guy call Lord Hayne!"

"The guys in the painting!" Randy exclaimed.

"Correct my friend. Lord Montague Hayne, the 1st to be exact! He was a fleshy… ya know, from your world. We all know the stories. He came here by accident in the olden days.

"His family used to mine the grounds around his home back in your world, gold, precious gems, you name it. One day, whilst looking for these gems and rocks, one of his workers stumbled upon a strange blue stone. He said he hadn't even realised he was looking for it, it was like it had called to him, like a siren's song or something.

Next thing he knows he's being transported to our world. He freaks out, a few creatures nearly eat him, it was a mess. These were dark times in history, we're not all that bad now."

"Huh, could have fooled me!" Said Randy, waving his arms like wings and pulling a face like the bat lady.

"Our people had never seen a fleshy type before. He goes back home to his life and naturally, he tries to tell his family. They don't believe him when he can't prove it. Now, he works out that he can only use this stone to travel to our world and vice versa on one special night, what we call Crossover. I'll give you three guesses when his guy found the stone?"

Marshall felt cold, he knew what stone Jimmy was talking about. It was the amulet.

"Now flash forward to the next year and guess who comes knocking, only this time, he has with him a whole bunch of these stones. He's been busy and he got greedy. He knows we have things here that would make you a powerful ruler in your world, says he wants to make a trade. So, in return for him taking home some... *unique items,* to enhance his standing, our ancestors get to keep their own stones. Thus, allowing us to visit your world too. This continues for a few years but then the guy says he wants to bring his empire here, a retirement home shall we say, hence the current abode to which you are standing in."

Jimmy raised his hands and fanned them out showing the mansion to the boys.

"So, he imparts his secret to his only son, Montague the 2nd, and he carries on the legacy back home while father sits it out here. Until he in turn grew old and came to the family home t*he tomb with a view,* as I call it. And so on, and so on. Each generation more spoilt and greedier than the next. That is, until Samuel Hayne."

"The last guy!" Randy whispered with excitement, totally enthralled with the story.

"Correct my costumed counterpart!" Jimmy exclaimed.

"Now he wasn't like his ancestors, he wanted to do good. He had been researching cures for illnesses in your world and he discovered that using stones from the ground might help certain conditions. But what he stumbled on was something far greater than he ever hoped and far worse."

"Is that really him in all the other paintings?" Marshall asked. "No way he didn't age in two hundred years!"

"You're jumping ahead, don't worry kid, I won't miss out the good part!" Jimmy Continued as he floated into a seated position, mid-air.

"Now he was told, as was his father, about the opportunities and riches it would bring but, unlike his father, he decided to try and use its power for good. To harness its powers to help those less fortunate somehow. He had taken it to his workshop to test its properties. He heated it, he tried to melt it, he even tried to open it. That's when he slipped and his hammer opened up his thumb instead." Jimmy made an exploding sound and a wave with his hand.

"Ha, I tell you, you fleshies are so delicate. Anywho. So, his finger bleeds all over the stone and whoosh, he lands in our world, right here on the spot where this house is but not on Crossover. He was the first person to be able to travel outside that night!"

"How come only this one night?" Asked Joe.

"Now you see, once a year, the power of these gems builds up or the cosmos aligns or the veil is at its thinnest or something, I don't know, but basically its strong enough to let us jump to your world... just for one night. If we don't come back before midnight the pathway shuts and we are stuck in your world until the next Crossover and if we try anyway it hurts like mad. Let me tell you my cousin, three finger Jake... well you get the idea."

"So, after some initial screams, a visit to the family museum here and some travel advice. Samuel grabs the stone and boom he's back home in your world. Now here's where it gets tricky and where the real history lesson begins. So, he lands right back in his little village right and he's spotted by a lady, one Aylse Young."

"Hey, we studied her in class!" Marshall exclaimed. "Mr. Neidernaim made us write an essay on her and the history of Salem."

"I'm not surprised, she's responsible for quite a bit of history here too!" Scoffed Jimmy.

"Now, she and Samuel are in Love but they can't announce it due to her being... how do you fleshies say it... *out of his league?* From a social hierarchy standing anyway. She's a lowly town washer woman, he's a lord. It's forbidden. Now, she sees him appear from thin air and lights in the sky and she's freaking out and so he shows her the stone. But there's nothing, not even a flinch of movement, she doesn't believe him of course and fears he's absolutely crazy but then she notices his blood-stained hand. Now he realises it wasn't fire or pressure, it was his blood. The stone requires a sacrifice to make it work outside of Crossover. That's why it hurts us so much to try, it takes a part of us each time. So, he pricks his finger,

183

grabs her by the hand and whatta you know, he has frequent flyer miles on Monster Sc-airways."

"How do you know all this?" Asked Marshall.

"I told you kid. We all get told the story of Crossover when we're kids. It's a yearly tradition. That's not the last of it though. When they returned-"

Jimmy stopped abruptly. They heard a clattering up ahead from one of the rooms.

"Quick hide!" whispered Jimmy.

They ducked down, around the corner from the direction they came. They all held their breaths until they could hear the noise had stopped.

The noise brought the boys back to their present predicament.

"So, Jimmy what does all this have to with us." Asked Joe.

"Sorry guys, I have a tendency to rattle on and I don't mean my bones."

Even Randy couldn't muster a laugh at the poor attempt at humour.

"Not funny? Ah tough crowd."

"What happened to Samuel?" Asked Marshall. "And the Stones." Marshall thought if they could get hold of one of the stones in this world, then they would be able to return home once and for all.

"Hold on now, there's more to it than that!" Whispered Jimmy.

Another clatter, this time a little closer, came from up ahead.

"We don't have time, Jimmy!" Marshall replied "That's why we teleported here!"

"What's that?" Asked Jimmy.

184

"Well, you see, this stone I think we used it. What I mean is, it's not a stone now it's an amulet but we were taken from our world and we somehow ended up in the middle of a man-eating jungle."

"That's impossible." Said Jimmy.

"We didn't know how, why or where we were until now! We were being chased by this bully, Josh Butcheson and his gang and we were trapped see, then the amulet I found in the store-"

"That he stole!" interrupted Joe.

"I did not steal it, I was gonna– never mind, what's important is that we were trapped but I read the words on the edge aloud! I think that's what brought us here!"

"Oh my, kids you've messed with a power far greater than you guys can imagine it's not safe!" Said Jimmy with a look of terror.

"Ow!" Marshall let out a cry, as a pain jolted through his arm. He turned to Joe, who had just hit him.

"What was that for?"

"That's for getting us trapped in the town from hell with a bat lady with an appetite for kids, turning me into a pinata and bringing us to this haunted house." Said Joe.

"Well it was that or be Josh's punching bag, I still think we're better off here."

"So how did it get from Samuel Hayne to being on sale in a creepy antique store in middle of nowhere Maitland?" Asked Joe. "And why did we all come through and not just you?" Joe asked.

"I had hold of you guys when I read the words and thought of escaping." Replied Marshall.

Jimmy interrupted. "If that's so, then you have your ticket home already! You can use it to get back home right now. And take it with you too, it can't stay here. We may all already be in trouble."

"That's the problem." Marshall said, embarrassed and a little panicked. "We *had* it, but it must have dropped on the floor back home, because when we crashed here, it was gone!"

Jimmy held his skeleton head low and sighed a breathless sigh.

"The rest of the story can wait, we need to get you guys out of here and to a friend in the woods, a doctor."

"A doctor?" Asked Joe. "We need a travel agent not a medical."

"He's not that kind of doctor, he uses... more unusual methods but he may be your only hope of returning home. At least the amulet isn't here, the last thing we want is for it to wake up the worst kind of company."

Chapter 13

"Mmm mm mm, can you smell that?" Asked the large, dark purple creature. The first creature to emerge from the rocks he was the leader. He sniffed the air around, like it was his first time.

"All I can smell is... Crudge." came a thin, high pitched, gravelly voice from the small red creature with the sharp teeth and claws.

"You try being stuck in a rock all that time Ravage. See how you smell." Growled Crudge, the hefty green beast that had emerged second. He spoke slowly, in a dull voice.

"He did... we all did actually." Remarked the towering, spindly, blue giant behind them. He was better spoken than the other creatures and wore a pair of old glasses but he was still just as devilish and sinister. The Engineer, as he was known.

"That de-lightfull smell, my brothers, is freedom!" Said the first creature, ignoring the others. "Freedom from our imprisonment and freedom to unleash our power once again on this world. The freedom that was taken from us when that wretch stole my amulet."

187

"How come we're free boss." Replied Ravage, the smaller, crazed monster with the high-pitched voice.

"How indeed Ravage, there was only one power strong enough to free us... *it* must have returned!"

"Engineer... can you see that little human here, I want my amulet." He growled.

"Negative." Replied the Engineer. "It looks like this place has been empty since we fell into our untimely sleep!"

The Leader growled a low, guttural growl in disgust. He raised his head and yelled into the night as it echoed around the cavernous, dungeon walls.

"I am Kassir! And I shall not be denied my revenge for what that creature did to us!"

"But Kassir... given our current status, it's safe to assume that the amulet must be closer than it has been in a long time." The Engineer quickly added, noticing his leader's obvious anger at the situation.

"Good, our essences won't last long out here without the amulet's power and fresh souls. We must find it and soon before we fall back into our stone prisons."

Ravage shuddered at the thought. "I aint goin' back in there, nope, nope. I'll find 'em boss I'll seek 'em out." He began sniffing the air, then the ground, for a scent to track as he hopped about the cavernous floor. "I'll sniff em, I'll find them. Then I'll *play* with them." He said as he grabbed a handful of soil and then crushed it with his bare hands, flashing an evil grin and mimicking his intentions.

As he did so, his large ears pricked up and twitched in time with noises coming from above. He listened intently for a second, then as his ears lowered, an evil grin rose.

"We're not alone."

The others could hear the dull beat now as well.

Kassir raised his head up as if looking up through the ceiling above, through layers of stone and mud and he smiled.

"Looks like somebody's thrown us a welcome back party."

Chapter 14

"Okay so how do we get to this doctor?" Marshall asked. "Do you have a map?"

"You won't need one kid. I'm coming with you!" Jimmy replied, with as much of a smile a skeleton could give.

Just then, a louder crash of wood and metal came from the room just up ahead.

"Shh, someone's definitely coming this time!" Whispered Joe.

"They must have realised I'm not back yet." Said Jimmy "Quick, third door on the left up there is unlocked. Just wait in there. I'll be right back!"

The boys ran as quickly and quietly as they could to the left corridor, as the footsteps could be heard getting closer from the right corridor.

"Hey boneman, where's the food?! Boss is hungry, just 'cos you can't eat, doesn't mean we can wait!" They heard a grizzly voice shout at Jimmy.

As their Hearts returned to their chests and their breath regained a normal pace, they heard another crash in the distance, from the other direction. It came from up ahead, from the room that Jimmy had told them to wait in. It was followed by something calling out in pain.

"Aarrghh!... stupid, stupid." Came a deep, mysterious voice in a low, rasping tone as it cursed in pain.

They crept behind a dresser that was up against the left-hand wall. Randy held his hand over his mouth, trying not to make a sound in case they were spotted. Marshall tapped Joe's shoulder and pointed in the direction of the creepy voice and motioned with his hands to ask if he could see anything. Joe shook his head and leaned further from the dresser to get a better view.

As the lanterns flickered their light in the cobweb ridden hallways, the room lit up momentarily again and Joe's eyes grew wide as he caught the outline of something monstrous and spindly coming out of the room up ahead. He spun round to the brothers and beckoned they should retreat hastily down the separate corridor to the right, opposite the dresser that they were crouched behind. It was coming their way!

They heard it crash through another door, too impatient to open it properly. Now was their chance. They turned, in their crouched form and readied themselves to make a dash down the side corridor.

First Marshall, making sure the path was clear. He peaked his head out and made a dash on his hands and knees across the hall, into the shadows. Once safely there, he checked to see if the coast was clear and, satisfied the creature wasn't looking, he motioned for Randy to follow next. Randy shook his head. He was too frightened to move and he pointed to Joe. Joe took a deep breath and waited for Marshall's signal. Marshall gave him the thumbs up and he darted along to the corner, in the shadows, to join his best friend. Now it was Randy's turn. He was still frightened but he knew he had to move now or else he might be spotted by whatever was lurking in the hallway. He looked to his older brother and he put his thumb up to give the all clear. Just as he got the courage to make the dash, he saw Marshall's hand change to a stop with his palm held up, out flat, then disappear into the shadows. He heard the floorboards creak and he leant back as tight to the dresser as he could. The creature sniffed the air and looked around the hallway, as if searching.

As Randy waited and readjusted himself in his hiding spot, his costume caught on a splintered piece of wood on the bottom of the dresser. He got ready to brave the journey once Marshall had given him the signal, but his costume briefly snagged and caused an old ornament on top to wobble slightly and topple off with a thud, as it rolled along the hallway and came to a stop at the base of the large, clawed foot of the monstrous figure.

The boys gasped and the creature peered down to enquire what the object was and to its origin. It picked it up, sniffed it with its large snout and growled a menacing grin. It flexed out its right hand and its long needle-like claws shone in the candlelight as he dragged them along the wall, tearing through the old paper as he made his way slowly, along the corridor, towards the dresser.

"What's we got here then?" It snarled in its rasping voice. "Littul sneaksters is it? Come to spy on us has it?" It sniffed the air again with its large bony snout. In the moonlight Marshall could see its long muscly legs and spindly arms, they were covered in dark tufts of mangy fur and as it turned to catch a scent, he saw ridges running down it's back through holes in its ill fitted clothes. It was unlike anything he had seen on TV or in books.

The creature paused. "Or maybe it's a littul treat fa' Grax is it? I was wondering where I could find something ta eat." It licked its crooked pointy teeth with its long, thin tongue and ran it along its lips, tasting the air. "All that talk, it's supposed to be a party but Grax is hungry he is, yes very... very... HUNGRY!"

He thrashed at the dresser ripping it away from the wall and smashed the wooden carcass against the wall. He looked down ready to grab his meal but to his surprise the hallway was empty. He shot a puzzled look and scratched his head with one of his long pointy claws. Then all of a sudden, he heard a tiny scurry behind him coming from the direction he started. It was a diggul, a small red rodent like creature, peaceful in nature but covered in small spines down it's back. But to the trained predator it was a tasty snack.

"So, it was you was it?" Grax smiled. He turned and swung for it. It squeaked in a frenzy as it swung from its tail between Grax's claws.

"A furry littul diggul is tasty!"

He spoke softly to it as he held it up above his open mouth and with one swift flick of his wrist, he threw it in the air and devoured the unfortunate diggul. He wheezed as the spines tickled his throat going down. Then, satisfied there was nothing more to eat or find out in the dark hallway, he retreated back through the corridor and out of sight.

Marshall looked from the shadows with tears welling in his eyes, where was his brother? Then, as soon as Grax had moved out of earshot, the door behind where the dresser used to sit next to, slowly creaked open and a small face with curly hair popped out with a cheeky smile.

Marshall felt an immense sense of relief and they quickly joined him in the room and closed the door behind them.

"Phew..." He said to the other two with a smile. "That was a close one!"

Randy looked at the bottom of his costume and poked his finger through the torn hole in his costume.

"Ah man!"

Candlelight flickered in the corners of the room from large antique candelabras. They made the whole room glow a low orange. The room smelt musty and everything was covered in a layer of dust.

Joe peered through a set of old red and gold curtains to the view outside. As he parted them, a cloud of dust erupted into the air and he coughed. He waved the air clean and stepped back towards the old window. The storm was wild outside. He was glad they were out of it but he wished he was safe at the diner with his uncle and mom. He'd give anything to be sat watching Charlie Brown right now and he resented ever mocking it.

The room itself wasn't that special, it was an old-fashioned office with bookcases full to the brim with old, leather bound books. It must have been where the family paintings were made Marshall thought. Then he spotted something out of place. In the centre of the room, was a large square object, covered in a dusty sheet. Next to it was an old bowl with remnants of something that might have passed for food but it hadn't been touched.

Joe looked at it and turned to Marshall, keeping his eyes on the mysterious shape.

"What do you think's in it?" He asked. "Should we take a look?"

As he finished his sentence the shape shook and a low grumble came from within.

"Whoah, No way!" Shouted Randy as they all took a step back from the object. "I'm tired of things trying to eat us. Whatever it is, it must be in there for a reason!"

"H... Hello?"

A soft voice came from inside the object. The boys looked at each other in surprise.

"Hello?" Marshall asked.

"What are you doing, are you crazy?" Joe cried. "Randy's right, who knows what's under there. I say we leave it alone and we find somewhere safe to wait out this storm, then we make a run for it."

"To where, huh?" Replied Marshall. "We have no idea where we are and if the things that live in those houses want to eat us, then what do you think is going to be out there? In the dark... in the woods. We need to be smart. We need to find a map or-"

"I can help!" came the soft voice again. "Let me out and I can help!"

"Oh, nooo chance." Answered Joe.

"What if they can? What if they're nice?" Replied Marshall.

"Wasn't it you that told me that the woods whispered what you wanted to hear when you thought it was me? That doesn't just happen in normal life" Argued Joe.

"To be fair, it wasn't the woods it was the crazy old bat lady who wanted to eat us that whispered to us." Randy added.

"Oh, that makes me feel much better." Joe replied sarcastically.

"Look..." Said Marshall. I don't know what's in there but right now we don't have much options while we're waiting out this storm and so far, Jimmy and that thing in there are the only ones who have offered to help us and seeing as Jimmy is currently steering danger away from us, I'm gonna take a look."

With that Marshall ripped off the dusty sheet covering the object and to his surprise, underneath, was a large wooden crate locked securely at the top with a padlock. There were no holes save for a small rectangular opening at the bottom, just big enough to pass the bowl of food through.

"Hello?" he asked cautiously.

Randy shook the top of the crate inquisitively. Marshall shot him a look and he stepped back.

"You said you could help? We're not here to hurt you..." Marshall tried to reassure the creature inside the crate.

"But we will, if you try anything!" Joe quickly added from afar and out of reach, should things go wrong. He was scared but it was easier to sound tough when the mysterious creature was locked away.

There was a pause, then the creature inside the box spoke softly.

"I can get you out but you need to get me out of here."

"How do we do that? it's locked!?" Asked Marshall.

"And probably for a good reason." Joe added. We should leave it where it is, it could be dangerous."

"There's a key!" Whispered the creature. "The creature in charge, the one who owns this mansion, the one who caught me. I saw it on their belt when they threw me in this crate. They must have it on them still."

Marshall looked at the door as if mapping out the route in his mind. Lightning cracked overhead and the boys all jumped in fright.

"They'll all be in the main hall." The Voice whispered, undeterred by the loud thunderous crashes from outside. "They mentioned something about a feast, a party or something I couldn't make it out. But if you can get that key and help me out, I can get us all out of here and far away."

"That's crazy!" Argued Joe. "We wouldn't even get close, you saw that thing out there, whatever it was. I don't know about you but things aren't normal around here-" He paused and with a sudden inquisitive look he stepped closer to the crate. "Come to think of it, how do we know you're not some sort of monster, like one of those things and this isn't some sort of a trap?"

There was silence again. The boys looked at each. Marshall knew Joe was right.

"You just have to trust me." Came the voice within the crate. "Do you think this is my idea of fun?"

"I guess not, no... but still, how do we even get close to the key without being spotted?" Asked Marshall, choosing to trust the stranger.

Then, as he sat on the floor beside the crate looking for ideas, he heard a loud bang from behind him in the room. He looked behind him as a pile of books came crashing off the shelf. Next to the fallen stack, stood Randy with a guilty expression written all over his face.

"Oops...Sorry." He grimaced, as he looked at the other boys. But before Marshall could tell him to sit down and not touch anything, he noticed his white ripped costume and smiled.

"Randy, you're a genius!"

Randy looked confused but before he had time to ask any questions Marshall had leapt up from his spot besides the crate and its mysterious occupant and was rushing over to the window, by the books that Randy had toppled over. He grabbed the thick red curtains.

"Randy, c'mon give me a hand! Pull on three, okay! One... Two... Three!"

The pair fell on the floor. As they stood up and brushed the dust off them from the ground, they held up the large curtains that were now free from the rail that was attached to the wall.

"Perfect!" Marshall Smiled "Now Joe, see that up there?!" He pointed to the mounted skull of a strange beast on the wall, behind him.

"Uh yeah..." Joe said nervously, wondering what Marshall was thinking.

"Bring it over here. Randy grab the curtain ties from each side."

"Eeugh!" Joe tried to hold his face away from the large head as he lifted it off the wall.

"Gross, gross, gross!" He repeated to himself, as he grabbed the base of the four spiked horns that sat, two on either side of its head and carried it over to Marshall. Randy laughed as he watched Joe struggle.

"I think it's looking at me." Joe whined.

"It's probably never seen a dork before." Randy teased.

"Quick." Marshall tried to rush him. "Randy, you have those ties?"

"Got 'em." He said as he held them up high for his brother to see.

"Great! Right, now Rand, how much do you weigh?"

Joe and Randy looked at each other confused. Then they both realised Marshall's plan. Randy grinned in excitement whilst Joe's head dropped.

"Why me?" He asked Marshall.

"This is never gonna work." Joe sighed as he held his arms out and Marshall draped the old dusty curtain around him. "This is ridiculous!"

"Trust me it's gonna work." Smiled Marshall, as he tied the sheet over Joes head with the curtain tie. "How's it lookin' Randy?" He yelled over his shoulder. "Almost done?"

"Almost!" Randy called back. He had attached the creepy skull to his head with some fishing line he had in his pocket and flipped his Ghost hood up. "I can barely see though!"

"That's okay." Said Marshall. "Joe's the one doing all the walking, now climb up here on his shoulders."

Randy laughed as he stood on the desk and lifted his legs onto Joes' shoulders.

"Now I really do wish we had Dad's Camera!"

"Okay, so everybody knows the plan yeah?" Marshall asked.

"We got it." Replied Joe.

"Randy?" He asked his brother, who was too busy with his arms out, practicing ghost noises. "You know what you're doing, 'cos we're only gonna get one shot to do this!"

He lifted the skull up. "I got it, I got. We dress as one of those monsters, so we can slip into the party all casual and undetected. Then, when we see big ugly, we get the key, give it to you so you can come back and unlock the mystery box!"

"And?" prompted Marshall.

"And... erm..." He looked at Marshall for a prompt. "Line?"

Marshall sighed with a smile, as he fastened the last few parts of the costume. "The most important bit. You guys cause a distraction, so that I can unlock our friend here and we can escape unnoticed."

"Oh yeah... that bit!" Smiled Randy remembering.

"We're dead!" Sighed Joe, as he closed the parting of the curtain around him.

Marshall opened the door into the Hallway.

"Okay all clear!"

"Giddy up." Randy clicked his mouth as he kicked his heels into Joe's shoulders to make him move like a mule.

Unsteady at first, the boys wobbled out of the room and into the hallway. Randy had to steady them with his left hand against the wall to begin with but they managed to get the hang of it, with the odd hiccup along the passageway.

"Okay, I'll be back as quick as possible!" Marshall said to the creature in the crate.

"Be careful! Their leader is a sneaky one, that's how they caught me."

"I will... and thanks".

Marshall grabbed an old sheet and covered his head in a hood fashion. He followed the others down the passageway. They had walked past three or four doorways before they noticed the familiar eerie, blue glow shining at the end of the corridor, around the corner.

"They must be down there!" He said. "Be careful and keep your eyes open!"

"Easy for you to say." Joe said, muffled through the thick red curtain.

"Don't worry I'll keep an eye out." Said Randy, beneath his skull mask. "Now giddy-up!" He said as he clicked his tongue and kicked his heels into Joe's Shoulders.

As they rounded another corner, they could hear the feint sound of music and voices. They were close, thought Marshall and the Crossover party was in full swing.

They made their way to the end of the corridor, where they emerged onto a balcony much like at the front of the house.

It overlooked a large, open ballroom. Large, candle covered chandeliers lit the spacious, open room and in the middle were the townsfolk. They were all glowing blue, some dancing, some talking.

There were, what appeared to be children in one corner, chasing each other, playing games with small creatures. In-between were a melting pot of creatures of all shapes, sizes and limbs. Some that looked like the ravenous Grax who nearly spotted them earlier. Some looked gentler and more refined with their Victorian style clothing. There were some who couldn't be described using the human language. There must have been hundreds of them, Marshall thought. The hall was a mix of music and grunts, shrieks and chatter. He couldn't tell which were the friendly type, like Jimmy had described and which were the other, like Grax.

There was a set of stairs leading down to the left of the boys and another identically the same, over the back, against the far wall opposite. Next to the other set of stairs was a large rounded stage where a mixture of ghouls and creepy characters were playing music. It was a band.

For all the evil and spookiness this world offered, Marshall couldn't help see the similarities between their two worlds. This was just like the parties the town hall would put on for the community of Maitland at various events of the year.

Marshall turned to the wobbling tower behind him that was his best friend and brother.

"Okay, we need to get in and find this guy, he's gonna be important looking and the thing in that crate said he was big and ugly."

"Mmmph Hurgmpph." Came a muffled noise from the midriff of the tower.

Marshall pulled the curtain open and Joe tried again.

"Like that narrows it down!"

"Let's split up, we'll cover more ground, besides I don't think we'll have any trouble fitting in with this crowd!" Replied Marshall.

Marshall led the group and descended the stairs. Close behind, Randy and Joe pulled the curtains closed on the costume and were about to head down the stairs when they heard a voice from the right call out.

"Hey, what you doing up here!" A deep voice called out to their right. A large slimy beast with a round belly came bouncing over to them on his tiny feet. He had a small, dark Purple trunk for a nose and his arms were covered in thick brown fur.

The boys froze.

"We... I mean I needed to use the little monsters' room. All finished" Randy turned his head and replied. He tried to put on a deep voice. "You know how it is!"

The creature eyed the towering shape, trying to make it out.

"Actually... I don't... I'm a sneep, we don't eat, drink or use the bathroom."

"So, how'd you get so fat?" Randy quickly shot back, completely forgetting where he was.

"Hey!" The creature roared.

Joe took a step back in fear and gripped Randy's legs.

"Sorry..." The creature replied from under his trunk. It's a glandular problem... on my mother's side... I get touchy about it." He said, as he lowered his head in shame. All the other sneeps make fun of me for it but I'm just as scary as them.

"Oh, for sure." Said Randy. "I mean if I hadn't have just used the facilities, I'd have totally peed my pants right then!"

"Really?! You're not just saying that?" The sneep replied, with a smile. "I always get left out of these things 'cos everyone thinks I'm useless. No one respects me but I still try real hard."

"No way, are you kidding? It's not the monster outside that counts, it's the monster inside!" Randy reassured.

Joe hit Randy's leg under the curtain to make him stop talking and hurry him up, before they got caught.

"Well... better get down to the ol' feast now! Don't wanna miss it!" Randy replied, getting the hint.

"Okay well g'bye!" The monster waved goofily and smiled a crooked grin. "And thanks."

"You got it!" Randy called back."

As the sneep walked back to his guard position, he gave a little fist pump in the air and mumbled to himself.

"You are scary, just like Momma said."

As Randy and Joe turned and walked down the stairs, Joe whispered under the costume.

"What was that?!"

"What?" Randy whispered back, under the skull mask.

"You, stopping to give life coaching to a monster, we could have been caught. What part of inconspicuous don't you understand?" Cried Joe.

"Erm... all of it." replied Randy. "Is it a topping? Besides monsters are people too."

"No... they're not!" cried Joe sarcastically. "That's why they're literally called *monsters!*"

"So ignorant!" Randy mumbled to himself.

"Look, forget it, Marshall's gonna be wondering where we are and we need to find this dude. Let's go, lead the way."

The boys made their way down the large staircase and into the party. They mingled amongst the guests that gathered along the back walls. The floor glowed a brilliant blue from the various ghost like figures but there were creatures of all descriptions in the hall.

"This is amazing!" Said Randy as he looked about the room.

"Yeah until they decide to eat us!" Said Joe, overwhelmed by the surrounding creatures as they moved around the room.

"I honestly think we're okay!" said Randy. "Look they're just like us, talking, eating snacks, dancing."

A pack of tiny balls of fur came scuttling between their feet, their little teeth gnashing away at the guest's ankles as they ran across the dark, wooden floor.

"Excuse me, sorry, excuse me!" Came a voice from behind, trying to chase the tiny creatures.

One of the creatures screamed as the miniscule biter latched onto their foot and she threw herself at Randy who caught her in his arms. She had a lime green sheen to her skin with gills on either side of her neck. She stared up at her horned skull saviour.

"My, my, my... so lucky to be rescued by such a handsome ghoul. Would you care to dance?"

She gave the boys no chance to answer and without warning, she flung them into the middle of the crowd.

The band noticed and changed the pace of the music to something a little fierier and fast paced.

Meanwhile over the other side of the hall, Marshall had been looking for the owner of the Mansion. He walked through the sea of faces and tusks and wings, trying not to let his fear get the better of him from under his hood. He spotted the band playing their tunes on some very interesting looking instruments, he noted the large chandeliers above reflecting the various greens and purples of the lights around as if dancing themselves.

He was taking in all the sights when all of a sudden, a silver tray of small, round, furry looking items was thrust under his nose.

"Hors d'oeuvre, Sir?" Came a voice from the glowing blue arm attached to the tray.

Marshall gasped and jumped back in horror as the furry mounds spun on the tray and brandished a set of needle-like teeth. He through the tray away from him, scattering the creatures who scurried into the crowd, he heard a rattling on the floor.

He lifted his hood slightly and saw it was Jimmy who had offered the tray and, in the outburst, he had knocked his skeleton head clear off his bones. Marshall dropped to

205

the floor and picked up the skull, Jimmy's body still wandering aimlessly looking for his head.

"Jimmy, I'm so sorry, what were those things!?"

"Gorgonian Biters, very rare, very expensive. Now turn me around you mook!"

Marshall spun his head round to face him.

"Oh, hey kid, sorry I thought you were- hey wait, what are you doin' down here? I thought I told you to hide."

"We did, but there's been... some developments since. I'll tell you all about it but we have to do something first. I thought you were coming back for us!"

"I tried but I couldn't get away, I hoped you'd have sense and wait it out 'til I could sneak back out. Hey, wait, we? You're all down here? This ain't good, we gotta get you out of here. But first I need to catch lunch or I'll be nothing but a toothpick for these guys!"

Marshall rose and lifted Jimmy's head back onto his body. He twisted and clicked the skull in place.

They heard the crowd make a commotion.

"Quick they must be over there." Jimmy shouted.

"Excuse me, sorry, excuse me!" He called as he parted the crowd then came to a halt. Marshall came running up not far behind him just in time to see a lime green skinned woman taking the dance floor with the tall masked figure that was his brother and best friend.

Marshall looked on with his mouth open.

"Oh no!"

The crowd of monsters cheered as Joe, Randy and the gilled lady took to the centre stage. She pulled them this way and that as the crowd clapped their hands and tentacles in excitement. She let out a shrill call and smiled as she beckoned them to her again with a wink of her eye.

With that, the towering costumed figure burst into step with her.

"What are you doing?" Whispered Randy to his lower counterpart.

Joe whispered back. "Six years of Salsa lessons with my mom. It's this or we die. You tell anybody and you'll be wearing a skull for real!"

Jimmy and Marshall looked on in horror, as the odd couple took the floor. The crowd parted to a circle round them and the band kicked into full swing.

"What are they doing?!" Thought Marshall. "And who knew Joe could actually dance."

"Joe?" Asked Jimmy turning to Marshall, his sockets forming a shocked expression.

"Yeah that's Joe and my brother under there, dancing with the creature from the black lagoon. They're supposed to be helping me find a key from the dude who owns this place. Typical Randy, goofing off!"

"Oh no, no, no. This is bad, real bad!" Jimmy muttered.

"You're telling me." Agreed Marshall. "We're supposed to be lying low, incognito. Not parading in front of the entire hall."

"You're not getting it kid, that ghoulish green diva out there with your friends... she *is* the dude that owns this place. That's Feldma!"

Marshall looked in horror at his brother and Joe, his mouth dropped.

"What!"

"Shhh." Whispered Jimmy trying to calm him down. "I thought I was gonna get the can when I dropped those biters at her feet, but bringing humans here... If I had skin, she would tear it from me. She's bad news!"

Marshall watched the show that the trio were putting on. As he did, he noticed a small brown hessian pouch, tied to her waist. That's it. That had to be the key!

"Jimmy, maybe luck's on our side after all!"

Chapter 15

Joe was in the zone. His hips on fire, his feet glided across the floor. The hostess was loving every minute of it. She pulled them in tight and let out her forked, wet tongue that oozed up the cheek of the skull Randy was wearing, then she propelled them back.

"Ew, gross!" Randy whispered to Joe below.

"I know right, that's gross. Fish lady drool!" Joe replied.

"No, not that! That's *cool*, I mean ew, I got kissed by a girl!" Randy replied in disgust.

"You got issues man. Anybody tell you that?" Joe replied, bewildered.

Feldma, clapped in the air and shrilled out loud again.

"Maestro let's take it up!"

With that, the skinny, pale faced singer shouted behind him and the large, purple skinned drummer proceeded to produce another set of tentacled arms as he let loose on the drums.

"*Bum ba dum dum, Bum ba dum dum...*"

The fiery dance sped up.

"Ahhh yeah!" He shouted into the air with a smile, as he struck the kit.

The party broke into full swing and everybody joined the dance floor. From fur to feathers, tentacle to horns, it was a jamboree of music and merriment.

"Now's our chance!" Marshall said to Jimmy.

He ran over to the boys.

"Psst." He whispered. "Hey!"

"Hey Marsh!" Randy called down.

"So much for *low key*!" He called back.

"Sorry man, one thing led to another and... well, the girl can dance!" Joe laughed.

"It's okay." Marshall whispered. "I think it worked in our favour. She has the key!"

"What?" Joe asked, unable to hear clearly over the loud music coming from the band and the noise of the crowd as they danced.

"The Key!" Marshall repeated a little louder. "She has it, on the cord around her waist! I think you can get it!"

"Why would she have it?" Asked Joe.

"*She's* the guy who runs this place!"

"What*!!*" Joe shrieked. "Are you for real?!"

"Yeah, but no, it's okay see I think she likes you! I think you can get it from her if you can get close enough. Then you can pass it to me and I can free that thing in the cage! You guys are the only ones that can get that close to her!"

"Ah man, I don't know about that!" Joe shied away to the back of the dancefloor into the dimly lit part of the hall.

"Ow!" He called out as Randy dug his heels in to his shoulders.

"Hey!" Called Randy from Joe's shoulders. "When Love comes knocking you gotta boot down the door! That's what they always say!"

"Randy, like, nobody and I mean *nobody* says that... ever!" Marshall said as he looked in confusion at his little brother. "But he does have a point. The quicker we get this done the sooner we can go home!"

"Okay, but I wanna go on record-"

"We know, we know." The brothers said in unison. "You don't like it!"

Marshall left and headed back to the side of the hall he came from.

Joe and Randy danced their way back to the centre of the floor and took the creature by her cold, smooth hand. Randy spun her round and Joe danced back and forth on the spot.

"There you are, my handsome stranger. I thought you'd left me!" She smiled.

"Who us?!... I mean Me?!" Randy corrected himself after Joe gave his leg a squeeze. "Never could I leave someone as beautiful and... scaly, such as you!"

"Well aren't you a sweet talker!" She grinned and pulled the figure in close. She grabbed Randy by the Skull mask and gave a long lick on the other side of the face.

Joe knew he had to be quick and he seized his chance while she was close. He rummaged under the curtain, but it had twisted, he couldn't find the gap.

In all his excitement and showing off his dance skills, he had twisted the curtain round and now he couldn't reach out to grab the keys. He hoped Randy could stall long enough to sort out the problem.

"Ah man! C'mon, c'mon!" He said to himself as he fumbled under the heavy fabric to get his hand free. He could feel Randy tapping him trying to speed him up but it was no use he couldn't get free.

I got it! He thought to himself. He needed to reverse the tangle so he could get his hands free. So, he spun round on the spot, twisting Randy as he turned.

"Ooh how spirited" Feldma yelled and spun on the spot too.

"What are you doing?" Randy whispered.

"The Curtain, it's stuck! I can't get my hand out!" Joe replied.

Randy gave a sigh then confidently he replied.

"Okay, I have this!"

"What? wait, what are you gonna do?" Joe asked, nervously.

But it was too late Randy spun them around and directed Joe. He took them back to Feldma, took her hand then spun her around and as she came back to face them.

Randy bent over on Joe's shoulders and leant in and lowered her for a kiss.

As he held her with his right hand, he grabbed the pouch with the left. She locked on to the Skull of the costume and Randy could only close his eyes and hope she would let go soon.

"Gross, gross, gross!" He repeated quietly from inside the mask.

While she was preoccupied, he dropped the pouch to the floor and Joe kicked it over to Marshall, who was waiting eagerly to their left. He had a pale expression and felt sick watching the show on the dancefloor but he knew now was no time to get queasy.

Marshall picked up the pouch in a flash, before anyone noticed. He shielded it with his arms and peered inside. There, among a few other items, was a large silver key.

They did it, he thought. He was secretly impressed it had gone so smoothly, well relatively he thought, as images of the amorous, gilled beast and the tray full of biters flashed to mind. He disappeared into the crowd towards the stairs.

He left the ballroom floor and sped up the stairs as fast as he could without looking too conspicuous. As he reached the top of the staircase, he glanced over his shoulder to check on the others. They were in the midst of a lively dance and no one had spotted him. But, as he turned back round to head to the room with the mysterious box, he felt a warm, wet, heavy slap on his left shoulder.

"Hey, where do you think you're going!"

The large booming voice came from behind. Marshall turned with a fright then sighed. It was the guard whom Randy had befriended earlier. He had a big, goofy grin slapped across his large, round face.

"You're gonna miss the best part!" The Creature insisted.

Marshall panicked at first but he knew he had to get to the room, the others had done their part and then some. He couldn't let them down and he didn't have time to waste chatting.

"I... uh... I ate some bad food, I'm allergic to... tentacles?"

He didn't wait for a response. He ran as fast as he could to the room with the box and its mysterious contents.

He slammed the door shut behind him once he got there.

Lightning flashed outside from the bare window where the curtains used to hang. It lit the box up with an eerie white light. It made it look creepier than he remembered and now being here on his own he started to wonder if unleashing whatever was inside was a good idea at all.

"H... Hello?"

He asked cautiously. It was eerily quiet.

"Are you still there?" He asked. Instantly realising there was no way of it escaping and glad the others weren't there. Joe would have teased him about it big time!

"You came back?" The creature replied softly. It sounded almost sad.

"I thought you might have left me... thank you!"

Marshall was nervous but he still trusted his gut.

His grandma had always taught him, never go to sleep on an argument, and always trust your gut instinct. He considered her a wise soul and he lived by those words.

And so, he carefully opened the pouch and took out the silver key. His hands trembled slightly as he walked towards the box.

"I'm gonna let you out, okay! But please... don't eat me, okay? Do you think you can do that?"

"The soft voice from inside giggled a little at his words, then the creature calmed itself and replied.

"I promise!"

"To..." Marshall wanted to hear it say all of his request.

"To not eat you, or your friends... including the annoying sounding one. Is that better?" They asked in an amused tone.

Marshall sighed a heavy sigh. He was as satisfied as he could be with the answer, besides they had to leave soon. He couldn't leave Randy and Joe down there much longer.

He held out the key and slowly walked the remaining steps towards the large box.

He took hold of the large padlock. It was heavy in his hand. He turned it to face him and pushed the key into the keyhole.

No going back now. He thought to himself.

He turned the key counter clockwise with a satisfying *click.*

He removed the padlock from the latch of the box and tipped the lid back, opening the container. Lightning flashed its monstrous shapes across the walls and the creature stood and stretched to its full height with a groan.

Marshall stood back a little. His mouth dropped open a little and he couldn't believe what he saw as the flashes of lightning lit the creature up.

It had long, scraggly, brown hair that reached to its shoulders. Mauve fabric covered its torso and two arms and looking down to its two legs, Marshall could see... denim jeans.

Huh? He thought.

The creature raised its head slowly and as the storm subsided and the moon's light filled the room once more, he saw a pair of glistening brown eyes from under the scraggly hair. As it parted it back and tucked it behind its ears, he saw the creature, standing there with a gleaming white smile. Almost in tears. It was a girl!

Chapter 16

"Thank you!" She said softly. Tears of joy welling in her eyes. She lifted her leg over the box and stood before him with a humbled smile. Marshall, still in shock, stood in silence with mouth agape. He was expecting something creepy, something slimy, with fangs and wings and horns, something... not like her.

"I've been trapped in there for so long and I was beginning to think I would never be free. I was minding my own business over in Ghastly Gulch looking for some supplies when Feldma's goons caught me. I'm usually smarter than that to let my guard down but nevertheless that's how I ended up here and on my way to Trader's Alley or who knows where.

She took a breath.

"So... Thankyouuu...?" She looked at him with her big brown eyes questioningly.

"Uh Marshall!" He replied, realising what she was asking.

"Well, thank you Marshall." she replied with a kind smile.

"And you are?" He asked with his hand out to shake.

She measured him up with her eyes and smiled.

"Name's Ava." She said and took his hand and gave a hard shake.

He smiled as she shook his hand. Now she had managed to get out of the box he could see she stood slightly taller than him and her dark brown wavy hair, now tucked behind her ears, looked less dishevelled. She had big brown eyes and a button nose and he noticed two little dimples on her cheeks when she smiled. She was the nearest thing to normal he had seen since they had arrived here... he just hoped she wasn't secretly a bat creature or blob monster or something else in disguise.

"Ghastly Gulch... Trader's Alley? These are all real places? How big is this place?" Marshall asked.

"You're not from round here are you?" She asked curiously.

"No, we're from... well, let's just say a long way from here." She seemed genuinely nice but if what Jimmy said about what they thought of humans here was true, then he decided he should leave out the part about being from another world just for now.

"Well, Marshall from a long way from here, we don't have time to go into that right now, we need to get out of here while we can!"

Marshall suddenly remembered the other two boys still in the hall entertaining and distracting Feldma. He agreed with her and explained where they were.

"We need to get them away from her, then you can lead us out of this horrible place!" He said.

They crept to the door and it creaked as they opened it slowly. Marshall stuck out his head and looked both ways. Satisfied, he turned back to Ava.

"Okay, I think it's clear!" He said.

As he stepped forward, she grabbed his hand and followed from behind and he tried to hide a little smile.

They started down the corridor back towards the party but as they did, they heard a clatter of metal and heavy objects coming from one of the other passageways up ahead.

"Quick!" He said. "Let's go this way instead. I think it will still lead us to the main hall!" They ran down the other corridor and around the corner and-

Bam!

Marshall felt his face hit something furry and bouncy. He looked up into the menacing, bony snout of Grax, who snarled in anger then licked his lips.

"Tasty littul treat!" He said, smiling at them.

"Run!" Ava shouted.

They turned and ran just as Grax swiped at them with his clawed hands, ripping the wood panelling from the wall next to him.

"C'mere!" He snapped as he took chase. He dropped to all fours and pursued down the labyrinth like hallways, bouncing off the walls and bashing into the corners as they turned, with so much force that the plaster and paper cracked away from the derelict walls.

As the chase grew longer, he grew angrier!

Ava looked behind as they ran and turned back to Marshall.

"Friend of yours?" She said with a chuckle.

"We've made a habit out of bumping into horrible beasts since we arrived here." He shouted back as Grax thundered down the hallway behind them. "Present company excluded, of course."

"Of course!" She repeated with a laugh.

"In fact, you're the first one who hasn't tried to eat, maim, kill or cover us in goo so far!" Marshall found himself laughing at his own sentence. Just hours ago, he was concerned with homework, being cool and parties. Now... well, a lot had changed.

****

Back in the ballroom, just after Marshall had climbed the stairs with the pouch. The creature let go of the costumed figure and called out into the air with a smile. As she did, she spun them around in excitement, then she propelled them outwards with a wave of her hand. They bumped in to a few creatures dancing, who pushed them back into Feldma. She laughed and twirled them back out, the kids were getting dizzy. The monsters at the side pushed them back but this time the antlers of Randy's Skull mask caught the shoulder of a tall, glowing gentleman with large tusks and red skin as he passed, who gave a little grunt then walked on.

Randy hadn't realised and was enjoying the fun. It was like the teacup ride at the fair back home, he thought. That was until he saw the look on Feldma 's face.

The music stopped and the crowd were standing still, save for Joe, whose legs were still dancing under the curtain.

Randy's mask had been cracked and half of it was missing. Feldma yanked the curtain from the midriff of the figure and Joe's face dropped as he stopped dancing. Their they were, exposed on each other's shoulders for the whole hall to see.

Small pores on Feldma head started pulsing with rage like little green balloons. She let out a piercing hiss as her gills rattled in anger! The guests all gasped and muttered to themselves. Whispers travelled round the hall.

"Humans."

"Look it's a real human."

"Stand back."

"What is the meaning of this!" Feldma bellowed.

"Who dare let a *human* into my hall?!"

She looked around the room with a vengeful scowl. The guard that had spoken to the boys slunk back out of sight from atop the balcony.

"We all know what happened to the last occupants when they messed with humans!"

She turned back to the boys who stared at her in fright. She hissed at them in rage.

"We can explain!" Randy called out with his hands up in protest.

"Silence! I thought you were too good to be true, such an evil little creature." She scorned them.

"We're just trying to get home, we don't want to bother anyone, you can let us go. We just wanted to find a way out of the rain and to our own home! Please!" Joe Pleaded.

She lowered her head to the side.

"To play with my emotions, to make me feel so... so alive! Only to be made a fool of. In my own home nonetheless!!"

"We didn't mean to-" Randy was cut short.

"Shh! Little ones, I'm not going to hurt you." She smiled playfully. "No, no, no... You see I deplore violence. It's a ghastly thing. You see when this place became... *vacant...* I realised I could turn it into something different. Not just as my home, but as my kingdom... my empire. And what is an empire without loyal subjects?!"

She motioned with a flick of her wrist to a creature nearby, who immediately came and grabbed randy by the shoulders with a pair of large, muscly, orange skinned arms. He then produced another set of identical arms and grabbed a hold of Joe. The boys struggled but it was no use.

Now, the previous owners led with fear, with anger... with hate. Whereas I am a creature of the people and my people demand entertainment. Ever since the Crossover times stopped, we've been looking for something to fill our curiosities, our sense of fun and adventure. Until we took this place, this wonderfully evil little home!"

She spun with her scaly arms in the air as she walked over to the side of the hall. She settled her hands on a large chrome lever. She gave it a squeeze and yanked it down. A loud rumbling and scraping sound came from underneath them. The floor shook and split apart at the centre. The crowd quickly parted to the sides and cheered with their fists and claws in the air.

As the floor came to a halt, a large pit, ten feet below became exposed. The boys could see bones of all shapes and sizes down there and a large set of metal doors.

"Doeggul, doeggul, doeggul." The crowd cheered in unison.

The boys looked at each other.

"What's a... *doeggul*?" Joe asked Randy.

Randy shrugged his shoulders.

"Beats me, but I think we're about to find out!"

Feldma turned to the boys and raised her voice over the spectators.

"I had a feisty little bag of bones locked up ready to play tonight's game. But seeing how you evil little brats decided to trick me and make me look a fool, I think the people deserve a double feature! You've danced your last dance vermin. This will teach you to make a fool of Feldma.

Randy, still on Joe's shoulders, tried to break free of the four-armed creature.

"Hey wait, I thought you said you raplored violence!" Said Randy.

"She said deplored, genius! It means hates." Joe corrected him.

"That's what I said. So, why are you doing this?" Randy shouted at Feldma.

"I said *I* hate violence, but my doeggul *loves* it!!" She said with a devious grin.

"Bring out my beautiful pet!" She signalled to two other guards who pulled a set of levers together.

A large clanking sound came from below and the large pair of metal doors opened in the pit below.

The crowd fell silent in anticipation.

The boys tried to peer from their restrained position.

They heard what sounded like a large boulder being dragged across sand from inside the dark, cavernous hole.

222

Then a low rumbling from the throat of something huge filled the room.

Joe gulped. Randy leaned in, eager to get a good view.

Two giant red hands attached to long spindly arms launched out of the shadows and came crashing down on the dirt floor in front. The sinuous muscles in the arms flexed as the doeggul lifted its hulking red body forward into the light. It looked like the little diggul that Grax had devoured back in the hallways but this was 50 times bigger. It had no hind legs or tail and had to move on its hands and knuckles but the spines in its back were significantly bigger and sharper than ever.

As it landed into the light, it roared a mighty roar into the air and the crowd broke their silence and cheered.

"Doeggul, doeggul, doeggul!"

Randy and Joe looked at each other with mouths agasp.

"We're doomed" Said Joe in a high-pitched voice, unable to hold it in.

"For once, I agree!" Replied Randy, unable to take his eyes off of the slobbering monster.

"Throw them in!" Feldma called out.

"Wait, no! We can talk! What about that kiss?!" Randy called out in desperation, as the four-armed guard gripped them tighter.

"Wait!" She called out to the guard with her hand up. She walked over to the boys.

"What are you doing?" Whispered Joe, through gritted teeth.

"I don't know but the longer it works, the less we're playing with Rizzo the radioactive rat over there!

Feldma came over in a huff.

"It's because of that kiss you monster, you dared to make me feel, make me think I was more than a cold blooded... lonely lady." She lowered her temper.

A blob like creature next to her coughed and spoke up.

"But, m'lady you are cold blooded, you come from the swamp!"

"Aaaagh" She screamed a high-pitched scream and with one stroke of her hand she shot a blue bolt at him from her fingertips and he exploded into thousands of tiny blob-like pieces.

"You see how hard it is to be loved! And you came in here and purposefully tried to trick me. That's why you're going in, not because you're human but because... I can't bear to look at you my prince."

"Dude what's happening?" Joe whispered to Randy.

She looked at Randy then, in a twist of events, she bent down to Joe and stroked his face.

"What!? Me?! Your prince?!" Randy called out as she gently stroked his face with her cold hands.

I've never seen anyone move like that. She purred. Are you sure there's no golgotham beast in your family tree, somewhere along the line? You move with such-"

She stopped herself, her subjects knew her as a tyrant, she had a reputation to uphold.

"I have decided!" She screamed. "The boy with feet of fire shall not be harmed, he will not face the beast!"

The crowd booed. The boys sighed.

She continued. "Fear not!" She held her hand up for silence. "For the masked imposter will face my pet alone!"

The crowd erupted. The boys looked at each other and yelled out.

Randy had waited long enough, he had to escape. He turned his head to his left and sunk his teeth deep into the orange skin of the four-armed guard. It let out a bloodcurdling yell and Randy whipped his head back hitting the guards chin. He instantly let go and dizzily fell forward, straight into the pit below.

The doeggul leapt forward in a frenzy and made a swift lunch out of the big brute.

Feldma shrieked. "Noooo! Guards seize him! But don't harm my Prince!"

The boys didn't know where to go, they were surrounded by the screaming chaos of the crowd as they watched one of their own get devoured. Some out of pity, others in delight at the entertaining twist to the night's show. Some of the more questionable characters though, had circled towards them and were closing in. Baring teeth and claw as the monsters of varying shapes and sizes made their way towards them.

Then they heard a familiar voice shouting to them.

"Hey fleshies!! Over here!

It was Jimmy, he had been waiting for the right time to step in, still afraid of his boss. But it was clear, if he didn't do something then his new pals would be toast.

He was standing at the other end of the pit, opposite them.

Was he crazy, they thought? There was no way they could cross the pit without the doeggul spotting them and making them dessert.

But then Randy saw his plan. Jimmy pulled out a handful of the Gorgonian biters and started throwing them like furry tennis balls into the pit to distract the beast.

The boys looked left and right. They were surrounded by groups coming around the side of the pit.

"Quick lads, now's your chance!" Jimmy yelled and beckoned them his way.

"We gotta go!" Randy said to Joe.

"What, are you crazy?" Joe replied "We'll never make it!"

"Suit yourself!" Shouted Randy. "But hey, don't forget to invite me and Marshall to your wedding fish boy!" He smiled as Joe groaned and grabbed his hand.

They ran towards the pit as both groups of monsters began to pounce. Horned, hairy titans, little goblin types and ghosts all surged towards them, narrowly missing their legs as they ran towards the pit.

They jumped down into the dirt below. Their eyes darted about looking for the doeggul. He was off to the far-right hand side. They could make it, thought Joe.

"Let's go." Joe shouted!

Jimmy was up ahead waving them forward. They were half way across, they had nearly cleared the distance.

"We're gonna make it! We're gonna make it!" Joe screamed.

But his excitement was short lived when he saw Jimmy's face drop, up ahead. He turned his head behind to see the doeggul had finished the last of the biters and was now in hot pursuit of the two kids.

"Ruuuuuuuun." Jimmy shouted. Beckoning them forward.

But as Randy and Joe grew closer, Randy realised a huge flaw in the plan.

He turned to Joe as they ran and shouted.

"How are we gonna get out the other side?"

Joe's eyes widened as he too realised, they had jumped ten feet or so down and now they would have to jump ten feet back up.

"I, I don't know!" He called back in a panic.

They reached the thick rocky wall and started scrabbling up but their footing kept crumbling away.

"What are we gonna do?" Shouted Randy.

They looked behind. The doeggul was only about twenty feet away and it was charging quickly.

The boys stood, ready to be giant rat food. The doeggul closed in the last few feet and pounced, teeth out ready to strike when a rattling came from above. A voice came down, in between them.

"Going up?" The familiar, skeletal voice came.

It was jimmy he had floated his bones down and formed a makeshift ladder. The boys jumped as quick as they could and climbed up the bony escape rope.

Jimmy floated back up into shape as they heard a huge thud from back down in the pit. They peered over and could see the body of the doeggul slumped on the ground, knocked out unconscious from hitting the stony wall.

The two boys jumped up in celebration and high fived the skeleton. Before they could leave though, they were grabbed by another four-armed guard, waiting for them and lifted high into the air.

The guard spoke with a deep gravelly voice, they could tell he meant business and that they were in trouble.

"You puny little pipsqueaks have messed with the wrong-"

Poof!

The guard turned to smoke mid-sentence and the boys fell to the floor.

They saw the creatures all around them cower away from them and Jimmy. They trembled with fear, muttering words as they slowly slunk into the shadows. Feldma was on the other side of the pit and Randy saw her kneel down.

"Enough!" Came a deep, booming voice.

Randy and Joe turned back to face the direction everyone had been looking at, the direction they were going to escape.

Four large, grotesque shadows came to life as they entered the room, smoke still rising from the pile of dust on the floor as they trod through it and into the light of the large hall.

One by one they entered, scrawny and deadly Ravage, the thundering footsteps of Crudge, the unmistakable, towering Engineer then lastly, almost gliding across the floor, came Kassir!

His lip quivered as he snarled and looked at the chaos around him.

"Somebody had better tell me what you're all doing in *my* home!!"

"It's the guy from the painting!" Whispered Randy from the floor.

"Shhh!" Joe replied.

Kassir stomped in fury towards Feldma and the group that was now huddled at the back of the Hall.

Jimmy waited for the evil, foul smelling foursome to pass him, then he floated over to the kids.

"What is the meaning of this. Trespassers, in the mighty lair of Kassir!" He bellowed

"And co!" Ravage quickly added, as he slithered his way through the crowd with a smile.

Kassir groaned. "Yes, *and co!*"

Crudge loomed over the guards, his brutish form shadowing theirs and they stepped back.

"Ah, Feldma, so it's you who woke us is it? Brought us back to find you jumped in our graves so to speak?" Kassir leant down to her height and lifted his huge finger under her chin to make her face him.

He gave a grin, hiding his anger.

"N... No, your darkness, I... we... I would never. I merely acted as *housekeeper* until your return." She stuttered in fright, as she faced him.

"Good." He replied. "Because I'd hate to see what Ravage would do to anyone who dared cross us!"

Ravage hopped on all fours where he stood, in excitement. He was eager to unleash his maniacal side. It had been so long.

"He he, let me do it Boss, let me do it!"

He licked his long lips and scraped his claws along the stone floor, they screeched as they sharpened and the crowd shuddered.

Now Ravage, come come, we have Feldma's word she was just... *housekeeping* for us. We must reward her, no? Besides she wouldn't dare lie to us now, not if she remembers what happened to her brother!"

Feldma hung her head low in sadness.

Crudge and The Engineer circled round behind the rest of the crowd of misfit monsters and four armed guards.

"But why, I wonder?" Mused Kassir, slowly and calmly, as if talking to himself and toying with his prey as he walked up and down the front line of creatures in front of him. "Why would it take so long for someone who is *looking after us* to bring us back from that wretched stone prison of ours. Like an eternal waking nightmare, stuck behind those walls." He turned back to Feldma in a flash and roared.

"Why now?!"

Her frills and scales rattled as the force of his roar shook them with force.

"We... I, never woke you sire. We didn't know you were still here. Or we would have! But I have to tell you this all started when-"

Kassir held up his hand in silence and turned, sniffing the air. He sniffed a couple of times then he snarled, his top lip curled up in anger and he glared around the room.

"I smell humans!" He growled...

He grabbed Feldma by the neck and lifted her up with one hand.

He spoke slowly. "Where... are... they?!"

She couldn't speak, he held her so tight but she raised her scaly, cold arm and pointed out across the hall behind him.

Kassir growled and turned to face where she had pointed and his eyes grew wild with anger.

"Lies!"

Feldma looked puzzled and moved her head as much as she could in his grip. They were gone, the floor was empty.

"Jimmy!" She said to herself in disgust.

Then she spotted his glowing body to the left, from the corner of her eye they were running up the stairs, towards the way they entered.

"Sire, there!" She pointed.

Kassir dropped her on the spot and shouted for Ravage and Crudge to take chase but he started coughing, he was struggling to breath, he glared at Feldma who understood his command and she sent her guards after them.

Jimmy, half way up the grand staircase, heard her and looked behind. Four or five of the four-armed guards were coming their way and they didn't look happy.

"Er, guys, we got company, scram!"

The boys took flight. As they reached the top of the staircase, they were blocked by the same guard who Randy had spoken to before. They backed away, unsure what to do.

"Quick!" The guard cried. "Down that way!"

"What?" Asked Joe, confused. "Why are you helping us?"

The guard looked at Randy. "It's hard to make a friend when you look like this! Even in this place. You never judged me or nothing. You're the only one who ever did that! Now go, you need to get out of here, Kassir don't like humans!"

Randy smiled at the guard and nodded.

"Thank you, friend!"

Jimmy wasn't far behind but he had to try and slow the other guards or they wouldn't get far.

That's when he realised. The Chandelier! He quickly untied the knotted rope that attached the giant chandelier and held it up, above the dance floor. He released the knot and let go of the rope quickly. He raised his fist in the air.

"Take that you lousy, good for nothing-"

A chandelier came crashing down about twenty feet to the right of the guards, completely missing them and nearly hitting the crowd of hidden party goers.

"Ah man, that's not good, wrong rope! Sorry guys, my bad, that was an accident I uh... Ruuuun!!!"

He charged past the good guard and floated straight past the boys who were down the hallway. The rest of the crowd that were hiding in the shadows burst into pursuit after Jimmy and soon monsters and ghouls of all types were flooding the hallways in chase of the trio.

They came to a crossroads and decided to take the right passage, then the left, then right, then-

Bam!

They fell on the floor after crashing into something coming the other way. They stood up and shook their heads.

"Eurgh." Joe rubbed his head then jumped for joy. It was Marshall, and a girl?

"Marshall, you won't believe what happened! But we can't talk as we're being chased!" Joe explained.

"I know!" Marshall replied. As he pointed from the direction they had come, Joe and Randy heard a loud thumping getting closer as the ravenous Grax burst through a wall and down the hallway towards them.

"Quick, we gotta go!" Shouted Ava.

"Who's this?" Asked Joe.

"No time!" Shouted Jimmy.

The five adventurers ran as fast as they could down the last few corridors, they were following Ava's lead and behind, came the rumble of dozens of creatures in pursuit. There was the hungry Grax, the four-armed guards, ghosts, ghouls, furred beasts that stood six feet tall and winged spooks. All in pursuit of this unlikely band of heroes.

"Look, that's It!" Ava called out behind her.

Up ahead was a dead end, just a straight corridor covered in the same dreary, torn wallpaper that adorned every other wall in the building.

"Uh, Ava that doesn't look like a way out!" Marshall called out in front.

"Ava?"

But she ignored him and instead ran faster. As she neared the end of the hallway, she braced herself into a charging position and-

Wham!

She shoved the wall open. It was a secret door and behind it stood a plethora of trees, shrubs and flowers, the likes could never be found in your own garden. Behind that, were the thickest sheets of glass Marshall had ever seen. The storm outside had completely cleared, Marshall noted and moonlight shone brightly through the giant panes of glass and bathed the foliage in a soft, eerie glow. Under the top layer, the place was as dark and cold as the air about them.

The boys and Jimmy skidded to a halt and were in awe at the mysterious beauty and melancholy that surrounded them. For although filled with life, there was an air of sadness that surrounded the glass walls.

"Whoah!" Cried Randy. "What is this place?"

"It's the Conservatorium." Ava replied. "Now quick, we don't have long, follow me!"

She was right. The group of monsters were thundering their way through the halls, on their heels as they spun round the last corner, down the final few feet of the halls.

The group of five fled into the darkness, along the narrow path in front. As the mob of creatures spilled out into the entrance of the Conservatorium, they came to a halt with unease.

"*whaatttt iisss thiiisss plaaacce?*" Rasped a floating spectre with long grey arms and skull like face covered in silver floating hair.

"It looks like a forest but in a house." Came the deep, simple voice of a creature whose stomach and head met with no need of a neck or upper torso, almost like a ball but with arms and legs.

"Which way did they go?" Called out one of the four-armed guards, as they pushed through the crowd to get to the front.

In front were three paths that took them different ways in this huge indoor jungle. The leader of the guards turned to the group.

"We need to split up."

Chapter 17

The kids and Jimmy ran on down the dark path. Every now and then a shaft of moonlight shone through the darkness, just enough to make out the path in front.

"How big is this place?" Marshall asked Ava.

"I don't remember exactly but big."

"Wait, didn't you say you were captured not long ago? How come you don't remember if you saw it then?"

"I've been here once before, a long time ago. I escaped through here. I don't think Feldma and her goons know about this place, last time it was all lit up, doesn't look like anyone's been down here in years!"

As they continued, they came upon a man-made pond. Joe saw bird shaped skeletons standing in the water with their stilted legs, like flamingos. When they noticed the group, they slowly crept into the bushes.

They walked on. Randy hit a leaf here and there as they made their way down a nearly invisible path, when all of a sudden, he struck at a leaf and a bright red glow illuminated the whole area like a ripple. Lighting everything along the way in a deep, bright red.

"Wow!" They all smiled, the path had lit up and they could see where they were headed, they were on a long straight path that went on for ages but up ahead was a large metal door in the solid glass wall that looked like it opened to the outside.

"Look there's the exit!" Ava shouted. I knew it was this way. "C'mon! Ten minutes and we'll be out of here!"

As they continued on the long straight path, the leaf that Randy hit, started to pulsate and bubble as it grew in irregular shapes and expand. It spread up the vine to the main tree and it began to shake all the leaves around it.

Back at the entrance, the group of four-armed guards took the left-hand path with a few other monsters. A second group, consisting of the spectre, a beast whose head was replaced with a black circle of thick, black smoke and glowing red eyes and a few of the Victorian clad townspeople took the middle route and lastly the ball shaped creature with no neck joined the last group which included a horned beast with wings a few other creepy spooks and their leader, Grax.

They all walked on their paths, twitching at every little night sound. They knew of the wild beasts of the world, most of whom could be worse than them and as thick as the glass was between them, they weren't completely satisfied they were safe.

The four-armed guards marched along, undeterred by the dark, they were trained for such things and nothing would stop them finding the band of trouble makers. A small creature slithered along behind them about four feet tall it moved like a worm but had two forearms that it brushed the bigger leaves away with.

"I can't ssssmelll them!" It hissed. "I thhhhink we're on the wrong track!"

"Nonsense!" Replied one of the guards. "We're trained soldiers, we know what we're-"

The guard fell silent. The group stopped and spun round.

"Where did he go?" Another asked.

The leader who was at the front of the path had spun round with them, there was an empty spot in the dark where the guard had been. He looked up at the slithering creature and others behind it and saw their eyes grow wide.

Oh no, he thought and before he knew it, he felt something grip his ankles and he was tossed up into the air.

From the far-right path Grax and his men could hear a group of screams. He stopped and turned his head in their direction and grimaced.

"What was that?" One of the monsters asked nervously.

"It was nothing, now keep moving." Grax snapped. "You, with the wings!"

The winged beast pushed through the group to Grax. "Uh huh?"

"Get up there, see what's goin' on and where those littul brats are."

"Uh huh." The creature replied obediently and he stretched out his wings, kicking up dust and leaves all around. He took to the tops of the trees to scout what was the matter. From above he could see the room was long and the end was far away. They had to be near somewhere but in the dark, even with the moon's light, it was impossible to see through the trees. Then he glanced up ahead as he saw the middle of the long building slowly glow red, like an element slowly heating up. He called out with a roar below to signal he'd seen something and pointed but then to the far left, where they had heard the cries, something shot out of the canopy and the winged beast disappeared from sight!

Along the middle path the spectre had lit the way with himself and the townspeople and they could see the path clearly ahead and what's more they could see the footprints of the others in front of them.

"*Thissss wwaaaayyy!*" The spectre cried. An evil, crooked red grin came from the black smoke faced monster and the skull faced, Victorian clad townspeople shifted towards the kids and Jimmy. Not long after, they heard a group of bloodcurdling shrieks to their left, then the same to their right, the roars and cries of pain in the night.

"*Quuiiiiickk, maaake haaaaaaste!*" The spectre rasped, urging them forward at great pace.

They began to run but then the jungle ahead grew red like a summer Sun glowing at Sunrise. The leaves, the vines they were bulging and growing, they uprooted themselves and came crashing down on the path swiping at the monsters. It took out a couple of screaming townspeople, then it lunged at the spectre but it fell through the ghostly form.

"*Ruuuuuun!*" The spectre shrieked, then zigged and zagged as it flew up the path beyond, leaving the others to their fates.

The smoky beast took out an old sword and slashed at the pulsing vines, cutting and hacking away limb after limb but they grew back quicker and thicker than he could cut, until eventually, they coiled round his body and the red eerie lights of his eyes went out and the smoke blew away.

Marshall and the gang heard the awful noise in the plants behind them in the distance, they decided to run the remainder of the distance. As they took flight, they saw the roots and branches around them trembling and shaking as the red glow consumed them and they grew and mutated and began to chase them.

"Just don't look back, okay!" Ava said to Joe, she could see how terrified he was.

"Don't look back, don't look back!" He repeated to himself. But he couldn't help it. Curiosity and fear got the better of him and he turned his head as they ran.

The entire network of trees and bushes were moving and growing and shaking as they chased the gang along the path, like thousands of vine-like snakes. Then, like a screaming banshee, the white spectre came shrieking up the path from out of the darkness and passed straight through Joe and off into the distance.

"Aagh!" Joe screamed and run as fast as his legs would carry him.

"We're nearly there!" Marshall called out.

But then a loose vine shot forward from the encroaching forest and wrapped itself around Randy's ankle.

"Ah, Marshall. Help!!" He called out in pain.

The forest was close. It would swallow him up any time now. Ava acted quickly, she grabbed a few leaves and flowers dotted around. Then she pulled hard on the bark of a dagglewood Tree and she dropped to the ground.

She rolled up the hard bark, then crushed the flowers over the leaves and as the seeds and pollen fell, she tipped the leaves into the curled-up bark and took aim.

She paused with the makeshift blow dart ready to fire. She waited for the right moment. There, just behind the vine came the small opening that it was trying to drag Randy towards. She took a deep breath and blew hard down the pipe.

The seeds and pollen flew, like a natural dart. The moment they entered the small opening, the trees erupted into a twisting, creaking moan. They dropped Randy and slowly froze in shape.

Marshall ran over to his brother.

"What... how... thank you!" He smiled at Ava. "How did you know to do that?"

"I said I was captured... I never said easily though!" She smiled and gave him a wink. "C'mon let's go, the door's just here.

Marshall turned to his brother.

"Are you okay?" He asked, relieved.

"Are you kidding, that was so cool!"

Marshall rolled his eyes. "He's okay!" He helped Randy up, then they all joined Ava towards the door.

The copper toned metal door was set into the thick glass with a thick, steel frame. There was a small, circular porthole at the top and Marshall could see the world outside. It felt ages ago that they had been walking out there, all alone with no idea what to do or where they were. Now there were the five of them and they had a goal, well partially at least.

Under the porthole was a large, round wheel.

Ava tried to turn it but it was stuck, she leant all her weight down on it but it wouldn't budge.

"Here." Marshall said. "Let me give you a hand." He took the wheel with her and together they pushed. Joe joined in and with their combined power, the wheel slowly twisted and the door creaked open.

A gust of air blew through, as if it had waited years to enter. Ava stepped out, then Joe. Joe pulled the door all the way open and looked out across the world beyond.

"Woah!" He said softly.

To the left, behind them, was the large wall of trees and thorns that they had passed through but in front of them and spanning the rest of the view, they looked down on to the top of a giant jungle and in the very distance they saw a glow of multicoloured lights. The night sky was a mix of blues and purples that reflected in the dark.

"Hey Marsh, com look at this!" Joe called out.

He turned around and noticed the door from this side had no handle. Weird he thought. Why would they make it so they could only be able to open it from the inside? At first, he thought it might be to stop intruders breaking in but he figured with what they'd seen so far it might be to stop unsuspecting victims falling in.

Marshall and Randy followed outside.

"Wow, ah Marshall are you seeing this?!" Randy exclaimed.

"I know buddy, it's pretty awesome Huh?!" Marshall replied.

Ava was confused, she looked at the sky and the forest. "Don't you guys get any of this where you're from?" She asked.

241

"Er... Not exactly, not as many trees at least." Marshall said shyly, still not able to bring up their home.

They began chatting and talking about which direction to go next, when they head a large cracking from inside the conservatorium.

Jimmy was propped against the doorframe and he spun his head round on his shoulders to see what the noise was. A large log in the distance that had fallen across the path cracked and then he heard a low groan as two hands pulled a bedraggled body up and over the log. Covered in cuts and bruises the body lifted up onto its legs. It was wheezing and barely able to stand. It was Grax!

Jimmy spun his head back round on the spot.

"Psst, get down low, trouble." He whispered.

Marshall and Randy dropped behind the metal rim of the outside of the conservatorium and Joe and Ava crawled over and hid behind a nearby rock.

Jimmy turned to face the approaching Grax, limping his way.

"Hey... you... you made it too!" Jimmy called, pretending to be from the mob of beasts.

What, aren't you with them humans?" Grax Said suspiciously.

"Me? No, definitely not, can't stand those human types. I was with er, the other group yeah the other group who also got walloped good."

"What's out there?" Grax asked, leaning over Jimmy's Arm to see out the door.

"Nothing, I was just looking but I don't think they got this far, must have been zapped by those tree things. Ya know, you don't look too good! You should get looked at."

"Yeah I'm feelin' a littul whoozy, now that you mention it."

"How about I keep checking here and you head back to the house?" Jimmy said.

"How kind of ya!" Grax replied with a sly smile. "Say." He said looking at him. "How come you ain't got anything wrong with ya?"

"Nothing wrong with me? Nothing wrong, this guy says, ha, you need to speak to all my exes. Ha"

Jimmy gulped he clearly wasn't fooling him.

"Like I say I was with the other group, I ran as soon as I saw it coming, no guts you see. Ha."

"Which group you say?" Grax leant right up into Jimmy's face.

"Er you know the one... with... the one with the big guy, had wings, Wingy...McBig Guy... think he said his name was. So anyway, I'll have a look here and I'll catch you back at the house." Jimmy stepped towards the door. He had one foot out. Then he felt Grax's claw slam down on his shoulder.

"Nice try sunshine! That fella was with me, you're the traitor! We'll see what Feldma wants to do with you and we'll make you tell us where those brats are!"

Jimmy quickly kicked back and hit Grax on one of his many bruises. Grax cried out in pain and Jimmy pushed him away just long enough. He ran to the door and whispered to Marshall.

"Remember! Find the doctor kid, use the amulet! If you don't make it, none of us do!"

Then he slammed the door shut and turned the wheel tight. Marshall peeked over the porthole and saw Jimmy flash a smile before Grax attacked him and dragged him into the dark depths of the conservatorium. He tried opening the door but it was no use. He watched as Jimmy's glowing light slowly dwindled into nothingness.

****

"What's taking so long?!" Kassir growled. He kicked a nearby critter across the room in anger. He knew they needed the power of the amulet and soon or they would be locked back in their stony prisons. They were weak and the magic he had used to eviscerate the guard had drained him further.

Ravage came to his side. They all felt the effects and he glanced at the people in the room.

"Boss, the guards will be back soon with the humans and they will know where it is. Then we will have a whole buffet ready for us!" He grinned.

"What can I do?" asked The Engineer.

"I have a special job for you but first let's see if any of our old friends are left in the vaults. We're gonna need all we have if we have any chance of finding that amulet."

The four beasts entered the cold room. The walls were black and a low green mist floated above the stony floor. The small amount of light, coming from the small illuminous bugs that were in the air, reflected off the shiny surface and lit the room, dimly.

"It's pretty empty Kass." Crudge said, as he looked around the black cave as they passed through its tunnels.

"We just need enough to find the amulet then-" He stopped and smiled an evil grin as he spotted what they needed. "Then we can make more!"

He walked to the back of the room and knelt down. There, amidst the dark slimy walls and cold hard ground was a small, black, goo like substance waving in the air like a dandelion in the wind. Kassir put his thick fingers together and plucked the strand of goo from the ground. Suddenly it wriggled in his hands and a pair of dark, cold, angry eyes surfaced in the black mass. It snapped with a set of black, tar like teeth at Kassir's fingers as he tried to poke it.

"My, my, my we have a lively one here. I thought you had all gone. He's a little small, but you'll have to do... for now."

He clenched his fist suddenly, with might and the black, tar like liquid oozed down his hand through his closed fist. He lifted his hand above his head and he drank the liquid that seeped out. He felt barely envigored.

"Argh, this won't do at all!"

They returned, hungry, to the hall to find Grax had returned, alone.

"What is the meaning of this! Where is everyone else? Where is my amulet?!" Kassir called out between coughs.

"There is no one else!" Grax replied, his head held low. He gave a glance to Feldma, who was also disappointed.

"I did find this littul one though!" Grax replied with a smile as he threw Jimmy to the ground. "He's the traitor what let them in!"

Kassir snarled. "One of yours?" He looked at Feldma who nodded.

"We cannot leave the confines of this house unless we are sure we have the amulet. It looks like we may need you after all Feldma. Well, you're magic anyway! I hope that sits well with you. I'd hate for you to lose any more of your people if we had to *persuade* you!" He smiled.

Ravage bounced up and down. "Maybe just one?"

"I'll do it, if it means you will leave my people alone."

"You have my word!" Kassir smiled. "We need to know the whereabouts of those humans, so I can find my amulet! Awaken the eye and let me know when they have been found!"

Feldma stood up and with a wave of her hand, she sent a pulse out into the world that would affect all corrupt souls in the area. If Marshall and the gang were spotted, they would alert Kassir.

"Now, as a reward I will let you pick the half you like!"

"I don't understand! Which half of what?" Feldma asked.

"Which half of the people in this room you will save and which half will restore our power, to avoid a stony prison for now!"

"But you said-"

"I said I wouldn't hurt your people! But you see, these are now my people! And I only have people, to feed on!"

Kassir looked at The Engineer, who nodded in return at him.

"Ah, the old machine is ready. Now granted, without the amulet the souls don't stretch as far but a normal stone will do the trick until we catch those thieves! Now, who will it be?!"

Chapter 18

Marshall and his group climbed down the rocky outcrop that hung from behind the large mansion and plunged down into the basin of the jungle below.

They reached the floor as they descended into the lush tropical basin. The path ahead was covered in vines and tall trees, with big wide roots sticking high up out of the ground. The treetops went on for miles in every direction. There were noises and bird calls all around.

"Wooooow."Said Randy, with a huge smile, grabbing the nearest stick he could find, as subtly as he could, without Marshall noticing.

"I can't believe Jimmy did that! To save us!" Marshall said quietly as they reached the bottom of the hill.

Ava started walking on into the jungle.

"Hey wait a minute. Where are we? Who are you? What's going on?! Said Joe, exhausted and freaking out a little.

Marshall sat for a moment, on the large root of a tree, to take in everything they had just been through. He could

247

hear the wild forest noises, they were eerie, almost hypnotic. He took in his surroundings. The trees grew in twisted bizarre shapes, lights flickered from little bugs here and there and he could see strange bugs and odd-looking creatures flying in the skies above. Then he looked up at Joe.

"Guys, this is Ava. Ya know, the creature from the box!"

The others looked in shock.

"She helped us escape, just as she promised!"

Randy came back over to the group with his stick.

"Ava, this is Joe and the terror over there is my little brother, Randy."

She smiled. "Nice to meet you all."

Randy walked up to her and took her hand and gave it a little kiss.

"On shark grey!" He said with a little wink and a smile.

She giggled in confusion.

Marshall sighed. "It's 'enchante'!" He corrected him.

"That's what I said!" Said Randy using his stick as a walking cane.

Ava looked at Marshall.

"Is he-"

"He was like that before all this, yeah."

They both laughed.

She looked at Joe and could tell he was still distrusting of her.

Marshall saw the sad and hurt expression on her face.

"Don't worry about him, again he's always like this too! He'll come around!"

She smiled a little and felt a bit better. "Thanks Marshall." She flashed a grin.

Marshall walked over to Joe and gave him a nudge to make an effort with their new friend.

Joe Rolled his eyes. "Okay, Okay!"

"So..." He struggled to think of anything. "How'd you end up in that box?"

A small rustle in the leaves above set Ava into a state of alert.

"We don't have time for that!" She replied and motioned for them to start walking.

"Wow, and I'm the rude one?" Joe said to Marshall.

She was looking about the spot they stood.

"What is it?" Marshall asked. "What's wrong?"

"Are they still after us?" Asked Joe.

"I doubt it! Did you see what those plants did? Pow!" Randy punched the air.

Ava ignored him, she was still searching the canopy and skies.

"Is everything okay?" Marshall asked calmly, placing his hand on her shoulder as she looked around.

"Yeah, what's so interesting up there?" asked Joe as he ambled over the rocks and vines on the jungle floor.

"The things in these woods are far worse than those in that building!"

Joe gave a loud gulp. "Of course they are, we wouldn't want it to easy would we! Why couldn't we have landed somewhere with roads, with people, somewhere where everything doesn't want to eat or destroy us. Somewhere with a day time for starters. That would be nice... a little light?"

Ava turned to Marshall, ignoring Joe's complaining.

She gave him a smile. "If we get through this you can buy me a gabthrop juice okay? That's if Megamouth doesn't get us killed first."

"Hey, I heard that." Joe replied, taking a pause from his rant.

"C'mon, we need to get going. We can't stay here!" She called out.

"A gabthrop juice? What's that?" Marshall said with a look of disgust, as if he had just smelled something foul in the air.

"You know… It's not *quite* a shake but you get used to them." She smiled. "Where are you guys from anyway?" She asked, as they picked up the pace again through the trees and bushes, looking for some sort of path. "Ghoul's Gulch, Vampire Valley, Monster Plaza?"

The boys looked at each other. Marshall shook his head. She was nice but so far everyone apart from Jimmy had hated or wanted to kill a human. They couldn't tell her, not yet.

"Erm... yeah like around that area... we move a lot!"

"Are you guys from the circus? That would explain a lot actually!" She laughed.

"No, we're not circus folk!" Marshall replied. "Wait you have circuses here?"

"Ah that's a shame, I've never been." She said a little sad.

"How about you are we near your-" Marshall started to reply but with a sudden motion the girl had dropped to the floor. She looked back up and slowly stood on her feet.

"Hi, welcome back..." Marshall said as he laughed. "You okay?"

"Yeah..." She paused, she looked uneasy. "It's just I thought I saw..."

To the untrained ear, or that of someone who is just unlikely to take note of their surroundings, you would have been forgiven for not hearing the tiny sounds in the trees. Amidst the wild creatures calling out into the night, filling the air with an eerie ambience, and the howling winds that rustled amongst the trees, there was one noise that hid in the shadows. One that silenced them all when heard. It was only then that the novices among you would hear the faint scratching of tiny clawed feet on the hard bark of the trees or course surface of the rocks but by that time it would be too late. The ever so slight ruffle of thick fur against itself, growing faster and closer. Then finally, maybe even too late, came the small, sinister giggle and chatter and haunting growls that swept through the branches and leaves above.

The boys and Jimmy continued talking.

"Shhh!" Ava Whispered, with her hand out to beckon silence. "Do you hear that?"

Randy lifted his ear in the air and strained hard.

"I can't hear a thing!"

Marshall felt a shiver, where were all the noises, the birds, the creatures. The silence was deafening. What scared them away?

She closed her eyes and hung her head low, as if letting the forest in.

Almost instantly, her eyes opened wide in panic and fear.

Small silhouettes dotted the trees against the moonlight above. They crept through the trees and over the vines that hung from them. Ava slowly rose her head and whispered.

"When I say, we need to run!"

"What? Why?" asked Joe, suddenly panicking.

But he was denied an answer, it was too late.

"Run!" She called into the night. In response the trees and night air around her erupted into haunted laughter and the chatter of tiny teeth from every direction.

She grabbed Marshall by the shoulders, yanking him forward into a sprint. The other boys followed blindly as they ducked and dived through the tangle of vines hanging low and the roots that lifted high off the ground. As Marshall ran through the bushes, he could hear the hysterical giggling and laughter grow louder. Through the dappled moonlight that crept through the leaves and branches he could make out the creepy silhouettes of dozens of tiny creatures lunging through the trees around him. Chasing along the branches and hopping from vine to vine in steady pursuit. The tangle of vines grew thicker and they slowed their escape.

They carried on through the thick jungle as the creatures closed the gap between them through the trees. Some of the braver ones left their spots in the trees and scurried down the branches to the lower vines that ran like miniature pathways, through the creepy forest.

As they descended, Marshall could see their features clearly and he felt his stomach turn as he saw their horrifying faces. They stood a foot off the ground, with pure white fur running along their short fat bodies, their faces were distorted with large round eyes, red at the rim, set into dark, black sockets as if they never slept. Beneath their eyes were a set of yellowed, misshapen teeth. They weren't sharp like those of the bat lady but Marshall could tell they weren't chasing them for a conversation.

One of the creatures at the front leapt from its vine and landed on Marshalls shoulder. He could feel the needle like claws of its feet crimp on his shirt as a hot, sharp sensation filled his skin. He knew why they didn't need sharp teeth. He let out a yell in pain, then batted it off his shoulder as he carried on running.

He turned down a slope in hopes that they would lose them. Another jumped from its high perch above Joe who managed to duck last minute. It hit a branch that stretched over the path and it shook itself off as it stood back up and screeched at the escaping prey.

"I wish we had our bikes!" Randy called out

"Quick, this way!" Ava yelled from in front, as she turned right through a path that had been invisible to the boys.

"You know where you're going?" Joe Yelled out from behind.

"No!" She replied, just as scared. "But I know where I don't want to be!"

"Oh, great!" Joe rolled his eyes. "We're gonna be turned into hamster food!"

"Hey have a little faith, I'll make sure they only eat some of us!" She laughed nervously, then all of a sudden, the laughter went silent.

"Where'd she go?" Shouted Joe. "I told you she'd leave-"

Before he knew what was going on, the floor beneath Joe gave way and he found himself falling down a large, muddy tunnel. He screamed as he slid down the muddy slope. It was pitch black inside but he could feel the ground and roots all around him as he shot through the tunnel. He tried to dig his heels to slow himself but the earth was too wet and slippery and he could do nothing but slide. He could see a light growing at the end of the tunnel, it was approaching fast. He screamed as he plummeted towards it into the open.

Up above, the brothers both turned, as they ran, to see what was wrong.

"Joe!" Marshall called. He had vanished just like Ava.

They turned a corner but came to an abrupt halt as they saw the path ahead was obscured by a large rock face, covered in vines. They spun around to face the oncoming pack of evil, white faces as they closed in, laughing menacingly.

Marshall picked up a stick and started swinging in front of him trying to keep them at bay but more and more dropped down from the trees around them. They all smiled an evil grin. Full of crooked yellowed teeth, their tiny claws extended and slowly they closed in around the brothers.

Marshall hit a couple as they got within reach but it didn't slow their approach. One of these things might be manageable but working as a pack, they would turn Marshall and Randy into mincemeat in minutes. They stepped back against the large rock face. Marshall was so busy keeping any of the brave ghouls that tried to break forward at bay, that he hadn't noticed the white patch of fur lowering down behind them from the vines that covered the rock.

The beast opened its crooked jaw wide as it hovered about Marshall's head. It was about to sink its teeth in when Randy hit it hard with his stick. Marshall looked behind, startled at the noise. He saw the dazed and bruised creature on the floor and gave a smile to his brother, who raised his thumb back at him.

They looked back at the circle of vicious, crazed creatures who were slowly pinning them against the large wall of rock.

Randy reached out and grabbed Marshall's hand and squeezed it tight.

They could hear the haunting giggles and evil growls growing closer. They could see the feral, matted fur on the beasts as they slowly stalked closer, gnashing their teeth. They could hear their heavy breathing. They were toying with them making it slow and unbearable.

This couldn't be it, Marshall thought. This couldn't be how his night ended, he needed to get home, to get his brother and friend home safely, to get to his date with Vinessa, to-

He was stopped in his thoughts by an almighty light, then everything went black.

Chapter 19

Marshall's head was pounding. He tried opening his eyes but they felt so heavy. He could smell a weird smell and he heard cluttering around him like bamboo hitting each other.

The creatures, he suddenly remembered. They must have attacked or something, he couldn't remember but they could still be in danger.

He tried forcing his eyes open again, this time with success. He slowly opened them and the blur soon disappeared. He could see small, orange lights and browns then it all came clear. He was inside.

He was in a small, rickety, wooden hut. He looked about the room in which he had awoken. There were wooden shelves, filled with strange looking items. All different colours. Jars filled with all sorts of strange things. Some purple, some green. It was pretty dark inside but he could see the flicker of flames through the archway leading out of the room and it reflected the colours to an eerie glow. He had been laying on a straw bed on the floor.

It felt soft under his feet. Where was he? Where was his brother?!

Then he spotted something moving. In the lowly lit hut, a hand crept round onto the open archway, into the room. The skin was mottled, turquoise and yellow. The skin was stretched across the bones and the marbled colours continued up the arm as the figure stepped in, slowly. Marshall pulled his legs in close as he cowered against the wall in fright.

It looked like an old man to Marshall, hunched over almost double, he wore nothing save a pair of scruffy burlap shorts. What was most strange, was what he wore on his face. It was a large, solid mask, about two or three feet long. It looked solid like wood but as though covered in tanned leather. The eye and mouth holes were minimal and dark. Too dark to make out any features. He stood there facing Marshall for a while in silence, deadly still. Then he shuffled off back to the front of the hut, near the fire and placed some herbs and items in a pot. Marshall heard it spit then bubble away as the ingredients were consumed.

Despite being cautious of the stranger, Marshall sensed he was okay for now and decided to stand up. He was a little wobbly at first and his head felt light. That passed and he stepped into the room with the fireplace.

"Oh Marshall, you're awake!" It was Randy, he was here too and he was safe.

"Where are we Randy, who is that guy?"

"I haven't a clue but he has *tons* of neat stuff, look!" He jumped off his seat and showed Marshall a rack of trinkets and knick-knacks. All looked strange but none looked out of place there, in the shack. It looked creepy but a kind of fun, creepy Marshall thought. Harmless, just odd looking. The purples and greens and blues that lit the dark hut, danced through the shelving and all the odd items. It was eerie and mystical.

"Er, excuse me but-" Before Marshall could ask any questions, the strange creature pushed a bowl towards him and motioned to drink.

"I don't think he talks." Randy said, sadly. "But he is *real* smart! He has a book on everything."

Marshall looked at the bowl and could only think of the crazy bat lady. Randy turned to him and showed him his empty bowl. Marshall's stomach was rumbling so much, he was so exhausted he decided to try whatever it was. He took a sip. To his surprise it was delicious and he felt strangely envigored.

"See, it's good huh! Kinda like medicine but without that gross taste!" Randy laughed.

Marshall turned to the silent creature.

"Thankyou!"

The creature bowed slightly, acknowledging, then turned to fuss with some things in the back.

Marshall continued to drink as he asked his brother about why he thought he was smart.

"Well like I say, he has books on everything, plants, medicines, he has one with all the monsters we've seen in it. Do you know terror squirrels are afraid of Sunlight!"

"So that's what that was in the forest!" Marshall said, remembering the bright light and the creatures. "So, this guy saved us?"

"Yup, he knew we were there, he has powers!"

"Powers, how? Like super powers?"

"No, like mystical powers. He knew we were in trouble."

Marshall put down his empty bowl, and looked at the creature. He pondered to himself about Jimmy's last words. He got up and walked slowly over to the creature who was silently stirring the pot.

"Hi... um... thanks again for saving us both. This is gonna sound a little strange but we had a friend, his name was Jimmy and he told us to seek out a... doctor... of sorts, here in this forest. See we aren't from around here and I just wondered if you're-"

The creature raised his arm whilst stirring and facing the pot. He pointed to a large bookcase filled with old books.

"Yes, books, it's very impressive and you must be very clever but see what we really needed-"

The creature raised his hand again this time though a book fell from the shelving onto the floor.

Marshall looked at Randy a little shocked.

"Did he just make that book fall?"

"I don't know but I think he wants us to read it."

The creature bowed again, as if nodding.

Randy smiled. "I hope it's a picture book, I hate words!"

Marshall ignored him and went over to the book and picked it up. He opened it but the pages were all blank.

"I don't understand?" He called over to the creature. "There's nothing in it!"

"Let's see!" Cried Randy.

Randy got off the raggedy old sofa like seat, took the book and sat down again. Marshall sat down next to him.

"See, what'd I tell you no-"

"Hey!" Shouted Randy. "Look, it *is* a picture book."

Right in front of their eyes the page started swirling, like water down a drain, it was mesmerising!

Marshall looked up at the creature. He held his hand up with his palm out flat.

"I think he wants us to touch it?" Randy said.

Marshall and Randy held their hands out on top of each other and pushed down onto the vortex on the page.

Marshall and Randy felt themselves being pulled forward, there was a bright light then they seemed to be floating over a small town.

"Hey, there's people!" Randy shouted.

"Where are we?" Marshall asked.

They were hovering over a small town, it was old, he could see stables and farms and there, just as Randy said, were people. No monsters or spooks and it was day time, it felt ages since Marshall had seen the Sun.

"Marshall, what's going on?!" Randy asked.

With that they were whisked away into one of the small houses like a fly on the wall.

A young Man walked in. He was dressed a lot nicer than the rest of the townsfolk. He was swiftly followed by a lady.

"Aylse, I told you we have to be careful my love." The man raised his hand and stroked her face softly. Soon we shall be together I promise.

"Aylse!" Marshall said to Randy "That's who Jimmy told us about. So that must be..."

The boys looked at each other and in unison both replied "Samuel Hayne!"

"Randy, I think somehow we're in the book, a history book or something. This is the story Jimmy was trying to tell us... but why are we being shown this?"

"This is the best history lesson ever. I wish we had some popcorn though!" Randy said with a smile.

The brothers watched on, as they saw the events unfold just as Jimmy had described.

They watched as Samuel and Aylse returned from their trip together.

"We can't tell a soul my dear." Samuel said. "We'd be committed or hung for lunacy. But you see we can finally live the life we've always dreamed of. We can finally be together. Now quick let us grab a few things then meet back here when ready!"

Samuel gave Aylse a kiss and took her hand as she was about to leave.

"I love you my dear Aylse, in this world and the next, beyond the stars, my heart shall forever belong to you!"

"And I, you, Samuel Hayne. They may try to keep us apart but together we are stronger than anything."

She crept out and Samuel remained behind to pack his things but poor Aylse Young was seen reappearing from Samuel's workshop by another woman from the village. Stricken with jealousy by her own desires for Samuel, the woman condemned her as a witch and before she could return to the workshop, the brothers watched as she was taken away and locked up. They watched as Samuel learnt of her fate and he tried to break her free but he was caught and chased until he could find a spot to use the stone and escape. Despite his efforts to save her, Samuel returned to find she had been placed in the village square and was to be hanged. He raced to get through the crowd, to save her.

No one would, move they all were jeering at her and throwing items at her, calling her a Witch. He pushed through as he heard them call out her crimes, he couldn't get through the crowd of people, as hard as he barged.

"Stop, stop I beg of you!" He called. "She is but innocent!!"

The same women who had been infatuated and condemned the poor woman, cried out.

"Look, she doth even now, possess the poor mind of our Lord. No great man would cast his eye upon such a lowly woman as she!"

"Witch! Witch!" The crowd called out.

"No, stop!" Samuel cried. He fell through the final row of people, tears in his eyes as he knelt before the woman he loved. He looked up at her. She too had tears but she bore a smile and looked at him.

"Remember my Love. In this world and the next, my heart belongs to you. They may try to keep us apart but together we are stronger than anything." The boys saw her try to whisper over the noose as it tightened but the crowd overpowered her voice.

The signal was given and Samuel looked on in horror as she swung to a halt.

He yelled an almost animalistic cry into the sky.

"Marshall, we did this in school." Randy whispered. "We were told slightly differently but this is it. This is what starts 'The Salem Witch Trials'."

The kids' mouths gaped open and Randy felt sad.

Marshall was in disbelief.

"But she wasn't a Witch at all!"

"Look Marsh, I don't think it's over!" Randy pointed at the crowd as they circled around Samuel.

Now under suspicion himself, he fled the square as they chased him. To evade capture, he ran to his workshop and used the stone to cast himself far away, for sanctuary.

They watched as he carefully made the trip back and forth over the years that followed. Many times, to try and bring a little piece of their world and technology with him. But panic and hysteria had infected the townspeople instead and he no longer recognised the unforgiving nature of the town. They scorned him and accused him of witchcraft too and the hunt began again. He was helped by his three closest friends to escape the clutches of the town and in return he granted them passage with him to the other world. They decided this was their home now and only returned to catch a glimpse of their old families, or to bring back some homely treasures but they made the journey whenever they wanted and the sacrifice they made each time, left them weaker with every use.

As the boys were transported through history watching the events unfold quickly, they noticed a familiar face.

"That's the guy!" Randy said. "The guy with the Mask! That's here!"

Samuel became consumed with hatred towards the town and sadness for the loss of his beloved Aylse. He told his comrades he would seek out a very powerful witch doctor to heal them and cast a spell on the stone, so that they didn't have to pay with their health.

"He is the witch doctor!" Marshall said smiling. "But why did he help them?"

The witch doctor refused to help though, he knew no good would come from it, exposure to the amulet outside of Crossover had started to turn them, not just physically

263

but in their soul with anger. They grew darker with each use. Samuel grew tired of the witch doctor's refusals and was ready to beat it from him when the tallest of his friends, an engineer, noticed his books. They had it, absolute power! He would create the casing to protect them, without the help of the witch doctor. The Engineer set up a powerful workshop in a nearby town and encased the stone in an amulet sealed by powerful words, allowing them to make the trip without sacrifice to themselves, so that they could walk freely between the two worlds.

But the boys watched on as they saw how the witch doctor had tricked them. As soon as they left with the book, he cast a powerful spell to conceal all his powerful magic and knowledge, making the books blank. So only those he allowed could read them.

The Engineer watched as he added the finishing sections to the amulet. The words began to fade from sight. He knew Samuel would cast him out if he didn't finish it so he did the best he could from memory, leaving out one important, final word.

The words became cursed and the sacrifice was only transferred. Instead of draining their health the amulet now stole a piece of their souls, slowly turning poor Samuel and his crew evil, with every trip over the years."

"I wonder what happened to them?" Asked Marshall.

With every piece of their soul that was taken, they became changed. They grew greedy, power hungry and their hearts slowly twisted. They resented the creatures of the world for being able to travel unaffected and the bitterness grew. Samuel Hayne grew conflicted. The man he was, resented the evil monster he was becoming and the monster he was becoming liked pushing the weak man he was, down. He liked the strength it made him feel and he wanted it more. Samuel became obsessed with the idea that the creatures in the world must all be more powerful than him to withstand the amulets affects.

So he realised that if the amulet could take his soul then maybe there was a way he could steal that of the creatures of this world and stay powerful forever and so he charged his taller friend, "The Engineer" to come up with a device that could harness the amulets power to transfer the life force of one creature, to his own."

The boys looked at each other solemnly.

"This doesn't look good!" Randy said, with a fearful expression.

The Engineer was successful in making the machine and the brothers saw it being tested on one of the groblins who worked in the big mansion. Samuel placed his amulet into the new machine and when it was turned on the amulet glowed a mighty blue colour and the soul was sucked right from the centre of the creature. Samuel uttered the words around the edge and it gave him what he desired most, power!

"I think I know why it worked for us!" Said Marshall solemnly. "The sword!"

"Huh?" Randy was confused. "What sword?"

"In the store, the first time. There was a samurai sword. I cut my finger on the blade. It must have been my cut that brought it too life. It called to me. Joe never heard it. I thought I was going mad but it must have called me because it was my blood."

"Ah man, Joe's gonna blame you even more now, you know that right!" Randy said calmly as he turned back to the show.

Now for those of you who hadn't seen a groblin before. They are a cute, happy little critter, eager to please and loyal to a fault. They taste good in a stew so I'm told but basically, small, fuzzy little creatures you get the idea.

Once the smoke cleared all that was left of the groblin was a small, tar like creature, pure evil. Snarling and snapping its jaws at the air around it. Samuel and his friends locked the creature in the dungeon and they decided to "take care" of the rest of the creatures residing at the mansion. But they didn't stop there. Blind with power, greed and the darkness brewing in them, they knew they had to destroy all the other stones in the world as they feared others would make a similar contraption and become more powerful or leave completely and then they'd have no souls. And so, they unleashed their pets on the towns nearby until all the stones were found and anyone who resisted, joined the pack of black, oozing critters. All the stones were collected and the four took control of the amulet.

As the story came to the last chapter for the boys, it showed the paintings that Randy had pointed out. The family history, up until the last painting!

"So, Samuel was defeated by this Kassir person?" Randy asked. "He's super scary by the way, in the hall he was all like *I'm a gonna get you* and Joe was all like scared and screaming like a girl."

Marshall laughed. "Yeah I don't know how he fits in to all this yet. What's this?"

They saw the events unfold and how Samuel was lost the moment he took the soul of that first Groblin. His heart twisted and his own soul corrupt, the transformation took over. One night he fell to the floor and called for his comrades. They came in, in a panic and they too dropped to the floor. They gripped at their chests and writhed on the floor. Then, all at once, they lay still.

"Was it a Heart attack? Marshall asked.

But then they burst to life and changed before the brother's eyes. As they began to mutate, their screams turned to roars and their hands turned to claws. They watched as the four men from 1600's America were finally consumed, evil manifested itself and Samuel was lost as he became Kassir!

The boys' eyes grew wide in shock.

"Say what now! You're telling me that man, he *is* the monster in the painting!" Randy said trembling.

And his three henchmen with it. "The Engineer" the smartest of the three but just as menacing, "Crudge" The brawn of the three, a pillar of muscle with half the brains and "Ravage" the smallest but the scariest. He was all teeth and claws and a furious rage. With Kassir at their lead they made a formidable group and with the only stone in their possession they called the shots.

Those in the closest towns to the mansion lived in fear and servitude after that. Including some of those Marshall recognised from the party. Some of the wild beasts of the forests remained untouched but they say they had no souls anyway and that they were always to be avoided. But despite their looks, for the most part, it seemed to Marshall and Joe from the vision that most creatures there were actually good folk, happy to help. After a while they ran out of "good souls" and so they started taking people from their old world, on the day of the Crossover each year.

But then the vision went hazy and it showed Feldma. She went to the house one day to speak to Kassir but the four abominations had up and vanished without a trace. Some creatures said they moved on. Others said they took so many souls, they simply exploded. Some said that it was the human side of them that had gone bad and they were dangerous.

"So that's why Jimmy tried to hide us! Why they thought humans were to be feared." Marshall understood now. "And why Feldma ended up taking over control of the mansion, there was no one there to oppose once they disappeared."

Marshall turned quickly to Randy, interrupting the story.

"We need to get to that town!"

"But why?" Asked Randy trying to take it all in and what the story meant.

"Don't you see, we don't have the amulet anymore but if we can get to that workshop maybe we can find another stone and the witch doctor can send us back home. Maybe they still have them there, after all these years.

We have until morning to find one and use it to get home or we're stuck here! Let's find Joe and get out of here!"

At that moment the door of the hut flew open and the boys were thrown from the pages of the book.

"How are you guys here?" A voice came from behind them.

They both spun around to see Ava standing in the doorway.

Chapter 20

"We thought we lost you, or you got eaten or-" Marshall stopped himself, he could see she was fine and he was getting over excited.

"I guess what I mean is, it's obvious you can take care of yourself and its... it's really good to see you safe... and hadn't run away." He went shy.

"Aw shucks, you missed me eh Marsh?!" She teased him.

"Hey Randy." She waved, he waved back with a smile.

"Hey where's Joe?" She asked.

The boys looked at each other.

"Oh no, Joe! We forgot he disappeared just after you, he isn't with you?" Mashall panicked. He knew Joe wouldn't do as well on his own. Back home, he got lost camping in their back garden.

"Relax, Mookey will find him, won't you!" She said as she slumped onto the sofa. "Ah that feels so good!" She sighed as she stretched out, finally able to unwind. The switch doctor gave a grunt.

"Mookey? That's his name?" Marshall asked, trying not to laugh.

"Oh, I have no idea what his name is, the dude doesn't talk but he looks like a 'Mookey'." She got up and grabbed both sides of his mask and tussled it. "Don't you, my Mookey!" She giggled.

The witch doctor, flustered, batted his arms to shoo her, then he ushered her back with his hands and silently, he gave her a hug.

"And you know him too?" Marshall asked, unsure if he was disturbed or endeared by her treatment to the mysterious creature.

"Yeah, we go way back. He saved my life you know!"

"He seems to make a habit of it!" Marshall smiled to himself.

"But you mentioned being able to find Joe, 'cos that's probably really important right now, if he isn't somethings dinner already!"

"Oh yeah Mook, this guy is hilarious, they must be living under a rock in Stromp's Pond or something because the way they reacted to some of things we've seen. Man are they sheltered."

She laughed as she mimicked their faces with her hands in the air. "Aaargh! Haha!"

The witch doctor chuckled a silent chuckle then instantly stopped and he went on his way to the boiling pot.

"Okay, so that's gonna take just a few minutes for him to sift the ether and find him. Hey Randy, why don't you grab some rest, you must be tired?"

Randy hopped up onto the sofa and slunk down against the arm. "Nah, I'm okay, I'm way too excited to-"

As soon as his head hit the soft sofa he passed out and began snoring. Ava and Marshall laughed.

"And that is my brother, we're in the middle of madness and he can find time to power nap!" Marshall laughed.

"Poor little guy!" Ava smiled. "You guys are close, huh!"

"Yeah." Marshall responded with a thoughtful smile as he watched his little brother asleep.

In that moment he was peaceful and calm. He remembered how he used to be when they shared a room, when they were younger. Before he grew so random and odd in his ways, when life was simpler.

"I mean, he's a complete pain but yeah... we are. We always have been but lately it's felt, I don't know, like it's getting less and less. He's only a few years younger but it feels like he's not old enough to understand my world anymore and I'm outgrowing his. We used to spend every day together but now..." He paused. "I don't know." He stopped himself short. "Sorry, I don't know where I was then... I mean we haven't done something like this in... years!"

"Getting chased by monsters?!" Ava asked with a smile, seems like my daily life.

"No, I mean spent actual time together..." He paused and thought to himself. He had missed it, the exploring, the adventures and not worrying about trying to look cool and what the other kids thought.

"I guess I've not been the world's best big brother lately." He felt guilty and sad, he had been too preoccupied with school and Vinessa to want to *hang out* with his little brother. He smiled to himself as Randy slept, then he heard a noise behind. He turned around and saw Ava step out of the hut and he followed.

The torches around the hut glowed orange and yellow in the dark forest it attracted fireflies that danced in the air. The air was still and the night warm, as they stepped onto the wooden platform under the star filled sky. The moon shone so bright that the torches were almost unnecessary.

He walked over to where she was standing on the porch area of the old hut, looking out into the night sky.

"So, how do you know... *Mook*?" He asked. She seemed a little sad herself but he couldn't work out why.

"He saved me, a looong time ago." She smiled softly looking at the stars.

"From those little creatures?"

"No something much worse, much scarier! I was out here all alone. I had been running for what felt like days. I nearly didn't make it. I just remember running until I couldn't anymore, I wanted to get as far away from them as I could. But I got so tired I fell and hurt my leg. I couldn't walk or even stand up. I was out here for what felt like forever, scared that the creatures in the night would take me but then Mookey found me and he took me here. He healed my leg then showed me a few tips to survive on my own out here."

"The blow dart trick." Marshall remembered.

"Yeah, he taught me what I could use, what I could eat. I was lost out here and he was my only friend. Eventually I left and made friends in Hallowed Haunt. Despite the name it has the best stores and the fried food is outta this world! Just don't ask what it is and you'll enjoy every second of it." She laughed. Marshall knew none of these places but he wanted to hear her story.

"That was until a few days ago when Feldma and her goons captured me and took me to that town. I don't know what they were planning but I'm sure glad you guys came along!" She smiled and placed her hand on top of his.

He startled, as he felt her hand touch his and looked at her. "Well I'm glad Mook saved you... and I'm glad we let you out of that box!" They shared a glance at each other. Then he tried to cover the new feelings of happiness, stirring in his stomach. "For all our sakes... we were really lost!"

She retracted her hand, embarrassed. He felt strangely at ease talking with her, but even though she was the most "Normal" looking creature they had met since arriving here, they were from completely different worlds and hopefully sooner than later they would be leaving this place behind, Including Ava. Which made him just that little bit sad.

She smiled at him bashfully and hid her face behind her hair. She stood up abruptly and held out her hand. Puzzled, He took her hand in his and stood up.

"The Gloom Woods is a creepy and dangerous place... but it can also be amazing and wonderful. Follow me." They ran down a little path, through the trees to a clearing along the edge of a lake. The blue tinted moon reflecting perfectly in its calm, flat surface. Fireflies skimmed its

274

surface and lit the night air as small winged creatures flew from the nearby trees and chased them into the night.

As Marshall followed them with his eyes across the lake, he noticed a whole host of strange and wonderful beasts along the far shores of the lake. Some resembled small deer, a family of them by the looks of it. They grazed peacefully and lapped at the water. Large herds of bocine moved through the plains and overhead, blue and purple lights filled the sky like a flickering oil painting.

"I have to admit, when I first got here, I was creeped out by pretty much everything... but here?" He paused as he looked around at the view in front of them. As the moonlight reflected in the water, the luminescent bugs danced and made it ripple.

"It's a pretty amazing view huh?" Ava replied and stared out across the water. Marshall turned to face her. He saw her face in the moonlight. Her smile at the natural wonder in front in such a harsh place was mesmerising. He noticed her eyes glistening, as they reflected the cool moon's light and he found himself smiling.

"Yeah... yeah it is."

"So, what brings you out here then?" She asked with a quizzing tone. "I thought all your type were townies. Not ones for living the country life."

"My type?" Marshall asked, confused.

"Oh, I'm sorry I just assumed you were... it's just that you look... sorry, you just don't look like most of the freaks out here that's all." She replied, embarrassed.

"Oh no?" He asked. "What kind of freak do I look like then?" He asked with a smile.

She giggled.

"Erm, it's kinda a long story. But yeah, I guess you're right we're not from around here... but trust me if you see my brother sometimes, you'd swear we borrowed him from here!" They both laughed.

"Ooooh, you're not a skin shredder, are you?" She asked excitedly. "I've never actually seen one, that would be cool.

"Skin shredder?" Marshall asked in confusion at everything she had just said.

"Yeah you know, disgusting, hairy monster hides under another skin?"

The Bat lady! Marshall thought.

"Er, no, I'm not, I mean we're not skin... shredders! All my own see!" He pinched his arm, showing her, it was indeed firmly attached.

"That's good, I suppose!" She said a little disappointedly, then she smiled at him shyly. "Some skin is too cute to be shred!"

"So." She spun around in her seat and faced him with eyes wide with excitement. "Where you from?"

"You wouldn't believe me if I tried. I'm not even sure I believe me." He said. In truth he still didn't know whether to tell her they were human and how he would even begin their tale of how they ended up here.

"So, did you run away or... ?" She ignored his protests.

Marshall thought back to how they ended up here in this strange world with no way home. With this girl who scared him how strong she was but also found himself liking, which made him fear her even more. She had made him forget about Maitland, about school, about bullies... then he remembered Vinessa and the amulet. The reason they were even in this mess.

"Erm... Actually, it doesn't matter..." He said, feeling a little stupid.

"No come on, I gave you my sob story. You gotta tell me now Marshall, from somewhere far away." She giggled and pushed him gently, teasing him.

"I came here be Mookey's new best friend, actually!" He laughed.

"Oh, really Mister! I can see I'm gonna have to have some words with him later!" She giggled. "No, c'mon, really!"

He laughed a little and sighed.

"So... I went to this store... in the town where I'm from, to get something. I thought it would make someone happy. Anyway, me, Joe and Randy we kinda got caught up with some creeps who trapped us and next thing we know we're out here, lost and looking for a way back home. It was our friend, Jimmy, who told us to come find the witch doctor. He thought he might have a way for us to get back."

"I'm not sure I follow." Ava said, trying to piece together the story.

"I'm not sure I do either, in all honesty." Marshall laughed.

"Why do you need Mookey to get home? Surely someone can show you the way back?" She asked, unsure why they needed him at all. He was mystical and hard to find. A road map would have been easier and far less perilous.

"It's not that simple!" Marshall skirted around the subject.

Ava wasn't buying it but she knew she wasn't going to get any answers soon.

"Hmm." She frowned, teasing him. "Okay, Chatty Chatterson. I can see you're not gonna open up but whatever it was must have been important to risk all that."

"I guess so..." Marshall pondered.

"You don't sound so convinced? Was it something to help someone who was ill or return a lost item?" Asked Ava trying to work out what would have made him risk so much.

"Umm... no actually, see there was this girl-"

"Oh..." Ava said sounding disheartened. She backed away slightly. "She must be special... I mean to risk so much. You two must be very close." She tried to sound sincere but she couldn't help feeling a little upset.

"Well, I don't know about close." Marshall replied, thinking back to all the times he had tried to speak to Vinessa and failed.

"Well, what's she like?"

"Um, she's pretty..."

"Yeah? And...?

"And... her eyes..." He couldn't remember the colour of her eyes. He stopped himself to think of something different. "Well she has this hair that..." He felt silly but for the life of him he was struggling to imagine anything significant about Vinessa, the girl he had obsessed over all these years.

Ava looked at him. "So, she's pretty and she has eyes and hair... I can see why you like her... I mean what do you guys talk about, what do you share?"

Marshall frowned, thinking to himself. Being so far away from his normal life and now sat out on that rock, overlooking the view he suddenly thought to himself, had he been blind all these years, had Joe been right? The laughter, the mocking, the cruelty to others. She *had* used him to do her homework... how could he have been so blind?!

"We've barely even spoke." He said in a flat voice to himself, looking out over the water in sudden realisation.

"Wow, she sounds a keeper." Ava replied, feeling sorry for him and also a little hurt. She was enjoying her new friendship but she was too stubborn and hard faced to admit she was also secretly falling for this stranger from out of town.

Marshall changed the subject, until now he had been so focussed on surviving and getting home. He had forgotten all about the trivial things like missing the Horrorthon and whether his parents would be angry that Randy was out late and finally, trying to impress Vinessa Marsden.

He spotted Ava sat on the rock, looking dejected and a little sorry for herself. Why was she so sad? Maybe she was upset that her troubles were worse than his, he thought. He tried to cheer her up, he was far too shy but with all they had been through in such a short time he found himself liking her, not that he would ever tell her. It was nice to have someone he could talk to that actually talked back.

He spotted a flower, by the edge of the rock, to his right and he picked it for her.

"For the lady!" He smiled his goofy grin, trying to cheer her up.

To his shock, Ava pushed the flower away and leant back in disgust.

"Oh no, get that away quick, please."

"What's wrong are you allergi-"

Before he could finish, a cloud of green smoked filled the gap between them. He spluttered, she laughed.

"You really aren't from around here, are you?" Her eyes ran with tears of laughter.

"What was that?" Marshall asked, still coughing. He threw the plant to the ground.

"That's a nightflare." She replied. "It sends out a gas when it's threatened." She wiped her eyes and calmed her laughing.

"At least your smiling now." He laughed, clearing his throat again.

She stared into his eyes, concentrating on him intensely.

"Marshall, from somewhere-" She stopped and composed herself, becoming more serious for a moment. "Marshall... can I tell you something? I kinda feel like I can-"

Waaooggaa

Before she could say anymore, they were interrupted by a loud call coming from back in the hut.

"That's Mook!" She turned quickly and faced towards the Hut.

"He must have found Joe!" Marshall shouted with joy. "Quick, c'mon!" He helped her up then ran towards the hut.

As he sped off back down the path, Ava looked down and sighed. She whispered to herself.

"I'll have to tell you my secret some other time Marshall from far away! And I hope you don't run away!" She gathered herself and followed him back up the path.

<u>Chapter 21</u>

Randy was at the doorway to meet them when they arrived back.

"He's found Joe. Look!"

Marshall and Ava ran into the hut and circled around a pot that the witch doctor had placed on a large wooden table. purple and orange smoke rose from the boiling stew-like, gooey substance. In the middle of the steam and vapours that rose was an image of Joe. They could see him in the mist and he was screaming. He was tied up against something and he was screaming. It looked to Marshall like he was being tortured, thrown this way and that and he looked in pain!

"Oh no! What are we going to do, whoever has him is going to kill him!" Shouted Marshall.

"Where is he?" Randy asked the witch doctor.

Then Ava caught a small sound between Joe's screams. *Ding!*

Then there was the feint sound of music!

She rolled her eyes and gave a smile.

"You gotta be kidding me!" She laughed as she grabbed a nearby rucksack and started filling it with items, like rope and strange fruit.

"What is it?" Asked Marshall. "Can we save him in time?"

"Oh yeah!" She said with a smile. "I just hope we have enough coins!"

"Coins?" The brothers mouthed to each other, both just confused as the other.

Ava had finished packing the rucksack and was getting ready to head out.

"Hey Mook, you still got the hatch that leads to Ghoul's Gulch?

The Witch Doctor nodded his oversized head to signal it was still there and then waved them out.

"Okay cool, now guys, we have a short trip but remember keep your arms and legs tucked in okay!" Without a word Ava grabbed the brothers and led them outside. They reached a set of thick trunked trees. Up until now Marshall hadn't noticed anything out of the ordinary to make them stand out from the thousands of other trees that grew in the woods. But now he could see they were all the same thickness and they were all completely straight.

Ava brought them in front of the trees and let them go. She struck a nearby rock with her foot and with a gravely rumble, the third tree in began to shake and a section of bark, about three feet tall, came crashing down like a draw bridge. It revealed a hollow inside. She threw the rucksack into the dark hole.

"Wait, what are you doing!?" Called Marshall.

It was too late, she grabbed them and one after the other, she pushed them in and shouted.

"Remember keep your arms and legs in at all times!"

Then she herself jumped in, not before running over to the witch doctor and giving him a kiss on the top of his masked face.

"Don't worry, I'll be safe!" She shouted, as she jumped down the hole.

She disappeared into the abyss and was gone. The witch doctor waddled over and lifted the bark door up, off the floor, then slammed it shut and waddled back up to the hut in silence.

Meanwhile, not too far away. A hole opened up in the ground and shortly after, out, shot the rucksack followed by the three kids like a waterslide. Shooting them out into a pile on top of one another.

"That was so cool!" Shouted Randy underneath his brother.

"Woah!" Marshall called out as Ava climbed off him and he could see where they had landed.

"What are we doing here?" He asked.

They stood up and dusted themselves off. As they stood, they saw their surroundings. There were bright lights in front of them and eerie music being played all around. They could hear the laughter of children and crowds of people.

All of a sudden two long, stick like legs walked either side of the three kids and as they looked up, a face looked down and smiled a crooked grin and laughed as the creature walked over their heads and into the crowd. Marshall felt a large surge of heat to his right and heard a large *whoosh* as a ball of fire erupted into the air near them. It came from a man dressed as a clown as he blew it from his mouth! They could smell the unmistakable smell of cotton candy. The brothers smiled in amazement. It was a carnival!

"I don't get it?" Marshal asked Ava. "Why are we here? We need to find Joe!"

"Follow me!" She said, as she smiled knowingly.

They joined the crowd of creatures entering the carnival. It was like the ones back home Marshall thought. But with an eerie spin on it.

As they walked through the entrance and under the sign, the brothers watched with awe at everything going on around. The noises, the smells, the lights. It was a hive of activity especially compared to the dark, unwelcoming places they had visited so far. Monsters were selling strange looking food from purple and orange striped tents and others had sideshows like a coconut shy but Randy noticed they weren't coconuts at all. They were shrunken heads! As they carried on, taking in the sights, they watched as creatures played some of the games.

A large, muscly, furry beast had hold of a large oversized mallet. Marshall could tell he was trying to show off to another smaller, female, furred beast as he picked up the mallet, proving his strength. He stood in front of a large set of blue gums opened wide with a full set of bright white teeth. Randy noticed the teeth were like his, regular human except they and the gums attached to them were ten feet tall and were opened wide. The furry monster stepped up to the small square in front and shuffled into position, twisting the large mallet in his palms, getting a firm grip and with a final wink at his girl, he raised the mallet high above his head. With one swift swing, he struck a back-molar tooth with all his might. The tooth shot out and the creature celebrated with his hands in the air, his girl impressed, gave him a kiss on his furry cheek and the game's owner passed the monster a prize. A wriggling, squirming creature with six legs that squeaked as it was handed to the winner.

"Alright!" The furry monster called out. He passed it affectionately to the female monster as a token of love who was beaming with happiness. But not for long as the aggravated set of teeth opened its jaws and shut them hard, over the furry beast. The furry beasts' legs, in their shorts, squirming from the mouth. Marshall watched the game owner and the girlfriend take a leg each and pull hard as the jaws chuckled with content. Marshall walked on. He was slowly getting used to this place.

Small creatures walked upright through the footsteps of the crowd, making little chattering noises to themselves while large eyeball shaped objects flapped their tiny black wings overhead. They whizzed around the kids' heads, chasing one another and off into the distance. They drew Marshall's gaze up, as they flew away, to a host of rides.

There was the Tilt-a-Hurl, The Tunnel of Ooze, The Hall of Mirrors that oddly made all the strange creatures look normal and that's when he realised why they were there.

There, in the centre of all the rides, was the largest rollercoaster they had ever seen. And right in the front cart was Joe, strapped in and screaming his way along the tracks.

The ride came to an end and the kids walked over.

"I don't believe it!" Marshall cried as Joe exited the ride.

Joe looked up and suddenly his face lit up. "Guys!" He said with a wide grin and his arms up in the air as he ran towards them. "You're alive!"

"Yeah, no thanks to you!" Randy cried.

"We thought you had been captured and were being tortured!" Said Marshall in a panic. He was relieved his best friend was safe but angry that they were worried for no reason.

"Tortured?" Joe said, confused. "Why would you think that?"

"We have a lot of catching up to do!" Said Marshall, who knew he needed to tell him about the vision they had had in the hut and the events with Kassir.

"Okay, but first, can we go on a few more rides?!" Joe said smiling a playful grin.

"Yeah!" Randy shouted in excitement, jumping up and down.

"No way!" Marshall shut them down. "We don't have time for this we need to-" He looked down at his brother who had stopped jumping and wearily hung his head low. This was exactly what he had been doing back home. Too busy to spend time with his little brother who looked up to him. All he wanted was to spend time with Marshall and he always made excuses for being busy. He crouched down to meet his eye level and put his hand out on his shoulder.

"Which one you wanna go on first?" He said softly.

Randy's eyes widened with joy and a huge smile shot across his face. He launched himself onto his brother and hugged Marshall tightly, wrapping his arms around his neck.

Marshall looked at Ava and she gave a little smile. Their night was looking up and she found herself being able to relax for the first time in ages.

They jumped on all the rides, some twice! Whizzing this way and that. Randy was laughing, Joe was screaming

Marshall was having fun! They decided to stop and get something to eat. They could smell the irresistible smell of southern fried chicken which was strange as they hadn't noticed a Chicken the whole time they'd been here. Nor a Cow, Pig anything that looked familiar. So, Marshall was apprehensive when they approached the food stand. But after seeing Randy tuck into "whatever it was" on a stick, he gave in to his hunger and took a bite. He was pleasantly delighted and they got one more each for the road. Although his suspicions were once again raised, briefly, when a family of smooth skinned, slimy monsters with a head full of eyes scoffed in their direction.

"I hope this wasn't a relative!" He whispered to Joe and Randy who laughed then suddenly grimaced at their meal.

The four came to the centre of the carnival and looked around at all its little alleyways.

"What do you say guys, shall we get going?" Marshall asked the group.

Randy burped and put his stick, cleaned completely of meat, into a nearby bin. Which in turn burped, as it gobbled up the trash.

"I'm good!" He said, Joe agreed.

"Wait!" Said Ava. "Go where?"

"Er, we need to get to a town, it looked nearby, cobbled streets, a few shops and a big workshop with a tall tower made of metal." Said Marshall.

"Shockton?! Why would you want to go there? There's nothing but trouble there." Ava pleaded with them.

"Ah great, just what we need and I thought we were on our way to the better side of town, ya know the side that doesn't want us captured or as dinner." Said Joe, sarcastically.

"So, you've been there? You can show us where it is?" Marshall said, excited.

"Not exactly." She confessed. "I've never been, but I've heard the stories. But we're safe now! Feldma won't come this far just for some escaped pets."

"It's a long story." Said Marshall. "But we need to get to this Shockton, otherwise we may never get home. It's our only hope!"

Ava grew sad, she was about to reply when a deep, growling voice interrupted them.

"Steeeepp right up folks, step right up! Cast your eyes out over the best view you'll ever have, on the Monster Wheel!" A large green monster with bobbly skin and small white hat that matched his ill-fitting, white shirt had burst through the group and with a smile on his face and a spring in his step, was trying to fill the Monster Wheel ride. His large belly poked out of the bottom of his white cotton shirt and over his white trousers. The seams of his uniform bursting at the sides.

"Small print folks, please keep your eyes in your head. Don't actually cast them out!" He gave a deep, low pitched chuckle and a snort as he laughed.

"Sorry, who are you?" Asked Joe.

"Name's Kleb." He smiled as he pointed to his name tag. He slid his finger along it and tapped it. "I run the Monster wheel, *the* best viewing platform in all the world! When she reaches the top, you can see for miles in all directions! Why don't you take a look!"

"Er, we don't have time, thanks though man." Joe said as he turned, ready to leave the way they came.

"Hold on." Marshall said, as he thought, we could use this to see where this town is. He just said, you can see everything, so maybe we can use this to help us." He turned to Kleb. "Four tickets please Kleb!"

"It's on the house, my little friend! Courtesy of the carnival!"

"Wow thanks!" Randy said as he stepped up into the first carriage. "Can I ride one to myself?! I wanna swing it when it's at the top!"

"Why sure you can sonny! The best part is rocking the cart!" Kleb patted him on the head and locked the bar across as he stepped in.

"Oooh, I see we have a couple of *lovebirds* here, allow me, you two!"

Marshall and Ava went red in the cheeks with embarrassment and before they could protest, they were ushered in to the next cart by Kleb as it circled round.

"Oh sure, don't worry guys I'll just ride alone too, I'm okay!" Joe said as he waved them off. "Don't worry about me!"

He felt a bump as something brushed his legs. "Hey!" He cried as a group of six furry balls with no eyes or faces rolled up passed him and cut the queue. They laughed and mocked him from somewhere under their furry bodies and they were taken up by the wheel.

"Here ya are fella!" Smiled Kleb, opening the next kart as it passed. "Plenty of carts still free, take a popcorn for the ride, put a smile back on your face."

Joe stepped into the cart and Kleb handed him the hot carton of corn. The cart started moving.

"Gee, thanks man!" Joe called out, as he started lifting into the air.

"Not a problem!" Kleb waved as he watched the carts rise up to the summit. "Anything for a human!"

Joe felt cold and nauseous, had he just said *human?* Kleb smiled as he waved them up and as he blinked, Joe could swear his eyes flashed red! Joe gave a large gulp and dropped the popcorn to the floor.

As the carts lifted higher and higher, Kleb held out his hand and black ooze poured from the palm of his hand. It crawled off his hand and fell to the floor where it began winding through the grass and the hordes of creatures, into the distance back to the mansion.

"That's it let them know!" Kleb smiled as his eyes shone Red.

Up above Marshall looked out as they slowly rose up, they were almost above the tree line. He couldn't wait to see what was out there and whether they could see Shockton from their view point. He hoped it wasn't far, then he could put all this behind him and they could get home.

But as they rose high above the carnival, with all its noise and music and monsters having fun, he suddenly felt Ava's arm grip his. He turned to her. She could barely bring herself to look over the rim of the cart.

"Are you okay?" He asked.

"Oh yeah, I'm good!" She responded quickly.

"Are you... surely not!" He laughed amusedly. "Are you afraid of heights?"

She shot him a glance.

"No, no, no... not at all..." She breathed heavily through her nose. She gave a timid grin. "It's the falling from them I can't stand!"

"Wow!" He said with a smile. "I didn't think you were afraid of anything, you're like the toughest person I've ever met. Okay just try not to focus on it. Tell me more about you. You said you were lost out here before the witch do-*Mookey* found you." He corrected himself when she gave him a look. "What did you do before then, friends, family, interests. It can't all be monsters and gloom?"

She kept her eyes down as she spoke but she tried to do as he said and not focus on the height.

"I er... I don't know, I wasn't like most kids around here. I mean I had your typical family life, I guess. But mine was a bit different. That doesn't matter though, I'm used to being alone now." She let out a little yelp as the cart tipped slightly as it climbed higher.

Marshall held her and listened. He sensed there was more but he didn't feel now was the time to ask. He tried to take her mind off it.

Just then as they climbed higher, a gust of wind rocked the cart a little. She gripped his hand tight.

"It's okay, it's okay!" He said, trying to comfort her. "I won't let you fall." He took her arm and wrapped his around it then he took her hand and held tight.

She turned to him and gave a little smile. "You know, Marshall from somewhere far away, you're quite the hero after all."

He felt a warmth grow inside him. He was lost in the middle of a monster filled world. He'd nearly been eaten, maimed and captured to name but a few of the night's escapades and here he was, sharing a cart with a beautiful creature that actually spoke *with* him, not at him and actually remembered his name. He watched the view unfold in the night sky. He would give anything to keep this moment saved as it was, perfect and simple. He gave a smile then he heard his brother above shout out.

"Look Marshall!"

As they climbed, almost at the peak in the rotating cart, they could see above the trees and in the star filled night they watched as the world was alive with fireflies and purple glows in the background coming from unknown parts of the world in the distance. It was stunning.

" Ya know what?" Ava said as she smiled, watching the view unfold. "This is the first time I've felt I've done something normal and been part of something in a very long time... it's been pretty lonely!"

Marshall turned to her and smiled. "Well you're one of us now!"

She gave a little smile and he felt her grab his hand.

To the right were a large range of mountains that looked jagged and wicked. Ahead and to the left, in the far-off distance, were lights coming from some mystical place but all across the forest canopy was a melting pot teaming with life and light and there, not too far away in the distance was Shockton. Marshall filled with happiness when he spotted the town but then suddenly became conflicted with sadness as he realised the closer that they got to finding a way out, the closer he was to having to say goodbye to Ava and he suddenly realised just how much he was going to miss her.

At that moment Ava turned with a smile, but it was a sad smile. He could tell she had something to say but was troubled.

"Are you okay?" He asked, as if she needing comforting.

"Marshall, there's something I wanted to tell you but I'm not sure if I can. I just... I just feel like I can trust you and apart from Mookey, it's been a very long time since I've been able to say that about anyone."

"Of course." Marshall replied a little taken aback. He turned to face her and listened.

"What I told you earlier. I was telling the truth but... but I wasn't alone... at the beginning... I had a sister. I haven't spoken about her in a long time."

"What happened?" Marshall could see how hard it was for her to talk about it. Her eyes were sad.

"She was younger too, like you and Randy. We were close... we were on a holiday with our parents. We had been staying at a place..." She paused a little and gave an ironic smile to herself. "Similar to this spot right now actually. We had been out all day in the woods, playing games looking out for creatures in the woods. We were so tired our eyes closed the moment our heads hit the pillow that night. It was a perfect day."

Marshall saw her reliving the moment in her mind. Her eyes welled up as she smiled softly to herself. Then her eyes changed, became more focussed and her smile faded.

"We uh... we had run so much that day that we didn't even stop for food when our mom called us in."

She laughed remembering how silly they'd been behind her tears.

"I'd barely drunk enough water all day so, when I woke up in the middle of the night with the driest mouth ever, I went straight to fetch a drink for me and my sister." She let out a deep sigh and lowered her head between her knees for a second. Then she looked back up, staring blankly ahead.

"When I returned to bring my sister a cup of water, I saw it standing there, over her while she slept. It was dressed all in black with a hood over its head, I couldn't make out the shape at first. Then, under the cloak I saw a long thin hand stretch out, its nails were long and sharp. I dropped the cup of water and tried to scream but nothing came out. The figure heard the cup and turned around and all I remember are those long, glowing red eyes and the flash of white from its horrible pointed teeth. It picked my sister up without any trouble and then it hopped towards me and grabbed me before I even had a chance to move. The next thing I know it was carrying us out into the woods and that's all I remember." She wiped her eyes.

Marshall was listening intently.

"I woke up and we were in the most horrible place. The smell was-" She motioned a vomiting gesture.

"We couldn't see a thing. I called out for my sister. She was crying. She hadn't seen the beast but she was scared all the same." We tried to stand but the floor was sticky. We could hear echoes and moans all around us but we didn't know where from. It was so dark. As our eyes adjusted, we could see that the walls were moving, then we realised they were alive. Hundreds of creepy faces snapping their mouth at us from the side of the wall like a black ooze-like substance. We managed to stand and pry ourselves from the floor. Then we heard a small scuffling near us. It was the patter of little feet on rock. We called out and something answered back. It told us to be quiet, we couldn't see it, it just kept repeating to keep quiet. We were scared and wanted to get out of there, then a small light flickered. It was a little creature. He stood on two small legs and was covered in long hair. He had two black eyes and a mouth full of tiny teeth but he looked just as scared as we were."

"So, he wasn't trying to hurt you?" Marshall asked in relief and curiosity.

"No. He was really friendly, kind actually. We realised he was creating the light. Deep in the centre of his little, round belly was an orange glow. My sister said he was like a living nightlight. He could see we were just as scared in the dark and so he tried to help. He told us his name was *Davithireo*- we couldn't pronounce his full name so we just called him Dave." She laughed, remembering him. "Dave was very kind to us..."

She paused.

"It was hard to see but we managed to find our way towards the front of the room to a large door. It was locked. Dave panicked and told us to keep away but my sister banged as hard as she could, that was our mistake. We heard the booming of footsteps from the other side as Dave extinguished his light. He knew what was coming next. We heard a large bolt being slid open and *he* walked in."

"Who?"

"The most hideous and evil creature you'll ever see." She paused. Her Eyes filled with fright at the mention of him, then it was replaced with anger, then finally sadness and she took a breath before continuing.

"He had his henchman with him. The smallest was the one I hate the most, he was the one who took us. They laughed as they came through the door. I was so scared but I had to be brave for my sister who was crouched behind me. I could hear her sniffling."

"What did they want? Why had they kidnapped you?" Marshall was totally engrossed. He could see how hard it was for Ava to tell her story but he wanted to know more.

"They wanted our souls! That's when I realised what was with us in the cave. All the little creatures on the cave wall were bad souls, he called them *lost souls*. The remnants of the creatures he had taken before us."

"How did you know, what happened next?" Marshall asked, he almost wished he hadn't but he wanted to know what happened to Ava's sister. The creatures sounded worryingly familiar to him.

"The beasts crawled into the room, smiling their evil smiles and talking about how hungry they were. They played with the black ooze on the wall. The mouths snapped around their fingers but they barely flinched. Their leader clicked his fingers and they stopped playing about. He told them there was no need for scraps when they had fresh food to go, right in front of them. We had a bad feeling and I clutched my sister close. But that creep with the hood who took us from our room grabbed her away from me. He held her up by her leg. As she dangled there, he poked her stomach with his long, sharp claw. He said she looked tasty. I cried out I didn't want them to take my sister, I didn't want them to hurt her. That's when Dave jumped forward, he started hitting at their legs and shouting at them. The smaller beast dropped my sister and lunged for Dave. He had him in his long claws as he wriggled to break free. He saved her, but at a terrible price."

Marshall knew what was coming next, he thought back to the books in the witch doctor's hut and the poor Groblin.

They were taken to the machine and watched as Dave's soul was taken with the uttering of the words.

"Ramus
Venke
Hudo
Danray"

With a bright flash of the stone Dave was gone and all that was left was a black ooze creature in his place snapping at the air.

"But that's when I remembered the flash!" Said Ava trying to focus without getting too upset. "The same flash I saw when the smaller one took me and my sister! So, while they were preoccupied, I took my chance and grabbed a nearby rock. I threw it as hard as I could at the machine. There was a loud crack as sparks flew and they jumped back in shock. I reached up and grabbed the stone and we ran as fast as we could. We climbed a stair case and came out into a large room filled with plants and glass."

"The conservatorium!" Marshall said in shock. "That's how you knew where the secret doorway was!" He realised, she had been taken to the mansion, it was as he feared. The creatures she was talking about were Kassir and his gang.

"We heard the creatures coming from behind, we saw the walls come alive as bugs and little black rat-like creatures fled from the cracks as the four beasts chased us from that dungeon, they were almost on us. I knew we wouldn't get much further. We didn't know where we were, how to get home and no time, those beasts were nearly on us. So, I did the only thing I could do to stop my sister from being in danger."

She wiped a tear from her eye.

"The rat-like creatures were nearly on us then we saw the four beasts crash down the corridor, they clawed at the walls and paintings as they tried to catch us. I thought I could use the stone to transport us home and away from this nightmare so I took the amulet and began to say the words. I didn't know if it was going to work or make things worse but I knew I had to get her out of there. But then I felt something on my foot, I couldn't move. I turned to see what it was and one of the little creatures had me by my foot. I couldn't move. We had no time. I was stuck on the spot and the beasts were just feet away from us. So, I spoke the last of the words and as the light grew bright, from the centre of the stone, I grabbed my sister tight and whispered to her that I loved her. She looked confused then scared. She knew what was happening. As the light grew, I put the amulet into the pocket of her nightie and pushed her threw!"

Marshall sat with mouth agape.

"The light disappeared and my sister with it. The room went dark and I heard the beasts loud breathing behind me like a bull ready to charge. *What have you done?!* The leader cried out. I thought it was the end for me. But then something strange happened. The four creatures ran! They ran back towards the dungeon with the machine and the lost souls. Shortly after I heard loud shrieking and screams and then silence. I went to look and there in the centre of the room, where we had been held captive were four giant stone statues. Somehow, they couldn't live without the power of the amulet. I ran, I ran as fast as I could back out into the room with all the plants and out into the jungle... the rest you already know I guess."

Ava felt a big weight lift from her and she felt better for being honest with Marshall. It was nice to have someone to talk to about the worst day of her life. But she began to panic when she saw his reaction. He looked white as a ghost and was eerily quiet. Had she scared him away, was it as she feared and she had made him hate her for what she had done to her sister.

She took his hand and looked into his eyes with half a smile and a concerned look in her eyes.

"Please say something Marshall... I have nightmares about that day and I worry everyday if I did the right thing... please don't freak out on me now!" She pleaded.

But then Marshall did something she hadn't expected. His mouth curled upwards and he began laughing.

"Wow, I'm glad my pain is funny to you!"

She backed away, confused and hurt but he grabbed her shoulders reassuringly.

"No, sorry!" He carried on laughing excitedly. It's not that. What happened, it was terrible. But, it's okay! She's okay... I think anyway!"

"What do you mean... my sister?! You've seen her, oh no is she still here?!" She panicked as she imagined sending her someplace even worse and this time she would be on her own.

"No, I've never met her!" Marshall said as he calmed down. "But I need the truth now, where *exactly* are you from!"

She hesitated, she had never told anyone, she was too afraid to. But she trusted Marshall somehow, even with this new, weird behaviour. She closed her eyes, sighed a long heavy sigh then opened her eyes.

"Dennison, I came from a town called Dennison!"

Marshall couldn't help but smile. He could get her home to her sister, Sheriff Johnson was right, he didn't have to miss her, he didn't have to leave her! So many thoughts and emotions filled him. He wanted to tell her everything! She was the missing Dennison girl and her sister was safe. She was human! Then he remembered her Sister's current location. She wasn't mad! The locket

Sheriff Johnson had mentioned! It wasn't a locket. It was the amulet. The shopkeeper must have found it somehow! The Monsters were Kassir and his gang. The black creature his dog, Dash, had chased and the sheriff had spotted. They must have been the rat-like creatures in the halls and had gone through with the girl, when the portal was opened. It all made sense! He had so much to tell her and the other boys.

He grinned at her in excitement. "You'll never guess wha-"

Scrrreeeechhhhh!!

The wheel came to a sudden holt and the cart swung back and forth as it abruptly stopped moving! The various creatures that were riding it, called out in disappointment, with their various roars and squawks.

"Marshall!" It was Randy from the other cart, he was peering over the top and pointing to the ground.

"Look! It's Kassir!"

Marshall stretched over as far as the bar holding them would allow.

"Oh no!"

He was here and the trio of terror.

"We need to get out of here!" He said to Ava, she looked over.

She fell back into the cart in shock. "W... What are they doing here, alive! Marshall that's them, that's the creatures-"

"I know, Ava there's so much I need to tell you but for now we need to get out of here or none of it will matter!"

They tried lifting the bar but it was no use, the locks were secured by magic. The operator had tricked them. He had lured them there so he could capture them and deliver them to Kassir.

"Marshall, you and the others need to go, it's me they're after!" Ava said. She was scared but couldn't allow anybody else to get hurt.

It was too late. The ride was in motion again and it was pulling them down to the ground. Like a shark cage being lowered slowly into the sea, they could see their predator's cold, dark stair as they grew closer and closer.

They reached the bottom and in turn they were grabbed from their cart by Crudge with no effort. Randy looked at Marshall, he was scared but he wasn't showing it as much as Joe who was trembling.

"Looky here!" Smiled Crudge, looking at Joe and Randy. "If it isn't Feldma's little dance partners! We have to stop meeting like this!"

Ravage grabbed Ava from the last cart and dragged her to Kassir and dumped her at his feet. She looked up at him with a defiant look. She wasn't going to let him see how scared she was. She was stronger than that.

"Let her go!" Marshall yelled.

Without warning, the large, fat arm of Crudge gripped Marshall from behind and he was powerless.

"You ain't going nowhere pipsqueak." He chuckled as Marshall tried in vain to wriggle free from the large beasts' arms.

"Relax Loverboy, we just want the girl... well the amulet that the she has anyway." Crudge replied in his deep voice.

"I don't have it. You know I don't." She shouted in protest.

"She lies." Whispered Ravage in his shrill voice.

"Even if I did have it, I wouldn't give it to you!"

"Lies!" shouted Ravage again, growing impatient, he wanted to "play" with his food.

Kassir spoke for the first time and leant down to face her. He spoke calmly but with anger to his voice.

"We've waited for years to be released after you imprisoned us in that stony cage." His anger dropped and his crooked white smile flashed menacingly in delight. "And as you can see, we are very much back in the flesh. Now the only thing powerful enough to do that is the power that's still inside that amulet." His temper began to flare again through his gritted teeth. "So be a dear and hand it over!" He gave a pleasing smile and held his large hand out in front of her.

"She's telling the truth!" Marshall yelled out.

"Stay out of this." Crudge bellowed as he squeezed Marshall in his grip.

"Leave them alone, okay!" She pleaded. "They have nothing to do with this."

Crudge gave a squeeze of his arms as if teasing her and Marshall let out a groan. The Engineer prodded the other two in the back and they protested.

"Hurt them again and you'll be sorry!" She called out.

Kassir smiled. "Such a brave and fiery little mortal. Much different to the scared little thing Ravage brought to me all those years ago!" He looked at her, with an evil smile and pondered his next move. "Maybe this warrior could have saved her sister when she couldn't before!" He smiled and she lunged at him. Ravage stopped her from reaching him and held her down.

Kassir laughed. "It's simple my girl. Hand over the amulet and we spare your friends." He grabbed a small creature that was passing nearby with a swipe of his hand. "And if you don't!" He squeezed the creature tight, it started gasping. Then he released his grip and the creature darted away to safety. "You get the idea!"

Ava bowed her head. What was she to do, she had lost the amulet with her sister, all those years ago but she couldn't let her friends get hurt.

"Hey, how many times do we have to tell you, she *doesn't* have it, you oversized ape!" Marshall called out, without realising fully what he was doing. But he knew he didn't want them messing with Ava any longer and upsetting her.

"It's not here okay!" He shouted in anger. "I... I lost it!" He said in shame. He knew if he had kept a good hold of it then none of this would have happened.

"It's true!" Joe added. Sticking up for his friend.

The creatures froze and turned their gaze to the boy. Ava stopped her struggling and looked in shock at the trio that had come into her world. How could they have it? She thought.

"Maybe we do need you after all, loverboy." Ravage whispered as he leaned in towards Marshall with his bony fingers pointing into Marshall's chest. "You'd be wise to hand it over boy."

"That's what I'm saying!" He said angrily, as he stared into Ravages eyes, the one who had taken Ava and her sister and caused so much pain. "I... don't... have it." Ravage's face curled up in anger and snarled. Marshall gulped as he explained.

"Don't play games with me." He said as he placed his long, razor sharp claw against Ava's cheek. "It would be a shame for something to happen to this pretty one!"

Mashall froze in horror as he saw Ava wince, as the claw pushed against her face.

"Hey!... Hey, calm down okay, I'm telling the truth." Marshall protested frantically trying to stop him hurting her. "We found the Amulet in a store but it somehow transported us to the middle of the woods. But it must be in our world still because when I got up it was gone. I don't know what brought you slimy creeps back to life but I can guarantee you it wasn't that amulet!"

Randy took a slow, uneasy step back.

"Your world?" Ava asked, ignoring everything else.

"*Llllies*!" Kassir growled in frustration.

"Crudge, Ravage drop them. We've wasted enough time. We will just have to take the girl and find a way to *make* her talk." He turned and walked away slowly.

"No!" She cried out. Marshall and Joe yelled for them to stop.

"Wait!" Randy shouted from behind. The first noise he had made the whole time since being captured by the brutes.

Kassir smiled a deep, evil grin to himself and turned back to face the boys, adopting a stern face. He walked over to the youngest boy and bent down to match his eye level.

"Yes?" He asked slowly.

Randy went quiet and bit his lip. He glanced at Marshall, then he stared back at Kassir and looked him in the eyes and softly said.

"I have it..." He faced the floor in shame.

Kassir turned his head a little to show his ear to the boy. "Speak up shrimp, don't be shy."

Randy lifted his face, with a look of defiance and tears and shouted.

"I HAVE YOUR STUPID AMULET!"

He reached into his pocket under his costume and slowly pulled his hand out. As he unclenched his fist Marshall saw the familiar metal shape and the blue stone set inside. He looked over to his brother in shock and disbelief.

Randy turned to his brother. "I saw it on the ground when we fell here. Before you found me. I just thought it looked shiny and cool so I took it for my treasures, then you said about how powerful it was, I wanted to have one as well. To be like you." Marshall and Joe stood in disbelief.

Ava looked in disbelief at the small metal object. She never thought she would see that thing again. Her eyes began to fill with tears.

"Wait, where's my sister, is she okay!"

"Silence!" Called Kassir.

"No wait, who gave you that? Where is she?" Ava called out again, desperate for answers.

"Keep her quiet." Kassir roared. The Engineer placed his hands over her mouth.

Marshall didn't know what to say or feel. He wanted to explain everything to Ava, they needed to escape and now he was trying to deal with the fact that Randy had the amulet all along!

Kassir turned back to Randy and smiled with delight as he crouched back down to his level.

"Ahhhh, I see you're the brains of the gang. I'll tell you what. You hand it over like a good child and we can be done with all this. And if it's treasures you like I can make sure you have more than you can count! What d'ya say?"

Ava bit down on The Engineer's hand hard.

"Aargh" He cried out in pain and shook his hand.

Ava screamed out to Randy. "No! Don't trust him."

Kassir spun his head round in anger and glared at the girl. He nodded to The Engineer to silence her and he wrapped his four arms around the girl, covering her mouth.

"We both know I can just take it, but I see no reason for such unpleasantry. I'm a reasonable creature!" Kassir said to Randy with a wicked smile.

Randy was deep in thought. Then he looked back up a d met Kassir's gaze with a stern expression.

"I don't want your treasures but if you want it so badly then nobody hurts my friends!"

"Randy no!" Marshall cried out!

"My brother and my friends go free and you can have it! Do we have a deal?"

Kassir smiled a sly grin. "You drive a hard bargain master shrimp, such a funny young boy... but I like you. Deal, we don't hurt your friends and in return you hand me over the Amulet."

"Randy no!" The other kids shouted.

But it was too late, Randy held out his hand and Kassir's beckoned Ravage to take the amulet to safety. Ravage clenched his fist shut, tightly around it and Kassir grinned a large smile showing his rotten, pointy teeth. He laughed to himself with joy.

"Brothers we are back and we have the stone." He raised the amulet high above him and it glinted in the carnival's light.

The other creatures cheered and laughed. Crudge dropped the boys and he and Ravage barged past the kids and joined Kassir at his side as he turned to leave.

"What shall I do with this one?" The Engineer asked.

"Why, she's coming with us of course." He smiled fiendishly at the group of boys.

"What! but you said..." Shouted Marshall.

"I said I wouldn't hurt *his* friends! But you see, she... now she's *my* friend. We go way back. Now I am a character of my word and so I shan't harm you, but... It's a long road home and we're gonna be tired when we get back. And I can't think of a better person to help us get back on our feet. So, we can retake what was ours!" He smiled and hollered to The Engineer.

"Wrap it up, let's go!"

The Engineer threw Ava over his shoulder.

The boys ran over as they left but Kleb stood in their way blocking them from saving her.

"No." Marshall shouted.

"Marshall!" Ava called back as they disappeared into the jungle.

Marshall turned around to face Randy. Anger in his eyes and utter disbelief his brother had been lying to them all. And now Ava and their ticket out of there was gone.

"What was that! You had it all along?!"

Joe stepped in. He was angry too but he could see the look in Marshall's eyes.

Marshall pushed him away as he made his way over to Randy.

Randy opened his mouth to speak.

"No, I don't want to hear it. You always do what you want to do, with no thought to others. And I'm always left to fix things. I'm tired of always having to look after you, or sort things with Mom and Dad when you mess up."

Joe took a step back he had never seen Marshall this angry before.

"You give no thought to what you do and what's worse is you don't care about anyone else. Always taking "treasures" but not realising they belong to other people. What you do affects other people and now, because of your selfishness we've lost the only thing that might get us home and Ava is in trouble and she will *die* if we can't stop them in time. What was so important that you needed to steal the amulet and lie to us about it huh? Especially when we found out it was our only way home?!" He took a breath as years of built up frustration left him in a powerful outburst.

Then he looked at his little brother's face and felt the deep sharp sting of guilt, instantly, as Randy's eyes began to well and his bottom lip trembled.

"You're gonna forget me!" Randy shouted back, behind the floods of tears he was trying to hold in. Marshall looked at Randy and saw he was staring back in a way he had never seen before. Randy was scared, his little brother looked up to him and he had obliterated that in one brief outburst.

"What do you mean?" Marshall asked.

"You're gonna be big!" He wiped his eyes with his sleeve.

"You never want to play with me anymore! We used to always play figures or board games. We did EVERYTHING together. But that stopped. Now you hardly want to spend time with me anymore, 'cos you're getting big!... I know you're getting older and all you want to do is parties and talk to girls. You're so worried about being *cool.* But you were always the coolest person I knew. I always wanted to be like you!" He sniffed. "I don't want to lose my big brother. I don't want to lose my best friend...

I don't want to lose my only friend!"

Marshall was speechless, he didn't know his little brother had thought that. Joe stood uncharacteristically silent. Being an only child, he couldn't imagine but he knew what it was like to be alone and how the brothers stopped him feeling like that.

Randy wiped his tears, getting more and more upset as he unbottled his fears.

"I saw it on the ground when we landed and I took it, at first I just thought it looked cool but then I kept it after we found out what it did... 'cos I knew we could stay here!"

"That's ridiculous, why would you want to stay here?!" said Marshall, still confused at his actions.

"Because! I wouldn't get grounded anymore, people listen to me here, I fit in here and..." He drooped his head. "You wouldn't leave me."

Marshall felt tears welling up in his eyes as he listened to how much his little brother was hurting.

Randy continued. "We would always be best friends and I won't be alone."

Marshall's face dropped in sadness and regret. He had always been close to his little brother but he hadn't realised how that had been strained since starting high school and trying to impress Vinessa. He stopped and realised just how much his brother loved him. He began to reach out to grab his brother and give him a hug but it was too much for Randy who still looked just as scared of

Marshall and who couldn't control his tears any longer. He flipped up his ghost hood, to hide his tears and upset and ran back into the thick crowd of strange creatures and out of sight before Marshall could say a word.

Chapter 22

"Quick Joe!"

Marshall and Joe chased Randy into the crowd. It was hard to see between the darkness, the flickering of torches, the dazzling lights from the rides and stalls and all the different looking creatures. The horns, the frills, the wings. It was almost impossible to spot Randy's white hood as it plummeted deep into the depths of the carnival.

"Which way did he go?" called Joe

"I think this way!" Marshall pointed off to the right.

"Wait, over there!" shouted Joe, as he spotted the top of a white object to the left.

"Let's spilt up!" said Marshall. "Meet back at this spot okay?!"

"Okay." Said Joe and nodded as he pursued the white object to the left as Marshall covered the right.

"Randy" They began to yell as they split and searched the crowd.

Randy, brimming with tears, ran as fast as his legs could take him. He just wanted to get as far away as everything as he could, it was all too much. He was scared, upset, he felt guilty that the creatures had taken Ava. She had saved them so many times already. He ran down the bazaar like market with its stalls and games stands. He knocked into a purple creature with horns as it tried to win its girlfriend a stuffed creature from one of the games.

"Hey, watch it!" The creature yelled, shaking his fist in the air.

Randy ignored him, as he continued to barge through the pillars of monsters. He zig-zagged between the mix of scales and feathered legs and feet of all shapes and sizes. Suddenly he tripped and he came crashing down into the stall to his side with a crash. He stood up and saw that the stall had collapsed on it itself, the canvas of the tent draped over the broken wood that held it up and some form of large tentacles were erupting from the centre of it. He wasn't sure if the tentacles were the food that was sold there or if they belonged to the customer that had been stood there but he didn't stop to find out, as he dodged down a path to the right. He could hear his brother calling from behind, not too far away. He came to a cross roads and hesitated in the middle. A creature with long legs, taller than a giraffe and thicker than an elephant, crossed his path and its huge head, with it's one large eye ducked down and stared at him curiously without a sound as it walked past. He watched the behemoth stride past him in awe.

"Randy." Marshall called. He was getting closer but he hadn't spotted him yet.

Hearing his brother, he took flight and chose which of the four paths he was going to take. He spotted a group of creatures that looked like kids with their parents. The four, squat children with their flat, chubby faces and bald, slimy skin were all wearing stripy t-shirts and shorts and fighting with each other over who's turn it was at the game stand. They had to fling a small, furry creature at a series of creepy looking plants that stood on a shelf at the back of the stall. The plants were waiting to catch them with their crooked mouths. The one who filled up the most plants would win a prize.

Their mother was pre occupied with paying the stall owner so Randy snuck into the group of little monsters, with his hood over his head to blend in with the crowd. He ducked as Marshall ran past the crossroads, he stopped to turn and look but with all the avenues and creatures, he couldn't see him and he carried on his way.

The first of the creepy looking children threw the little furry creature with a wind-up arm and although nearly knocking the plant from its soil, the mouth closed firmly and the furball bounced onto the floor. The plant opened its mouth back into its starting position and the little furball tried running off but the eagle-eyed games operator scooped it up and placed it back into the bag. The next child took aim. Randy deduced it must be a little girl but only due to the pink bow that was stuck on the top of her equally bald head. They all looked alike save for this minute detail.

The smallest child at the back teetered on its two legs and turned to face Randy. With no neck it had to turn its whole body. He looked at Randy in his costume, up and down as if not sure what to make of him. To the creature, Randy was the odd-looking character. Randy flipped down his hood and the child startled and made a cry in surprise.

"Maaaaah." It yelled.

"It's okay, it's okay." Randy said with his hands out in front to calm it.

"Mah?" it replied blankly.

"It's okay." He repeated calmly.

The creature quietened down and tilted its head to the side, trying to make him out.

"I'm Randy!"

The creature looked at him then opened his mouth.

"Mah, Maah" He called out as he patted his chest.

"Your name is MakMar?" Randy asked, trying to understand him.

The creature bounced up and down on its short legs in excitement and smiled.

"Nice to meet you MakMar, what are you playing?" Asked Randy.

The creature teetered back round to look at the stall and then back to Randy. "Mah Mah, Mah Maaaaah." It held out it's hand and offered Randy the furry creature.

"For me?" Randy asked.

The creature bowed its body up and down in agreement. "Ma Maaaah." It was giving Randy its turn.

Randy held out his hands and giggled when the fury creature was placed in his hand. He couldn't make out a proper shape due to all the fur but it tickled his palm so much that he couldn't help but laugh, which made the creature laugh too.

"Okay, here goes." He mimicked the older creatures wind-up arm technique and stuck out his tongue in concentration. He brought his arm back and held it there while he focussed on the plant. He took a deep breath and he launched the little creature with all his might, sending it hurtling towards the plant and it's gaping mouth ready to pounce and snap it from the air. The kids all cheered and he gave his new friend a high five.

The furry creature was gone and the plant gave a low gurgle as it digested the furball.

"I didn't know plants could burp!" He giggled, as he turned back to his friend who was smiling with praise at his win. He forgot all about his upset and started to enjoy himself. The large operator gave the group of kids a prize. It was a creepy looking stuffed toy. It looked like a creepy bear, there was a zip running down the middle from head to toe and back round. One side was jet black the other, a deep purple. The Eyes were made of two odd sized buttons one green, one red.

Makmar turned back to his family and bundled with its nearest sibling. The mother cackled to them to motion they were leaving and they stopped their games and picked each other up.

Randy remembered when him and Marshall used to play fight and mess around. He missed his brother. He was upset still but he missed him. The creatures all started walking off when Randy's new friend turned back around to see where Randy was. He saw him still standing at the game stall and motioned for Randy to join them.

"It's okay!" Randy said with a smile. "I need to find my family too. But thank you!" He smiled at his new friend.

MakMar paused then bopped his sister on the head she turned around and they had a brief conversation that Randy couldn't work out but he saw MakMar's sister hand him the bear and he brought it over to Randy. He held it out to him and smiled.

"For me? Randy asked with a sincere smile. He had never been given a gift before by anyone other than his family. All the kids at his school thought he was odd. Makmar unzipped the bear and the two sides unfolded into a black and purple stuffed toy.

"One each?" He grabbed MakMar's hand and shook it hard. "Thankyou... Friend!" He smiled. Then he thought to himself as he rummaged in his pockets. He had his treasures from home, he fumbled through various bits and bobs until he found a small plastic Dinosaur, it was his favourite but he wanted to give something to his new friend in return.

Makmar took the small plastic toy in both hands and looked up at Randy.

"Mah, Maaaaah??!"

"Yeah, it's for you!" Randy smiled.

MakMar held it up and studied it, then erupted into hysterical laughter at the strange object.

"I'm glad you like it!" Randy laughed.

MakMar went running over to his brother's and sister and displayed his new trophy with pride and with a final wave they wandered off into the crowd

Joe looked at this odd family and realised he shouldn't be running from his family. He should be helping the other two boys in finding and rescuing Ava. He began to catch up to Marshall in the direction he saw him run. As he joined back onto the crossroads and took Marshall's path, he heard a small whisper.

"Psst..."

Randy looked about and could see nothing but the wandering crowd and the sounds of the big wheel and rides in the distance.

"Psst... Hey over here."

There it was again. But where was it coming from, he thought. He turned and looked about but all he could see were traders crying out their wares and kids asking for food or games. Then he spotted it, through the passing carnival goers in a darkened corner, a large, yellow eye glaring at him through the small opening of a blue and white striped canvas tent. He looked into the eye, it was yellowed and cloudy looking and staring straight at him, unblinking. He was always told never to follow strangers and he begun to turn back and find Marshall, when the voice hissed to him again.

"You look lost!?" It spoke from behind the tent. His voice deep and crackling.

"Uh yeah... my brother, he went that way though. I'm just going to catch up with him, thanks."

"Won't find him that way!" The voice came from behind the tent. The yellowed, beady eye sticking out, watching him intently.

"How do you know?" Randy asked curiously.

"Why don't you step inside and look at my *treasures*."

"Treasures? Like what?"

"Bit of this, bit of that, lots of treasures inside, could get your brother something nice."

"Um, no thanks... Besides I don't have any money!"

"First ones free!" The mysterious voice insisted.

Randy was cautious the ominous looking eye was all he could see of this creature and the voice sounded creepy. His parents had always told him to stay away from strangers but that was hard in this place as nothing was normal, everything was strange.

"Maybe something for my brother, to say sorry." Randy said to himself.

"Randy!" A voice called out from behind him.

Randy turned and saw it was Marshall and a huge smile spread across his face, he was so happy to see him.

Marshall gave him a big wave. He had never been so relieved and happy to see his little brother than right now. All he wanted to do was apologise and let him know he would always be there. Marshall carried on waving across the crowd, smiling even more when Randy had waved back and he realised he wasn't going to run again. He would make sure he would be a better big brother from now on.

Randy was waving and smiling back. He was just about to run towards Marshall, when all of a sudden, the large blue and white striped sides of the tent lifted up, outstretched and a large feathered head swung round and grabbed Randy in its jagged beak.

The tent was alive and the beady eye was joined by another, as the canvas-like wings that formed the tents side, wrapped tightly around Randy. Covering him completely into a little ball on the bird like creature's back. The creature rose onto two thick stilted legs, nine feet into the air. With its package wrapped neatly on its back. It hopped over the rooftops of the tents behind, crushing the last one under the sheer weight and sprinted across the clearing, into the woods beyond, with Randy securely held on the back.

"No!" Marshall cried out as he watched his brother get scooped up and kidnapped into the jungle. He tried to chase the evil looking bird but he couldn't push through the crowd quick enough. He dropped to his knees as he reached the edge of the carnival and saw the bird speed off on its two legs across the grassy plain and into the jungle.

"Marshall!?" Came a voice from behind, closing in. "Marshall are you okay?" It was Joe.

"Joe..." Marshall replied, still in disbelief at what he'd seen. "The tent... The tent stole Randy!"

"What?"

"The tent... it wasn't a tent it-"

"It was a Shadix!"

Came a voice at their feet.

Marshall looked down confused.

From under the tent that the creature had crumpled, came a rustling as the canvas moved. A set of blue hands came out from the edges and a strange creature coughed and wheezed as it pulled itself from under the mangled mess. It was covered in red.

"Yuk shenkarow soup! Boy this is gonna stain the ol' skin! That wasn't a tent, it was shadix, we get them every so often. They camouflage and try to blend in. I hadn't spotted this one but yeah it was a shadix alright."

The creature held out its hand, dripping with red sauce.

"Fimple, nice to meet ya! Oh sorry!" He wiped his hand on the remains of the tent. He was about Marshall's height and gangly. He had blue and green skin which dangled low under his pointed chin like the wattle of a rooster. He was wearing a pair of loose blue denim jeans with a tie died t-shirt under a cooking apron.

"We haven't had one for a while but with all the hustle and bustle here, who know how many creatures are really here lurking, you can't tell any more. Before it used to just be the circus and rides and us legitimate traders but now... it's gone too commercial."

"What was that thing and where did it go?" Cried Marshall.

"I told you it was a shadix. Ya know, speedy birds with beady eyes. They sit and wait until *bam* they catch you and then- woah, wait. You don't know... hey... hey you're human ain't ya? Wowee hey Chip... Chip? Where the?"

The creature stopped, to lift up the edges of the tent, looking underneath. A loud grown came from under the material on the floor behind Joe. He lifted the corner up and there sat Chip, upside-down and crumpled on his head. Chip was a lot shorter and his belly poked over his dark trousers. His skin had more of a peachy tone and he had a bristly moustache like the end of a broom. Above his moustache sat a single horn, rounded more than pointy and only a few inches long.

"Hey, get up. We have company!"

The second creature stood up and rattled its head. It looked at Fimple, saw the that he was covered in the red soup, pointed and laughed a huge laugh.

"What are you laffin' at meatball!" Fimple said as he pointed back at him.

He looked down, his arm still out, pointing and stopped laughing abruptly when he saw he was also covered in shenkarow soup, from head to toe.

"This, guys, is my esteemed colleague and business partner Chip. Chip meet the guys, they're *humans.*" He said with excitement.

"Get outta here!" He said, fascinated as he climbed off of the wreckage. "Well, would you look at dat!" He spoke in a deep, gurgling voice. He shook himself off like a dog splattering red sauce everywhere. "Nice to meet ya!" He said holding out his hand to shake.

"I was just telling these guys that we were the unlucky victims of a shadix."

"Well dat's no good!" Replied Chip. "Dey're humans, dey won't know what a shadix is, idiot."

"Welcome to the room genius!" Fimple replied sarcastically! "That's just where we got to before we found you lying down on the job."

As friendly and entertaining as these two characters were, Marshall needed answers!

"So, these guys are nasty?" He asked the food vendors.

"I don't know!" Fimple replied laughing. "I never met the guy before!"

"No, what I mean is, he kidnapped my brother. Will he eat him?" Marshall specified, trying to get a serious response.

Chip and Fimple looked at each other in confusion.

"Will he eat him?" They repeated to each other, then they both collapsed into laughter on the floor.

Fimple could see Marshall was serious. He stood and wiped a tear from his eyes and calmed himself.

"No, my friend, he won't eat him. Shadix's don't eat meat."

"Phew." Marshall and Joe sighed and smiled at each other.

"That's a relief." Joe said, relieved.

Fimple continued. "But... he will be taken to the kingdom of the beasts and be held there as a slave for all eternity by their master, Landis." He replied casually.

"What!" Cried the boys.

"Yeah, shadix's eat creepy crawlies and the kingdom of the beasts has the biggest and strangest. From the glowing fireflies we get here and the ghost moths to the giant shadow spiders, found only in the northern parts. They have trouble catching them due to their crooked beaks and feathers but they're incredibly sly and sneaky and so they capture other creatures and take them back to their lair to forage for the bugs for them."

"Who's this Landis you mentioned?" Joe asked.

"He's their leader, a fierce and powerful shadix. He rules with an iron fist. They live on the outskirts of the kingdom of the beasts, a place where no one goes, unless they have to. You think the forests around here are wild! There are places there that's said never to have been visited by anyone, ever, it's too dangerous. That's why they stay there. They can steal who they like and never have to worry."

Marshall's heart sank. "So how do we get my brother back?"

"You're not listening kid!" Fimple said. "Your brother's already gone! Nobody ever comes back from there!"

Chip nudged him. "Go easy on him!"

"We need to get him back, now!" Marshall said.

"Well good luck with that boys, we wish you well" Fimple waved them on as he started picking up the broken stall.

"Wait, you're not going to help us?" Asked Joe.

322

Fimple sighed. "If you hadn't noticed your brother's chariot completely destroyed our business, we got a lot to do!"

"Your business was all in one tent?" Marshall asked. "What *was* it?"

Fimple stood tall on the collapsed stall, with his chest out and cleared his throat.

"Ahem. You, my fine fellows, are in the presence of the owners, managers, proprietors and *head honchos* of-" He looked at Chip and whispered. "Drum roll!"

Chip began to strike his belly like a drum.

Fimple raised his voice with pride.

"Fimple and Chip's Food Emporium!"

"Hey!" Chip stepped in. "You mean Chip and Fimple's Emporium of Food!"

"The name doesn't matter, what does, is that we've lost a days' worth of shenkarow soup, not to mention our equipment is completely ruined because of bird brain there!"

"Please?" Marshall asked. "We have no idea how to get there or where *there* even is!"

"I'm sorry." Fimple sighed. "Look, even if we could help you. It's too dangerous!"

Marshall felt sick, he needed to save his brother so they could rescue Ava and somehow get the amulet back and get home. Then a thought occurred to him.

"How can you know what the kingdom of the beasts is like, if no one's ever come back before to tell anyone about it?" Marshall asked.

Joe smiled. "Yeah, that's a point!" He raised his eyebrow at Chip and Fimple with a smile. "I think they're just scared Marsh!"

Chip and Fimple dropped the pieces of tent and wood they were clearing and shot a look at the boys.

"Nice try, you think we're dumb enough to fall for that!" Fimple said, seeing through Joe's plan. "We have been there, well, partly. A long time ago. And we ain't ever going back."

"Besides." Said Chip. "If you're gonna get your brother back."

"Which you won't!" Fimple added.

"Shh!" Chip told Fimple. "*If* you're gonna get your brother back, then you'll need to get there before the shadix carrying him does."

"Why's that?" Joe asked.

"Because, once Landis has you, there's only one way out."

Chip motioned a noose around his neck and stuck his tongue out.

"So, how do we beat the shadix there? Won't it just take the same route?" Marshall asked, trying to understand and aware that all the time they were talking, Randy and Ava were in more danger.

"No." Said Fimple. "The shadix are the fastest thing on land but they're cowards. So, it'll take the long way around. The only way to beat the shadix and get your friend back is through The Forbidden Valley."

"The Forbidden Valley?" Joe asked hesitantly. He didn't like the sound of that.

"Yeah, but no one *ever* goes through, I heard it's haunted!" Said Chip.

"Isn't this whole place haunted?" Said Marshall.

"True, but this is where the darkest things come out to play!"

"So far, we've been thrown into an unknown world, had a bat lady try to eat us, been chased by ghosts and creatures I can't even explain. Attacked by plants, rabid squirrels and Soul takers. I don't care what it takes, I'm not afraid, I need to find my little brother and if this shortcut is what it takes then we're doing it!" Marshall shouted.

Joe looked at Marshall with a smile.

"There's the Marsh I know! I'm in whatever it takes." He said as he high fived his best friend.

"So, will you guys help us?" Marshall asked confidently.

Fimple looked at Chip then back at the kids.

"Wow you're incredibly brave and your honour is motivating..."

"You're being sarcastic right now, aren't you?" Marshall sighed.

"Oh yeah, for sure. Yeah, there's no way we're going through The Forbidden Valley." Fimple replied.

"Please?! We need to save my brother as quick as we can then hopefully, we can still save our friend Ava, she's been taken-"

Chip dropped the items in his hands and stared at Marshall.

"Ava?" He looked at Fimple.

"C'mon it must be a different Ava!" Fimple laughed nervously. "Remember a few years back everyone was calling their baby Flungus? Huh, remember that?" He tried to convince Chip.

Chip didn't change his expression.

Fimple sighed "What does this Ava look like?"

"Why? I didn't think you wanted to help!" Joe replied.

"Just answer him kid." Chip shot back.

"I don't know. About my height." Said Marshall. "Dark brown hair... pretty I guess..." He smiled "She's got these dark brown eyes that glisten in the moonlight and a soft caring voice. She's tougher than she seems, but I think secretly more scared than she lets on." He chuckled to himself as he thought about Ava and if he'd ever see her again.

Joe made a puking face. "What he means is, normal looking, has a tendency to be pushy and definitely been out in the woods too long."

Chip looked at fimple with despair. Fimple sighed a heavy sigh and nodded. He turned back to the boys.

"We're coming with you!"

"What... really?" Asked Marshall in shock and delight.

"Yeah, really but we need to go now!"

"How come? I mean thank you, but what made you change your minds?"

"Any friend of Ava is a friend of ours and if she's in trouble then we'll do everything we can to save her. So ya know, let's go get your brother." He turned to the pile of debris on the floor, and kicked it half-heartedly. "Might as well leave it here Chip, 'cos I doubt we're coming back."

Chip kicked the site too for good measure.

"Ah I was getting bored of the carnival chef game anyway. I feel we should expand our horizons and go into da mobile eatery world! *Chip and Fimple's Travelling Extravaganza!*" He said as he envisioned their name in lights.

"*Fimple and Chip's* you mean!" Fimple shot back as he walked over to a nearby beast and yanked its long trunk into a wooden bucket of water, that had been left for it to drink from. With a long stretch of its nose, he squirted the water out over himself, washing the soup off him.

"Ah that's better, hey Chip c'mere." He hosed down the soup covered Chip and shook dry.

The four set off across the grassy plain, towards the edge of the jungle, leaving the lights of the carnival behind.

Chapter 23

Chip and Fimple used the time crossing the plains into the dark jungle, to describe the route they would need to take if they were to arrive there before the shadix. Each step made Joe and Marshall shudder harder and gulp louder. But Marshall knew they had no choice. They needed to rescue Randy and Ava and get the amulet back so they could all leave together and end this nightmare once and for all.

Not long after setting off, they found themselves entering the first area.

"Here we are!" Chip said.

"Where?" Asked Joe.

"The Restless Valley!" Fimple whispered.

As they looked out in front the forest became thinner slightly and they could make out various stone ruins dotted all throughout, that were surrounded by an eerie, white mist that covered the floor. They also noticed it was surprisingly quiet compared to the bustle of the carnival and the animal sounds they had come to get used to in the other parts of the jungle.

"Seems pretty dead for a *restless valley*." Joe joked. He had a bad habit of making poor jokes when he was nervous.

"You got one part right kid!" Chip said calmly as they entered the misty valley. "Dis ain't New York but dis old city certainly never sleeps."

Joe looked at Marshall and smiled. "Hey, you could be doing Mr. Neidernaim's essay right now so you know... *every cloud* and all."

Marshall shook his head and laughed a little. He turned to Chip and Fimple.

"So, why *is* this called the Restless Valley?" He was almost afraid to ask.

Chip said nothing but motioned with his finger to his lips to be quiet. He led the way through the low ferns and bushes, towards the heart of the stony graveyard cautiously and silently. They were careful where they were treading, on the uneven ground. Even with the moon's glow reflecting off the mist, it was hard to tell where to step.

They came to a slow-moving river. The water was thick and dark like tar and as the swampy stream bubbled, purple and blue gasses spewed from the murky waters.

As they passed through the various sized stone ruins, the path grew thinner and the grass grew taller until it passed their heads. All they could see was the person in front. The night air was silent you could hear a pin drop. The only sounds were the soft footsteps of the boy's shoes and the patter of Chip and Fimple's feet, on the bare ground.

They had walked on down the grassy passageway for a few minutes, being careful to listen out for any signs of trouble. All of a sudden, a short gust of wind blew through them and bent the long blades of grass back and forth.

Marshall turned around to look at Joe and his face froze. In the blinking gaps of the long grass, as it moved briefly back and forth, he saw various shapes surrounded by different coloured smoke. They were twenty feet away. The only visible parts were the tops of the skulls and the piercing eyes underneath that were gliding through the long grass, in a straight line, towards them! They were being hunted!

Chip spotted them too and tried to warn the boys.

"Don't make a sound. Don't make a sound!" He whispered fast but it was too late. Joe spun round and saw the silent shapes, like a shark fin sticking out of the water.

"Run! They're coming!" He yelled and the night sky filled with a shriek from the surrounding circle of ghosts.

They leapt into full sprint, Chip running as fast as his little legs could carry him. They heard the ghosts pick up pace as the grass whooshed all around them.

Before they knew it, they had exited the long grass and had emerged into an open landscape of old stone ruins. It looked empty but almost as soon as they fell out into the open land, Marshall watched as a small flicker of purple smoke appeared over by a cluster of rocks in the distance. The plume of purple grew and rolled outwards across the floor as it took form. Thin arms and long fingers sprouted in the air and in a flash the small flicker of purple smoke had grown into a fully formed being that floated silently and still. Marshall couldn't make out the shape or its face, it was turned away from them. It slowly rotated on the spot where it was floating. Marshall's breathing almost slowed to a halt as he saw the floating creature had been there a long time. Its jaw was loose and the sockets, where there should have been eyes, were as dark and empty as the silence that surrounded the whole ravine.

Before Marshall could say anything, he saw the valley come to life with pockets of tiny smoke that started to grow too. Some purple, some lime green others blue and red. All different, no two ghosts looked alike. They floated back and forth, some on the ground, slowly and others through the air with great speed. Then, they all turned when they sensed the four intruders and let out an almighty screech.

The chase resumed and they took a turn to the right where they could see a wall of rocks in the distance.

"Quick!" Marshall called out. "Through there!"

They ran as fast as they could. Fimple twisted his long neck around and screamed as one of the ghosts zoomed right at him. He quickly ducked and the ghost shot passed him. It spun over in a loop like a fighter jet, flipping mid-air. It was coming at them but they could see the rocky wall and in the centre was a passage, about six feet deep.

Marshall thought if they could just get to the other side maybe they'd have a chance to hide.

The kept on, their legs aching and breath getting heavier but they made it just in time. Marshall and Joe charged through the gap, Fimple just behind but Chip, the shortest of them with his squat legs, was lagging behind. His arms outstretched and his mouth open in fear as he screamed the whole way! The rest all cried out to cheer him on.

"C'mon, this way."

"Nearly there, c'mon!"

They all shouted. He was followed by dozens of the floating spirits, all aglow and surrounded in smoke. He leapt in as he made the final few feet and just as they all began to run again, the ghosts disappeared!

"What happened?" Asked Joe.

Then a few of the lights re appeared in the distance. They remained motionless, just watching the group in the rocky cave.

"They... can't... leave..." Chip panted in exhaustion.

"What?" Fimple asked.

Chip tried to regain his breath and explained with a wheeze.

"The Ghosts... they can't leave the valley. They're cursed to haunt it forever... hence the name *restless!*"

"And you knew this?" Fimple cried out as he collapsed in a pile exhausted.

Marshall heaved fimple to his feet and laughed. "C'mon, we need to keep going, which way now?"

Chip and Fimple led the way. The cave was small and it wasn't long until they were exiting the other side.

They carved through the low-lying vines and various enormous leaves that hung over the crude pathway. They stepped out onto a clearing that dropped away, beneath them, into a gaping black void. The chasm ran as far as they could see to the left and right. Tropical trees and roots dotted the edges of the cliff-like drop and there, some 40 feet across the gap, was their heading.

"Great!" Said Joe. "Where now?" He turned to Chip and Fimple. "How do we get across?"

The duo looked at each other, perplexed, and smiled back at the boys sheepishly.

"Wait, you *do* know where we're going right, you've been here before!" Joe questioned.

"Er... We said we knew how to get there. So... it's like we've been there before. Technically this our first time actually... you know... coming here... in the physical sense." Fimple grinned.

"I mean, we don't even know if *anyone's* been here before really..." Added Chip, brushing away an exposed bone he had noticed on the floor, into the bushes by his feet.

Joe groaned and slumped to the floor. "We're doomed!" He buried his face into his hands as he shook his head.

"Maybe not!" He heard Marshall say from his right. He was clearing a path through the bushes. He had spotted something.

Joe stood up in hope and looked at Marshall's discovery as he smiled back at him.

"Yeah... we're definitely doomed!"

There, in the distance, behind the tangle of vines and leaves was an old, rotten rope bridge.

Joe shook his head as they neared it. Marshall smiled. This had to work, he thought.

Chip and Fimple brought up the rear and smiled when they saw the bridge.

"Looks dangerous!" Said Chip, softly.

"Looks broken!" Chirped Fimple.

"Looks fun!" They both said in unison. They pushed past each other to get there first.

"Hold up guys!" Marshall said, as he held his hand out in front of them. "We should check it first. We need to go one at a time. I don't think it will take all of us at once!"

"Good idea!" Fimple spoke up. "Exactly what I was thinking!"

Chip shot him a look. He was always taking credit where credit wasn't due.

"I'll go first!" Marshall said tentatively, as he placed his hands on the cool, damp rope that guided either side of the rickety wooden bridge.

"Wait!" Joe called out nervously. "Shouldn't the biggest go first? If it can hold the biggest of us, the rest of us should be fine?!"

They all nodded and they turned their heads one by one looking back until it came to Chip. He followed suit and turned but there was no one behind him. He spun back around.

"Hey wait! Why me?"

Fimple and Joe looked down at him and Chip dropped his gaze towards his extended, round stomach.

"Oh!" He said, with a slight air of embarrassment. He sighed and dragged his knuckles across the floor as he sulked his way to the front of the queue.

He carefully placed his toe on the first wooden plank. It gently touched it and a loud creak came from the bridge.

"Nooooope!" He ran back behind the group.

"C'mon, it's our only way!" Marshall begged. "Besides, Ava's counting on you!"

Chip sighed. He made a slow walk back and tried again. This time his whole foot managed to set down firmly without so much as a groan from the bridge.

He made his way, three, four, five planks in. He held the rope for support. Every now and then a small gust of wind blew through the canyon and the bridge teetered a bit but it soon steadied again. He could see a gap in the middle planks, where they had completely rotted away. He managed to step over, holding the rope, then a quick dash the other side over the last few planks and he had reached the safety of the other side.

"Hey guys I made it, it's not that bad!" He called out. *Bad bad baddd...*

His words echoed throughout the valley and a flock of winged animals, in the distance, flew up from the trees in surprise.

A few rocks on the edge of the ravine fell loose and tumbled down, into the darkness below. It was so deep that they never heard them hit the floor.

Joe went next, following Chip's path and in no time he was across. The only time Marshall had seen him smile so much was when Joe knocked on his door, holding his new Gameboy that he had got one birthday.

Fimple pushed Marshall forward. "You next my friend!"

"No." Marshall paused. "If something happens, Joe will need you both to get him to Randy and Ava. You go, I'll be right behind."

Fimple made his way across, he hopped over the gap in the middle, something he found easier to do than Chip with his longer legs. He was almost at the end. He turned around to signal Marshall over but instead, he looked in shock as he saw a few more rocks crumble from the edge just under Marshall's feet.

"Kid, you need to go now!" He yelled.

Now, now, now ow ow

The echo reverberated through the valley and a low rumble came through the trees. It was followed by a chorus of squawks and the sound of heavy flapping. The sounds grew closer and the trees behind Marshall erupted

335

with a plume of feathers and beaks it was a flock of white, stork like birds. They had crooked necks and a large pouch under their beak. They flew over with such force, Marshall leapt forward onto the bridge as he fell to his knees. He grabbed the cold, damp rope and held on tight as they continued to swarm over his head and into the valley. But now that the beating of wings and the deafening cries had subsided, he could hear another sound. A lot closer. He turned to face the rope he was holding in his left hand. He could feel the slow, uncurling with every creaking sound.

"Oh no!" He said to himself.

He jumped to his feet as the first rope began to fray and let out a loud *ping* as it spun away from the wooden brace in the ground.

Marshall forgot all caution and charged down the wet, wooden bridge. He could hear the twisted rope coming loose as though it was following him as he ran. He felt the right-hand side of the bridge come loose and he heard the first wooden planks begin to fall against the rocks, down into the abyss.

"Must go faster, must go faster!" He told himself.

He was half way. He leapt across the hole in the middle. The rotten wood crumbling as he landed the other side but he picked himself up and pushed on. He was nearly there, two planks left!

All of a sudden, he heard the worst sound he could imagine. The left-hand side of the bridge let out an almighty *twang,* as it too snapped from its fastening. He felt the floor pull from under his feet and he let out an almighty cry as he watched the edge of the canyon drift away above him.

Chapter 24

Ava hit the ground with a thud, as The Engineer dropped her into the workshop floor. She rubbed her arm to try and stop it from stinging.

"Thanks for the ride, Stretch!" She called out sarcastically to the towering Engineer. She realised where she was, a room she hadn't been in for a long time.

It was the room she had last been in with her sister, before they escaped that fateful night.

"Now, now. Is that any way to treat our guest?!" A deep voice spoke from the doorway, as it burst open. It was Kassir.

"You!" Ava said with her mouth open, she felt her blood go cold, she thought back to her sister.

"Surprised?!" He asked with a playful grin. "So were we when we awoke to find our home overrun with vermin and our vault of... *friends* emptied. We thought we had been resurrected anew only to return to our stony slumber straight away. You see without the amulet, without the souls, which keep our immortal coil intact, we are nothing. But would you believe our luck? Not only did we find the rats who stole the amulet of power, they were looking after the very cause of our demise. You!"

He coughed.

"Hey Boss, you don't sound too good!"

"Quiet fool!" Kassir scolded Crudge. "Our feast earlier sufficed for a time but now we can return to our former glory. And what's more fitting, than to start our new reign with the life force of the one who imprisoned us to begin with!" He smiled, devilishly at Ava.

"How long until we're ready?" He asked The Engineer, who was hopping between mechanisms getting the machine set up.

The spindly beast turned with a smile.

"She's good to go Kass!"

"Finally! Crudge, bring the girl."

Ava kicked and lashed out as the large beast picked her up. He placed her in the seat and strapped her in to the machine as Ravage took out the amulet. He placed it in the slot and took a step back.

The Engineer began to turn the handle, rotating it faster and faster as it began generating electricity. Bolts of electric zapped down two coils and into the device. He laughed maniacally as he watched Ava's eyes grow wide with fear.

A loud whirring sound began to ring out as the electricity built up. The four creatures jeered and laughed in excitement.

"Now!" Kassir shouted to the Engineer.

He pulled the lever with a scream of laughter as he waited for the electricity to enter the amulet and drain Ava's soul, leaving her as nothing but a black ooze monster.

The electricity shot down the machine towards the amulet. Ava closed her eyes and thought of seeing her sister.

Just as the electricity ran down and touched the amulet, they heard a loud-

Bang

Smoke filled the room and the four monsters began to cough. The Engineer was covered in black. The machine was destroyed!

Ava opened her eyes in disbelief, she was still her normal self.

"What!" Kassir roared, filling the room.

He growled towards The Engineer in anger.

"Kassir, I... I don't know what happened!" He pleaded, completely unaware of what had caused the problem.

"Fix it!" He yelled.

The Engineer continued checking every connection for a reason for the fault.

"You realise you have destroyed us all!" Kassir growled at The Engineer.

The Engineer snarled when he spotted what was wrong.

"Here's the problem!" He took the amulet from the device and handed it to Kassir.

Kassir looked in anger at the object. It had completely melted. It was made of plastic and bits and pieces of scrap.

"Those sneaky little brats tricked us!" Kassir roared as he threw the fake across the room.

Ava smirked. "That's twice you've been bested by a child!"

"Lock her away!" He screamed at Crudge.

Crudge lifted her from the machine and carried her to the dungeon.

"Ravage!" Kassir yelled. Ravage cowered. He hadn't noticed the fake but he knew he was in trouble. He began to run but Kassir swiped and grabbed him by the scruff of his neck.

"Fool! How could you not spot the real amulet for a child's toy?!" He growled and threw him into the broken machinery. Ravage sat up in the pile of metal and shook his head.

Kassir looked out the window over the old town and sighed. He could see his reflection and he had begun to grow weaker. It would be getting light soon and without the amulet they would be stuck in that realm, in that house and fall into their stony prisons once more.

"All this wealth and material goods and not one beacon of hope!" He muttered to his friends.

The Engineer paused when he heard Kassir and peered over the top of his glasses with a menacing smile.

"There is another way!"

"Go on!" Kassir said.

"We need to travel to Shockton! Bring the girl!" He cackled.

Chapter 25

"Mmphh" Marshall groaned, as he hit the side of the ravine with force.

Something had swung him into the side of the large canyon instead of dragging him down. He looked up and saw Fimple dangling from the ledge, arms outstretched. He held on to Marshall with sheer determination.

Marshall looked below as he watched the remainder of the bridge fall into the dark, gloomy mist and disappeared forever. He gulped as he held onto Fimple's arms.

"Don't look down, kid!" Fimple laughed. "I got ya!"

Fimple pulled with all the might he had in his long arms and lifted Marshall up, on to the edge of the cliff. They collapsed onto the floor with a heavy pant.

"Are we there yet?" Marshall asked, exhausted as he lay on the floor.

"Nearly kid!" Chip said, as he parted the bushes in front of them. "There it is, The Kingdom of The Beasts!"

Marshall looked through the bushes into the ravine below. The forest was covered in webs and strange flowers. He could see small monkey like creatures

341

crawling through the trees and birds flying through the low canopy, it looked just like any other part of the jungle they had crossed so far.

"It looks quiet!" Marshall said as he looked on with relief. "Where to no-" But he cut himself short as he watched the troop of apes swing into an unseen web and in seconds, the eight, black legs of the giant shadow spider had scurried from its hiding spot and had cocooned them in its web, upside down. The shadow spider faded back into the dark as if disappearing altogether.

"Okay, so we have no chance of getting through!" Said Joe. "If we can't see danger, then how can we stop it?"

"We tried to tell you!" Fimple said. "But luckily you have a secret weapon!"

"What's that?" Marshall asked, looking around.

"Us!" Chip said with a wide smile.

They disappeared into the bushes for a few minutes, leaving Marshall and Joe in the dark entrance.

"Where do you think they've gone? Joe asked.

"I've no idea! Maybe they ran away!" Marshall laughed. He looked at his friend. "I wouldn't blame them! Joe, I wanna say I'm really sorry I got us into all this! If I hadn't have taken that stupid amulet!"

"Are you crazy!" Joe replied. "This is the most fun we've had in ages. I mean yeah, it's dangerous but look at what we've done! No one at school is ever gonna believe us!"

"That's if we ever get back to school!" Marshall sighed.

"We will!" Joe smiled. "You'll get us back, I know it!" He smiled at Marshall, who smiled back.

"Thanks man! I hope you're right! And for what it's worth, I'm glad you're here!"

"Hey do you smell that!" Joe asked.

With that, Chip and Fimple came from out of nowhere carrying a mixture of leaves and berries.

"Gross, what's that smell?" Joe asked, covering his nose and mouth.

"Camouflage!" Fimple replied with a cheeky grin and they started covering the boys in the smell without warning.

Within minutes, the kids were covered in the stench.

"Okay, so what is the plan with all this?!"

"Shadow spiders work on movement and smell. They can feel the movement in their webs or sense a nearby creature and shoot its web at it to trap it. So, as long as we avoid the webs, we can sneak past undetected and get to Landis's lair."

The four traversed the dark opening of the kingdom and slowly made their way through. They crept along an old path. They could see the long, spindly legs in the trees above them. Each, as long as them. But they were resting. They kept quiet and hoped the smell would stay on them long enough to make it through. Though not too long, thought Marshall, who was trying not to breath it in too hard.

Eventually they arrived at Landis's lair. Flickering torches lit the area. The entrance was quiet. There was no need for a guard out here, Marshall thought, as only certain people would be stupid enough to try and sneak in. They crept inside and through the tunnels. They could hear digging up ahead. As they entered the main area, they could see dozens of different creatures digging, they were mining giant grubs from the ground. They looked like large termite grubs, Marshall thought.

He scanned the area. The workers were mesmerised as if in a trance. There were a few mangy shadixs, sleeping around on the dusty floor. He couldn't see Randy, or the bird who took him.

"Okay, I don't see Randy here. It looks like we beat it here, what do we do no-"

They stopped where they were. A bright orange light beamed down from above, cutting through the darkness. It swirled around them like a fog. The four stood underneath, shielding their eyes.

"It looks like we have some more guests!"

A rumbling voice spoke from above, awakening the animals nearby and causing a commotion. The nearby shadixs hissed and screeched as they woke to see the intruders.

"Is this what you were looking for?"

A second light shone onto the metal bars of a nearby cage.

"Marshall!" A voice called out. It was Randy and he was locked inside. He tried to push through the bars. He held his arm out to reach for his brother. His eyes welled up.

"Marshall I'm sorry, I'm sorry I ran away, I'm sorry Marshall!"

"It's okay buddy!" Marshall reassured him. "We'll get you out!" Truthfully, he had no idea what they were going to do next but he was just so glad to see his little brother safe and in one piece.

The spotlight flicked off of Randy's cage. Marshall turned back to the voice above.

"Let my brother go! He doesn't belong here!" He called out.

There was silence, then from atop a nearby rock stepped a figure. The shadixs huddled to the floor in silence.

"Landis!" Chip gulped and bowed. Fimple copied with Joe in tow.

The figure stepped into the moonlight and Marshall saw he was another shadix, but he was a lot older and larger than the slender limbed birds. His feathers were tatty and he bore a scar across his right eye. He was extremely large, compared to the agile shape of the others and Marshall had trouble spotting his legs from under his padded, feather covered belly.

"You dare enter the Kingdom of the Beasts and make demands! What monster would have the audacity to enter my realm and not bow!

"I'm not a monster." Marshall said, trying to hold it together. He knew that any of these beasts could tear him in two. "I am a human, and I want my brother!"

The shadixs hissed and cringed at the word.

"Silence!" Commanded Landis. "How interesting, I've never seen a real human up close! He will make an interesting addition to my workforce, once I've *conditioned* him!" He laughed as two slave workers dragged a slithering beast towards the cage.

"That's how he does it then." Fimple whispered. "Venom, to control them!"

Marshall didn't know what to do. He needed to get his brother to safety and they needed to save Ava and time was running out. He stepped forward and shouted.

"Take me instead!"

"What, no Marsh. What are you doing?" Joe shouted.

Chip and Fimple looked on afraid.

"You heard me!" Marshall shouted again. "I'll trade you! Me for my brother! You can lock me away and I'll work for you just let my friends leave!"

"And why would I do that?!" Asked Landis, intrigued but sceptical.

"I'm stronger and can work harder, I have larger hands to grab the food you seek!"

"You think I'm a fool! The fact you would trade yourself for your brother must mean he is of more value than I thought! Why would I accept your trade?" As he finished, shadows flickered and they saw more shadixs appear around them. Soon they would be on them.

"He is more valuable!" Marshall shouted towards the voice. "He's worth far more than you'll ever know!" Marshall's eyes began to well up. "To me!"

He wiped his eyes and turned to Randy. "I'm so sorry I yelled at you bud. I'm your big brother and it's my job to protect you, to look out for you. Keep you safe, you're supposed to test me because I'm supposed to teach you! I'm sorry I got us into this mess! All of it. The shop, the amulet, the ghost town. It's all my fault and now you and Ava are being punished for it."

Randy began to shed a tear. "You try so hard to make people like you Marsh! You give me more time of day than any other bigger brother and all I want to do is grow up to be just like you! That's why I took it, to be like you... to never leave here... so we can stay brothers. I'm sorry!"

"I know I'm growing up!" Said Marshall. "But that doesn't stop you being my brother! I just got mad that you traded the amulet and risked Ava's life too. You could have told me that you had it. We could have made a plan...

together! Whatever happens here now I promise you we do everything together from now on okay!"

Randy wiped his tears from his eyes and gave a little smile through the bars of the cage. "Okay!" He sniffed. "Even if we get locked away forever or murderlated in a creepy forest?!"

Marshall tried not to laugh. "Yes bud, even... that... What you just said, right there. Together! I promise!"

Randy smiled at Marshall and put his thumb up through the cage at him. "Also, I didn't want you to get mad, I told you I get *breaky*." Then he winked at his brother.

Marshall suddenly froze and looked at his brother... What was he up to?

"Enough!" Cried Landis. "I will agree to no trade! My subjects are faster and stronger than you and outnumber you ten to one! You shall all work for me!"

"Then you shall all die!" Marshall shouted!

Landis chuckled. His henchman joined in.

"Whilst your bravery amuses me, I grow tired. You think you could best my flock!" He called out into the night and dozens of shadixs emerged from the shadows. Chuckling, evilly from their crooked beaks and staring with their yellowed eyes.

"We can't, no, but Kassir will!" Marshall shouted.

The beasts fell silent and cowered as they looked at Landis!

Landis hopped down off the rock for the first time and stood eye level with Marshall.

"You're either brave or stupid! But in either case, you're a liar! Kassir is gone!"

"He was! But he's back and if we can't leave here to stop him then the entire world is at risk! And you shan't have any more workers to power your mines then soon he will come for you and with no food you will be too weak to resist him and his men! If you don't let us go, you're condemning yourselves!

Landis stood, silent in thought. "How do I know this is true and not some trick to escape!"

"He speaks the truth!" Chip said, we've only just met him but they have taken our friend, the one who sent him packing the first time and they have the amulet of power! We wouldn't be out here with them if they didn't.

Landis thought hard. I will not get involved in this, if they are returned then I wish to be left here, where I am safe in secrecy. But I cannot allow my workforce to be affected if they are indeed back. You may take your brother, and two of my subjects to return you swiftly. But if I find you are lying then my ears and eyes of the forest will find you and you will wish that you had chosen to work for me!"

Marshall held his hand out to shake and seal the deal. Landis obliged and they agreed. He signalled for the cage to be unlocked.

Randy ran up to Marshall and wrapped his arms around him.

"I'm sorry Marsh."

"Me too, forget all the stuff I said about you ruining things at home okay I didn't mean it I was just angry because we let Ava get taken, with our only way home.

"That's what I was trying to tell you Marshall! Before you got mad. I tricked them!"

"You what?" Marshall said, confused.

348

"Sooooo, when we first arrived here, I fell in the bushes and what did I see hanging there? The amulet! I didn't know then that it was the reason we got zapped here I just thought it looked cool and I could be like you. So, I hid it in my pocket but then Jimmy told us it was our way home and I figured I would hold on to it a little longer so that me and you could have just one more night together, having fun. I know this was supposed to be our last year trick or treating together but we were going to miss it because Mom grounded me. Then we arrived here and it was like living *in* Halloween! And I gotta say besides everything trying to eat us, this place is really cool. I'm not a freak here! Then Kassir came and I knew I had to give it back or else lots of people would be hurt... or worse!"

"The book!" Marshall realised, in the witch doctors hut!

Yeah and I remembered my treasures. I had the pouch from Feldma-"

"Hey wait a minute, I had that pouch!"

"Let's not focus on that right now, like I was saying I had the pouch and there were all these shiny things in there. So, I made one out of that and some of my own treasures. I was gonna give you the real one back, we could go home and we could have one each and I could still be just like you. Everything was perfect." He let out a big sigh. "But that's when we got chased and that's when it happened." Randy hung his head low.

"When what happened?" Marshall asked.

"It broke!" Randy replied.

"It what?" Marshall said in horror.

"It broke! I always break things, but this time I didn't mean to, I promise! I must have landed on it and it broke. I was scared to tell you in case you were angry and we couldn't go home but then Kassir came and he said they'd hurt Ava unless we gave it back to them.

"So, what are you saying man?" Joe jumped in. He and Marshall starting to smile.

Randy pulled out his hand and inside was the Amulet.

"I wanted to protect Ava so I gave them the fake! I didn't know they were gonna lie though!"

"Rule number one of bad guys kid, you can never trust a villain to tell the truth!" Fimple said.

"Randy, you genius!" Marshall and Joe grabbed him and lifted him into the air!

"If we can fix this, we can save her and go home!" Said Randy with a smile.

"Guys, we can go now and forget all this even happened!"

"Wait, what!" They all cried.

"You're kidding right! We need to save Ava!" Marshall shouted.

"No, hear me out. You heard them. They have her but they only have 'til morning to use the amulet and steal the souls. Otherwise they turn back to stone. So, if we have the gem and they can't use it, then we can leave safely and they will be destroyed in a few hours and Ava will be safe!"

"We can't just leave her!" Chip and Fimple shouted! "After all we did to help you!

"They're right, Joe! We can't!" Said Marshall with a sigh. "She's the missing Dennison girl, we need to bring her home!"

"What!" Joe shouted back. "You're crazy. I can't believe you always make the bad decisions for a girl!"

"What's that supposed to mean!" Shouted Marshall!

"You like her! It's obvious, and now you'd rather chase her into the mouth of evil, than go home and sort this all out! You want her to be the Dennison girl, so you can take her home, I get it. But she's not!"

"She is! She told me everything, she didn't know we were from our world. She's been out here alone since 1990 and now her only hope of getting home to her family is us! And I'm not gonna let fear get in the way of that, cos she wouldn't leave any of us behind!"

Marshall jumped on the back of one of the shadixs in a temper!

Joe was quiet, deep in thought.

The others climbed aboard the other bird and got ready to leave.

"Wait!" Joe said softly.

"You coming?" Marshall asked, flatly.

"Your riding into a world of evil on the back of a talking bird that steals people for a living to save the world from soul stealing monsters from the 1600's!"

"You still think we can't do it?" Marshall said, disappointed in his friend's lack of faith.

"Oh, no, I know you can do that! But I know you're gonna need me there to be able to talk to a girl!" He gave a wink and a smile.

"Get on Marshall smiled as he held his hand out to lift him up.

"I really do just wanna go home and watch Charlie Brown, in boring Maitland!" Joe laughed. "I'm sorry, let's go!"

As they left, Marshall caught a glimpse of himself in the reflection of a pool of water. He saw just how dirty and dishevelled he look. He wet his hands and ran them through his hair trying to fix the jungle look.

Chip noticed and nudged Fimple on the other shadix. He gave him a glance and smiled. Fimple caught on and smiled back.

"Who you tryin' to impress kid?" Fimple replied with a knowing smile.

"What, oh, me? No one! I uh..." Marshall startled.

"Relax kid!" Chip said. "You gotta be yourself!"

"I don't know what you're talking about!" Marshall protested. He turned and looked at them trying to hide the truth. They looked straight back at him with a raised eyebrow.

He gave in with a sigh. "What if she doesn't like *myself*."

"You always gotta be yourself kid, no use pretending otherwise!" Fimple said softly. "If you're always trying to be someone you're not to make others happy, then you'll never have true friends. Look at me and Chip, he makes no effort and I'm his best friend!" He smiled.

Chip grunted, then he smiled.

"It's true kid, my taller, dead weight here is right! If you're always changing to make someone like you, then people will never get to know the real you and the people that matter will miss that!"

Marshall looked back at his reflection and smiled as he pushed his hair back to how it looked before, with confidence.

They thanked Landis and headed towards the safer route.

"Where to?" Shouted Randy.

"We need to visit mookey! He's the only one who can fix the amulet! Then we go pay Kassir a visit at his mansion!"

Chapter 26

As they reached Shockton, the creepy quartet took Ava into a large building off of the main street. The Engineer began flicking various instruments on as the room powered up and came to life.

"Where are we?" Ava asked in amazement.

Various gadgets spun and beeped with their various lights.

"Welcome to my workshop!" The Engineer cackled. "It's where I do all my best experiments, or at least it was until you came along and put us in that infernal slumber you little brat."

"Silence!" Kassir commanded. "Show me your plan!"

"Yeah!" Ravage added. "What is it that is so important we had to sneak everyone here?!"

Crudge rubbed his fist in his hand. "If we were at full strength, we wouldn't have to sneak. I'd pound them all."

"Well," Interrupted The Engineer. "The fact is we don't have our strength and we don't have the amulet, which is the only thing that can restore that!"

Kassir growled in anger. "We know that, now why are we here?!"

"Well it was something you said actually, it was genius!"

"Something I..." Kassir thought back to their previous conversations.

"Yes, we need our strength to get the amulet and the amulet to get our strength. Now, we know that without the amulet, the stones won't allow us to steal the souls properly out of the wretched creatures of this world. *But* we can still use them." He opened a small vault under one of the workbenches and inside was one of the blue stones that had been collected all those years ago. "You see, I had been working on an experiment to test the properties of the stones further, before we were imprisoned, and I had made an interesting discovery."

The Engineer turned to ravage and whispered in his long ear. He went scurrying off out of the building.

"The stones seem to have a unique effect on the creatures here, watch!"

Ravage came hopping in with a smile and a poor creature that he had just taken off the streets. The furry individual was kicking and thrashing his arms. The Engineer signalled and Ravage dragged him over to the corner.

The Engineer picked up a crude looking metal helmet, made from scraps of metal. It was connected to a strange generator looking device. He placed the stone in the centre of the helmet, it clicked into position then he placed the helmet tightly on his head and grinned as he turned the generator on.

Bolts of electricity flickered from the machine all the way to the helmet. The stone began to glow. Ravage and Crudge took a step back as Kassir took a step closer with a smile of intrigue across his face.

The Engineer looked at the furry creature. Its eyes began to glow the same colour as the stone. The Engineer lifted his right arm slowly and to Kassir's amazement the creature also lifted his right arm. He dropped his arm and tilted his head side to side. The creature followed suit and copied his every action. Then the Engineer closed his eyes. The creature bowed in front of Kassir then opened his mouth with a voice that seemed to speak many voices.

"We are at your service, Lord Kassir"

"We?" Kassir questioned.

The possessed creature raised his arm and pointed out the door. Kassir and his group opened the door onto the busy road of creatures and he grinned from ear to ear, menacingly. All of the creatures in the vicinity of the workshop, were stood facing them, with eyes that glowed a radiant blue. From the smallest vermin to the tallest of the monsters that were going about their business, they all were frozen awaiting their leader's command.

"You said we were *without a beacon of hope* and that's exactly what we have here!" Smiled the Engineer from under his helmet. He pointed across the street to a large energy tower that powered the town. It was the largest in their world enough to power the city and all around it.

"There's your beacon Boss!" The engineer smiled. "Once we have hooked it up, we can amplify the power and we can control all of the creatures in the area. We don't need our strength. They will capture the brats and when we have the amulet back, we will take the souls of the entire world and they will already be standing in line, waiting for us!" He laughed.

Kassir laughed with a roar and grabbed his friends. Ravage and Crudge laughed maniacally.

"Brothers, we will rise again and now no one can stop us. But my friend," He turned to The Engineer. "before we drain the souls of this world, we will march our kin into the human world and we shall have our vengeance for all the years of hurt and destruction they have caused us! No longer will they ruin our plans for supreme power!"

Ravage, almost afraid to put a spanner in the works, turned to Kassir.

"But boss, how do we get the humans to come to us? We don't know where they are!" He cowered, waiting for Kassir to strike him for suggesting the plan had a flaw.

Instead Kassir patted him gently in reassurance, too overwhelmed with eagerness to execute his plan to be put into a bad mood.

"Relax Ravage. We shall send the grundlehounds!" He smiled devilishly. "They will sniff out and deliver a very important message."

Ravage clapped his clawed hands in excitement. The hounds were a personal favourite of his. Kassir turned to Ava with a grin as the night air filled with the haunting howls of unseen creatures.

Take her away, she will be our first feed when the amulet is back with us!

Crudge took Ava to one of the nearby rooms. He placed her inside then he slammed it shut and locked it behind him. He gave a deep chuckle to himself as he left the poor girl alone in the room.

Ava ran to the door and tried to pull it open, despite hearing the familiar click of a key being turned in the lock. She needed to escape, she needed to find her friends and she needed to know how come the boys knew so much about the amulet!

She slowly approached a bed that was in the corner and sat on its edge.

What was she to do? She thought to herself as she stared out of the barricaded window.

Then she heard the familiar clicking of the key in the lock again. She braced herself to see which of the brutes was going to enter but she was pleasantly surprised when a woman stepped in. She was dressed in a long, brown gown with a hood but Ava could clearly see it was a woman, probably in her forties, she thought. She couldn't tell the type of creature she was, as the hood covered most of her face.

She didn't know why she was there or whether she intended to harm her or not and she backed shyly, across the bed, against the wall.

"Don't be frightened little one!" The soft voice came from under the hood. "I won't hurt you!" She held her hands out to show she was unarmed. She took out a small fruit from her gown and ripped it in two. She took Ava's arm and placed the fresh fruit on her grazes.

"Who are you?" Ava asked nervously, still unsure who or what was under the hood. She could feel the fruit taking effect, she could move her arm without any pain! "Why are you helping me?"

"I'm a friend!" The voice replied calmly. I used to be a slave for Kassir and his henchman before they vanished. I was left here, long ago. I thought my life was rid of them but now they're back, I know it will only be a matter of time before they will notice me and I shall be prisoner once more."

"Why haven't you run?" Ava asked. "They'll be back any moment now!"

"I heard them when they first arrived and my first instinct was to leave here and find a new home so I hid until I knew it was clear. But then I saw you and I knew I couldn't leave you here, all alone. Not like I was!"

The woman scurried over to the barricaded window and looked out! The coast was clear.

"I know a way out, follow me!"

Ava didn't need convincing. She was already on her feet and following the woman like a shadow, across the room and out the door. They snuck down the corridor. They could hear Kassir and the henchman talking up ahead in the workshop.

"Quick, they're in there. We can leave through the back-" The woman was cut short as they turned to flee. They were face to face with Ravage who had just let the grundlehounds free and had returned to join the others.

Kassir was going through his plan when the two were thrown in front of him.

"Well, well, well we have a stowaway!"

He lifted the woman's head up softly and flipped the hood down. His eyes changed, as if scared and relieved all at the same time. Then he gathered himself in the next moment.

"It looks like someone's still loyal after all these years!" He lifted her up for the others to see. They gave a gasp and a smile. "We lost our home, our creatures, but you, you remained! Why!"

She began to weep. "I thought you were gone for good!"

"Guess again!" Ravage smiled, as he ran his long claw down her arm. It scratched against her gown.

She gave a yelp and Kassir roared, flinging the smaller monster across the room. Crudge and The Engineer backed down.

"I'm not going to let you harm this poor girl Sam!" She spoke softly behind her tears with defiance.

"*It's Kassir!*" He bellowed and she shook. He calmed himself and took her hand. "We're back now and we're *never* going to leave again. So, why don't you take our guest and clean her up. We're getting hungry!"

Crudge went to escort them both but Kassir held his hand out to stop him. She took Ava and they walked back on their own, to the room that she been locked away.

They arrived and Ava went straight for the windows. She tried pulling at them in anger.

"It won't work!" The woman spoke, she sounded as though she had given up.

"I don't understand?" Ava asked her in frustration. "Just a second ago you were ready to leave and now you're doing everything he tells you?! That thing is going to kill us, I've seen it happen!"

"He won't kill me and I won't let him kill you!" She replied calmly.

"Oh yeah, and how are you going to stop him?!" Ava answered back.

"He has never harmed me, all these years I've been trapped in this nightmare working for him, cooking whenever those beasts want and cleaning up after them. But he's different, he's... gentler with me."

"But why?" Asked Ava. "Why you?... No offence!"

"He took me from my life, I thought he was going to hurt me but he brought me here. He said I reminded him of her!"

"Reminds him of Who?" Ava asked.

"His wife!" She replied. "Before he was... he was different!" She paused, sad. She sat down on the edge of the bed and Ava joined her.

"I was at the mansion, working as usual like I did every day. I was cleaning one of the hallways when I heard voices in one of the side rooms. I wouldn't normally have followed as those beasts terrify me but something drew me there. A sadness to the voice that made me curious. I peered through the crack in the door and there he was. Kassir, stood by the roaring fireplace. Talking to a small painting, holding a piece of cloth. He called her Aylse and he couldn't stop apologising to the picture. He sounded sad to begin with but he kept repeating it to himself, torturing himself until he got angry. He made me jump with his outburst and I gave away my hiding spot. He spun around, furious but then his eyes dropped and his mouth quivered when he saw me. He saw that I'd seen the cloth in his hands. The small, soft, woven piece of clothing. He held it tightly in his hand as if he'd never let go. It was far too small for an adult and that's when I realised what he was holding. I nodded to him in understanding without saying a word."

"What was it?" Ava asked.

"He told me they had gotten married in secret in another lifetime. That they were forbidden to be together by class but destined to be together by love. They were going to run away together. But the morning they had planned to leave, she was taken by the local law and she was to be killed for witchcraft. He tried to stop them and was nearly captured but he was pulled away by his three closest companions. He watched her die that day. He heard her tears, then he heard her confession. With her final breath she managed to whisper to him." The woman's eyes began to fill.

"What did she say?" Ava asked, eager to hear.

"She whispered to him-*'Remember my love. In this world and the next, my heart belongs to you. They may try to keep us apart but together we are stronger than anything.*

Please don't cry for me, please don't cry for our unborn baby. You would have been the greatest father. We love you and we will be a family one day.' And then the gallows dropped and she was hanged. The piece of clothing was for his unborn child. That day was the destruction of all three of them. The pain consumed him and he became the monster you see today!"

Ava was speechless. This monster who had tried to take her and her sister, that had devastated the land, was born from one evil doing. She didn't know what to think.

"But how come he has kept you here, unharmed?" She finally asked.

"He says I remind him of her, her innocence and the light she bought upon the world. He can't destroy me like the others but he can't allow himself to return to what he once was. He saw himself as weak then, and so he is consumed by the unending need for power."

Ava felt sad. She wanted to go home. She wanted her sister. She lay down on the bed with the woman and closed her eyes.

Chapter 27

The heavy pounding of the shadix bird's feet rang out as Marshall and his group traversed the land. They made their way through the longer but less perilous route back to the carnival. Through the jungle to the witch doctor. Where, after a short and heated discussion with his hands as to why Ava wasn't with them, he agreed to fix the cursed amulet. They ran over their plan to get Ava back and return to their world and set out for the mansion.

When they arrived, it looked just as eerie as it did before but somehow Marshall felt less afraid than he had when they had escaped through the conservatorium just hours before. They slowed as they reached the large glass building. They took a left turn, down the side of the building, to find a back-way in.

As they walked past the large, solid glass panels, he could see the lifeless roots of the large plant creatures that had attacked them before and couldn't help but think of poor Jimmy.

After a few minutes of searching, they found a side entrance. They dismounted the shadixs and entered the mansion cautiously. It was eerily quiet. The music that had been playing at the party was no more and the sounds of the guests had disappeared. They continued through the lower level corridors into the large hall where they had last seen Kassir and his men. They prepared themselves for confrontation as they entered but instead, they were met with an empty room and silence.

"Where are they all?" Joe asked.

"I don't know, something isn't right. Let's keep looking!" Marshall said as he scanned the hall for any signs.

"Maybe they've you know..." Randy said as he posed in a statue form with a scrunched face, mimicking them.

They decided to check upstairs and followed the large stair case up. They saw scratch marks in the carpet floor of the steps. They were going the right way but now they weren't sure that was a good thing.

They traversed the corridors until they heard a sound up ahead.

"Can you hear that? It sounds like... crying!" Randy said.

They walked slowly over to the room that the sound was coming from and Fimple pushed his ear against the door. He heard the sobbing from inside and slowly creaked the door open.

The kids stood in shock. There, in the corner of the room was a single creature sat in the shadows.

"Feldma?" Marshall whispered.

She spun round in shock, not hearing the intruders enter.

"Who dares disturb- Oh what's the use?!" She sighed. "Take what you want now, before *they* return!"

"What happened here, where's Kassir!" Joe asked, checking the room to make sure she was alone.

Feldma's gills raised as she heard the familiar voice. She turned to face the doorway.

"My Prince!" She stood and walked over to the group. "I suppose you've come to kick a lady whilst she's down?" She said, feeling the hurt all over again from the dancefloor fiasco.

"N... No! We came to rescue our friend and... and put a stop to Kassir and his men." Joe said, he could see she was hurt. "What happened to you?"

"That doesn't matter, it's nothing compared to the pain of losing you, my prince. I thought you'd left me for good!" She grabbed his arms.

Joe got embarrassed and tried to pull away. "That's nice an' all but you know I'm a kid right! And a human and... not to mention I live in a completely different world it just would never work okay! I'm sorry"

"Minor details that's all my love!" She insisted. "Why, I myself am only a young gorlap! Compared to our lifespan I am but a child too! Plus, long distance relationships can work. For those dancing feet alone, I would travel the Fields of Gloom and beyond!"

Marshall could see he was needed and interrupted the happy couple before she could wrap herself around Joe any further.

"So, where did Kassir go and where is everyone who was here earlier? It's so quiet!"

"They left!" She replied in a sombre tone as she let Joe go. She pulled open the curtain and looked out at the world outside. She looked sad. "They left the mansion with the wretch I had captured and took those they decided they could use."

"What about the rest?" Asked Randy.

She hung her head then looked up with heavy eyes at the group. They understood their fate.

"Wh... What about Jimmy?" Marshall asked, almost too scared to find out. "Is he..."

She looked at him with sad eyes. "I don't know child. It was hard to tell who survived and who was taken. I don't know their plan but it might not matter. They may all meet the same fate. They left me here alone as punishment. They wanted me to suffer, knowing I had failed my people!"

"That wretch is our friend!" Chip piped up.

"Yeah, you better not have hurt her fish face!" Fimple added angrily.

She hissed and rattled her gills at them. "Or what!"

"Guys, we need to work together!" Marshall shouted, coming between them. He turned to Feldma. "We really are here to stop Kassir, once and for all. You can start a new life too, maybe less of the death pit but that's just a suggestion. But we need to rescue our friend first and before Sunrise! Now, do you have any idea where they might've gone?"

She hung her head, she didn't. But before she could answer they heard howls coming from outside. She raised her head in fear. Chip and Fimple also knew all too well that they were in trouble!

"Grundlehounds!" She said.

"What's a grundlehound?" Asked Randy.

"Bad news kid!" Fimple answered.

"Kassir used to use them as his messengers. That message was usually 'you're lunch'!" Feldma added.

"We need to leave!" Chip joined in.

They flew from the room and down the corridor. They emerged into the large ballroom. It was tattered and the once elegant hall was now full of ripped fabric and busted woodwork. As they pondered which exit to take, they heard the clicking of claws against hardwood flooring from behind them. As they turned, they met with the icy stare and snarling jaws of several of the grundlehounds! Marshall stood, frozen in fear, in front of Randy like a shield. Feldma pushed through and stood at the front of the group, her arms out either side to protect them. She hissed and rattled her gills as they let out their slobbering growls.

They stood on all fours. Their shoulder blades ridged and bony, with a dark mane down the back of their spine. Their battered and torn faces permanently set in a face that ushered terror. Bright green eyes shone from the sockets of their flat faces and rat like tails met the black, scaly fur that covered their bodies. They drooled as they stood in front of the group.

Marshall stared at the pack.

"Joe, they look like the small creature Dash chased back home!"

"I was thinking the same thing, it looks just like Sheriff Johnson's drawing! Just... you know... a lot scarier when they're right in front of you!"

The leader of the pack stepped forward, growling at them as it moved. Then suddenly, it stopped in its spot and started reaching. It coughed and made a sound that even Marshall found hard to stomach. Then, with a single motion, a black pouch slipped out of the creepy dog's mouth, onto the floor.

It steamed on the cold floor as the slime dripped off of it. Then, with a cracking sound, the pouch opened. The other hounds stepped forward and soon there were four black, slimy cocoons on the floor.

They each opened and out crawled a black, blob like creature. They oozed along the floor, towards each other and grew into miniature shapes, before the group's eyes. They watched the scene unfold.

Four figures stood over one smaller, all without faces like tiny mannequins.

The smaller one knelt on the floor. It was Ava, Marshall thought. He watched as the four larger characters swirled into bars that the smaller figure was now gripping hold of.

She was trapped, he thought.

The black bars transformed into jagged teeth that formed an evil smile, closing down on her. Then the whole lot started spinning until it circled into the shape of the amulet. Marshall looked at the black replica of the stone. He knew they wanted to trade. The amulet for Ava or they would kill her. But where were they?

Then, with a final push. The amulet lay flat on the floor and slowly stretched out and in the centre of the shiny, flat, black surface came the image of a town. There was a tower and houses and stores, it was bustling with creatures.

"It's Shockton!"Chip shouted. "I'd know that town anywhere. Good food! They're in Shockton!"

With that, the grundlehounds pounced on the black mass and devoured it within seconds like ravenous vultures.

The leader snarled at Marshall who nodded to it in understanding.

"Tell them, we're coming!" Marshall said with a defiant look on his face.

The leader growled and snorted then howled into the air to signal the pack and they fled the mansion.

"Are you crazy! Now they know we're coming!" Joe shouted.

"The hounds would have torn us to shreds if we didn't tell them." Fimple said. "There's only two responses they'll accept. 'Okay', or 'dinnertime'!"

"But how are we gonna stand a chance of rescuing Ava and getting home if we don't have the element of surprise." Asked Joe, knowing how much harder this already impossible task had just become.

Feldma spoke up. "They know we're coming, that makes it harder. But now we know where they are and we didn't say how many of us were coming!" She smiled sneakily.

Marshall looked at her, trying to work out what she meant.

She smiled for the first time since the return of the fearsome four.

"We're gonna need some help!"

Chapter 28

The winds blew the scattered, dead leaves across the cobblestones of Shockton, the banging of window shutters echoed through the quiet street as the neon signs of the bars and eateries glowed to an invisible audience.

"Where is everyone?" Asked Chip. "This place is usually teaming with people."

Marshall led the way as Randy, Joe, Chip and Fimple followed. They walked past the shops and houses. The lights were still on but the buildings were empty. Cars were strewn across the street. Their doors opened and abandoned.

"I got a bad feeling about this!" Said Joe.

The wind whistled through the empty streets, the neon lights flickered over the bars and the odd stray creature scuttled through the shadows. Steam rose in the cool air from the sewer vents in the ground. The place was deserted.

Randy looked through the various shop windows for any sign of life. Chip and Fimple scoured the rooftops for any signs of a trap or the gruesome foursome but there was nothing.

They all made their way up the high street towards the large, tower at the back of the town. Marshall looked about at this new town. It was very similar to those back home. There were monster clothes shops, monster restaurants, T.V.s even. There was so much of this place they hadn't seen. It was like his neighbourhood back home just with a slight eerie spin on everything. He reminded himself he wasn't there to sightsee though and he continued looking for any signs.

"Bob would love this place!" Joe said out loud. "Could you imagine-"

All of a sudden, they heard a group of laughter coming from up ahead. It was the Kassir, Ravage and Crudge.

They stood on the roof of a single-story diner. Ravage was laughing menacingly, Crudge flexed his knuckles and Kassir stood silent, grinning at the group as they approached.

"Welcome Marshall." He said with a sly grin. "You've caused me quite the stir tonight! But I suppose I should be thanking you! For you see in just a few moments all our hardships will be at an end forever and you will have helped us destroy this world so that we can live forever in a world of our own design. Without limitations, with all the power we could imagine. Never again will we be stopped. I mean you won't be alive to see it but I assure you I will name somewhere after you. Some smoldering, burnt land full of desolation! How does that sound?"

Ravage laughed a wicked laugh and Crudge chuckled.

Fimple looked around with a side glance.

"Looks like you're a little outnumbered. How about you just give us the girl and we be on our way!

Kassir burst into laughter.

"Outnumbered? Us? Please forgive me, where are my manners? I haven't introduced you to the rest of the family."

With a whistle of his fingers the town came alive.

From the bushes and the shadows crept the glowing eyes of the townsfolk as they illuminated the street, it was hard to tell where they began and the neon street signs ended.

They were gruesome. Creatures of all sizes came to the call. Half man, half beasts, floating ghouls wrapped in chains. Grubby blob like creatures spilled from trash cans and sewer grates and things that could only be imagined in the worst of dreams.

"Oh, you had to say it genius!" Scorned Chip as he looked around at the glowing eyes surrounding them.

"Where's Ava!" Marshall called, ignoring the sights around him.

"She's safe... for now." Kassir grinned. "We wouldn't want our dinner to spoil! Where's my amulet?" He shouted back.

"We don't-"

"Do not test me boy!" Kassir roared, interrupting Marshall.

"I know you have it, you wouldn't be foolish enough to risk her life again by further deceiving me!" He snarled as he shot a glance at Randy. "Besides I can feel it. Calling to me. I can almost hear it's song!" He nodded to Crudge at his side who bent down to grab something. "Now hand it over or Crudge here will have fun with your precious friend!"

Crudge lifted a bag above his head and with a swift tug he pulled the bag away and they saw he was holding on to Jimmy.

He was okay Marshall thought!

"Jimmy!" Marshall shouted. But it was no use he was tied and gagged.

"One more step, one more lie and Crudge will crush his bones to dust! Now, give... me... my... amulet!"

Marshall paused. He looked across the street at Jimmy who was mumbling to try and tell them to run but he couldn't with the gag in his mouth. They needed the amulet to get home and they also knew if they handed it over, they would be dooming everything that was in this world once Kassir had the power. Marshall stopped and gave him a little wink and jimmy frowned, confused.

"Now, see I feel rude." Marshall said calmly to Kassir. "Here we are, guests in your town surrounded by all your... friends... and I forgot to tell you I was bringing *our* friends!"

"What's he talking about?" Ravage mumbled with a laugh.

Crudge looked more confused than normal.

With that, Marshall turned behind him and called out. "Now!"

There was silence.

"Now!" Marshall shouted again a little louder.

Randy and Joe looked at Chip and Fimple in despair.

Kassir began to laugh sarcastically. "What is the meaning of this?" He growled! "Tricks will not save you this ti-"

The street began to rumble, the winds picked up. The air filled with shrieks and moans. The sounds grew closer and the street signs and metal trash can lids began to rattle.

Clouds of blue smoke rose from the trees and swarms of birds came from overhead.

Kassir's mouth dropped as giant beasts poured through the streets led by a charge of shadixs.

Feldma had arrived just in time and she had used her fierce leadership skills to convince Landis to join them. With him he bought his workers and his beasts.

It was true he thought, should they lose he would lose everything anyway. They had to fight.

Kassir erupted into anger. He spun to Ravage and Crudge.

"Get them!"

Crudge dropped Jimmy and they ran down into the crowd.

Kassir signalled the creatures of the town under his spell to attack and retrieve his amulet.

The town was thrown into chaos as creatures stacked onto each other. Spectres flew through the air grabbing the possessed townsfolk below and whisking them away. The townspeople scurried, and flocked towards the creatures. Some climbed the red brick walls of the town and jumped down on to the tops of the larger beasts in an effort to slow them down.

"Quick!" Shouted Marshall to Chip and Fimple. "While they're distracted, you guys find Ava and get her to safety!"

"Righto!" Shouted Fimple and they ran off towards the back of the town where Kassir had emerged from.

"Right." Marshall said, turning to his brother and best friend. "You two distract Kassir so I can find what's making these people act-"

"You're going nowhere!" The unmistakable deep voice of Crudge bellowed as he grabbed Marshall, launching Randy into the nearby bushes in the process.

"You leave him alone!" Yelled Joe! Marshall and Crudge both looked at him in shock! This was uncharacteristically brave or stupid Marshall thought.

Crudge laughed while he held Marshall up by the ankle dangling upside down.

"Get out of the way... loser!" Crudge laughed.

"No!" Joe stood his ground.

"What did you just say?" Crudge sneered.

Randy appeared from the bushes.

"Joe, just run!" Marshall called from midair.

"No Marsh, not this time! I've run away from problems my whole life. I've been scared, I've been worried and running never solved any of it. Marshall I've watched you do more brave things in one night than I've ever seen in my life. You had to and you did it for your friends, your family. Well I'm not gonna let some overstuffed, half brained monkey push me around anymore! So, for the last time, you leave him alone!" Joe yelled and pushed his glasses firmly back up his nose.

Crudge was taken aback a bit by him, he wasn't used to being talked back to. He didn't like it.

"Or what?" He jeered dropping Marshall to the floor.

"Or, I'll make you!" Joe stood fast in his spot.

"Yeah? You and what army?" Crudge called back.

Joe looked slightly panicked now there were only feet between him and the giant beast.

"This one!" A voice yelled from behind.

They all spun around to see Feldma bounding towards them on the back of the doeggul. She called out with a shrill into the night and leant forward with her hands out. A continual stream of energy shot forward from her hands as she pushed Crudge's giant mass back.

He flew back with a cry into the base of one of the buildings.

"I told you I wouldn't let anybody hurt you, my love!" She cried out then charged forward into the battle that had ensued in the streets.

Joe couldn't help smiling. "You see that Marsh! A girl likes me!" He had stood up to someone, not backed down, received the attention of a girl and not gotten beat up. This was his greatest day ever.

The moment was short lived though, when Randy called out. He had spotted a small rat like creature possessed by the stone and creeping up towards Marshall, who was still on the floor.

In the confusion the amulet had fallen from his pocket when Crudge dropped him and the small creature was headed straight for it.

Joe couldn't get there quick enough but Randy jumped in and toe punted the rat-like creature, sending it splashing across the street into a stone fountain in the center. He grabbed the amulet, holding it above him for them to see but it was knocked from his hands by a flying creature with tattered wings and a reptile like head as it chased through the air after another beast. The amulet fell to the ground and rolled along the path. There, it was kicked by the scuffling of creatures fighting and sent deeper into the crowd. The boys split up and headed through the crowd. Joe went around the side to see if he could see it clearer from there.

Marshall spotted it but the rat creature had sprung back and was hopping across the shoulders and heads of various monsters towards the spot.

It ran down the tentacled arm of one of Landis's workers and onto the floor, just as Randy had crawled through the sea of legs, where it managed to pick it up in its teeth. It chuckled to its self then before they could reach it, it had scurried up a bench leg, along the bench and up a street lamp. It leapt out and glided across the street, over the fighting monsters and landed at the foot of the large tower. It ran up the grassy bank and was picked up by The Engineer who was stood with his helmet, controlling the townspeople. He had been waiting to receive it to place it in the tower.

Marshall, Randy and Joe went to chase the creature but they were stopped suddenly as Ravage broke through the crowd and launched himself in front of them, teeth and claws bared.

The Engineer slammed the Amulet into the machine, without hesitation and started it up.

The loud noise caused by the mechanism made everyone stop what they were doing. Some of the creatures ran away back into the forest. Others stood there in despair or frozen in their possessed state.

Kassir arose, on the ground as he lifted Crudge back onto his feet. He signalled for Ravage to join him and the boys shrugged free of his grip.

Kassir laughed as his peers joined him. "You fool! You've stopped nothing! If anything, I should be thanking you for bringing us our first meal!" He said as he motioned with his arms at all the creatures in front of him.

Marshall looked at his friends, then at Randy.

Kassir raised his arm then slammed it down.

"Start the machine!"

The Engineer cackled as he pulled the switch down on the device. A low whirring noise started then got faster. Bolts of electricity ran down the machine, into the amulet. It began to glow brighter and brighter as more energy syphoned down into it.

The Engineer laughed in a craze as he moved to the last switch.

Kassir gave a grin. "You see boy! You've already lost!"

He turned to the Engineer and yelled. "Light it up!"

The Engineer pulled hard on the last switch and laughed hysterically at what was to come.

As the switch dropped, the energy was released from the amulet and it expelled into the sea of monsters. The first wave struck and the townspeople and Landis's creatures alike started shaking. They all began to call out, as they started changing. Marshall could see Feldma and Jimmy and the guard who had let them through at the mansion, all succumbing to the energy from the amulet.

Marshall knew that in minutes they would all be turned into the creepy black ooze creatures and their souls would be taken by Kassir. Then he would be too strong to defeat.

He had to do something and quick.

"Marshall what are we gonna do?!" Randy shouted. "We need to think of a plan to turn that switch off." Marshall replied.

"We don't much time. This isn't like catching frogs back home. We can't spend all day thinking how to-"

Then it hit Marshall, it was exactly like catching frogs back at their spot. Well, it was like their last attempt, he thought.

"Randy you're a genius." He said, interrupting him. "Quick, hand me that trash can!"

Randy suddenly saw his plan and tipped the trash can upside down, emptying its contents on the street. He threw it to Marshall.

Marshall charged towards the fountain, avoiding the suffering creatures that were trapped in the amulets beam. He sped towards the fountain and with a lean he scooped the water into the empty trash can as he passed.

Kassir spotted him and although unsure of his plan, he wanted him stopped. He sent Ravage to stop him but Randy held him at bay, throwing the trash that had been emptied at them. Joe joined in, throwing all they could to allow Marshall the gap he needed. Marshall ran up the grassy bank towards the tower and The Engineer and with one final push he reached the machine and threw the metal bin and its watery contents at the power source.

"This one's for you Jeremiah!" Randy shouted, as he watched his brother.

The water hit the switch and The Engineer and instantly there was a humungous spark followed by a loud bang and Marshall was thrown into the air, back onto the grassy bank.

"Marsh!" The boys called out together and they ran over to the spot where he had been thrown, which was covered in smoke.

The machine was destroyed. It was completely fried and the energy pulse disappeared. The townspeople slipped from the grip of the machine and were themselves once more. All that was left of The Engineer was a tall, black char mark on the wall of the tower and a pair of broken glasses.

The boys reached the spot where Marshall was thrown.

Maybe he had managed to get far away enough before it blew? Randy hoped. The smoke cleared and there was just a patch of empty grass.

Joe's mouth dropped and Randy eyes started to well up as his bottom lip quivered. He couldn't take it, he leant in to Joe, who grabbed him and he started to cry.

"What's a matter bud, miss me already?" They heard a voice from behind call out.

They spun round and there was Marshall, the other side of the smoke as the last of it cleared. He had a big grin and what's more he had the amulet in his hand!

"Marsh!" They yelled and ran up to him and bundle him to the floor. "We thought you were toast!"

They laughed and smiled as they got back up. The townspeople started to gather too. He had saved them all.

Then they heard the familiar roar of Kassir as he yelled in anger. The remaining three had rushed to the spot where The Engineer had met his demise.

"No!" He screamed. "My faithful engineer! My friend! You sniveling brats destroyed him. Now it's your turn!"

Angrily, he turned to face them, his eyes wide with rage. He was about to leap forward when all of a sudden, a large blue bolt shot forth and hit the damaged tower above.

"Not this time you don't!" It was Feldma, she screamed as she used all her energy on the giant metal structure. "This is for my brother." The beam intensified as she gritted her teeth. "For my people!" She shot forth more power. "This is for all the lives you ruined!" She screamed as she released the last beam and sent the metal structure crumbling down onto the three beasts. It crumbled down in a heap on them and they were lost in a plume of dust and metal.

"We did it!" Joe shouted. He laughed as he shook his hands in the air.

"Marsh you did it!" Randy said excitedly.

Marshall ran over and gave his little brother a big hug.

"No buddy, *we* did it!! He smiled and gave him a high five then he laughed as he turned to Joe. Feldma had picked him up and given him the wettest kiss on his cheek.

"You're not so bad for a human!" She laughed.

Joe blushed. "Gee thanks." He laughed. "I guess you're not so bad for a *gor... gorla...* you're not so bad." They laughed.

All of a sudden, they heard a loud yelling coming from the right. They turned to see Chip and Fimple with raised fists, screaming as they ran. Then they slowed to a halt as they saw it had ended.

"Well, looks like our work here is done!" They high fived each other and dusted off their hands. The others laughed then Marshall smiled as he saw Ava emerge behind them. She was safe, he thought.

He ran over to her and she ran to him when she saw him.

"Are you okay?" He asked. "Did they hurt you?" He couldn't help but panic.

She laughed and then gave a shy smile. "I'm okay, Marshall... from Earth." She looked up at him and gave a big smile.

He smiled back. "Have I got so much to tell you!"

"It's gonna have to wait, fleshie!" A voice called from behind. It was Jimmy, he was smiling his skeletal grin.

"Jimmy!" Randy yelled.

"I thought we lost you for sure!" Joe said as he came over with Feldma.

"Nah, takes more than some goons to beat ol' Jimmy!" He said with pride.

"Hey." Marshall called to him. "Thankyou! For what you did back at the mansion! You saved all of us!"

Jimmy shook his hand. "Aw shucks guys you're gonna make me cry!" He said wiping at the dark sockets where his eyes should be.

"Can he do that?" Asked Randy.

Marshall laughed.

"I was just saying we have to get Ava up to speed on a certain sister and what she's missed in the last five years!"

"Well, you're gonna need to do it on the flight home. It's nearly sunrise, you need to get back home before you're stuck here!"

The kids agreed but it was bittersweet as they had come to get used to this crazy, bizarre world and their new friends.

Jimmy walked over to say his goodbyes.

"Thankyou!" Marshall said as he shook his hand again.

"You take good care kid, okay!" He said to Randy as he ruffled his hair. "And never stop askin' questions okay! Never change!"

Randy put his thumb up.

"Sorry again about the whole goo thing!" He apologised to Joe.

"Don't sweat it man." Joe smiled, as he shook his hand.

The sneep guard who had let them through gave a wave and bounced on his little feet back with Jimmy into the crowd.

Chip and Fimple made their way to the group. "Let's do this quick!" Fimple said with a sniff.

"Are you crying?" Joe asked.

"No." He sniffed. "You guys need to get back quickly that's all!" He sniffed again.

Chip winked at the kids, Fimple wouldn't say it but they were going to miss their new human friends.

"Who knows, if your uncle needs a couple of chefs for dat diner of his. You know where to come!" Chip said with a smile as he hugged them each.

The pair walked up to Ava and gave her a hug.

"I'm gonna miss you guys so much!" She said with a tear in her eyes. "Thank you for everything!"

They both burst into tears on her shoulder in a loud cry.

Marshall and Randy laughed then Marshall gave a discreet cough and nodded behind Joe.

Joe turned around to see a very sorry looking lady.

Feldma had never looked so fragile.

"I will miss you my prince! And if you tell anyone I shall kill you!" She said angrily. Then she burst into laughter as she grabbed him and gave him a big hug.

"You are the bravest human I have ever met and the best dance partner I will ever have. Maybe one day I can visit your *Mait... land?*" She said with a kind smile, then she licked the side of his cheek.

Joe wiped his face and smiled silently. He saw her face drop. She knew he didn't share her feelings.

"Well, we do have next Crossover?!" He said with a smile and she grinned as she called out in excitement into the air, her gills rattling with joy.

The kids laughed and they made their way through the group of people towards the fountain where there was a gap. Marshall looked at Randy, he looked sad.

"I'm gonna miss this place too. But you know what?"

"What?" Randy asked.

"I'm looking forward to spending a whole lot more time with my little brother!" They both smiled.

"Okay, let's do this!" Marshall said.

He held the amulet out in front of him as he grabbed Ava's hand. She, in turn, took Randy's and he grabbed hold of Joe's.

They all breathed a deep breath and looked around one last time at the see of faces and creatures in this creep and bizarre world.

Marshall took a breath and started to read the words aloud.

"Ramus..."

"Venke..."

He felt the amulet start to get warm and come alive.

"Hudo..."

The bright light began to return. Suddenly, they heard a tapping at their feet. Ava felt a tug at her jeans. She looked down and gave a smile as she burst into tears.

"Mookey!"

The witch doctor beckoned her down to his level. She knelt down quickly in front of him!

"I didn't think I'd get to see you again!" She said through tears. "You saved me. You helped me. I can never repay you but I will always love you Mook, you were my family here, all these years!"

He placed his finger on her lips to let her know she didn't need to say it. Then despite all his protests in the past, he pulled her in tightly for one last hug.

She wiped her eyes and kissed the top of his leathery masked face and he stepped into the crowd beside Feldma.

Marshall smiled. "Okay, here we go!"

They joined hands again. The morning sunrise was just starting to show over the mountains, in the distance.

"Ramus,

Venke,

Hudo...

Danrayyyy!"

The light shone bright from the centre of the amulet and in a flash, they were gone.

Chapter 29

Marshall opened his eyes and spluttered, he was lying on the ground. He felt with his hands and could feel the cold earth beneath him. It was soil. Had it not worked? He thought.

Then Randy grabbed him and lifted him upright.

"Marshall, we did it! We're home!"

Marshall stood up and he saw his brother was right. They were back in the basement under the store. Joe came running over with a huge smile.

"We did it man!"

Then out of the shadows he saw her, Ava had come through with them. He gave her a smile. She was scared and confused. She hadn't seen the basement before. They walked up the steps, no one else was around. He led her out of the store, past all the knick-knacks and items that looked oddly more familiar now and took her out to the main street towards town as they told her the story of what happened all those years ago and how they got there.

Joe looked down at his watch, it had started moving again.

"Erm guys, according to my watch, we've only been gone an hour!"

"That can't be!" Said Marshall. "We were gone all night!"

"That means we didn't miss Halloween!" Randy shouted with Joy.

"Boy, I can't wait to see my family and relax with some chilli and Mr. Charlie Brown!" Smiled Joe.

As they came into town, they saw the lights at Futterman's. The party was in full swing and they could make out all the costumes from a distance.

Joe was right! Marshall thought. They hadn't missed Halloween. They hadn't missed the Horrorthon. They could enjoy it, once he had gotten Ava back with her family.

Randy jumped into the middle of the street and yelled as loud as he could.

"Last one there buys the ice cream!"

Marshall sighed and rolled his eyes. "Randy, isn't that a little childish-" He stopped and looked at his brother then realised what he was saying. "You're meant to count to three first!" He laughed and started to run as he pushed Ava back jokingly, to give himself a head start.

They all began to make a mad dash towards the diner. They soon passed Joe, then randy. Then they heard a shout, then silence.

They turned around and Marshall felt sick. There, in the middle of the street, *his* street, here in Maitland. Stood a badly injured Kassir. His clothes in tatters and covered in cuts and bruises. His eye was badly damaged and he stood with a limp. Out of the shadows crept Ravage and Crudge. Equally as injured.

"How?!" Joe asked.

"Surprised!" Asked Kassir, with as much of a grin as he could muster. He was wheezing heavily and coughing.

"The machine!" Ava said with a heavy sigh.

"But we destroyed it!" Said Marshall in shock.

"Not that machine, the machine The Engineer was wearing! He was powering the helmet with one of the old stones!"

"Precisely!" Sneered Kassir. You destroyed him but the stone survived, luckily we had the fortune to use it before that oversized goldfish brought that tower down on us fully."

"Hey, you leave her alone!" Joe shouted, surprising himself with his chivalry towards her.

"It's been a long time since we visited home but unfortunately, we can't stay and chat. It's not sunrise here for hours yet but as you can see-" He coughed, hoarsely. "we don't have that long left! So, let's try one last time and I'm warning you Marshall, my patience was the first thing to be destroyed in that accident, so choose your words carefully! Give me the amulet"

"And you'll let Randy go?" Joe asked.

"Of course!" he smiled a thin smile.

Marshall wasn't buying it, neither was Randy. He knew the moment he gave them the amulet he would take Randy and he would never see his little brother again. He looked at Randy, he loved him, he would never let anything or anyone harm him.

He sighed heavily.

"Take me instead!"

"What?!" Kassir shouted in surprise.

"Take me! There's three of you, he's small and weedy! He wouldn't even be enough to feed small and ugly over there!"

"Hey!" Ravage shouted.

"Take me, I'm bigger and you can last longer. At least until you get home, then you can take more without us stopping you. By the looks of that leg, you need it soon." He said, pointing at the exposed cut on Kassir's shin

"No Marsh!" Randy shouted.

"Yeah man, what are you playing at?!" Yelled Joe.

"We can find a way!" Ava replied.

Kassir looked either side of him at his remaining men. They nodded and he smiled.

"A clever human after all! We accept, but no tricks. You and the Amulet for the short one!"

Marshall pulled the amulet out of his pocket and dangled it on its chain to show them he had it for real.

"Okay, slowly let him go and I'll come to you!"

Kassir loosened his grip slightly and when Marshall was in grabbing distance, they made the trade. Marshall smiled at his brother, as he walked back to the others sadly.

Kassir brought him in close. He coughed hard as he laughed.

"Brothers, it's finally ours!" He held the amulet up high to show them.

Marshall looked at Randy and winked. Randy looked puzzled this time.

"Hey Rand! Sometimes I get breaky too!" He smiled at him then with all his force, he kicked his heel back into Kassir's exposed shin. Pain shot through the beast as he doubled over, lowing his body. Then Marshall brought his elbow back hard into Kassir's ribs, making him wheeze and splutter and drop to the ground. He grabbed the amulet from the ground and threw it to Joe.

"Ruuuun!" He yelled and the kids split up as Crudge and Ravage jumped into chase behind them.

Crudge ran after Joe and Randy as they headed in to the woods towards the north. They ran this way and that, through the low ferns and bushes and overhanging branches. Crudge struggled with the close-knit foliage. His size slowing him down but as he burst into a partial clearing by the lake, he saw the boys and he laughed.

"Nowhere to go, pipsqueaks. Nowhere to hide, no one to save you!" He chuckled.

"Randy and Joe looked at each other with a big grin on their faces. They held their hands open in the air with a smile.

"No amulet either, you big ape!"

Crudge growled in anger, he knew they didn't have time. He had to help Ravage find Ava before it was too late. He left the boys at the lake's edge and carried on into the forest towards the direction Ava ran.

Ava had taken the path that ran a little further south but, unlike Crudge, Ravage found it easy to hop and duck through the dense foliage. He chased her through the woods until he was swiftly right behind her. Then he pounced and knocked her to the floor.

She spun around, clutching the amulet tightly in both hands. She was scared. She felt him lunge over her. He dragged his sharp claws over the leafy ground and she could hear them scrape along, like sharp metal. He leaned over her with an evil grin. He chuckled and she saw the familiar red glow in his eyes, the same look that she saw when he was stood over her sister, the night that he took them both.

She winced as she felt him grab the amulet. She tried to push him off but she froze in terror it was like being back in the woods all those years ago, she couldn't move. He laughed as he tried to take it from her. She closed her eyes with fear as he grew close to her face and with a smile he whispered.

"This time, no one can save you!"

"Wanna bet!" They heard a voice from up ahead.

Ravage looked up.

Ava heard a loud shriek then an almighty *bang*!

She felt Ravage stop moving and a coldness on her face. She opened her eyes and she was covered in a green goo. She pushed Ravage's body off her to see a large hole where his evil had had once been.

She turned to see the smoking barrel of a shotgun. The smoke cleared and behind the gun was moustache faced smile of Sheriff Johnson looking back at her.

"You okay darlin'?" He asked, as he lifted her on his feet. He looked at her as he cleaned her face with a handkerchief. "I gotta strange feeling I've been waiting 5 years for you to show up!" He smiled and she smiled back at him. He picked up his torch and they headed back to town.

Just north of their spot, Crudge was ambling through the forest. He was getting turned around, left and right. In the dark, in this strange place, he was utterly lost.

"Rav! Hey Rav! Where are ya! C'mon this aint fun no more!"

He stumbled out into a clearing and on the ground, he saw a small black ball of scaly fur. As it turned around it stretched out. It was about the size of a squirrel. It had a flat face and green eyes. It was the same creature Dash had chased into Johnson's hut. It shrieked in fright at Crudge's bulking frame. Crudge laughed as he bent down and looked at the creature. He chuckled at its puny size and with a swift flick he launched it into the air and into the bushes.

"Stupid, tiny rat."

As he stood, he heard a large growl come from inside the bushes that the tiny creature had landed in. A sudden realisation dawned on him.

"Wait a minute, what are you doing he-" he turned to see two large green eyes glowing in the bushes in front of him, they were joined by dozens of others as the bushes came alive and as the night grew late Crudge's screams were lost in the swamp amongst the undergrowth as the grundlehounds devoured every last bit of him and disappeared back into the shadows.

Back at the roadside in the centre of town Kassir was enraged and had had enough of Marshall and their medalling.

"You've made a big mistake boy! When my brothers return with the amulet and your friends, we will devour them first so that you can experience the torment of watching them suffer. Knowing you failed them."

"I don't care what you do to me, but I won't let you harm the people I care about! You're weak and soon you'll be back in your stony prison forever!"

"You think you can beat me! Foolish child, I am more powerful than you, nothing can stop me!"

"I've been bullied all my life and there's something I've learnt that I should have realised a long time ago!"

Joe and Randy stepped out of the bushes and watched as the two battled.

"You may be bigger but I have my friends and that makes me stronger than anything. I'm not letting you take mine. Not today, not ever!"

Joe smiled. C'mon, there's the Marsh I know! He thought.

"You fool." Kassir snarled as he coughed. His wheezing was heavier now. "You confuse friendship with power!"

Ava and Sheriff Johnson emerged from the bushes with the amulet. Everyone turned to face them. Kassir's face dropped briefly in sadness.

Where were his men? He thought.

Then he saw the green all over Ava's shirt and knew they were gone. He turned back to Marshall with a face full of anger.

"I've seen your power!" Marshall smiled. "Where are your friends now? You can barely stand. You're the weak one here. No, I don't need your power." He looked at his friends. At his brother. His family. "I have everything I nee,d right here."

Kassir dropped to his knees, unable to hold his bodyweight up any longer.

Marshall paused a little and thought back to the vision in the witch doctor's hut.

"That used to be enough for you too!"

Kassir looked up at Marshall slowly with a puzzled look, then laughed.

"How would you know *anything* about me!" He coughed.

"I've seen what happened to you, it's not too late you can sti-"

Without warning Kassir lunged at Marshall and grabbed him by his throat.

He lifted him into the air as he stood on his feet.

Marshall could feel him using the last of his strength to squeeze the life out of him.

"Stop!" Ava screamed. "You're killing him!"

"Exactly!" Kassir yelled back.

"But why, you can't even take his soul!"

"It doesn't matter. I'm not long for this world but at least if I can take this wretch with me, my brothers and I will not have died in vain!"

"Stop!" They all shouted.

Johnson was reloading but Ava placed her hand on the barrel and he lowered it as she walked calmly over to Kassir.

She placed her hand on his bruised shoulder as he held Marshall high, off the ground.

"What would Aylse think?!"

Kassir instantly loosened his grip slightly. He turned to Ava. His face filled with remorse. She saw the moonlight glisten from the sadness in his eyes.

"What did you just say?"

"I said stop, Samuel! What would she think?!"

Kassir dropped Marshall onto the floor in a heap, as he gasped for breath.

Kassir dropped to his knees again, weary and tired. He knelt in thought, then he roared with rage. He arched back at the moon. Conflicted, he couldn't control the two forces within him. He grabbed his head, as the voices battled against each other.

Ava stepped forward and whispered in his ear.

"Remember my love. In this world and the next, my heart belongs to you. They may try to keep us apart but together we are stronger than anything.

Please don't cry for me, please don't cry for our unborn baby. You would have been the greatest father. We love you and we will be a family one day."

The words pierced through the battling voices and he fell still. He looked up at her with a glisten in his eye as if years of evil had been washed away and in that brief moment, he was his true self once more.

With a sudden lunge he grabbed hold of the amulet that Ava was holding and spoke the words.

He grabbed Marshall and pulled him close.

"Don't wait too long to miss out on something too good!" Then he whispered in his ear and he let him go.

The kids shouted in fear but as the light flashed before their eyes, they watched as Kassir threw the amulet into the light.

The bright light ripped through the night sky, then it vanished.

As they watched in surprise, they saw Kassir start to glow. Then with a final smile to the stars, he became stone. Forever smiling for he knew he would be with his Aylse in the next life.

Ava wiped a tear and turned back to the others. Randy was quiet. Joe and Marshall stood in shock. Johnson removed his hat and looked on at the statue, he could finally rest this case.

Ava cuddled into Marshall.

"That was kinda sweet, don't you think?" She said as they stared at the statue.

Marshall stood, still in shock. Both at the events and also at Ava. He was truly happy.

"What did he say to you by the way?!" She asked.

"Oh nothing." He replied with a smile. "But he might have told me where he hid the rest of the stones if we go back. Ya know so that everyone can come and go as they please equally."

She smiled. "That sounds a great idea!"

"What say we head to Futterman's and get ourselves a shake! My treat!" Johnson asked, trying to bring some normality back to the table.

"Finally!" Randy shouted and he ran to the diner.

As he reached the pathway to the diner, he could see everyone inside having fun, blissfully unaware of everything that had taken place. Then he heard a whirring sound, it was the sound of bikes. It was the sound of The Butcher Boys.

Josh's front wheel came zooming in front of Randy, blocking his entrance to the diner. The rest of the gang swiftly followed. Marshall and the others ran over to Randy. Johnson was steadily walking. He was too old to be running.

Josh grabbed Randy by the collar of his ghost costume. "You little punks have no idea the night we've had, running around trying to find you three, since your little trick at the store. You wait to see what we're gonna-"

"Let *me* tell *you* about rough nights!" Marshall shouted as he stomped over to Josh. "I've been chased, beaten, put on a menu. I've had to look evil in the eye, chew it up and spit it back out and now I have to deal with a moronic nobody of a thug who has nothing better to do than beat on smaller kids!" He slapped Josh hand away from his brother. Josh looked shocked and a bit angry. Joe couldn't help but smile, this was a long time coming!

"I have one thing for you Josh Butcheson!"

"W... What's that?" Josh said, taken aback by this new Marshall.

Marshall raised his fist and Josh flinched. Then Marshall smiled and pulled him in tight and patted him on the back.

Josh was confused and a little scared.

"Go home, stop bullying people and speak to your dad. Picking on those not as powerful as you, won't solve your problems. You'll just have bigger ones when you're older, 'cos there'll always be someone that's better than you at something."

Josh stood in a daze.

Joe was disappointed he hadn't gotten his comeuppance but proud of his best friend and Randy couldn't have looked up to his bigger brother more than right then.

"Nice work, Colonel!" Joe smiled as he patted Marshall on the back.

The door swung open and Bob let out a loud cry. Joe's mom followed.

"Where have you been, you've been gone over an hour I was getting worried!"

Joe ran up to his family and gave them a big hug.

"What's goin' on out here? Trouble Joseph?" Bob asked, eyeing up the gang on their bikes.

"No, we're cool!" Marshall said with a reassuring smile. He looked at Josh. "Right?"

"Yeah, right!" Josh agreed with a smile.

"Now what in the heck is that?" Bob cried as he pointed back towards the woods.

"Oh, we may have gotten you a new decoration for Halloween if you can lift the statue!" Joe laughed.

"Statue? I'm talking about the great big light."

The kids turned and saw the bright white light. They ran over to it.

"What's going on?" Randy asked.

"I don't know, but get ready in case!" Marshall said.

"We got your back!" Shouted Josh and the gang with a smile.

The light grew brighter then disappeared with a flash.

They saw a figure lying on the floor. It was covered in a brown robe and it was carrying the amulet.

Marshall looked at Randy, worried.

The figure came to and tried to stand.

Ava saw the face under the hood and recognised them.

"It's okay, she's a friend. She helped me when I was taken, she healed me."

The figure stood up and pulled back her hood. She smiled at Ava. Then she smiled even more when she saw where she was.

"What's her name?" Joe asked.

"I don't know!" Ava said, still surprised to see her.

"I do!" A soft voice came from behind the group.

It was Bob, he stood in silence as he looked at the mysterious woman. Then he gave the biggest smile he had.

The woman looked through the kids at the man in front of her in the dark. Then her eyes shone as she saw him!

"Bobby!"

"*Bobby*?" Joe and Marshall mouthed at each other. No one called him Bobby.

"It's My April!" Bob cried out over a mixed bag of emotions.

He pushed through the kids and picked her up and squeezed so hard that he didn't think he could let go.

"I never stopped lovin' you!" He gave her a kiss and pulled out the aged, white ribbon that he had kept on him.

"Still so sweet, I never thought I'd see you again my handsome man!" She wrapped her arms around him as tight as she could.

Joe and Marshall smiled in disbelief.

Bob welled up, confused. "I thought you left me! That I wasn't good enough"

"I've waited 25 years for you, my silly man!" She smiled at him as she placed her hands on his face. I'll have to fill you in on some of the details later hun, but I was waiting for you at our spot, all those years ago. When I was taken by a monster of a man. I reminded him of someone special."

Bob was already confused.

"I'm gonna need some more coffee, c'mon." They laughed and walked towards the diner.

April turned to the kids. She could see they wanted an explanation too.

"I was waiting for him that day but Ravage kidnapped me, he said they were going to have a feast but then Kassir stopped them and set me to work for them instead. It was later when I realised that I reminded him of his poor wife, although he'd never admit it to anybody. He said I wasn't to be harmed like the rest. I saw the amulet come through, on its own when I came out into the square. I didn't know if it would work but I just had to try!"

"Well I'm glad you did. I've not seen my uncle this happy ever. And that's kina his thing!"

They stepped into the diner and Bob introduced April to his sister and the other townsfolk. April recognised one old lady and asked to be excused just for one second. She tapped the shoulder of the elderly Ms. Thackery who was sipping a tea and watching the kids' film.

She looked up at April. "Oh, hello dear." She smiled. "Can I help?"

April smiled at her. "You're just like your photo!"

"I beg your pardon?" She asked with a confused smile.

April took her hands and whispered. "Your dad was a great man, he never stopped trying to get home to you. He called you his ladybug!" April smiled and walked back over to Bob.

Ms. Thackery grinned from ear to ear, that was their secret name. She didn't know how but she felt years of relief wash over her and a warm feeling of resolve suddenly.

"Finally, Ice cream!" Randy shouted as they all tucked into a special concoction Bob had made them all.

"Erm, excuse me!" A voice called out.

"What now!" Randy muttered. "I just want my ice cream already!"

Marshall and the others turned around. It was Vinessa!

"Oh Mitchell, there you are! I like thought I'd see if you got anything cool yet, the party was a snooze fest, so, like what have you got me?! Oooh Is it that cool necklace?!" She asked, looking at the amulet with a smile, it looked expensive.

Marshall looked up from his stool. "Hi Vinessa!"

Ava looked depressed. Oh, that's Vinessa, she thought.

Marshall looked at her, then laughed. "Actually Vinessa, no it isn't. Firstly, the name's Marshall, *Marsh... all!* It's not that hard. Secondly, the only thing I have for you is this!" He reached into his trouser pockets and pulled out a crumpled, soggy floppy disk and placed it on the counter. "You can do your own homework. In fact, you can do everything yourself. Now if you don't mind, I'm trying to enjoy some quality time with my friends, my family-" He looked at Ava. "and my girlfriend!"

Ava smiled and cuddled into him as she smiled at Vinessa.

"Like, Oh my God! I have never been so insulted, grr!" She stomped off in a huff, not noticing Randy.

He sat back on his seat and chuckled to himself. Marshall looked at him with a knowing glance.

"What did you do?" He asked with a smile.

"I just wanted to share my treasures!" He said with a cheeky grin.

"Wait for it!"

There was an almighty scream before Vinessa left the diner as she pulled her hand out of her handbag and attached to the end was a slimy creature that had latched on to her finger.

The kids and grownups alike all laughed. Marshall turned back to Randy.

"That was the only one you brought back though, right?!"

Randy remained silent as he sucked on his straw.

"Right?!" Marshall asked again.

Bob turned to April and the kids. "Why do I feel like I'm missing out on something big right now?"

"I'll tell you all about it in the morning hun, let's just enjoy tonight. You wouldn't believe me anyway. You finished the diner though while I was away! I love all the cute decorations!"

Bob looked at her, had she just called his house of horror cute?

"Cute! These are the scariest things you'll ever see in your life!" He replied.

April and the kids looked at each other and burst into laughter. Bob didn't understand but his family was whole again and he wasn't going to question it.

<u>Chapter 30</u>

The next morning, Johnson drove the kids to Dennison.

They drove through the country roads, down the tree lined route that was covered in rusted leaves. Ava couldn't contain herself. She had forgotten how beautiful it was. There were no monsters hiding in the shadows, there were no shadows!

Her parents weren't in the phonebook, they had taken themselves out long ago, due to prank callers pretending to know where their daughter was or what had happened that day but they had never moved in case Ava ever returned. So, she stayed with Bob and April the night before and they made a fresh start in the morning to surprise them.

As they got closer, she recognised where she was. She turned to Marshall. He'd never seen her smile so much. They must be close, he thought.

A little while later they pulled into a small suburban road.

"This is it! She exclaimed with Joy and started counting the house numbers!"

They got down to number 4 and she could barely wait for Johnson to stop, before she was unclipping her seatbelt.

"Wait, where's the mental hospital?" Joe asked. Marshall gave him a nudge. "Ow, I mean... the... happy place."

"Ava got out of the car and looked at the front of the house, it was just as she remembered it. It just needed a fresh coat of paint.

"What are ya talkin' about, mental hospital? Johnson asked, turning around in his chair.

"All the stories, you even said you used to check in!" Joe replied.

"Yeah, I did. But she wasn't locked away. Dennison doesn't have a place like that! You need to stop believin' everything you hear at recess, you hear me!"

"Yes, Sir!" Joe said with a sigh. He was glad Ava's sister wasn't locked away but secretly he thought it would have been cool, his imagination had been racing about the types of characters that might have lived there.

The boys all unclipped their seatbelts. Johnson turned back to face them again.

"Listen guys, I'm thinking at first you let me take Ava in okay. That family's got a lot of mending to do and last thing they need is someone with a lot of crazy questions, a little cat burglar and brand-new boyfriend, you understand?!"

The three boys looked at each other in the back seat and nodded.

They got out and waited at the main gate.

Johnson took the girl by the hand and smiled.

"You ready sweetheart?!"

"I think so!" She replied.

They walked the few steps to the front door together. Ava tried the handle and it opened in her hand. They stepped in and the door closed behind them. There was a short silence then Marshall heard the little voice of a younger girl that had remained silent for years.

"You're home!"

Thankyou for reading Maitland '95!

If you're craving more spooky goings on and want to stay updated with photos, info and news. Then check out Maitland online, via the following fun ways!

https://www.facebook.com/maitland1995/

https://www.instagram.com/maitland1995/

https://maitland1995.wixsite.com/maitland1995

https://twitter.com/maitland1995

Roy Peplow

Printed in Poland
by Amazon Fulfillment
Poland Sp. z o.o., Wrocław